An Agreement We Made

DAN KOLBET

ISBN: 978-0-578-86978-0

CHAPTER 1

I park behind the line of gleaming cars idling at the curb of Columbia Ridge Academy. It's the same as every other day, all the moms and one dad—me—line up to collect our kids. Heaven forbid they get a taste of freedom for even a few moments in the thirty feet they walk from the elementary school door to the backseat. We can't let that happen, now can we?

The three-story, red-brick Gothic revival structure was built in the 1960s but has been remodeled with modern updates several times since. The cost of admission alone is plenty to keep the place in pristine condition. It's covered in ivy and dripping in expectation—expectations of the students, expectations of the parents. I know this building and the people who helicopter-parent around it all too well.

It's 2:50 p.m., and I'm late, even though I'm here ten minutes before school lets out. I'm way back in the line of cars. My carelessness means I've been exposed to the moms who want to chat about room-parent duty, volunteer fundraisers, or which wine bar has the most generous pour. And I'm just not up for it today.

I flip the visor down in front of me in the naïve attempt to hide my face from the group of women assembling on the grass just outside the library. We know them as the 'Stay-at-Home Tribe,' and I'm an honorary member myself. The visor trick is useless and does nothing, of course, to hide my vehicle—a Mercedes-Benz SUV, which at eighteen months, is showing its age compared to the cars driven by the other parents at Columbia Ridge Academy. These are doctors, executives, attorneys, or dare I say, their stay-at-home spouses and a few nannies.

I have half a mind to visit the Mercedes-Benz dealer this week to find a suitable replacement. The lease is nearly up anyhow, and an early trade-in would be nice.

I look up and try to ignore the wave from Christy Woods. She is dressed in nearly identical attire as the other Tribe members, in her stay-at-home-mom uniform of black yoga pants, fitted cotton V-neck top, and white sneakers. I'd say they coordinate outfits, but they wear the same thing every day, so it can't be that complicated.

Christy makes a break for it. Apparently, my ignoring her has backfired. She's now striding toward my driver's side window, adjusting her oversized black sunglasses the entire way. The other women close rank and watch her while desperately trying to act as if they aren't judging her as she saunters over. They are judging, and we all know it.

"James, you're late," she says, tapping her manicured fingernails against the side of my partially open driver's side window.

I glance down at the faded pink and orange scars covering most of her left hand as she taps. She burned her hand in a kitchen accident a lifetime ago. Christy used to be a chef, but like the rest of us, she no longer works outside the home. I've always wondered what sort of chef gets burned like that; something about it just never added up. Nonetheless, now she stays home, just like me.

She often keeps her hand covered with long shirt sleeves with thumb-hole cuffs that partially mask the disfigurement. She pulls her hand back when she notices the attention I've paid to it, swiftly tucking it under her arm.

"James, you forced me to make nice with those Tribe creatures."

I roll down the window all the way while staying safely inside the vehicle. "They mean well."

"They do not mean well, and you know it."

I've known Christy since we were kids back in Shoreline, Oregon. And while there was a significant lapse in our friendship after high school, we've been close for the last fifteen years. If I could say so, I'd tag her as my best friend, but we're both married and that just wouldn't fly with anyone.

I've spent quite a bit of time with her and her husband Malcolm, too. Both my older boys played on the same soccer and baseball teams as the Woods' son RJ. And they've all attended the esteemed Columbia Ridge, then went on to public but respectable middle and high schools together. My youngest child, eight-year-old Paige, is in the same third-grade class as Christy's daughter Sophie.

Paige is the lone child I still must ferry to and from school.

"The ladies are still upset you didn't come to the school supply backpack stuffing party at Meredith Stonemeyer's house on Monday night," Christy says. "They never miss a chance to tell me I'm the luckiest married woman around, getting to spend such quality time with a hunk like you."

"My wife would beg to differ," I offer.

"Would she? Where is that wife of yours, anyway?"

She gives me a knowing look, of which I disapprove. I can't remember which city Tina is currently in, but I won't tell Christy that. After all, she knows I'm unaware. Tina is away from home more than she's actually home. I keep track on a calendar, but I haven't committed it to memory.

Then I remember.

"She'll be home tonight. We've got big plans for dinner."

"I bet. Good luck with that." Christy nods, noting the difficulties I'm likely to encounter with her return.

Malcolm is a commercial pilot, so he's gone as much as

Tina, who's in medical sales for Goodwin Labs. Christy knows the drill—spouse comes home, thrills the kids with tales of adventure, and promptly complains about the state of the house in their absence. An argument ensues and both sides retreat to their separate corners, only to have wild make-up sex the night before the spouse leaves again. Then we rewind and repeat it all over again during the next return home.

The bell rings, and parents hurry to their vehicles to wait for their kids to descend the stairs and run through the iron gates.

"We still on for coffee next week?" she asks, backing away from my window. "I want to try that new place in the Pearl District."

"It's your week to pick, so I'll reluctantly drive all the way into downtown Portland just so you can get your fancy osmosis coffee."

"*Gravity* coffee, not osmosis."

"If you can tell me the difference between the two, I'll buy," I say. "But you have to tell me right now."

Confident that Christy has no idea, I let my offer hang, which she promptly ignores.

"This is why the ladies love you, Mr. Mom. You're so funny," she says with a head tilt as she walks off to her car parked several lengths ahead. She got here on time.

Mr. Mom, ugh.

* * *

Paige climbs into the backseat, tossing her backpack on top of crushed graham crackers and string cheese wrappers on the seat. I make a mental note to vacuum the car. I would hate to let the Tribe see such normalcy. She pulls out her cell phone, not even looking up to acknowledge me. I keep the car in park and wait. And wait. I'm blocking the exit to the street. The car behind me honks once, then quickly twice. I see Paige finally look up at me through the rearview mirror.

"What did we say about the phone?" I ask.

She puts on a deep, annoyed voice, mocking me, "Emergencies only, Paige-bear. You are too young for a phone, anyway. I should have already taken it away from you. Blah, blah, blah."

I've got to admit, it's a pretty good impression, and we both laugh. She reaches up and places the phone on the center console next to me. Tina made me get her that phone, and it's caused nothing but problems ever since. Paige smiles, and I put the car in drive. And all is well in the world again until we hit road construction heading to the freeway. This is a delay we cannot afford.

Today, like every Friday after school, Paige and I race across town and try to make it to her weekly dance class on time. Most days, we're solid and on time, but it's not looking pretty today.

As I weave through traffic, Paige starts to change into her required dance attire—a light pink dress with a short soft skirt. I pretend the dark-tinted windows, blocking out prying eyes, makes this action acceptable. Sure, people can't see in, but at the same time, she's not buckled into her seat, either. I'm not sure what alternative I have—we've got a schedule to keep, and there's no dressing room in this Mercedes.

Paige is genuinely in love with her pink dress. She's had the same one since Pre-Ballet more than two years ago. It's carried her through to Ballet I and now Ballet II. The nylon and spandex mix, which includes a limp skirt at the waist, is Paige's full-time outfit away from school. I've given up arguing with her about it. 'Oh, you want to wear it to dinner? OK. And for bedtime, too? Sure. At the dentist's office? Well, of course, why not?' Don't judge me here. It's not that I've given up; I've just selected other battles to fight, like the phone.

Yet, the biology and growth of my child is no match for the venerable garment. Today, behind the tinted windows, she removes her school uniform—a white button-down blouse and blue pleated skirt—and yanks up the pink dress with a tug.

"Daddy!" she screams as I slam the brakes in panic. "No!"

The thread-bare seam on her right side gives up the fight and splits from under her arm to her hip.

I'm used to frequent, incoherent outbursts from Paige, so I don't crash the car upon hearing her wail. This is the little game we play where she acts like a wild animal and I play our favorite guessing game of 'what's wrong, honey?' This theater plays out most days. Honestly, we could sell tickets.

But I know her issue this time, it's obvious. Her dress is toast, and I find myself secretly pleased, knowing it will necessitate moving on and buying an updated outfit that will match her ever-growing, but still slight frame. But the timing is not right at all. The class starts at four o'clock, and it's now 3:20. Getting to Ms. May's Dance Studio will take at least thirty-five minutes without traffic, which only leaves me with five minutes to spare. Without the dress mishap, it would have been close, but now we are full-on screwed.

I contemplate purchasing a new dress at the mall, but quickly rule that out. No shopping trip with an eight-year-old, in the history of the universe, has ever taken less than five minutes. I weigh my options. We could skip class, but we had to miss last week because of a parent-teacher conference, and I can't do that again. I know Ms. May would veto Paige wearing her school uniform in class, even if she did have the right slippers on.

Ms. May had booted a sobbing girl from class last spring for not wearing approved attire. It wasn't helpful that the girl's hair was not in a tight bun—as per the Approved Attire Policy, along with pale pink tights and leather ballet slippers with elastic straps. And for heaven's sake, no tutus. For some reason, tutus and nylon slippers are blasphemous and not allowed, either. Don't ask me why. It's Ms. May's policy, and Ms. May must never be questioned. There is no wiggle room with her supreme authority.

So, where does that leave us? Time to improvise.

Ace Hardware is in the same strip mall as the studio. I'd visited it many times after Paige's ballet classes for odds and ends needed for woodworking projects. I cross my fingers as we rush into the store. Paige clutches her ribcage as if wounded on the battlefield. People stare. We ignore them. We are on a mission and have less than five minutes before we are officially late and out of compliance with the holy Approved Attire Policy. One strike against us, we might be able to slide. But two? No way.

I had already ruled out staples or buying a needle and thread and somehow learning how to sew on the drive over. I'm a realist. Thankfully, Ace comes through. Just past the paint aisle, there is an entire adhesive section full of choices. This leaves me with one good option—duct tape. Standard gray is my go-to for just about everything. I like the stuff with the gorilla on it, but when I pick it up, Paige gives me one of those looks that, well… she looks just like her mom. I've seen that look many times over the last twenty-plus years. *Not approved.* I quickly put it back and move down a few feet to the decorative tape section.

Paige doesn't hesitate. She makes a selection, spins on her leather slippers, and heads for the cash register. I grab the tape with the gorilla on it anyway because you can never have enough duct tape.

Three people stand in the line before us. We have three minutes. I kneel beside Paige on the dirty white linoleum floor, peel up a corner of the red duct tape with ladybugs on it, and wrap her up. As she spins, I overlap the tape around her midsection, covering up the rip as best I can without attaching it to her skin. On my fifth pass around her back, we start to attract attention from the other shoppers. Paige loves it.

The older woman directly in front of us is buying one small bag of wood screws. She sees our angst and impatience. With a knowing, grandmotherly look, she nods and allows us to skip her in line. I hold up the empty roll of red tape and my sturdy gray gorilla tape to the cashier and he scans them with his little gun. I see the price, $11.45. I toss a twenty-dollar bill on the counter, grab Paige's hand, and take off like a bolt of lightning.

"Put my change toward that lady's screws," I yell over my shoulder before we burst through the automatic doors and across the parking lot.

I feel the three rapid zaps of my cell phone in my pocket. A text message alert. I know it's my seventeen-year-old son Mason without looking. I set up a particular vibration for my most frequent contacts, and my pocket buzzes a lot. I ignore it for the moment. We have more significant problems.

Paige keeps up as we traverse the lot. We make it to the door of the studio with seconds to spare. I turn to Paige to give her the once-over before going in. Paige's eyes are wide.

"Dad," she pants, "I can't breathe very good."

She is taking in shallow gulps of air. Her chest is moving in and out rapidly. In my haste to cover her exposed side, I must have wrapped her up too tight.

"Hold on, honey, I got this."

I pinch the tape under her arm and cut a four-inch slit. She lets out a massive sigh of relief as the pressure releases from her chest.

"That's better," she says, sucking in a big breath.

Now we are ready to go in. We aren't late.

I admire how some children aren't fully aware of embarrassing situations. At some point in childhood, that changes, right? Anxiety or fear takes over, and they close themselves off, afraid to move forward or try new things—just like adults. Most kids, at least ones Paige's age, don't know any better yet and forge head-on into the world. So, my daughter, wrapped up like a little red burrito covered in ladybugs, is oblivious to how ridiculous she looks right now. She should be oblivious because it doesn't matter, and she's eight. It's just something that adults can't help but notice. Children, on the other hand, have the privilege of not seeing it.

I think she likes being different anyway, so this is okay. She admires her red tape and folds down the corners of the tape and says she's ready for class.

I turn to hold the door, only to be met by Ms. May herself.

Crap.

* * *

"That's quite an outfit, young lady," Ms. May says in that condescending tone that can only come from a large woman who wears a skin-tight leotard and shimmery tights five days a week.

"Thank you," Paige replies.

"It was an emergency," I offer. "She'll have a new, policy-approved outfit by class next week."

Her eyes narrow in concentration. Her expression is pained but condescending all the same. "Yes, next week. That's what I'd like to talk with you about."

"Is there a change to the schedule?" I ask.

"Only for you," she says flatly.

"I don't understand."

"These classes aren't free, Mr. Bell. You do realize that, right?"

"Of course."

"Then, we're on the same page?"

"I'm still not clear what we're talking about. I know the class isn't free. That's why we pay you."

"As I've told your wife several times, I'm a reasonable person, but I'm not here for my health. This is a business, and I require my students to pay for these lessons."

"Are you saying we missed a payment?"

"Two months of payments," she says.

My eyes widen. "Two months? Why didn't you tell me?"

"I've spoken to your wife several times," she whispers, then glances first left, then right, as if what she is about to say next is a state secret. "I'm not about to get in between a man and his wife. I know your situation is… well, unique."

I ignore the jab at me for being a stay-at-home dad.

"I'm sure this is just a misunderstanding," I tell her. "Paige has been coming here for over two years, and we haven't had any issues before. I'll get this straightened out right away."

"That's all well and good, but I'm afraid I can't let Paige into class today without payment. You see, this is a business and I require—"

"Payment. Yes, I get it. What do we owe?" I ask, pulling out my wallet.

"Your balance is $425, but I will require you to pre-pay for the rest of your daughter's Ballet II class."

"Fine, and what will that be?"

She pulls a folded, moist piece of paper from the bra latched around her massive bosom.

"It'll be $925 in total."

"No problem."

I hand her my faded MasterCard, which I use for all our household needs and purchases. I follow her inside the studio, and Paige frolics over to her classmates on the floor, who have just begun stretching.

Ms. May inserts the card, punches in the numbers, and waits for it to connect.

"Declined," she growls.

Confused, I say, "Try it again, please."

This has never happened before. We have never missed a payment on anything that I know of, but I don't handle the finances for the family. Tina brings in the money and organizes our finances. She gives me a monthly budget to manage, and this was not over that budget. This has to be some misunderstanding.

"Declined again."

I glance away from Ms. May's stern look to see that Paige

has joined the line with her classmates. She's twirling around, happy and wrapped in red tape. I pray that Ms. May doesn't yank Paige out of line and cause a scene. Paige would never forgive me.

After a brief lecture on financial responsibility, Ms. May lets us slide.

"Just this one time. Don't make me regret it, Mr. Bell," she says before commencing the class.

Paige's face is beaming as the class moves through the various arm positions and basic movements. I've seen this simple instruction dozens of times, but I smile despite myself while trying to ignore the churn in my stomach about the credit card.

That shouldn't happen… not to people like us.

CHAPTER 2

I have never been offended by being called Mr. Mom. It would be an insult to moms everywhere if I, a father of three, took offense to being likened to a woman who displays an undying love for her children. Most moms are invisible superheroes hidden away, because when mom's around, everything works and everyone else's life is more comfortable. Moms do so much more than they ever get credit for. And yes, I know the irony of me—Mr. Mom—making this claim, but so be it. It's true.

In my family, the central parental figure, or primary parent, isn't a mom. It's me. Yes, I'm a man, and I'm not special because of it. I volunteered for this role as a stay-at-home dad, and I don't feel stuck—regardless of what most people assume.

When Jaden was born, followed two years later by his brother Mason, I left the "working" world and became a homemaker. This was nineteen years ago. OK, homemaker sounds antiquated. Did I stay at home? Yes. But anyone who says having kids means you "stay home" is out of touch. If you stay home alone with your offspring for too long, you slowly devolve into a madness of PB&J and cartoons on repeat. That's not fair to moms or me.

The first few years were a breeze, just me and my two boys. We did 'boy things' like playing tag, shooting rockets in the park, tossing the baseball around, and building forts out of blankets and couch cushions. We also created one truly epic tree fort in the backyard, then built an addition onto it. It was the envy of the neighborhood, dare I say.

We frequently had peeing-distance contests in the backyard, too. We're in stay-at-home dad territory here. It's much harder, but I imagine not impossible for a female to win a peeing-distance contest—sorry, moms. I'd like to see that, but not in a creepy way. Just that it's a feat I think deserves some special attention, but obviously, some privacy, too. I would sometimes let the boys win the contest, because let's face it, I had a distinct advantage over the wee lads.

Back then, I was just a cool dad who was super involved. I volunteered in their classrooms and for school committees. I coached their soccer and baseball teams. The parent association usually assigned me tasks like building carnival booths or schlepping a U-Haul full of boxes of purple licorice to be sold to the sugar-deprived children at Columbia Ridge. I didn't mind; I had found a niche and I enjoyed it.

I was labeled Mr. Mom when Paige came along eight years ago. There is something that people just don't get about a father being the primary parent of a little girl. I've made tutus and painted pictures of unicorns and didn't bat an eye. We also built birdhouses and flower boxes in the garage. That's what we do. But the first time I was called Mr. Mom was by Meredith Stonemeyer, who was responsible for the Girl Scout Troop Paige had begged me to let her join.

Meredith had a bad habit of not preparing for the meetings or she would just not show up. She was one of the few moms at Columbia Ridge who had a full-time job outside of the house. *Gasp, the horror.* Her absence from the meetings occurred twice before I took any action. So, on the third no-show, in front of 13 seven- and eight-year-old girls, I stepped in.

In truth, I was just looking to fill the time, but the girls were excited by the project that I had proposed. We were in the multipurpose room of the county library, and just outside the hall were rows and rows of white cardboard boxes that had previously stored books. I put my construction management skills to the test and challenged the girls to build a small castle with the boxes. Had this build been for boys, it would have been called a fort, but when in Rome, right?

The moms sitting along the back wall snickered amongst themselves as I took charge, but I wasn't deterred. I enlisted the help of a terrified-looking dad who had to break away from some game on his phone to help bring the boxes inside the room. He did his job and returned to his phone, glad to be free. The moms watched, first for a laugh, but then slowly, they decided this wasn't the worst idea ever and joined in. Maybe a male could provide some value here.

Someone opened one of those insanely large boxes of colored markers, and soon each girl was decorating a square of our makeshift castle. I tied the boxes together with some yarn and a hole-punch left behind by the last group in the multipurpose room.

Was our castle structurally sound? Not a chance. But we weren't preparing for hurricane winds; we were just killing time. But then Meredith Stonemeyer abruptly entered the room—twenty minutes late—wearing the sensible business attire of a working professional. I like to call it a costume because people act differently when they wear it. She also wore the strained expression of an over-subscribed adult as she dragged little Maggie Stonemeyer by the arm toward the front of the room.

Displeased, Meredith surveyed our work. I ignored her but couldn't help smiling at the finished product. It was a fairytale; a lopsided jumble of decorated boxes that might transport young minds into a land where princesses attended elaborate balls and the basic economics of feudal land-holding society was overlooked.

The girls continued working on the project, which was probably what upset Meredith the most. She had arrived, and she was supposed to be in charge. How dare someone try to usurp her?

"I've got it from here, Mr. Mom," she said with scorn. "We have an agenda for the meeting. It's not just playtime."

And there it was. "Mr. Mom" was a bad thing, and forever tainted by the icy words of a real working mom who didn't like a man entering her tightly choreographed world of cookie sales, yoga pants, merit badges, and shaming stay-at-home parents.

I looked at the other moms, who were still actively participating and maybe enjoying themselves at these unbearable meetings for the first time. They looked ashamed and afraid. Was it because they agreed with her, and they were embarrassed for me? Or were they toeing the line as not to offend this Mamma Bear? Maybe it was a mixture of both.

What did Meredith Stonemeyer have that I didn't have? I can tell you one thing—I'd beat her at a peeing contest, for sure.

* * *

We're nearly a year removed from the Mr. Mom comment, and I've had time to reflect on it, and I get it, somewhat. But I'll get into that later.

I've gotten a little ahead of myself. My name is James Bell, and I am a stay-at-home dad. I haven't held a steady, paying job outside the house for nearly two decades. I'm in charge of raising the kids and running the place. That's my job. Yes, it's a real thing that men do—they just don't talk about it. When would they talk about it? At the office with their co-workers? Obviously not. At the Mommy-and-Me playdates? Again, no. We don't get invited to those.

If a man stays home, it means his wife wears the pants. She makes the money, and you—the man—are subservient to her. This is why nobody, especially men, talk about it. But it's just a gender swap, that's all. Families choose to have one parent at home quite often; it's just usually a mom.

Please don't get me wrong, I'm not here to judge parents who both work full-time. Lord knows we can only afford this lifestyle because Tina works a lot and earns more. She's always out of town, but her work allows me to be the primary parent to our kids.

This life is not exactly what I had envisioned for myself. I used to be a professional project manager for a construction firm. You might have caught that with the whole castle-made-of-boxes thing. But I have a great life. Sure, it can get lonely, but thankfully, I have Christy to pal around with. And that's all it is, despite the gossip in the Tribe. We're providing each other a healthy outlet for human interaction. We're both married, and our spouses know that we're friends.

This loneliness is something the stay-at-home moms and dads don't talk about outside their circle. Who would feel sorry for us? For feeling lonely and needing friendship? You wouldn't understand until you're in it. You're alone, devoid of other adults, except for those loons on TV talk shows, which serve as company and background noise while you work around the house. Trust me, you don't want to get hooked on those shows—it's a downward spiral from which you can't come back.

I've heard stay-at-home parents say their kids are their best friends. Um, no, thank you. I love my three crazy kids, but not like that.

Jaden, my firstborn, is nineteen and away at his first year of college. He's at the University of Oregon in Eugene, which is not far from our home in Lake Oswego, outside of Portland. He's a full-grown man and on scholarship for the baseball team.

Mason, whose text message I need to return, is seventeen and attempting to finish his junior year of high school. It's been an uphill battle with that one. There's always one, right? If video games were graded, I'm confident he'd be a valedictorian. But they aren't graded, and he's not on any honor rolls. Having money to provide your kids with a good education doesn't mean they will automatically get smarter. I think they fight it more. Is it privilege? Possibly.

So, my co-workers at home are my kids. It's not a manager-employee relationship. We're on the same team, but I can't fire them. I read something once about servant leadership—how good leaders serve others to help them succeed, which lifts the whole group—and I think that applies here. Not just a servant. Not subservient. Servant leader.

OK, we are moving on now. This is my life.

CHAPTER 3

I watch Paige's class but keep one eye on the studio door. I know that I will never see what I'm looking for coming through that door—Tina. Her flight was supposed to land at Portland International at two o'clock this afternoon, giving her plenty of time to make it to today's class. I had put it on her calendar—not that it mattered much. All the classes are on a calendar we share, although I'm the only one who adds to it. The appointment reminders always pop up on her phone, but it doesn't make a difference when she's in LA or Seattle or Salt Lake City. She just ignores them, routinely. Mainly because she's hundreds of miles away and can't attend, but not today. Today she's in town and available to be here, but she's not.

Tina has attended a grand total of one dance class in the last two years. That was one in thirty-nine chances, not a great average. And even then, she took a phone call and missed the second half. She always says there's something pressing in the world of medical device sales. She's an executive who still makes sales, mostly medical devices that get implanted inside people. But if you want the details, you've got the wrong guy, because she doesn't talk to me about that stuff, and I'm a little squeamish about blood.

Back in the day, Tina was better at going to events with Jaden. He played baseball, and there were seemingly hundreds of games to attend. She was in town more then, so the expectation was evident each morning when I set his clean uniform out, signaling game day. She probably came to half of the in-town games. When he started traveling on the weekends and summers with his club team, she didn't see one. Now that Jaden is at the University of Oregon, playing baseball for their Division I team, I've lost track of her attendance record—and I wasn't counting, either. It's not her thing—attending her children's events. I've long since let it go, or at least nagging her about it. She can go if she wants, but typically, she doesn't.

Mason isn't an athlete if you don't count Xbox. He never played an instrument. Never sang in a choir. He hangs out with his buddies from school. They skateboard and skip class, and that's about it. There's nothing for Tina to miss. Here is where I'm supposed to say something positive about my son, maybe something excellent he did. Sorry, I've got nothing other than he's not a total slacker. I love him to pieces, but he excels at very little. Tina and Mason probably have the closest relationship of all the kids, which is ironic since they couldn't be more different. She competes in triathlons, often placing in the top of her age group; Mason doesn't even own a pair of running shoes.

The parental separation of duties is the agreement my wife and I have, although it isn't written down, officially. We never signed on the dotted line, but it's an agreement we made—an unspoken contract. I never nagged her to do more after the first few years, even if it hurts my heart to see her miss every single significant event in our children's lives. I am in charge of the kids and the house. She works. And works. And works. That's the deal.

She has made one request of me concerning the kids and their many activities.

"Take a picture for me," she asked years ago when I dropped her off at the airport one day. Jaden was in the backseat in his baseball uniform; we were on the way to his game. He was smacking his fist into his new glove, trying to soften it up. His blue cap was askew. Tina watched him but spoke to me.

"Pictures of what?" I asked.

"Jaden. His game."

That simple request has become a Bell family tradition that has spanned over a decade. The kids stand for pictures. Baseball games. School dances. Boy Scouts. Ballet class. Swim lessons. Graduations—really, she never made it to those, either. I stand behind the camera and snap away. I previously used a nice point-and-shoot camera with an optic lens, but now I just use my cell phone and text each picture to Tina. She always replies, "Thank you, James," sometimes with a smiley face emoji.

I hate that stupid emoji.

I have thousands of photos saved on my computer, memories encapsulated on camera. I imagine one day printing them all out and creating a giant flipbook that I could thumb through, from the earliest days until now, watching them grow taller.

It makes me sad. Not for me and not for the kids. For her. For my wife. She's missed it all.

* * *

Paige scampers over after class, weaving between her classmates as they meet their parents along the back hallway of the studio.

"How'd I do, Daddy?"

"Perfect, as usual," I tell her. "Time for your picture."

Paige takes a step back, realizes she is standing in a shadow, then moves slightly to the right so she has a wide beam of light facing her. She cocks her head to the side and flashes a smile. It's a practiced routine, one she knows very well.

We hurry out of the studio. I do not want to present Ms. May the opportunity to have another one-on-one. Or promise again that I would pay in full the next time because I'm reasonably sure she wouldn't believe me, which I find incredulous given our two-year relationship with her studio. I'll call the credit card company tonight and get it figured out, but right now my priority is getting home and making dinner.

Mason's text message earlier was asking if he could sleepover at his friend Yoseph's house. They planned to play Call of Duty online with some other friends. It was a Friday night, so I agreed to let him go, but only after dinner together. He wasn't leaving until around seven o'clock, so he had time anyway. Due to Paige's various after school commitments and activities, we had not had dinner together all week. These dinners are essential to a cohesive family, even if the kids find them tedious.

There's always a chance Tina will be at the house too, and I'd prefer the place to be full of children for some of the night. A buffer of sorts.

* * *

I park the car in one of the three bays of our garage. Our home is in a gated community in Lake Oswego, just south of Portland. We purchased the 2,950-square foot, four-bed, three-bath home before Paige was born for just under a million dollars. Surrounding homes have gone for considerably more in recent years. The 10,000-square foot lot is small but treed on all sides except on the narrow private road leading up to it. The primary traffic on our road comes from walkers and joggers who come by early in the morning, often before the sun rises.

Just last year, we finished building a small shop in the backyard. I have dreams of filling it with woodworking tools and producing furniture out of reclaimed barn wood. We had a shop growing up, but I haven't built anything since I left my parents' home. I always loved the craft of building, but it wasn't a priority, so I kept delaying building the shop. It was pricy, given the sloped lot and poor access for construction equipment, but we managed. Unfortunately, I have yet to move any of my old tools from the garage into the shop. Currently, the shop is used as a workout area for Jaden, and now with him away at school, it just sits empty. I will get around to putting the shop together, but right now, my focus is on the kids.

It's a great family house. I think if we had couple-friends, they would be envious of the house we own or the lifestyle we live. Alas, we don't have couple-friends. Christy and Malcolm have visited occasionally, but it's not a frequent thing. Tina doesn't care for Malcolm, and on this, we agree. He never stops yammering about his service in the Navy. He's a bore, which respectfully, isn't a bad thing in a commercial pilot.

Lake Oswego is small, but still close enough to the big city to be considered a bedroom community or suburb with a life of its own. The private and public schools here are great, and the people are friendly. It even smells good here—no complaints on my part. We settled in the right place.

I wish I could tell our couple-friends about it.

Having grown up on the green, misty Oregon Coast two-hours away, I'm not sure I could have found a better replacement than Lake Oswego. The weather was an upgrade from the gloomy coast, painted a watery gray for nine months a year. When I go back home to see my parents in Shoreline, it is always gray, inside and out.

In the garage, I open the door of the SUV and squeeze by a rack of five old, unused kayaks. Well, four unused kayaks and one gently used one. I bought them on a whim one day when Tina said she'd like to try the sport. She occasionally takes hers out on the lake, but the rest still have the tags dangling from the tips. *Maybe someday.*

Paige is sound asleep. I unbuckle her seat belt and carefully lift her out of the car. Her eight-year-old body is heavier than I remember. I shut the door with my rear and shimmy past my dusty woodworking tools that I should have already moved to the shop out back.

Unfortunately, I don't see the item sitting on the last of three steps leading from the garage to the mudroom—Mason's backpack. I catch my right foot on the bag, throwing my balance off just enough that I lunge forward and slam Paige's head on the doorway.

Instant tears. A reasonable response.

When we enter the kitchen, Paige is crying into my ear, but I can still hear the laughing and conversation coming from the living room. Mason and Tina.

So, she is home.

Tina hears the crying and greets us in the kitchen.

"Oh no, poor baby," she says. "What happened?"

Tina takes Paige out of my arms, and I think that there aren't many days left when I will carry her from the car to the house. She's getting so big. Or maybe my arms are just not getting any stronger. I feel old.

Tina cradles Paige in her arms for only a moment before she lets her slide down to her feet and stands. She wouldn't want to comfort her for more than thirty seconds or anything.

"Mommy!" Paige says. "You're back. How long?"

"Just a few days, sweetheart," Tina says. "Through the weekend."

Paige looks to me. "I thought you said she'd be here for a week this time?"

Lately, Tina's schedule has become even more irregular. I've had a hard time keeping up. I look to Tina for the answer.

"You know how it is," she says, flipping through the mail on the counter. "Plans change. I have a commitment I need to get to. I need to leave Monday."

I do the math. I could either look at it as four days, part of Friday and Monday, plus the weekend. Or view it as two days. Tonight is shot, and Monday she's off again, leaving just the weekend for family time.

"And I've got that triathlon tomorrow, too," she said.

I had forgotten about that, even though it's on the

calendar. So, let's call it one day. *Yippee.*

Paige's smile beams, happy to see her mom. Even Mason, who would usually be hiding in his room right now, leans against the doorway like he is part of the family unit, even if he doesn't say anything. He wants to be near her. I get it.

They are excited to see her. It is always a show when Tina comes home. Disneyland Mom—always a party, Happiest Place on Earth mom. Her flame burns bright for a relatively brief period and then goes dark again. This time for one day. Again, yippee.

Tina has this way about her. Somehow, she can transform herself into the most interesting person in the room and hold the attention of everyone around her, even with strangers. She is sincere and actively listens. She can say a thousand words with one look and speak on an endless number of topics with expertise. In turn, she makes you feel like you are the most vital person in the world, if only for the brief time she spends focusing on you. You can keep that memory in your mind even when she is gone.

She does this at parties, weddings, and I can only imagine at meetings with hospital boards and the doctors she visits selling medical devices. Her tactic is excellent for sales when an instant connection is needed, but it's less useful for long-term relationship maintenance. I hate that she does it with the kids because they don't know any better, that's just how Mom is. Her con. Vibrant and full of life. And she can keep up this false front because she leaves before the light burns out and reality returns.

And I hate that she is beautiful, even in the harsh light of the kitchen. This has always been true. Shoulder-length dark brown hair with a natural wave. Soft skin. Toned body. Curves in all the right places. She stays fit and knows the treadmill very well. The early 40s have never looked so good.

"You've got a race, Mommy?" Paige asks.

"Yes, do you want to go?"

"I do. I do!"

Tina gives me a look that says *you can make that happen, right?* I nod, yes.

"Of course, you can come," Tina says, leaning down and rubbing noses with Paige. "You'll give me the energy to keep going. I'm going to need it. My training schedule has not been very consistent lately."

She takes a step back, finally noticing the red duct tape encircling her child.

Again, *the look* is aimed in my direction.

"The dress ripped. It was a quick fix so Paige could attend class," I say. "I'll get her another one next week."

"Good, because she looks terrible. Like a homeless person."

And with that, her bright light burns out in under two minutes—that had to be a record.

* * *

"Dad, can we go? Our Call of Duty mission starts at seven-thirty, and Yoseph and I need to get ready," Mason said.

All four of us were at the dinner table, finishing up spaghetti and garlic bread, which is my go-to meal at least twice a week. Tina would usually rebuff the carbs, but with the race tomorrow, she indulges.

"You have to prep for an online video game?" I ask. "What does that involve?"

"It's not like the old days, Dad, when you were an Italian plumber breaking blocks with your head, throwing mushrooms and saving princesses in 8-Bit. Call of Duty is like real life."

"Don't diss the classics; those games were revolutionary when I was a kid."

"Times have changed in the last eighty years," he says.

I ignore his historically inaccurate timeline and insulting exaggeration of my age.

"Apparently," I say. "So, you're a Marine killing bad guys now?"

"Sort of. We like the zombie-mode and play as a team on missions and stuff."

"Zombies are real life?"

"It's just a video game, Dad," Mason says. "Can we go?"

"Yes, as soon as I clean up dinner."

"But Dad, I said I'd be there already."

"You can wait ten more minutes. The zombies will still be dead."

"Undead," he asserts.

"I can take him," Tina says after staying silent for most of the meal.

Tina has three choices in this scenario. First, she could stay out of it because parenting isn't her strong suit, and she doesn't have any history of Mason's recent behavior. Second, she could have volunteered to clean up dinner so I could drive him as I'd already agreed. But she picked the third and not surprising option—she offered to drive Mason, which means she can leave the house immediately.

The two of them get up and leave the table. I make sure Mason knows he needs to secure a ride home from Yoseph's mom in the morning since Paige and I will be at Tina's race. He agrees.

They have already closed the garage door and backed out of the driveway before I have the dishes cleared. Yoseph's house is about twenty minutes away with traffic.

Time to get Paige ready for bed. She should be sound asleep when Tina returns, giving me the chance to ask her about the declined credit card.

CHAPTER 4

The buzz in my pocket wakes me up—three quick zaps against my thigh. I squint as the glare from Paige's purple princess nightlight enters my eyes from two feet away. I'm lying on the floor beside her bed, covered in a pint-size baby blanket that, for some reason, is still in my eight-year-old's room. Her stuffed brown bear, Mr. Hugs, is smashed under my head, giving me no comfort whatsoever. My hand is high over my head and painfully asleep, still clutching Paige's hand as she lightly snores.

I pull down my hand and shake my head to remove the cobwebs of sleep. I look at my watch. One-forty-five a.m. Paige asked me to lie next to her at bedtime. She does that sometimes when she's either not ready to fall asleep, or when she has had a rough day. I know that I shouldn't lay down next to her. I've read the books about your children growing too dependent on you to fall asleep, but I don't give a crap about what some Ph.D. says about it. When your little girl asks you to help her fall asleep, you do it—end of story.

Unfortunately, I was exhausted, as evidenced by the time of night. I roll on my side, pull my phone out of my pocket, and confirm that the message is from Mason.

Dad sorry. I need you to get me. Sorry.

The message is followed by the map coordinates that cell phones let you send people to tell them your location. I find this mildly amusing that Mason thinks he needs to tell me where Yoseph's house is.

Why?

The little dots appear. I can tell he's typing.

Just come. Don't be mad. Sorry.

I stand up. This isn't a battle I want to fight tonight. I'll just go get him, it's easier. We can talk about it when I'm not half-asleep. Then in the morning, he can come to the race too, something that I hadn't figured on before, but now in the dark of Paige's room, it seems like a good idea.

I gently close Paige's door and head down the hallway past the double doors of our master bedroom. A small blue Post-it note is affixed to the outside of one of the closed doors.

I didn't want to wake you up. You looked tired.

I have to be up at 4 a.m. Please don't wake me.

-Tina

Great. Now I'm not welcome in my bedroom, either.

* * *

I pull up in front of Yoseph's house. All the lights are off except a single light illuminating the porch. His neighborhood is a far cry from ours in terms of real estate value, but they live in a nice, tidy home. Yoseph's parents are very kind people. I've had many conversations with them at school functions, and years ago, birthday parties for the boys.

I text Mason and tell him that I'm out front.

Where? I don't see you

I tell him I'm parked in Yoseph's driveway and to come outside.

I'm not at Yoseph's

Then it dawns on me why he sent me the map and why he kept saying, "sorry." I scroll up in the text message string and click on the map. He's in Wilsonville, nearly thirty minutes away in a residential neighborhood near Merryfield Park.

I avoid a text message scolding and tell him I'll be there shortly.

It's three a.m. before I roll up to the location Mason gave me on the map. Every other house on the cul-de-sac is quiet and dark. The one exception is a house with the basement lights flashing red, green, and blue to a rhythmic dance beat that I can hear from the road. Of course, this is where Mason is. Six cars are parked in the driveway with another eight or ten vehicles lining the street.

I park a few doors down and text Mason. Five minutes pass. No reply. I text again in between watching teenagers stumble in and out of the front door. Most wander down the street like the zombies Mason was supposed to encounter on his Xbox tonight. I can only imagine that video games were never really a part of his evening plans.

Tired of waiting for Mason to text me back, I decide to knock on the door and see if one of the teenage zombies can locate my son. As I ascend the steps, the front door bursts open, and three teen girls rush out, chasing each other with silly string. They blow past me, but not before covering my jacket with blue goo. They collapse in an "ashes, ashes, we all fall down" heap on the front lawn, a drunken mess of flammable silly string covering them. One girl looks up to the sky and says, presumably to me, "Sorry, mister." They laugh and roll around on the damp grass.

I enter the house. Red Solo cups line the stairs to the second story. The floor vibrates from the bass of the music coming from downstairs. I follow the sound of voices toward the back of the house. Empty bottles of vodka and tequila litter the rest of the counter.

Something crashes downstairs, and the music stops for a few seconds. A boy yells at someone for not watching where he was going, then I hear cheers as the music resumes.

Finding nobody alive or undead on the main floor, I descend the steps to the basement. A couple in the throes of passion are going at it, fully clothed, on the landing halfway down. I gingerly step over them and find myself in a mancave filled with sweaty teens. A half-dozen kids stand around a pool table holding drink cups and shooting pool. A bar partially fills the back half of the room.

A movie screen covers the far wall with a grizzly scene projected—a desert battlefield that is littered with dead bodies. In front of the screen, several boys stand a move their bodies with the motion of their video game characters.

I see Yoseph on a couch facing the screen. He doesn't see me—none of them do. I cross the room to him and finally see Mason, slumped on the floor next to Yoseph's legs. His mouth is open and his eyes are closed; he's passed out.

"Hey, man! Watch it!" one of the gamers says when I pass in front of the screen. "We're on fire here!"

I kneel, and I put my hands on Mason's face.

"Mace," I say, "Wake up. Time to go home, pal."

His eyes open slowly. "Dad, hey," he says, his words slow and sloppy. "Sorry."

"Yeah, I bet, but not half as sorry as you're going to be in the morning."

"No, D.D.," he says. "That's funny. D.D. Like Dad. You're the D.D. and Dad. Ha!"

"What are you talking about?" I ask.

"I don't feel so—"

These are not words you want to hear from your drunken seventeen-year-old son in a stranger's basement. The sounds of graphic gunfire and growling zombies somewhat drown out the sound of Mason's vomiting. As an experienced parent who has watched Mason projectile vomit his baby formula and many other liquids, I react quickly and save my clothing. I can do nothing for the poor gamer standing closest to the couch, though.

* * *

I help Mason to his feet and tell Yoseph that he's coming with us, and luckily, he doesn't argue. The lovers on the stairs have moved to a more discrete location, so our path is less treacherous.

I am keenly aware that it may be my responsibility to break up this party and send the underage drinkers on their way. I am not geared up for that battle, not when I'm dragging my son out of the party.

We get outside. I lean Mason against the SUV as I dig my keys out of my pocket. Yoseph slides in next to him.

"Dad, Dad," Mason says, avoiding my eyes, but placing his hand on my shoulder.

"What?" I'm not in the mood for this.

"Take our picture, you know, for Mom… She wouldn't want to miss this one!"

I don't laugh. Mason closes his eyes and slumps to the ground.

Despite the rear windows being down and a lengthy trip on the freeway blasting cold air on their faces, both boys fall asleep on the ride home. Having them asleep is way better than being awake since they can't barf all over the interior of the car if they aren't conscious. At least, I don't think so.

I take the exit for our neighborhood and think about what just happened. Mason said there was no D.D. It took me a minute to figure out what he meant—a designated driver—someone who wasn't wasted who could take them home. When Jaden and later, Mason entered high school, I sat each of them on the couch and laid down the law when it came to parties and drinking. I told them that I knew they would attend parties and that alcohol would be there; both protested like that would never happen. Sure, boys. I told them that I hoped they would wait until they could legally drink before taking part, but I'm a realist, and I was a kid once, too. I knew they wouldn't comply one hundred percent of the time.

The request of my teenage boys was simple—don't hide your poor choices for fear of being caught. If you need a ride home, for any reason, you can call me, day or night, to get you. I'd rather find you wasted or get you out of some other tough situation than see you at the hospital or police station. Everyone makes mistakes; they don't define us but their impacts can be mitigated with better choices. Getting help when you need it, regardless of the consequences, is a better choice.

This is pretty much the same talk we had about the birds and the bees. These conversations were a part of my parenting series, titled in my head as "Dumb Stuff To Avoid So You Don't Screw Up Your Life." We also talked about school, honesty, and hard work, among other pressing subjects. But these were the big ones after drinking and sex.

So, am I pissed off that Mason is currently passed out drunk in my backseat? Yes, I am. Am I surprised? Not really. But I have to account for what he did when he found himself in trouble. He texted me. Through the syrupy fog of drunkenness, he made a better choice. That's probably the best outcome for which I could have hoped.

I pull into the garage and open the car door on Yoseph's side. He's awake now, but only because gravity made itself known when I opened the door and he nearly fell out.

"Where do your parents think you are right now?" I ask.

"Staying here," he says. I can tell he's trying to sober up.

"Well, I guess that worked out in your favor, then."

I get them both inside the house. Mason tried to go upstairs to his room, but I stopped him and re-directed him to our office on the main floor. The office has two couches that I'd prefer the drunk hooligans sleep on, mainly because they are leather, which is significantly easier to clean than a mattress. Also, the floor is hardwood. The advantages are fairly clear.

I make sure each kid is propped up on his side and with

a plastic garbage bin within arm's reach. I mentally prepare myself for vomit patrol in the morning, but at least I did my part.

"Mace," I say when he stirs on the couch. "Thank you for texting me."

"No, D.D.," he says in a whisper.

"Who took you to the party?"

"Mom."

Of course.

"Night, Mace. I love you," I say before clicking off the light.

It's almost four in the morning when I head for my bed. The little blue note on the door stops me. I forgot.

"Please don't wake me."

Must be nice.

CHAPTER 5

Conservatively, I probably got about four hours of sleep last night, which wouldn't be all together terrible if there hadn't been a three-hour designated driver break in the middle. I slept in Jaden's room, which remains unchanged since he left for college. The walls are covered with posters of baseball and football players. An Oregon Ducks flag is pinned to the ceiling with thumbtacks. His baseball trophies and awards are crammed onto a shelf above his desk.

On the nightstand next to the bed is a picture of my father, or as the kids call him, Grandpa Mitch. Jaden and my father stand in front of the Westcott Inn, the large bed-and-breakfast my father owns in Shoreline. They both hold fishing rods and several shore perch they caught just down the beach.

Jaden looks so young in that picture—both of them do—but Jaden is twice as big today. He was probably seven or eight years old in the picture, baby-faced with a shaggy mop of hair covering his eyes. In the ten years since that photograph, Jaden filled out and became a man. It's the only picture of himself in his entire room. With all the pictures I've taken over the years, Jaden chose this to leave up, just him and Grandpa Mitch.

It's five-fifteen in the morning and I hear a honk from a car in the driveway. I peer out and see an unfamiliar gold-colored Chevy Tahoe. A man sits behind the wheel wearing a white hat and aviator sunglasses that are not entirely necessary for the dim morning light. He watches the front door, which I hear open, then close again.

Then the garage door cranks open, and Tina wheels out her racing bike to the Tahoe. The man gets out, fiddles with a rack attached to the trailer hitch, and secures her bike next to another one already mounted there.

I don't recognize the stranger picking up my wife in his Tahoe. Tina and I don't really have any mutual friends, and we don't get out much together. I'm certain she couldn't pick out any of my friends from a line up, either. She knows Christy and Malcolm, and my buddy Seth, who still lives in Shoreline.

But I don't know this guy driving my wife, and the fact that she knows him well enough to pick her up at this early hour is not particularly comforting.

By the time they back out of the driveway, I'm in the kitchen attempting to make coffee in my sleep.

* * *

The Tentpole Triathlon is an annual event held in and around Pierce Lake, south of Portland. The lake is a reservoir created by an upstream dam on the Manzana River. A large 150-site beachfront campground spans a sweeping bend in the river that also serves as the swim, bike, and run exchange point. Participants and spectators rent campsites for the weekend, turning the sleepy campground into an overrun zoo for fit, affluent professionals who complete endurance races. It sells out every year in less than an hour. I learned all of this from the race's website after Tina forwarded me her registration email. Tina and I don't see each other much, but we're pretty good at email. It's the one-on-one stuff we're not great at.

I park my SUV behind an endless row of cars on the shoulder of a dirt road more than a mile from the campground entrance. I decided to let the boys sleep it off at home. This is not because I'm nice. It's because I didn't want to deal with their hungover attitudes, especially since I was already rather grumpy from our busy night. Had I not promised Paige we'd attend the event, we definitely would not be here.

Paige and I fall in line with hundreds of other spectators ambling down to the campground exchange point. I have one chair strapped to my back, and I'm carrying a second. Paige is carrying our lunch and a few "passing the time" activities in a backpack. She's skipping her way down the road, though I'm not as enthusiastic.

The sun is up, and it's already in the mid-sixties at eight in the morning. It's going to be unseasonably hot. By the time we get to the campground entrance and pay our Day Use fee, the swimmers are gathering at the water's edge. Massive signs say Sprint and Olympic, denoting the two distances participants can choose.

More than 200 athletes wearing swim attire stand in a roped-off area fronted by the sprint sign. The sprint distance amounts to a half-mile swim, 12.4-mile bike ride, and a 3.1-mile run. This race length is the most popular choice. People are actually smiling. These participants don't look as fit, nor as geared up as the Olympic-distance athletes.

A significantly smaller group is milling about near the Olympic sign. The collection is less because the Olympic distance is approximately twice the Sprint distance. More challenging race, fewer participants. The athletes are fit and serious. No smiles.

Tina is doing the Olympic distance, and I spot her immediately. She's wearing an all-black one-piece swimsuit like nearly every other athlete. Her dark hair is tucked under a bright green cap, giving her an otherworldly look. Green goggles sit atop her head, waiting to be worn when she enters the water. The number 904 is stenciled in black paint on her left shoulder and right calf.

She's pacing back and forth like a panther in a cage, head

down, ignoring everyone around her. She's not the only one in this mode. The assembled group is a swarm of ants on a hill, crisscrossing each other. I take note that the guy from the gold Tahoe is nowhere to be found.

Paige sees her mom and races over to the roped-off Olympic area to grab her attention before I can tell her that spectators aren't supposed to be in that section. I have no choice but to follow her. A volunteer gives me the stink-eye as we pass. Paige calls for her mom, who doesn't hear her the first or second time. Eventually, the shouts of *Mom* break her concentration, and her intense stare fades. I worry that she'll snap at Paige for interrupting her pre-race ritual, but she doesn't.

She walks to the edge of the rope corral and kneels so she and Paige are eye to eye. She puts a hand on our daughter's head, petting her hair. She smiles.

"Hi, Mom," Paige says. She waits, knowing that she's done a good thing by attending her mom's event and wanting the acknowledgment for it.

This is where many parents would say, "Hello, I'm glad you're here." But she doesn't. She launches right into a complaint directed first at Paige, then me.

"They moved the race to a staggered start, so we get released in groups of twenty into the water," she says to me, standing and ignoring Paige. "Apparently some people last year complained about getting knocked around and kicked in the water by the shotgun start. Ridiculous. That's what we all trained for, and they changed it based on a few complaints?"

Paige holds up a white poster board.

"Mom, I'm going to make you a sign. What colors should I use?" Paige asks, digging several bright markers from her backpack and offering up a selection.

Tina's eyes are still trained on me. I look down at Paige, refocusing Tina's attention and acknowledging that our daughter just asked her a perfectly fair question. No recognition.

"They're going to push me to the back, so I have to chase all these turtles out here," she says. "I hate that."

This is classic Tina, and I'm used to it. For better or worse, right? She's laser-focused on what's ahead, ignoring what's right in front of her.

"Tina, Paige is going to make you a poster," I say. "You can look for it when you get out of the water and switch to your bike. Isn't that great?"

Hint, hint. Earth to Tina. I've found that a gentle reminder of how people and parents are supposed to respond in such situations is best to course-correct her. Sometimes it takes several hints, but occasionally, she can flip the switch instantly.

"Yes," she says, realizing not her misstep, but the course-correction I've provided. "Yes, honey, that's great. Thank you."

"What colors, Mom?"

Tina kneels again, eye to eye with Paige. Paige blushes with unreserved attention.

Remember when I said she has a way to make you feel like the most important person in the room? Yeah, she's doing that right now.

"I will love whatever colors you decide, honey," she says as if reciting a script. "Just write really big. You're good at that. I'm going to be looking for you as soon as I finish my swim. I'll need a high-five when I come out of the water and up the path. Now give me a hug. They are just about to let us wade into the water to get acclimated to the temperature before we start."

Paige smiles and throws her arms around her mother. On instinct, I take out my phone and snap a photograph of the moment. Force of habit, I guess. Neither of them notice me doing it. I put my phone back in my pocket without looking at the picture.

Tina stands, holding Paige's hand under the rope. She looks at me. Suddenly, I'm the most important person, too. Her blue eyes are clear and focused on me alone. The world around us goes dark except her face.

"Thank you for coming. I know you're busy, and it was a long night. It means a lot that you guys came. I love you."

All I can manage to say is, "Of course."

"There are a few things I need to talk with you about. Pretty big things," she says. "I know the past few months have been rough for us. I can explain why. Tonight we should talk, just the two of us, OK?"

She never wants to talk, especially when it's just the two of us. What could be so important that she mention it now? I open my mouth to ask, but a whistle sounds, and she jogs over with her group into the water.

I watch her walk onto the beach. I set aside my questions and enjoy the flood of positive emotions that I don't often enough associate with Tina. Love. Trust. Partnership.

I don't want to walk away. Leaving this place might make those feelings disappear.

I don't get to feel this way enough, and I don't want it to end.

* * *

I need to take you back to before. Way before. Because I know what you think of Tina. And I get that. She's distant, self-absorbed, and certainly not self-aware. Maybe she's on the spectrum, perhaps not. I don't know. But there's more to her than labels. She wasn't always this way, and that's what you need to see.

I love my wife, warts and all.

I met Tina twenty years ago at a sticky bar counter in a café in Willits, California, while hitchhiking down Highway 101. I was twenty-three years old and rebelling against the small, humdrum life my father intended me to have. If he had his way, I would have never left Shoreline and would still be working for and living with him at the Westcott Inn. But that's a story for another day.

Yes, I hitchhiked down the coast and was once a total

badass. Insert sarcasm here about how it totally didn't stick.

It was the summer before Tina's senior year of college at UNLV. She was on one of those ill-advised road trips that students take on a whim. Neither she nor her college roommate had ever seen the Pacific Ocean. One weekend they blew off their part-time summer jobs and set out on an adventure to California. Somehow, they landed at the "Gateway to the Redwoods," the fair metropolis of Willits—population, who cares. This is where her roommate—who owned the car they took—got worried about being away from her job scooping ice cream and decided it was best to head back.

"I haven't come all this way to turn back now," Tina told me that day over burgers and fries. "I've lived in Nevada my whole life and never gone one state over to see the ocean. Just because Brenda decided to crawl home doesn't mean I'm going to follow her. No way."

Tina's wavy brown hair hung over one of her eyes, and she was continually tucking it behind her ear. She did that thing that guys won't tell you they like, but secretly pine for—she touched my arm while we talked. It was light and brief, but it made me feel different. Important. She wore no makeup and had slept in a car for three days at this point, but she was the most beautiful woman I had ever laid eyes on. I had a hard time believing that she was not being waited on hand and foot by some dolt who undoubtedly felt the same way about her as I did at that moment.

To this day, I don't know if she spread the charm on thick for me because of me or because that's what she does when she meets anyone. Back then, I didn't care.

Her gaze in my direction was enough to alter my hitchhiking path and head for the choppy waves of the Pacific Ocean.

We made up a story and played the part of a couple in love to convince a truck driver to let us ride with him up Highway 20. When I say we played the part, I mean we acted it out. Because if two strangers try to hitchhike together, outnumbering the driver, your chances of getting a lift go to zero. A couple in love somehow seems less menacing, and it was fun to pretend… a lot of fun.

We made love in a cheap motel room to the sounds of big rigs barreling down the nearby highway.

It was love at first sight, no question. We were destined for each other, and nothing could ever tear us apart.

No, that's bull.

We weren't in love.

We were two horny kids who didn't have a condom at a roadside motel. She took the bus back to Las Vegas the next day. I eventually returned to Shoreline. I only saw her nine months later, when I met my son, Jaden.

CHAPTER 6

The horn blows, signaling the start of Tina's wave. Tina and her competition are all in green caps. They leap into the water like a flock of geese landing in formation. Just the colorful caps on their heads break the surface, obscured by flailing arms and the rhythmic spray of a swimmer's stroke. I lose track of her almost instantly as the group heads for the first of four large inflatable buoys marking distances in the water. Kayakers float nearby and observe the swimmers as they make their way to the first floating marshmallow buoy.

Another group is released and I turn my attention to Paige, knowing that Tina won't be back on the beach for at least thirty more minutes. She's coloring in the letters of a sign that says, "GO MOM!" on it.

"You think she'll be able to see it?" she asks.

"Of course, honey," I say. "She'll be looking for it when she comes out of the water."

"I'm glad I'm not swimming out there."

"Why's that?"

"Sharks," she says, then puts her hands above her head to indicate a fin.

"I see. Well, that's a lake, and sharks don't live in lakes."

"That's not what Jaden said. He said if I swam out too far that the sharks would get me."

"I think your brother was just pulling your leg."

"What does that mean?"

"That he was kidding," I tell her.

"Well, that's not very funny."

"No, it's not, but if I remember right, that was last year when we went to the lake when you were still learning to swim without a life jacket, and Jaden was worried about you going too far from shore and not being able to swim back."

"What about those people?" she asks, pointing to the swimmers preparing to jump in. "Why don't they wear life jackets?"

"They swim a lot and train for being in the water a long time, so they're pretty good at it. Besides, if they get into trouble, there are people out there to help them."

I point out the kayaks and assure her that her mom is a strong swimmer who doesn't need a life jacket. She goes back to coloring in the block letters of her sign.

I take in the surrounding scene. From all around the cove, spectators wander out of their trailers and tents to watch the swimmers. Many of them hold coffee cups and squint at the early morning sun. A few people wear matching shirts with the names of participants printed on them. They cheer as the swimmers start, but quiet when the swimmers move on, far out of earshot.

The smell of smoke from early morning campfires lingers in the air. It's a distinctive aroma that will no doubt stick to my jacket and pants.

The smell takes me back to when I was a kid. My dad used to take me out to the Tillamook State Forrest, which was not far from Shoreline. He'd bring this little two-person tent and overstuffed backpacks, and we'd hike into the dense green forest to this small campsite he liked. He'd make a fire with the surrounding brush, which would burn continuously for days and would drench our tent and belongings with the smoky smell.

It's funny, thinking about it now. These weren't the most exciting camping trips. I read a lot, and he hiked, often alone. He'd take me on the hikes, but not every time. There was no schedule for each day. My younger sister Darla begged to come with us, but Dad always made it just he and I each time. I still have a fondness for camping, but unlike my father, I take all three of my kids.

The next wave of swimmers launches into the water. They wear blue caps and look to be a few years older than the previous group. Tina's wave has spread out quite a bit. The first green dot—the woman in the lead—makes her turn past the third buoy with a direct angle of return toward the beach. The other green caps trail behind, some in little packs but many alone, with no one to pace alongside them. The final green dot has dropped way back and, in a few minutes, could quickly be passed by the leader of the blue cap group.

I've watched Tina race before, and twice last year. She finished fourth in her age group on her first Olympic distance and then twelfth on her next attempt. Those races were local, too—one up in Vancouver and another in Eugene. She should be somewhere in the middle of the green caps. The swim is not her best event, and often she switches back from the traditional freestyle swim to breaststroke or even a backstroke when she gets tired.

The leader of the pack nears the shore with her competition far behind her. She swims to within fifty feet or so of the beach and stands. She pulls off her goggles and cap and strides through the water to the blue and white flags marking the path up the beach to the exchange point. A healthy round of applause breaks out as she jogs toward her bicycle.

Her path winds down the beach, then up toward a dirt softball field where all the racers have parked their bikes on metal racks in neat, tight rows according to age group. I can't see the area from here on the beach, but we passed it on the way down from the car.

The leader is gone, but the next swimmers exit and follow the same routine. Paige and I now stand behind a barricade, so we're within inches of each racer as they exit the water and take their first steps. A woman emerges from the water with her hands raised. She's pumping her fists and flexing for the crowd. A dozen or so people to our right—all wearing matching red shirts—cheer wildly. Their shirts say, "Elaine, You Got THIS!" Under the text is an image of an arm flexing its biceps.

The woman gives them a little curtsy and strolls over to the barricade with a huge smile. Her time for this race is not critical as she pauses with her fans. She hugs everyone in a red shirt, including a pale girl who is probably the same age as Paige. The girl wears a green swim cap too, but not for swimming—the cap covers her bald head. The little girl's shirt reads, "My Mom *Tri's* For Me."

I look at the shirts and notice a web address and a cancer fundraising organization listed on the sleeve.

"You're my inspiration," the woman says to her daughter. "If I could put you on my back, I would. And I know I'd go faster with you there."

"Mom, you're silly!" the girl squeals.

"Not as silly as you, Elle. I'll see you on the bike path. Wave to me!"

"Peddle hard!" she says before one final hug. The woman blows a kiss to the girl, then jogs off. The exchange between the mother and daughter has captured the attention of everyone nearby, including Paige. Such a sweet, honest, heartfelt moment. Two people rightfully unashamed of their affection for one another.

I wonder if Paige has ever had those moments with her mother? Of course, I don't wish those poor people's circumstances on us, but would Tina be that kind of mom if Paige got sick? I don't know. Or maybe I do know, and I don't want to admit it.

* * *

Women in green caps exit the water in a steady stream. Some of them stand and high-step to the shore. Others swim until their arms touch the bottom of the lake before getting to their feet and exiting the water.

I keep an eye out for Tina. I don't know how she will perform against these racers, but I know for sure that more green caps have now exited the water than remain swimming to the shore. She's behind for some reason. Minutes and more green caps pass, and I'm getting concerned. She'll be in a foul mood tonight if she pulled a muscle as she did at the Eugene race. She tweaked her right hamstring muscle on the swim, which slowed her considerably. She blamed the injury for her twelfth-place finish.

These races might be for fun and the pride of earning a medal and a finisher T-shirt, but she still wanted to do well enough to beat more people than she lost to. That idea is quickly slipping away as more green caps finish the swim.

Three women depart the water together. Among them is a blue cap, meaning Tina got passed by a swimmer who started fifteen minutes after she did. She will not be pleased.

I strain to try to make out the colors of the caps bobbing up and down in the water. The reflection of the early morning sun isn't helping. I notice a man to my left with a set of binoculars hanging from his backpack and ask to borrow them.

Knowing that most of the swimmers left are blue caps makes it easier to focus on green, but it's difficult even with the binoculars. Until I see her—she's past the last buoy, her face entirely above the surface like she's treading water, not swimming forward. Her expression is impossible to read from this distance, and then I realize that she's not wearing her goggles anymore. They are around her neck. After a few bobs, she plunges her arms forward, only to stop again and tread water.

A watchful kayaker hovers near her. I can see he's talking to her but have no idea what he's saying. Other participants swim around the kayaker.

"Daddy, what do you see? Do you see Mommy?" Paige

asks.

"I think so," I say.

"Can I see? Can I see?"

I show her how to use the binoculars, then point her toward the mostly still kayak.

"She's coming!" Paige's excitement is innocent but somehow makes me nervous. Something is wrong with Tina.

The man with the binoculars has moved on, so I can no longer zoom in on her face, but her pattern repeats. She swims a few strokes, bobs, then swims again.

I ignore the barricade blocking me from the water's edge and stand on the beach. I hold Paige as close as I can at my side and she clutches my leg.

Blue cap after blue cap jogs by us. The kayaker is now so close that I can make out the brand name on the side of the little craft.

They are about twenty-five yards out when Tina's feet touch the bottom of the lake, and she stands. Does she see us waiting by the blue and white flags? She never looks up.

She walks several steps and collapses face-first back into the water.

CHAPTER 7

I don't feel the cold rush of water sink into my shoes or leech through my clothes. I don't hear the shouts from the bystanders who, no doubt, see the same troublesome scene that I do. I don't see the kayaker flip and slither out of his boat, but he must have.

I take large, lumbering steps through the water and rush to Tina. I fall, and my face smacks the water, which enters my nose and throat and causes me to choke. I shake off the painful sensation in my sinuses and push on.

The kayaker and I reach her at the same time. She's motionless, with her face down in the water. I pull on her arm and try to flip her over, but this just pushes her away from me. The kayaker grabs the other arm, and together, we lift her.

"Her head. She said her head was pounding," he says. "We have to get her onto the sand."

We walk backward, pulling her toward the shore. The kayaker falls, and Tina's weight shifts. I fall again, too. This time, I notice the water in my nose and mouth but don't care. Several other people arrive and take her from me. Her hand slips through mine as I fall to my knees and choke the water out of my lungs.

Tina is dragged to the beach in slow motion and surrounded by EMTs who check for her pulse and breathing before beginning CPR. They are repeatedly thrusting down on her chest. I get to her side just as a trickle of water comes from her mouth and then a faint cough. Her eyes remain closed.

"I've got a pulse. It's faint. Let's move," someone says.

She's lifted onto a backboard and strapped down. The EMTs use the swimmer's jogging path to rush Tina off the beach and toward a waiting ambulance.

The blue and white pennant flags that line the path gently sway in the breeze as they rush past. I watch the flags for a split second, mesmerized by their indifference to the moment.

Paige is patiently waiting in the sand where I left her. She is still holding her "GO MOM!" sign at her side. She picked orange and purple for the sign that Tina never saw.

Paige is silent and alone. Tears stain her face. She's looking at me, but her eyes are empty.

She had watched the whole, horrible thing.

CHAPTER 8

I slam the gearshift into park outside the emergency room entrance. Tina's ambulance is just ahead. I quickly glance at Paige in the rearview mirror. She's staring out the window, still clutching her "GO MOM!" poster. Her look is one of bland disinterest. I've never seen that before in her. She must be in shock, and that needs to be dealt with, but I can't focus on it right now.

I hop out of the car and run toward the ambulance as the rear doors burst open. Half of me expects Tina to be sitting up on the gurney, laughing at all the trouble she caused by fainting. But the other half of me knows that it was much more severe than that. She didn't faint; it's not that easy.

"Sir, you can't park there," a security guard shouts in my direction. I wave him off, but he follows me. "Sir. Sir!"

One of the medics stands at the side of the gurney, leaning on Tina's chest. But as I get closer, I see that he's not just leaning there. He's performing CPR again. Steady, methodical pumps downward to my wife's body. There's a flurry of commotion inside the ambulance—lights from an instrument panel blink, an alarm buzzes, but I don't know what for. All I can do is watch.

"Sir. Sir! You can't park there," the guard says again. "Did you leave a little girl in your vehicle? Sir?"

Medical personnel from the hospital rush out of a door

marked "No Admittance." They quickly block my view as they gather at the open doors to render assistance. I see the legs of the gurney spring straight as they pull her out. Her body is motionless, except the pounding of the CPR.

I turn back to the car and see Paige. I want to tell her to stop watching this. She should close her eyes and think of something else. That this is all pretend. It's not real and should not be burned into her memories. Maybe the day Mom was rushed to the hospital can be forgotten.

The guard must realize why I parked at the emergency curb because he backs away.

I can't leave Paige in the car. I hurry to the back door to get her out. When I lift the handle, it doesn't budge. I try it again. It's locked. I reach into my pocket. No keys. Damn. The car has one of those proximity keys and is still running with the doors locked.

"Honey, unlock the car," I say, tapping on the window. She turns her head up toward me, but her eyes are vacant. "The door, honey. I can't get in. I need you to come inside with me. Open the door, Paige-bear, please."

She holds my keys in her hand. She must have taken them from the console and locked the doors. She shakes her head no and bursts into tears.

Moments pass like hours. The guard reappears, and I plead with Paige to unlock the car. Someone offers to call a locksmith, but I ignore them. I know she'll come around.

I don't see them push Tina inside the emergency room, but at some point, they must have because when I look up at the ambulance, all I see is an EMT filling out forms on a tablet.

By the time Paige finally hits the unlock button and lets me unbuckle, then carry her inside, we've drawn a little crowd of onlookers watching the father-daughter standoff. I push past them and go inside. The guard nods to me. Now it's OK to park there, I guess.

Paige rests her head on my shoulder as we enter the ER waiting room. Her little body is comforting to me. I want to hold her close because I'm scared, and this is how I'm hiding it.

The waiting room is brimming with early morning patients, the strain of late nights and long waits is evident on their faces. Nobody wants to be here, whether sick or waiting with someone who may be. I see a bandaged head and a man holding his bloody hand against his chest. But this is all I can register before an older man in pale blue scrubs calls for my attention.

He motions for me to follow. His look is solemn, like a veteran who has seen it all. But I don't want to follow him. I know what they are going to tell me. I know it in my heart.

The man in the blue scrubs breaks the news to me. They didn't ask to speak with me alone, so Paige is there when I find out Tina's fate.

She went into cardiac arrest in the ambulance. They did their best to revive her, but they couldn't. She was pronounced dead at the hospital almost immediately on arrival.

She's gone.

My insides twist and rip, and I hold Paige even tighter.

* * *

It's funny, the things you notice when the rest of the world is quiet—the clock's ticking on the wall, for instance. Ironically, this clock has a Goodwin Labs logo on it. The same company Tina works for. *Worked* for.

They put us in this little room with no windows and that damn ticking clock. I can hear the shuffle of feet in the hallway outside, a cart rumbles by. Paige is in my lap, her head on my shoulder. She hasn't left my touch since we walked in, and I don't want her to, either.

The blue scrubs guy was kind and explained what he could. They didn't know much. He promised to send in a chaplain or grief counselor for me. He asked about our religious preference. I told him we didn't have one, but he could send whoever they wanted. I didn't want to talk to anyone, though. Not now, and maybe not ever.

I guess this is the part where I should say that my world has fallen apart—that I will never be able to comprehend the loss of my wife. That's what normal people would say, right? But I'm numb, and I can't stop thinking about my lawn that's overdue for a mowing. I could have Mason do it tonight. I still haven't figured out a reasonable punishment for that kid, the teenage drunkard. I don't know if he's a drunkard, but he was drunk, so there's that.

I need gas for the mower, too. And I'm supposed to call the tree guy because Mr. Speight next door complained that the branches from our maple tree are growing over his shed and that if a powerful wind hit, it would take out the place where he stores his garden gnomes and shovels. I keep meaning to call the tree guy for the sake of Mr. Speight's small army of garden gnomes that rotate around his yard seasonally.

I see Tina a few times a month, and those days are tense and stressful. We're forced to talk to each other. No texting. No email. We're so good at email. It's madness having to speak. Her days in town are filled with activities outside of the house, thank God. Training for her races or shopping. When she's home, she's checking email, or she's locked herself in the office on the phone talking about things I don't understand with people I'll never meet.

The kids don't ask about her anymore. They know the score. So, she's gone permanently. How is it different now?

Tina doesn't ask anything of me. She brings in the money and pays the bills. We have a comfortable life. I spend the money and keep up the house. Oh, and I raise our children. We're just like every other couple, except which gender stays home.

She's only asked for a few things of me in all our years together. You could say that she's indifferent to the world around her—sleepwalking through life, keeping in light contact with her family. Go with the flow, I guess. I don't consult her on family decisions. I used to, but she would always just agree to whatever I proposed. No argument, so what's the point?

She's driven but distant, and this is all I've ever known. I've accepted her, just as she's accepted me.

I should have known this was how it was going to be. The second time I ever saw Tina, I should have known.

* * *

It was nineteen years ago, and we were in a hospital in Nevada. I'd just flown in from Oregon after getting the call that I was somehow the father of a child that I didn't even know was possible. She was in labor. I'd taken the first flight out. I can't say why I believed her so assuredly that Jaden was my child. I mean, I'd only spent thirty-six hours with the woman. One time. Not even enough time to ask, much less remember her last name for God's sake. Besides, that was nine months ago. It was before Facebook or Instagram. It's not like I could keep tabs on her from a distance or like her selfies and see her face over and over. I had a vague picture in my mind of what she looked like, and I had this crazy, sexy memory from our time together, but that was it.

Yet somehow, I knew the baby she was about to birth was mine and this stranger was the mother of my child. In the pursuing years, Jaden's crooked little nose and toothy grin mirrored my own, and any lingering doubts about Tina's truthfulness disappeared. He was mine.

I missed Jaden's birth by one day. When I first saw them together in that hospital bed, she held him to her chest, struggling to breastfeed him. A woman was standing by her bed, a lactation specialist, coaxing her to sweep Jaden's mouth over her breast so he could latch on. Be gentle, she said, it's OK. Tina held back tears after each pass, but Jaden wasn't interested in his mother's milk. The struggle continued for a long while. No luck. I watched from the door, unnoticed by everyone. It was beautiful. A young mother, coming into her own and feeding her child.

But then Tina saw me, and she stopped the effort. The pained expression relaxed. It wasn't happiness or excitement on her face, it was a relief—an exit.

"Can you just feed him?" she asked, pointing at the bottle on the end of the bed.

The lactation specialist scoffed, "The breast is best."

Her words were punctuated with tart ridicule. Why would any mother not breastfeed? Her scorn was palpable.

Tina lost it. What I didn't know at the time was that the ritual of coaching had happened almost hourly since Jaden was born. Tina was bewildered and defeated. This well-intended, but crass woman showed no sympathy for Tina's struggle or for how much this particular failure broke her heart.

But I did. I could see the pain on this stranger's face—the face of my child's mother. My mother made the same face when I perplexed her when we were kids. Exasperated.

I could also see on Tina's face that the plea for help reached far beyond a bottle feeding. She needed rescuing from this woman and this battle to prove she could be a mother. Somehow this was the defining moment; her first challenge with a newborn, and she was failing. It was one from which Tina would never come back.

So as the woman launched into her well-rehearsed sermon on the evils of baby formula, Tina sunk further into the bed and tried to hide under the tear-stained sheets.

"I think we need a break," I said. My words startled the woman, who had no idea who I was or why I was lurking in the doorway.

"But we need to cover the—"

"As I said, I think we need a break." I fully entered the room to make myself clear of my intentions. "I'd like to feed my son. So, if we can have a few minutes, that would be great."

I ushered her out of the room by her elbow. She scowled at me as she collected her giant binders of breastfeeding manuals.

"I'll find you when we're ready. Bye now," I said, practically shoving her out of the room and shutting the door.

Tina released a tension-trapped breath from her chest and the air finally came back into the room. She smiled.

As I approached the bed, Tina wrapped a small blue blanket around Jaden, who was cooing and still not upset for lack of a meal. He was so little. His skin pink and fuzzy. His eyes flashed open, then blinked shut in an instant, like he was playing peek-a-boo and didn't know it. I thought it was the cutest thing in the world. Him blinking. I was smitten.

I glanced from Jaden to Tina and then back again. She held her hand over her mouth and tried to hold back her sobbing.

"Our son," I whispered.

"Our son," she managed to say.

I paced back and forth across the room, cradling him and trying to figure out how in the world I got to this place, wherein the blink of an eye, I'm a father and my life was no longer my own.

I sat down and shook the formula bottle. Once it was ready, I brushed the nipple across Jaden's lips like the snippy woman said to do. He grabbed the bottle with his mouth and began to feed.

I looked up at Tina for approval, but her eyes were closed. She'd fallen asleep now that someone else was there to shoulder the load.

We got married and had two more children together, and this is how it went. I didn't ask to be Mr. Mom, but when Mom won't, Dad must. I don't blame Tina for it. That would imply I didn't want to be needed.

Everyone wants to be needed.

CHAPTER 9

Paige and I are still in the ticking clock room thirty minutes later. I decide not to call the tree guy. Mr. Speight and his garden gnomes can wait.

Paige found a coloring book and some broken crayons, but she still hasn't spoken. She's busy with coloring. She's never been one to run around the room like a maniac when she's not entertained. Somehow, that didn't pass from her brothers to her and for that, I'm thankful.

I'm watching the clock, wondering what I'm supposed to do next. I need to see Mason. I need Jaden to come home from college. He should be home. My parents will want to drive here, in separate cars, of course, from Shoreline. My mom will call my sister, and then everyone will be here.

Tina doesn't have any close family that wasn't my family first. Her mom died years ago, and she never knew her father. My family is all the family she has had for the length of our marriage. She adopted them, or they adopted her. Sort of a long-distance thing, though, because they saw her even less than I did.

My parents will know what to do when they get here. I feel inadequate and unprepared for this. What do you do when your spouse dies? Who do you call? I decide to Google it but a woman in chinos and a purple sweater enters the room, interrupting my search.

"Hello, Mr. Bell, I presume?"

"James, yes."

I assume she's the counselor, and I'm ready to say all the right things, but she's not the counselor. She's with the hospital billing department. I set aside my frustration that the money people showed up before the comfort people and try to pay attention.

I pull the insurance card from my wallet, and she enters the information into a laptop on a rolling cart in the corner. I fill in all the other information she requests, which is a rather long list.

"Yes, I see now."

I don't know what she means by this, but she looks concerned as she squints into the laptop glare.

"Has your wife recently changed medical insurance companies?"

"No. We've all been with the same company for the last... I don't know. A long time."

"Hmm, alright. You and three dependents are covered, but we're having trouble locating a current record for your wife."

"Maybe because she just died," I blurt out. Lord knows I want to be polite, and this woman is just trying to do her job.

My comment doesn't derail her. Either she already knew or doesn't care. She just looks harder at the screen, like maybe if she really gives it her all, she'll find what she's looking for. Working for the billing department must be thrilling.

"We're all covered under her insurance," I say.

"I'll contact the company directly and get this figured out right away, alright, Mr. Bell?"

I nod, trusting that she'll do as she claims. She leaves, and we're alone again.

We sit here, waiting for another forty-five minutes. The Goodwin Labs ticking clock tells me this. I don't even know what we're waiting for. We don't need to be here. I stand on the chair and pull the clock off the wall. I place it on the small table and remove the AA battery. I pocket the battery and hang the clock back on the wall.

No more ticking for this room.

I take Paige by the hand and we walk out to the car, which thankfully, is still sitting at the curb. The guard gives me a wave as if we're old friends.

A sense of unease rushes over me as we drive away. I need to call the tree guy for Mr. Speight and his gnomes.

CHAPTER 10

"She never loved you. You know that, right?" my sister Darla says. It's a statement, not a question.

Darla is a gem, super smart. Like Cal Tech, mathematics degree, ones and zeros on a computer screen smart. The intelligence in her head doesn't always show in the emotions coming out of her mouth. I love her to death, but she has the emotional intelligence of a desk lamp.

Darla, to my surprise, was the first to arrive at my house tonight. She's three years my junior and still lives on the Oregon coast, just up the highway from Shoreline, with her husband Kevin and daughter Meghan.

When we were kids, we were only together when our parents were fighting, and they fought a lot, especially at the end. It's a common ground we didn't ask for and didn't appreciate then, or now. Siblings, like it or not, bond over those shared experiences. Now that we're older, with kids of our own, we don't exactly hang out for fun. Holidays, maybe a graduation here and there, but that's enough Darla to go around.

It really didn't help that she never gave Tina a chance, either.

"She used you for those kids. You made some damn good ones, I'll give you that. But she didn't appreciate it, you know? Not like Kevin and me."

Kevin, with his flannel shirts and man bun, didn't make the trip. He's at home running their zip-line business. I like

Kevin. Dare I say that I like Kevin significantly more than I like Darla?

"What about Kevin?" I ask.

"That idiot appreciates everything I do for Meghan. Worships the ground I walk on, too."

Meghan, my four-year-old niece, is currently throwing my couch cushions at Paige, who has yet to deflect them and defend herself from the onslaught. I move next to her to serve as her guard, batting the cushions away myself.

"I don't mean to speak ill of the dead, you know that, right? I wouldn't do that, but she never did for you the things that she should have done, like ever. She was never around. How can you be a wife and mother if you're gone more than you are home? Her priorities weren't right."

"It's not like that, Darla," I say, collecting all the couch cushions and sitting on top of them so Meghan won't continue to pelt Paige. "What about not speaking ill of the dead?"

"Well, for your information, I speak of the dead. The ill is your interpretation of what I speak. Besides, I'm not sure what to say about the woman. Twenty years in our family, and she was still outside looking in."

"Darla, I'm really in no mood to argue with you. I'm grieving, remember. This happened hours ago. Isn't this where you're supposed to comfort me?"

"Yes. That's what I'm doing. Is it working?"

"Incredibly well," I deadpan. "Couldn't be happier."

"Yeah? About as happy as I was when Tina ruined Thanksgiving last year? The sweet potato fiasco?"

I knew she was going to bring up Thanksgiving. It's stupid and exactly why my family is insufferable.

The whole issue was about sweet potatoes. You could burn the turkey and drop the stuffing on the floor, but as long as you had sweet potatoes with caramelized brown sugar and little marshmallows on top, you were all set with the Bell clan. We peel the real sweet potatoes, not yams, then mash them with some orange juice concentrate and additional secret family ingredients before layering on the brown sugar.

Sweet potatoes are beloved, but of course, we only eat them once a year at Thanksgiving and only at the Westcott Inn.

Dad doesn't rent rooms to guests on Thanksgiving or the day after, so Darla and I and our families can stay there and have the holiday to ourselves. It's tradition, and you don't buck tradition with Dad. But for some strange, unexplainable reason, Tina decided to tempt fate last year. She offered to make the sweet potatoes—big mistake.

The plan was all set. She would make them in the inn's commercial kitchen under the watchful eye of my sister. Darla and Dad usually led the event and set the menu. While Tina didn't have cooking responsibilities at our house, she was perfectly capable of it. She could make a pot roast melt in your mouth. But sweet potatoes…? That's dangerous territory. It's not clear why she decided that year was the year she needed to be responsible for the most essential item on the menu.

The day before Thanksgiving, Tina was in San Diego, or was it San Jose…? I can't recall. Maybe San Antonio. Either way, her flight into Portland was weather-delayed, so she wasn't due to arrive until two hours before the meal. She texted me when she got on the road and said she had all the ingredients to make them, so not to worry. She knew it was a big deal, and that she was on the hook for it.

Of course, I was fending off darts from Darla all day, who kept repeating that if the sweet potatoes were wrong, then the meal was ruined. First World problems, for sure.

Tina arrived at the time she predicted. She even left her luggage in the car and rushed inside, toting several brown bags of groceries into the kitchen. I was watching football with Dad and the boys.

"Your wife's in the kitchen," Darla said. "You better get in there. It's a colossal screw-up."

I avoided the knowing look of my father and shuffled

into the kitchen to find Tina, her hair curled and makeup perfect. She'd primped before the flight and was beautiful as always. She was still in her work skirt and matching blazer, which was wrinkled from the flight and drive.

She was holding two cans of cooked yams in heavy syrup.

"Oh no," I said, deflated. "You didn't get the recipe I emailed you?"

"The store didn't have fresh ones," Tina said. "The guy at Q-Mart said that the canned ones were the same."

"That's what you get for going to Q-Mart," Darla piped in. "Randall Hasson wouldn't know a watermelon from a grapefruit. He's a beach hillbilly of the first order. Why did you go there?"

She didn't reply, unless bursting into tears counted as a reply. That's all it took, one question from Darla. Tina dropped the cans on the island counter and left out the back door.

"Darla, you know that's the only store open in Shoreline on Thanksgiving," I said. "Where else was she supposed to go?"

"How about planning and going to the right store, like the rest of us?"

"She's not like the rest of us," I said.

"Yeah? I hadn't noticed."

I found Tina on the front porch with her hands over her eyes. Her dark mascara dotted her cheeks. She wiped away the tears and sat up straight when she saw me.

"It's not a big deal, Tina. What you got will be fine."

"I really don't want the 'it's the effort that counts,' speech. OK?" she said, taking a big breath. "I just wanted to show them that I could contribute to this family, too."

"But you do, hon."

"How? How do I contribute? I show up here, late. The meal is cooked by someone else. After it's done, my offer to clean up is refused. 'Be with your kids,' they say. Every year. Every time. Then we go to bed and find the rooms perfectly made up by your dad. No matter how early I get up, your mom will be cooking breakfast tomorrow morning. She doesn't even live here. Your parents divorced years ago, and she gets the run of the place while I can't even crack an egg or pour my coffee."

Tina's description was frighteningly accurate. I'm not in the same boat. It was expected that I pitch in, but it's my family, not hers.

"It's a functioning bed-and-breakfast," I said. "They serve people for a living."

"And they will always see me as a guest."

Tina stayed on the porch until I convinced her to go inside and see the kids, who seemed genuinely happy to see her. The canned yams were fine, and we all choked them down without many audible complaints. In the big scheme of things, it should not have been a defining moment of any kind, but it was the first time Tina verbalized her frustration with feeling like an outsider at our family gathering. It took our entire marriage for her to say it, but she never mentioned it to me again after that day. Life went on.

Darla, of course, never heard Tina's concerns and wouldn't care, regardless. Darla only saw that Tina had messed up.

This was the sweet potato fiasco that Darla will never forget because, well, she's basically just like everyone else in my family, and nobody ever lets anything go.

* * *

Since Meghan couldn't throw any more cushions, Darla plopped her in front of the TV to watch Netflix.

Darla finds me in the office. My hiding place was weak.

"So, what now?" she asks.

"About what?"

"About you. About life. What about a funeral? When is that going to be?"

"She didn't want one. She made that clear when we did

our will. Who would go anyway? The people from Goodwin Labs? That would be great. Our family in the front row and a handful of work people who only saw her at the yearly retreat in Lake Tahoe?"

"But what about the kids? Isn't a funeral supposed to provide closure or something?" Darla asks.

"I have no idea. Nobody in our family has ever died," I say, knowing that, yes, people have died before, but no one I knew well.

"What about Great-grandma Fonzie?" she asks.

"Great-grandma Winkler," I say. "You were the only one who called her Fonzie."

"It was not my fault that I alone found the irony in that woman's name."

"I was ten, and you were, what, seven?" I ask. "And nobody asked me to plan that funeral, so that doesn't help us."

The funeral decision was taken out of my hands no more than forty-five minutes later by my mother, who had planned the whole thing with Christy over the phone on the drive over from Shoreline. We are having a funeral. No question. Tomorrow morning, because why wait?

* * *

As expected, Mom and Dad showed up in separate cars, but within moments of each other. Mom set about distracting Paige while Dad joined Mason in watching TV. It was as normal as you might expect. Darla took Meghan out for a while, so I was alone in the office again. I needed to call Jaden at school. He didn't know yet. It was late afternoon, and I had already waited too long.

I pushed send on his number.

"Dad?"

"Hey, bud," I say. There was a lot of noise in the background, making it harder to hear him.

"What's wrong? You never call me. I didn't even know

the talking part of my phone actually worked. I just get texts from you. Well, from anybody."

This was true; we rarely talked. Jaden video-chatted with Paige most Wednesdays and I'd talk to him then, but other than that, our conversations have been through quick little text messages. He seemed to be adjusting well to his first year away from home. Since he was on the baseball team that gave him a purpose and kept him busy, I assume that kept him out of trouble, too. He sent me a few of his English papers. The kid had his head on straight.

"Where are you?" I ask.

"The locker room. We have practice in like two minutes. What's up?"

Baseball practice. It sounded like a rock concert.

"Can you go somewhere a little quieter?

"Dad, you gotta speak up, it's really loud here."

"Can you go outside?" I ask.

"I'm not outside. I'm in the locker room."

This wasn't how I planned it. I quickly calculate how long it would take to drive to Eugene and talk to him in person, but I decide I can't be away from Paige and Mason that long, even if my parents are here.

"Practice is starting, Dad," he says. "I gotta go."

"You can't go. Wait. Jaden," I say. "It's important. Something happened."

"Hold on." The phone goes quiet, and I hear a rustling sound like he's holding it to his body. "What did you say?"

It's now completely silent, and I picture Jaden standing alone in a hallway somewhere. Maybe I should have talked to one of the coaches first so he could be there and comfort him. But I didn't do that, and now it is too late.

I'd like to say that I eased Jaden into the most difficult news of his young life, but I didn't.

"Your mom… She died this morning, and you need to come home."

There was a long pause. The rock concert was gone and filled by the sound of nothing except my breathing. I was a coward and waited for his reply, which seemed to take years to come.

"Dad, that's not funny." His voice sounds broken. He knows it wasn't a joke.

"I'm sorry, Jaden. She collapsed after a swim at a race."

I give him the necessary details of what happened. He asks smart questions, but his tears betray his mature response. I tell him that Grandpa Mitch would come down and pick him up so he didn't have to drive by himself.

"No, I—"

Another long pause.

"I can get a ride," he says. "Dad?"

"Yeah?

"What happens now?"

I have no idea what happens now, but that's not what he wants to hear.

"We just need to be together, and we can figure it all out," I say. "When can you be here?"

He sniffs, evidence that his nose is running from the silent tears. "I'll ask Evan to give me a ride. I'll see if coach will let us go now. We can be there in probably four hours. I need to pack."

Evan's a freshman too, an outfielder who doesn't see much playing time. The two had hit it off right away when school started and were seemingly inseparable off the field.

"We're going to do the funeral tomorrow. If you want Evan to stay for it, that's OK."

"Thanks, I'll check with him. I'm sure he'll stay. I'll see you in a few hours, Dad. I'm sorry."

"Me too, bud. Me too."

CHAPTER 11

My parents, Mitch and Ramona, split when I was in college, but the distance between them had been growing for some time before that. Darla was still at home, finishing high school. She never quite forgave me for not being at her side when the inevitable end of our parents' union occurred. An icy, but largely unexplained divide grew between them for years. We watched the cracks appear slowly—more time away, cold shoulders, angry outbursts. In the end, they rarely spent time in the same room together.

Darla took the split harder than I did. She was there to see every waning bit of it. Watching your parents divorce as a teen when you actually understand what's occurring, despite your powerlessness, changes your perspective on relationships and love. Unfortunately for her, and to a lesser extent me, we saw it all.

I didn't take a side in their divorce, but Dad didn't make it easy. His expectation of me from boyhood was to take over the family business. He wanted me to run the Westcott Inn. He employed me as a handyman at the inn ever since I was old enough to swing a hammer or change a sprinkler head. I played along for as long as possible, but I just couldn't bring myself to live and work in the same house that I was practically raised in. To never leave, to never do anything on my own.

I thought going to college and studying something other than hospitality would force the issue, or at least buy me four years away from the trap of the Westcott Inn. But he demanded my return every summer and offered me full management of the inn before I graduated. He had plans for developing condos and more rentals in Shoreline and needed me to run the inn for him. I rebuffed him and left Shoreline one summer night without any planning. I hitchhiked down the coast where I met Tina, eventually had Jaden, and found the courage to tell my father that I wasn't going to take over his business and live under his thumb. He's never let me forget how much I let him down for choosing a path that didn't lead straight back to him.

Like I said, I didn't take a side, but Dad wasn't exactly the soft, cuddly type. Mom was, well, a mother, and it's hard to not default to your mom, especially when your dad is continuously reminding you how disappointed he is in you.

So, after twenty-two years of marriage, they had had enough of each other, and they couldn't hold out until both kids had left the house. In their defense, there was no way of knowing if Darla would be leaving the house to become a productive adult anytime soon. With that specter looming, they just couldn't wait any longer. They announced it in the living room of our little house on McArthur Street on St. Patrick's Day. Darla was home, and they called me on speakerphone. Mom moved out that night.

They were equal partners in the Westcott Inn, which had been generating a steady income for our family for years. But Dad wanted Mom out of the business and out of his home, too. They mutually agreed to the value of the Westcott as property and as a business. Dad didn't have any independent savings he could dip into in order to buy her out, and no bank would loan him what he required to be rid of her entirely. So, they struck a deal where he would operate the business and pay Mom a portion of the Westcott profits until her half was satisfied or he just bought her out.

They both agreed, and at the time, I marveled at the civilized parting of ways between these two pillars in my life. I can't explain this other than to say that my parents are unique, and while they are divorced, I'm not sure they ever stopped loving each other—although neither could stand to live with the other. At least that's the story I've accepted. No hate or disdain, they just needed to be apart. If they were sad about the whole thing, they didn't show it. It was all so routine. Or it was until the lawsuit.

Mom was an art teacher at the local high school. She also sold or tried to sell pottery, jewelry, and some genuinely awful paintings at the Shoreline Farmers Market. I can't imagine those efforts ever brought in much extra cash. Still, she loved making the pieces and talking to potential customers who would politely decline to buy any of her work.

Aside from her full-time job at the school, hobby craftwork on the side, she worked non-stop at the Westcott. Mornings, evenings, and all weekend, leaving Darla and me home alone on McArthur Street. Success required it. She knew the business and the customers. Most of all, she knew that she could start her own bed-and-breakfast and do it better than her ex-husband. So, she did just that.

With the money Dad was paying her each month, combined with some settlement cash from a long-ago car accident that left her with a modest limp, she partnered with her friends, Susan Clark and Maureen Ellington. They bought the rundown Evergreen Trail Bed and Breakfast, located immediately to the west of the Westcott Inn. My parents became each other's competition for guests and, to this day, still battle for bragging rights over the best B&B in Shoreline.

Mom and her partners remodeled the Evergreen into an environmentalist's dream. It's completely sustainable, with compost bins in the backyard garden. Rain collection barrels sit along the side of the place. Everything is recycled or reused. It partially runs on solar panels. Guests are made to sign a pledge to avoid unnecessary waste during their stay. The guests appreciate Ramona's love for Mother Earth. They can also afford to pay a premium for the right to stay at the most environmentally friendly B&B on the Oregon coast. This drives my father insane since Mom can charge twice the price per night and make her guest wash their own dishes in rainwater.

So, Dad sued, claiming damages from the re-opening of the Evergreen. Such close competition and an owner with intimate knowledge of the clientele unfairly impacted the Westcott's profitability. He further claimed that the repayment arrangement between them was no longer valid because the agreement's conditions had been significantly and permanently altered. He would go bankrupt if things didn't change. An arbitrator agreed, forcing my parents to renegotiate the deal. Neither has shared the exact results from the renegotiation. Still, we know Mom and her partners had to pay Dad a sizable amount to end the whole thing.

The bitter battle pitted their very livelihoods against one another. Darla and I agree that Mom wanted to prove to Dad that she could do it independently, and maybe she didn't expect to be so good at it. Dad took it all very personally, which led to the lawsuit and their continual bickering.

Mom takes pride in fighting every environmental injustice she sees in Shoreline and surrounding area. Dad takes pride in being the one to challenge her, sometimes at public council meetings.

They see each other every day, often in the back alley, where trucks deliver staples for that day's meals. They argue every day, but not about he said, she said, former spouse stuff. Now it's about property lines, paint colors, and which guests used the other inn's parking spots without permission. Dad complains that Mom brags that the Evergreen is closer to the Pacific Ocean, which of course, it is. The Westcott sits one lot east of the Evergreen, which means Dad brags his B&B is the closest to the town's nightlife, as if there was any nightlife other than my buddy Seth's place across the street, Ranger Bar and Grill, known by locals as simply the Ranger.

They are rivals, and it's really not that much different from how we grew up. They don't necessarily dislike each other; they love each other in their own weird way, that much is clear. They just can't stand to be married and tied down to one another, but to this day, they can't really separate from each other, either.

So, having both my parents staying at my house today is a bit surreal. It's not quite a flashback to the old days, but also not familiar enough to become comfortable. They talk in hushed voices and stop when I come into the room. Everyone is treating me differently than the days prior. I guess that makes sense, though to be honest, I don't feel much different.

* * *

We're all in the backyard the next morning—my parents, Darla, Meghan, and late-edition Kevin. All three kids are here, of course, plus Jaden's friend Evan. Evan is probably fifty pounds heavier than Jaden, a big kid with shoulder-length hair tucked under a flat-bill baseball cap.

Seth, my friend from Shoreline who owns the Ranger, came too, along with Christy. Her husband, Malcolm, is working out of town and couldn't make it back in time. Seth and Christy dated briefly back in high school. Like oil and water, they didn't work out, and I still tease them about it.

The bright, still rising sun overhead casts long shadows. It's a quiet weekday morning, and the dew is still heavy on the grass. I pulled the kids from school. I'm not sure if that was the right decision, but Mom said we were having a funeral, and I don't think that's something that can be missed. Mason didn't protest. Paige shrugged and said, "OK," her first utterance in three days. *Progress.*

We're all in a circle around the dry, stone birdbath. It's white and cracked and belonged to the people who lived here before us. But Mom seems to think this is the spot to be. If we had a family dog, I feel like this is how his burial would go—right here in the middle of my backyard next to the birdbath. I'd dig the hole, and Jaden would fill it in after I took the younger kids inside. But I've never buried a pet before.

We're all holding yellow daisies with thick green stems. Christy handed them out as we stepped off the deck. I'm not sure what we're supposed to do with them. Paige holds hers to her nose, doing her best to hide behind it. If it was another day, I'd make mine into a mustache and try to get a few laughs, but I decide against it.

Mom takes a step forward to speak first, which is good because this is her thing, and I have no intention of giving a speech. As she does, Mr. Speight next door fires up the lawnmower, breaking the peaceful quiet of the morning. Mom clears her throat and prepares to talk over the noise.

The self-propulsion mechanism for Mr. Speight's mower is on the fritz, so we're forced to listen to the engine rev and ease as he navigates the wilds of his backyard. I'd ask him to turn it off, but he'd probably say no, and I don't want to murder him in front of all these people holding daisies.

"Tina was a daughter. She was a sister-in-law and a daughter-in-law. But more than anything, she was a wife and a mother," Mom begins, giving Tina's family resume. "She was taken from us too soon, and we're here to honor her memory in whatever way we can. Her body will be returned to the Earth so it can help complete the cycle of life. From it, things will grow anew."

Mr. Speight is right on the property line now. His slow walk is obscured by the fence but the engine rumbles.

Mom doesn't know Tina is being cremated as we speak. She won't be returning to the Earth except in a sealed container. This seems like the wrong time to bring it up, though.

I don't know what it was, but I catch Paige's eye, who is standing by Dad. She smiles at me, and I laugh. Which makes her and Meghan laugh, then Darla. Soon we're all laughing. It might be this ridiculous little ceremony or just the much-needed release of natural emotion, but it feels good. It feels nice to laugh in that way that you just can't help, especially when you know it's inappropriate, and some higher power has told you that you shouldn't let your true feelings out.

The laughter subsides, and with it comes the tears that essential release of emotion. Laughter and tears are an unbalanced combination floating its way out of all of us.

The mower stops and it's quiet again. I wipe my eyes.

"Does anyone want to share anything about Tina?" Mom asks.

Darla raises a tentative hand, and I instantly regret bringing the kids into the backyard. I know this was rushed. I should have insisted we wait a few days and hold a proper funeral, even if no one came and Tina didn't want one.

"She didn't know how to make sweet potatoes," Darla says.

"Really?" I say, not believing that she would choose this time to disparage her, even if she really didn't care for her.

"Hold on, I have a point here. Give me a little credit."

I nod my tentative approval though I still don't trust her. She speaks slowly and looks like she's talking to the kids.

"She didn't know how to make sweet potatoes, but that doesn't mean she didn't want to or thought less of us because we did. She had her flaws, in the kitchen or otherwise, but she wanted to do the right thing, I think. She wanted to be like us, to have the connections we have as a family. The ability to share and simply be together and enjoy the moments. She's the only sorta sister I ever had, and while we weren't besties, she was a hard worker and had a great career and provided for her children. And in the end, maybe that's all we should be judged for if we provided for our children, and she did that."

Darla stops, and her eyes meet mine, and I could tell she regretted saying that last part about Tina providing for her kids. Financially, yes. Everything else, no. We all look at the ground or play with the daisies.

One by one, we each say something. We skip Paige. Dad's words were short but compassionate. Mason and Jaden talked about a vacation we took to Crater Lake—one of the few vacations we ever took together.

I say that Tina was the only woman I had ever loved, which is right by all measurements. I can't bring myself to talk about her and the kids and their relationship. It would be hollow. For show. It makes me feel bad inside, but I just can't do it. I don't know yet what it will feel like to miss her.

Christy directs us to place the daisies in the birdbath and take a moment to silently reflect on our loss. It's quite peaceful.

As we stand around the birdbath, looking at the pile of flowers, I notice that Jaden and Evan are holding hands, fingers interlocked. Jaden leans into Evan's shoulder for comfort. He looks content, supported.

Well, that was unexpected.

CHAPTER 12

Jaden and Evan sit next to each other on the couch in my office. Like partners in crime waiting to be interviewed by the detective who busted them. Did I bust them? Not really.

The boys went right into the office on their own accord after my father burst out, "What the holy hell is that?" He saw the handholding right after I did. He pointed like he'd just seen a spaceship landing by the birdbath. Truthfully, similar words were forming in my mouth, and they almost made it to my lips, but my father beat me to it. I'm glad he did.

Hearing the words out loud made it wrong—calling Jaden out. Something had to be said, but I was grateful that my father took the bullet and not me. It was an ugly thing to say, but someone had to point it out, because well, it was different, and my family doesn't know different. We are the same. From top to bottom, we have our issues, but we know what they are. We know what to expect. Until now, apparently.

My father shook his head and walked away, giving Jaden a disappointed look. Jaden blushed and dropped Evan's hand—a reaction forced by Grandpa Mitch alone. I don't know if it was shame or embarrassment that he felt, but I didn't like it.

My mother managed to distract my father as only she can. She whispered something in his ear, and he obediently followed her into the kitchen without another word. She could do that. Happens all the time. Maybe because my father is a highly inappropriate man with no filter, or perhaps it's because my mother knows this and tries to head him off before he says something he'll regret.

Either way, now I'm the handholding detective with two suspects.

I sit in the chair across from Jaden and Evan, them nervously grinning and me trying to find the words to begin. I watch Jaden for a moment as he steals glances at Evan, this boy whom I know very little. That's not entirely true. He plays baseball at the University of Oregon. Outfielder. He's tall. He owns a vehicle of some sort because he drove Jaden home. And apparently, he's my son's, what? Special friend? What do they call it? What exactly is happening right now? I look around for a hidden camera because I'm getting pranked, certainly. On the day of my wife's birdbath funeral, this is the most exciting storyline. Unexpected, I'll say that much.

I think about the posters in Jaden's room upstairs. Athletes, that's what I always saw. Every inch of available wall space is covered by athletes at the top of their game. Some baseball players. A Portland Trail Blazers basketball team picture. A guy twisting his skateboard on a half-pipe. No bikini pics. That's not odd, right? Jaden's decorations are typical for boys. Sure, Mason's room doesn't have posters plastered on the walls, but I don't think they make posters of famous video gamers. Maybe they do, but I'm not sure how they'd determine the best ones. Who knows? My mind is drifting. I'm avoiding the elephant in the room.

"Dad, this doesn't have to be weird," Jaden says.

I shake my head back to reality.

"What's weird?" I respond, because that, you know, that's helpful.

"I didn't want you to find out this way. We kind of figured I'd come up on a school break and tell you, then you could meet Evan later. I'm sorry, Dad."

"Don't be sorry about who you are," I say. "That's—"

"Dad, no. I'm not sorry about who I am. I'm just sorry I surprised you like this. The timing isn't great."

"Oh, right. Yeah. OK."

"Mr. Bell, I really care about your son—"

"Whoa, wait there a minute, partner," I cut him off. I've never called anyone 'partner' before in my life. "Thanks, but I need some processing time before we go there, OK?"

Evan lowers his head, defeated. I feel bad, but only a little.

I find myself holding back a wave of emotion. I picture myself red-faced and screaming. I see this from Jaden's perspective, though. I'd be a monster looming over him and his friend. It would feel good to scream and showcase my fury. I could throw an impressive tantrum right now, one for the ages. But it's not Jaden or Evan who deserves that reaction, although it would be a relief just to let it out. It's this whole thing—Tina, and now this. I think I could lose it. My face is getting hot.

But Jaden is watching me. My boy. The kid I coached in every sport he played. The one who never complained a day in his life. The one who understands. He looks happy, and it's not as if he didn't have reasons to be that way before. So today, a weight was lifted off his shoulders. He's relieved and practically giddy on the day of his mom's funeral. That's not for me to take away from him with my reaction to his news.

Jaden will remember whatever I say for the rest of his life. What did his dad say when he came out? And what am I mad about? It's not this. This I can take. This is my son, and he's no different than who he was thirty minutes ago. Am I comfortable with it right at this second? No. Does that matter? Not really.

"You had a girlfriend…" I say.

Her name was Melody, and she played softball. I have pictures of the two of them going to homecoming and prom. She was tall and athletic, sort of big boned. Blond hair. They were always together.

"Yeah, about that... We kinda covered for each other," Jaden says. "Appearances, you know?"

"You knew back in high school?"

"Yes, I knew," he says with a chuckle. "You didn't?"

"No, of course not. You had a girlfriend."

"I had a *friend.* Melody had a girlfriend. Her own girlfriend."

It takes me a minute to do the math. Now that relationship makes sense—a convenient cover. "Why didn't you tell me?"

"To be honest, this has nothing to do with you. This is about me. And now it's about Evan, too."

Evan raises his hand and gives a limp wave, to which I chuckle. OK, partner. Probably not what he bargained for today, either.

I give Evan the bro nod, to which he returns. We're on the same page.

"So, Evan was your first?" I ask.

"You really want to dive right in, huh, Dad?"

"No, not that. Christ. Your first *boyfriend.* I don't need to know that other stuff."

"You remember Tyshawn Michelson?" he asks.

"The kid from summer camp who became your pen pal?"

He nods. "That's the one."

"So that's why you were so upset when baseball camp conflicted with summer camp," I say.

"One of the reasons," he says wryly.

"You knew that long ago, that you were—"

"Gay. Dad. It's called gay."

"Right, gay. Yes."

"No, I didn't know back at summer camp. I just figured it out as I got older. I knew that I didn't feel the same way about girls that some of my friends did. I was confused because they talked about girls when they walked by. Nothing dirty, just comments about how they looked. I didn't see what the big deal was. Those girls were my friends, too. It's not just a physical thing, Dad. I didn't let myself figure that out until I met Evan. It doesn't matter what someone looks like."

"Hey, that's not very nice!" Evan says, smiling.

I stifled a laugh.

"That's not what I meant," Jaden says.

He leans over and kisses Evan on the cheek. I expected to recoil. This isn't my scene. To my surprise, the kiss has absolutely no impact on me at all. Am I Mr. Cool Dad or what? My involuntary response is nil—just another day.

"When I got to U of O, I met other people. People like me, and I knew that I wasn't different from them, and I could finally be who I wanted to be. I like boys. Not every boy—just like straight guys don't like every girl. That's what I mean. When you connect with someone emotionally, that's what matters."

"Does Coach Long know?"

"God, no," Evan said. "That guy's living in the 1950s."

"So, you have to hide it?" I ask.

"In Eugene, it's pretty easy to blend in, but we decided to be private," Jaden says. "The other guys on the team know. There are a couple of guys who don't get it and probably never will, but everyone else knows and doesn't seem to care. They have their own problems and worrying about us just isn't one of them."

"I wish you would have told me anyway. I don't like that you had to keep something from me."

"Mom didn't think you could handle it," Jaden says.

Tina knew?

Evidently, I'm not Mr. Cool Dad.

* * *

I broke my leg when Jaden was six. It was stupid. I stepped wrong off a sidewalk and something cracked. They put a small metal plate and three screws in there to hold it together. It still hurts when it rains, and the site of the incision is always numb.

It happened near the end of Jaden's second soccer season. They played four-on-four. No goalies and the coach just ran around on the field with the kids to point them in the right direction. They didn't even keep score because the kids were supposed to be learning the game. I'd coached the team all year. Coaching is a defined word, and maybe not the right one. It's definitely not what I did. At that age, if the kids didn't run off the field crying, you've already won. I managed the kids at practice and on the field. We all had fun.

I couldn't put weight on my leg and was using crutches. Given my predicament, I couldn't coach the team. We had one game left. So instead of asking one of the other parents to step in for me and herd those cats around the field, I asked Tina, the one parent who had not attended a single game at that point. Remember, this was early on, and I thought that at some point, work would slow down for her and she would start attending Jaden's events. Jaden was our first, and all of this was new. The timing worked because she was in town for a few days taking care of me after my surgery.

She reluctantly agreed to coach for one game only. I spelled out her role and told her what to do. I even had us arrive at the field thirty minutes early to watch another game before our game started so she could get the hang of her role. Just herd them in the right direction and substitute the kids in and out.

It was a total disaster. Tina didn't know the game rules and repeatedly gave the ball to the other team or made our boys do a corner kick when they should have done a goal kick. Trust me, there's a difference. She didn't know the kids' names, so she just yelled out their numbers a few times. But six-year-old kids don't know their numbers, so they would just wander off trying to look at the back of their jerseys for what was printed there. Our boys were colliding like pins at a bowling alley. It wasn't pretty.

We were down 8-0 at halftime. I knew we weren't supposed to keep score, but what else was I supposed to do sitting on the sideline? I pulled my hat down low to the other parents. Their looks asked why in the world was this lady out there, letting their little angels get killed.

Tina saw none of the chaos or dirty looks.

"Oh, man, that's a lot of running. I need to get back in shape!" she said, taking a big swig from her water bottle before the second half. "They're doing great out there, right?"

I didn't have the heart to tell her the truth. We were getting slaughtered, and she wasn't helping. I didn't think it was possible, but the second half was worse, at least on the imaginary scoreboard. But at some point in the second half, I stopped watching the game. I quit looking at the kids running in a pack around the field. I ignored the score, and I figured out why Tina wasn't seeing the same game I had been watching.

She was only watching one player. Jaden. She'd follow him around at a safe distance, only paying attention to his moves. When the ball would go out of bounds, she was supposed to call out which team was awarded the ball, but she didn't know because she wasn't watching the ball unless Jaden had it. When Jaden took a rest break and sat on the sideline, she'd follow the players on the field, uninterested or unable to focus on the mechanics of the whole thing.

When the game ended, the players did the congratulatory high-five line with the other team, then ran to get juice boxes and orange slices. Jaden collected his goodies and went straight to his mom to give her a big hug.

"That was awesome!" he said. "Thanks, Mom."

Tina looked a bit bewildered at this attention from her son, as if she didn't know what to do with it. She patted him on the head as he squeezed her waist. To Jaden, it didn't matter that they lost 17-1 because his mom was there, and she only had eyes for him. The bond between mother and son. Despite everything, I was the outsider.

* * *

"When did you tell Mom?" I ask, my head spinning.

"I didn't tell Mom," Jaden explains. "She asked me. She knew."

"How could she have known?" I ask.

"I don't know. The same way you could have known, I guess. It's not like I was hiding anything. She saw it. I just didn't come out and label it."

I dig deep into my parental memory bank to see what I missed. How oblivious I was. How I missed the opportunity to help my son discover who he was. To make him feel more whole. But what irked me is that Tina wanted Jaden to withhold something from me. What else did I miss?

"You can tell me anything, Jaden," I say, working to keep my voice steady but doing it poorly. "I will always be there for you, no matter what happens. I want you to know that."

"I know, Dad."

"You're not too old to hug your father, either," I say, standing.

I open my arms and welcome him into an embrace. He's taller than me, and he puts his head on my shoulder.

"Thanks, Dad. I should have told you."

"It's okay. You just did. I love you."

"Love you too, Dad."

CHAPTER 13

Christy sets a cup of coffee in front of me. It's a ridiculously large cup, more like a soup bowl with a wooden handle. The small café is packed with caffeine lovers of all types enjoying extra-large drinks that require two hands to sip.

"Gravity coffee. It's from nature," she says with no hint of irony.

"Sure it is," I say, lifting the massive drink to my mouth to take a noisy sip.

It's just an over-priced pour-over coffee, but I'd be lying if I said it wasn't good. I savor the flavor for a minute, determined not to let Christy know how much I am enjoying it.

After dropping the kids at school, Christy and I drove downtown to the café. Every few weeks we try a new café or restaurant. I decided this week should be no different. Why change things?

It's been a week since Tina's birdbath funeral. All the kids are back at school, and I'm working my way back into a routine and trying to figure out what's next. Tina was cremated, per her wishes, and I've visited a few cemeteries trying to find a suitable plot. In the most polite up-sell possible, the cemeteries asked if Tina's plot would be a single one or would I be joining her when the time came. Even death is a business, and I'm sure a double plot is valuable for the bottom line. I'm still mulling it over.

For now, her ashes are still at the funeral home. They've left me two messages to pick up her remains like they were causing some type of trouble for them to store for a few more days while I determine her eternal resting place.

I've also been looking to book a vacation for myself and the kids when school gets out. I'm hoping the time together will be good for all of us. We haven't done an actual family vacation since before Paige was born. It'll either be a cruise in the Caribbean or renting a house in Hawaii. Somewhere tropical.

I know our family income stream has dried up, but once we get the life insurance payment, we'll be fine until Paige is a bit older and I can find my way back into the workforce. Our portfolio is solid, thanks to Tina's diligent investing. I need to be smart about it, no question, but not having to worry about money is an enormous blessing. I would feel like a heel telling Christy how well Tina set us up to live without her.

"So, how are things with you?" Christy asks after a few minutes of idle chitchat. She's asking with genuine concern. This is something I very much appreciate about Christy—sincerity and thoughtfulness.

We've known one another nearly our whole lives, and I think if anyone actually knows me, it's Christy. The reverse is true, too. We've spent a lot of time together as married individuals, but solo parents. We have our own families and priorities, but it's a lot easier to have another adult who understands the situation.

Her question is predictable, and I knew she would ask, so I've already prepared an answer. I don't want her to worry about me; she's got her own stuff to handle.

"The house seems emptier than usual," I say. "The kids are hanging in there. It's not going to be easy. I'm ready to book a vacation for this summer, someplace hot and tropical, or maybe camping somewhere without Wi-Fi."

She frowns, and I wonder if she is thinking of the same thing I am—the camping trip we took with our kids to Expo

Park in Southern Oregon several years ago. The one we never talk about and haven't repeated since. Our spouses were supposed to be there, but they weren't. I still remember the hangover I had that next morning. I let the memory slip away, wishing I hadn't mentioned camping.

If she catches the reason for my daydream, she doesn't indicate it.

"I've known you for way too long to let you get away with an answer like *we're gonna take a trip*," she says. "You're supposed to be the tough guy at your house, but you don't need to be that way with me. I get it, remember?"

I hadn't prepared for any follow-up questions, so Christy's response momentarily befuddles me.

I sip my massive bowl of coffee and try to find the words to explain how I'm feeling, like if I laid down on the therapist's couch, what would come out of my mouth?

I know what I'm supposed to say. It would be easy to lie to Christy, or at least try. I would say that I'm in a dark place and I'm sad all the time. I see signs of my dead wife in everything I do. I see her every day in my daughter's eyes. I'll never love again, that's for sure. These are the things I'm supposed to say right now, but I don't have those feelings.

I can't lie to Christy, although I feel like I should. I feel sort of numb.

"I don't get it," I say. "I feel fine. I know that there are stages of grief, but I feel like I've moved past that already. Tina was a part of my life for more than twenty years, but I don't feel like anything has changed."

"James, your wife is gone. A lot has changed."

"That's supposed to be true, yes, but nothing is different."

"You're on your own to make decisions now. No spouse to consult with. It's all on you. Who are you supposed to talk to about your kids when they screw up? How are you going to support the family?"

"Why does it seem like you've put so much thought into this?" I ask.

She looks away and chuckles. We both know she's had her issues with Malcolm. He can be cold and distant, and I know she's envisioned life fending for herself, absent from him.

"It's what we wives do, James. Get with the program." She smiles and tries to play it off. "You don't feel alone or worried about the future?"

"Alone? No. Worried? Not any more than usual."

Christy waits for a few moments as if she's holding back something.

"I want you to answer this question honestly. You know you can confide in me, and I think you need to do some confiding right now."

"This sounds heavy. Like gravity coffee."

"Please be serious for a minute," she says. "You have been married for a long time. This is the only woman you've ever really been with. You had three kids, and by all accounts from an outsider, your life looked outstanding. But what's bugging me is what I think you're afraid to say, or maybe even afraid to admit to yourself. I've known you both for a long time, and I believe I know the answer. So, here's the question. Were you and Tina happy?"

Happy? What's that?

* * *

Two years ago, Tina and I attended a lavish event at an upscale hotel in downtown Portland overlooking the Willamette River. Goodwin Labs held a black-tie holiday party in one of the ballrooms to celebrate a successful sales year. Tina turned heads in a sleek one-shoulder strap dress that hugged her in all the right places.

The night started with speeches from the executive team. Tina spoke for a bit, discussing her team and their accomplishments. I felt proud of her. She had accomplished something of which she was proud, too. She was succeeding in a male-dominated field, and her success wasn't unnoticed.

Her year-end bonus had been sizable, and our bank account was growing significantly.

I sat at our table and observed everyone around us. Mostly couples who were attached at the hip. Men introduced their wives to one another. The women would find some common ground and become fast friends—I was used to this. Tina was working the room, and the wives assumed that I was another Goodwin Labs employee alone at the table, so I didn't make any fast friends. I did my best to butt into the conversations at our table and received polite but uninviting responses. Who wanted to talk to me? And besides, there was always the fear that they would get sideways with their husbands for chatting up another man. One guy even pulled his wife away from me by her arm as we discussed the cost of childcare while standing in line for the shrimp buffet.

I stared at my plate of slimy shrimp. I couldn't bring myself to eat, but they kept refilling my wine glass. Conversations swirled around me. I spotted Tina standing with a group of men away from the cluster of tables. She held them in rapt attention the way she always could. They hung on her every word and laughed at her jabs at them. She owned them. Her smile was bright, and she looked incredible.

I took a deep breath and pulled my phone out of my jacket pocket, pretending to answer an important text, when in truth, I was checking in with my mom, who had come into town to stay with the kids overnight at our house. It was getting late, and she was most likely already asleep. Getting no response, I put my phone back inside my pocket.

At some point late into the night, Tina's gaggle of co-workers dispersed, and she headed back toward our table. I stood, holding my new glass of red wine. Our eyes met, and she playfully smiled as she weaved her way between tables and chairs to return to me. She seemed to be saying, *I've been looking for you all night. There you are!*

My heart was pounding when she was only a few steps

away. Finally, I would get the Tina treatment and confidence boost that came with it. Only when she reached for my fresh glass of wine did it occur to me what was about to happen. For a quick second, I rejected the idea as shallow and silly. No, it couldn't be.

"Thank you, James, that's very thoughtful," she said, taking the glass and sidestepping around me, continuing her focus and giving a playful smile to a man standing behind me. I turned with her, and like a crestfallen high schooler, I watched her greet him.

"Steven," she said. "I can't believe they let an old rascal like you in here. How's the Midwest division treating you these days?"

It turns out this Steven guy was doing great. The Midwest division was killing it. His family was fantastic, too. His oldest daughter was just accepted to medical school, and he was elated.

As this man went on and on about himself, I waited for my wife to introduce me, the person standing at her side, but now miles away. Maybe share about our three kids. The opportunity came and went. She talked about the new product lines coming out, and I stood there like an idiot with my hands in my pockets.

Steven eventually moved on, just in time for Tina to find another conversation to join. She walked away, never acknowledging me.

Standing there, I caught my reflection in the ballroom window, confirming that I was not invisible. At least not to everyone.

* * *

I ponder Christy's question. Were we happy? Was I? Maybe I was just content with things as they were. Happy never played into it. We had a longstanding deal—a division of labor of sorts. I ran the house and she worked. We had balance.

"Happy is complicated," I say.

"Marriage is complicated," Christy says. "Happy is not."

The steam from the expensive coffee swirls out of the mug as I ponder a reply.

"It's not that easy," I say. "How can I answer for her? How would I know? I mean, was I happy? Yeah, I guess. I was content with us and the way things were."

"But she was your wife," Christy says. "Your happiness impacts her, and her happiness should impact you. It's the pact of a marriage. You can't claim to be happy, but not know how it influences your partner. That's selfish."

The fact remains I can't say if Tina was happy, or unhappy for that matter. She came and went through my life as she pleased. She didn't ask for anything more than what I gave her from our marriage. Was that selfish? Was I selfishly happy, prioritizing myself over her? No, I refuse to believe that. We had an agreement. We stuck to it, and it worked.

"We were happy," I say.

But if we were, then why do I sound like I'm trying to convince myself?

CHAPTER 14

Earl Wrightman always wears a tie and sweater vest, at least every time I've seen him. I'm not sure if this is fashion sense, lack of it, or failure to pay attention to other choices available. Regardless, he's always in a tie and sweater in different combinations, no matter the occasion. He bleeds consistency.

Earl has been our occasional attorney for years. He mostly does real estate law. Ages ago, we bought two small houses for rental income and hired Earl to handle the paperwork. We sold them at a profit a few years later, and Earl took care of everything. We're not the kind of people to have an attorney on retainer or anything, but I've seen him enough to know about his sweater and tie fetish.

The portly man was pleasant and reasonably priced, so we kept in contact whenever anything legal came up. He was more of a utility lawyer than a specialist of any kind. If I were on trial for murder—not a likely event—I wouldn't call Earl, but for little stuff, like the practical, run-of-the-mill lawyer stuff, Earl was the right guy.

When I turned forty, he did both Tina and my wills, which is why he's sitting at my kitchen table right now in his blue sweater and green tie, ignoring the blueberry muffin I've offered.

"I'm so sorry, James," he says. "She was so young. So much life to live."

I say the standard lines I'm supposed to say because I don't have any original material, and I certainly don't want to use Earl as my sounding board for everything that I probably need to unload on someone else. I'm still trying to figure out the point Christy was driving at yesterday at the café, too. Marriages can be happy. Who knew?

These thoughts run through my head, and I wonder if I should set an appointment to see a counselor. Do I need it? I've never sought professional help for anything. I just never felt the need. I let the moment pass.

"As you know, the will is pretty simple stuff. Anything that was hers reverts to you. This is just a formality for me going through this with you today. That is why we're here and not in my office."

"Thank you. I appreciate that," I say.

It's just the two of us at the house.

Mason caught the bus to school this morning, and I dropped Paige at school an hour ago. It was all a bit routine, which should be a good thing. Nothing was missing, except something was, but maybe, definitely, it had been missing for some time, and everyone knew it but me. Tina wasn't missing from that routine because she wasn't a part of it. Today seemed like any other day.

Jaden is back at U of O. We talked more over the last few days about his situation. Is it a situation? Maybe. It was easier to talk when Dad left. Something inside Dad had snapped, and the news that his grandson was gay, or more so, that he was different from what Dad thought he was, had been just too much for him to handle. He and Jaden were always so close, but it was different now. Like I said before, different is not acceptable in my family. My mom promised to talk to Dad because it did no good when I tried. She knows his weak spots. It's better this way.

I was expecting a dramatic reading of Tina's will, but I guess that's just what they do in the movies. Earl handed me a few documents that matched the copy I had saved in our home office. The assets listed were slightly out of date since the market has grown, but the rest was in order. The house was the big one. Our savings accounts at the bank were there, plus our portfolio of investments with Charles Schwab.

Tina knew more about the money side than I did. We budgeted an amount for the general household stuff—mortgage, bills, all the standard stuff you have to take care of each month. Her paycheck, our sole income, was split between all our obligations. Each month a deposit was made in our bank account that covered our bills while the rest of her check, including any sales-related bonuses, would go to an account at Charles Schwab.

I'm not ashamed to say that I've become accustomed to not living paycheck to paycheck, and that's thanks to Tina. In that sense, her job was a blessing, allowing us to provide more for our kids than we were offered when we were younger. Private dance classes. Select baseball camps. The latest technology for the house. Safety and security. We're not clipping coupons to buy organic, I buy our groceries at Whole Foods. When the kids needed new clothes, I drive past the Old Navy and Walmart to Nordstrom or order higher quality items online. Why buy junk that would just fall apart?

This luxury has come at a price. Tina worked hard for it.

I'm not oblivious to supply and demand, either. How can we continue to live this lifestyle with the primary breadwinner out of the picture? That's part of the other reason that I'm meeting with Earl. Goodwin Labs took out insurance policies on all its executives. Something along the line of five times Tina's yearly salary. I'm fuzzy on the exact amount because bonuses typically balloon her final annual take-home pay, but the last I recall, she was bringing in about $450,000 a year. This puts us in line for a $2.25 million payment. We also had a term life insurance policy we bought when Jaden was born, but I can't recall the payout for that.

The life insurance meant I wouldn't have to touch our investments, which topped more than $2 million last year. I will continue to stay at home until Paige is in middle school at least, and Mason is away at college, then I can find work if for no other reason than I expect to be bored out of my mind when that day comes and my house is empty. I'll skip the organic groceries and maybe switch the clothes shopping to Target. That should reduce our spending quite a bit. I won't need to cut back much, but I don't want to be greedy.

Insurance is meant to make you whole again when something terrible happens. We did the right things and planned. The kids and I will be fine, which made this meeting so much easier.

Earl slides the blueberry muffin to the side and pulls a thin brown folder from his briefcase and plops it down on the table in front of him. He opens the folder and thumbs through some sheets of paper.

"I'm not your financial planner—that's not my role in this thing—but I knew you'd want the exact picture of where you are financially. You know Paul Thornton at Charles Schwab is in my building, so I had him pull up everything. I hope you don't mind."

"No, that's very thoughtful of you," I say. "That saves me from meeting with Paul and having to sit through an hour-long story about his latest fishing trip. Does he still have that boat?"

"Yes, the 'Running of the Bulls.' He told me about it when I met with him for these documents."

"Sorry about that," I say, feeling his pain. Paul was a first-class gas bag. Good guy, but he never shuts up.

"It's the cost of doing business, I'm afraid. Those investment guys love to chat about their toys."

"Can you arrange to get the check from Paul so I can avoid the headache of making an appointment with him?"

"I'm not sure what you mean," Earls says.

"From the insurance. I think Goodwin Labs will issue the check to me, but the term life insurance was handled through his office. Not Schwab, but they set it up. I don't need it right away, but I'd like to get this taken care of in the next few weeks so I can plan."

Earl flips through the papers again, looking for something. He doesn't find it.

"When did you get your P.O. Box?" he asks.

"We don't have a P.O. Box."

"Schwab has your address as a P.O. Box in Woodlawn by the airport. It's where they've been sending your statements."

"Maybe Tina opened it. She was on the road so much. I thought she just got everything through email. That's weird. Why does it matter?"

"So, have you seen your balances with Paul lately?" Earl says, timid to ask the question.

"Not recently, no. Tina took care of that side of things. Most of it was in her name anyway."

"I assumed you already made the withdrawal, though," he says.

"What withdrawal? Tina passed ten days ago, and I have only left the house a few times."

"But you transferred the money out before, right?" Earl stammered. "Paul was a little peeved about the whole thing when I brought it up. He was not happy when your business walked out the door."

"Walked out the door? What do you mean?" I ask.

Earl ignores me and studies his papers.

"What is on those sheets of paper you keep flipping through? What do they say?"

Earl pauses and won't look me in the eye.

"It's gone, James. She pulled it all. I mean, if you didn't. I don't know where it went."

Earl hands me an updated asset sheet from Paul, and I go cold. Something is wrong. All the accounts are listed, color-coded even, and they are all gone. The money market account. Our mutual fund investments. The Roth IRA. All of them say zero balance. There should be over $2 million in the portfolio. That's what Tina had told me. I'd never verified it myself. Why would I?

The accounts are empty.

"Where did it go, Earl?" My voice shakes. "This was everything. If this is gone, then… It just can't be gone. We've been sending Paul money for years. I didn't transfer it anywhere else. Doesn't he have records?"

"He does. That's what I have here," Earl runs his finger down a spreadsheet, looking for something. "But eighteen months ago, the deposits stopped. I see a withdrawal a few months later. Then several more—the bulk of your assets, then all of it. You didn't know about this? You took quite a tax hit on the retirement accounts to withdraw it."

I ignore his question because obviously, I didn't know about it. I take the folder and look through the papers myself. Shortly after the deposits stopped, there were three large withdrawals, totaling all our money. Three checks were issued to Tina Bell.

"It was all in her name, right?" Earl says. "She could do what she wanted with it and not need your signature."

"What did she do with our money?"

"James, maybe we should take a break here. This isn't how I expected this meeting to go. I thought you knew all this."

"Not how *you* expected it to go?! What the hell, Earl! This isn't exactly what I expected, either. We're not taking a break. I need to know where our money went. We can't be completely broke."

This can't be happening.

CHAPTER 15

I find myself thinking about Ms. May. Not about how she stuffed her meaty frame into that ballet teacher leotard each day, but how she told me at dance class that she had spoken to Tina several times about the bill for Paige's classes. And how, after I tried to pay for it, the credit card was declined.

A few things are off here. First, Tina didn't deal with the day-to-day expenditures of the family, that is my territory. I signed Paige up for the classes. It never went through Tina, and as far as I know, she had never dealt with Ms. May or the ballet classes. Secondly, the payment was a reoccurring charge on our credit card—the same card that was declined. For the charge to stop reoccurring, someone had to change that.

I make a note to call Ms. May and figure this out, but if I had to guess, Tina stopped the payments. But why?

I set this aside. I have more pressing questions, and I needed more information from Paul Thornton to answer them. I dial him directly, and he picks up immediately.

"Darn it, James, she told me you knew about this," Paul says before I even get a question off. Earl must have called him.

"No, I didn't," I say. "How could she withdraw all this money without my approval?"

"The accounts were all in her name, not exactly the norm, but I didn't have any reason to question it."

"Did she say anything? Did she tell you why?"

"She just said that the family finances had changed, and that she didn't need me to handle the investments anymore."

"That didn't raise a flag with you?"

"Well, not entirely. People make emotional decisions about their money all the time. Sometimes they have a change of heart and decide to move the money to another guy. As I said, it happens all the time. But that's the thing… She didn't do that. The tax implications alone were significant."

"How do you mean?"

"Well, she didn't transfer the money to another investment firm like Vanguard or Merrill Lynch. She cashed it out to herself. As you know, some of those investments were retirement-related. Pulling that money before you reach retirement age means taking a tax hit that could wipe out a significant portion of any returns. In the ballpark of twenty to forty percent, sometimes more. But that's what she asked for, so that's what I gave her."

"So, she just walked out with a check," I say.

"Three of them, but yes. This wasn't all at once. The first one was a year and a half ago. That was just a liquidation of the money market account with no tax implications. She never really explained that one, just cashed out. Then she came back two other times and pulled the rest, saying she had plans for the money. That's where the tax hit came from. Dang, James, I wish I could tell you more. I just assumed that you all had talked this over and now that she's passed on… I'm sorry."

"You didn't think to give me a courtesy call," I ask.

"I thought you knew and besides, your name wasn't on the accounts. I couldn't share her activity, even though you were married. You and I have never had those conversations before. She drove the investments."

"Please tell me the term life insurance is still there."

"James, I'm sorry. She stopped the payments."

Of course, she did.

"Paul, I didn't know about this. Now she's gone, and I can't ask her about it. Is there anything you can think of that would explain this?"

"Once it's gone from here, I can't track it. The only thing I can tell you is that she had to put it somewhere. You just need to find it. Just because it's not here doesn't mean it's gone. I'm sorry."

I'm getting real tired of hearing *I'm sorry.*

* * *

I stand in our bedroom and stare at Tina's dark blue Swiss Army suitcase. It's one of those carry-on ones that frequent travelers use so they don't have to stow their luggage and spend extra time waiting at baggage claim. It's frayed around the edges. I can only imagine the number of miles this thing has logged in the air or time spent flopped open at some hotel.

Tina didn't unpack it when she came home for the last time. She just rolled it into the corner and left it. I hesitate before opening it, knowing this was one of the last things that she ever did—packing her bag. She had a routine for when she traveled. She'd pack three days' worth of clothes every time. Different pieces to mix and match them in rotation after the hotel had them dry cleaned. A light blazer was practically a requirement. This allowed her to travel light. She'd pack two pairs of shoes for her various business meetings and running shoes for the gym and any other needs. A small bag, packed like a professional.

Crumpled on the floor next to the bag were black flats, black dress slacks, and a blue blouse—work clothes. I've been walking by this pile of clothes since Tina got home and stripped them off, dropping them onto the floor, never to be worn or touched by her again. I pick them up. They smell like her. I put them back on the floor. *Not today*, I tell myself. *Maybe tomorrow.*

I lift the bag on to the side of the bed and unzip the main

compartment to examine the contents. I remove a laptop, but strangely enough, it's not a Goodwin Labs computer. It's a Mac laptop that I have never seen before and I set it to the side.

I remove a day planner with dozens of little tabs sticking out the side. Despite my urging, she hated using the calendar on her phone to track appointments. However, it would have made my life a lot easier by seeing where she would be using a shared digital calendar. The way it typically worked was that she would just text me when she would be home. Or more frequently, she would not text me, because she just wasn't home very often. I set the well-used day planner on top of the laptop.

Two pairs of jeans and one pair of black yoga pants were inside the bag. A few casual T-shirts were wadded up in a ball, including her faded Rolling Stones tour shirt. She loved that shirt. She bought it after we saw the band perform live on what they claimed was their final tour, which was probably four tours ago.

I pull out the running shoes and toss her undergarments in a pile on the floor. Do I wash these clothes? What am I supposed to do with them? Save them for Paige? No. That would be weird. I don't think she would want to wear them. Maybe she would like the Rolling Stones shirt after I explained who they were. It will be ten years before Paige is big enough to wear it, though.

It's odd. I thought I knew her packing system inside and out, but the contents of this bag tell me that I didn't. I can't see how she was gone for as long as she was with only one set of professional clothes. It looked like she was packed more for a vacation than a business trip. There was also a swimsuit and sunscreen. Maybe she always packed that, I don't know. She liked swimming laps at the pool in the early morning hours before rambunctious kids made swimming in hotel pool lanes impossible.

I flip open the day planner, looking for any clue as to what type of trip she was on, but the planner was blank for the last few weeks. How could that be? How did she track her appointments? What was she doing? Where had she been?

Week after week, the pages are blank with an occasional notation on Saturdays for her triathlon club training sessions at a park in Portland. I knew she missed most of those because she was gone, but she never missed one when she was in town, except last Saturday for the race. There were a few hour-long appointments noted during business hours, but they were just company names. Probably sales calls. I stop looking through the planner since it wouldn't reveal anything more.

I power on the laptop. The login screen appears, allowing "Tina" or "Guest" to login.

I click on guest, but once I'm in, I see that it won't allow me access to Tina's part of the machine. Go figure. I log out and click on the picture of Tina. It's a photo I don't recognize of her wearing her swimmer's cap. This account requires a password to open, and I have no idea what she used for her password. This must be how very inept hackers feel when confronted with their first challenge—a brick wall.

I type in the code I use on the garage door keypad—one that she knows, too. It's the birthday of each of the kids. 16-02-30. No luck. I go downstairs and grab her purse, thinking that something inside might send me in the right direction, but knowing that the odds of that are incredibly slim.

I dump the purse on the bed. Cell phone. Keys. Mace. Some make-up. Various receipts. A half-dozen pens. A granola bar wrapper. Nothing special or out of the ordinary. I pick up the cell phone. It's dead, but it gives me an idea.

Our neighborhood is a gated community where you have to type in the keypad code or click an opener when you approach to get inside. Our code is the last four digits of my cell phone number. I try that password. Nothing. It really could be anything, and I'm fooling myself thinking I can simply guess it before the thing locks up on me.

I type my full phone number. Nothing.

But then I get another idea. I should have thought of this before. I type in her cell phone number into the computer login screen. It flashes to life. I'm in. Master hacker.

* * *

I click open the web browser. The homepage is Amazon.com, which makes me chuckle because that's the homepage on my computer, too. Sometimes packages she ordered would pile up in the entryway for weeks before she came home to open them. Although now that I think about it, that trend has slowed a bit. Much fewer packages.

I move the mouse over the link to browser history and pause before going any further. Am I invading her privacy by lurking through her web history? It feels wrong. Will there be things in there that she wouldn't want me to find? Something embarrassing? There's a reason we lock our computers, right? I wouldn't want my web history to be combed through. But then again, I didn't cash out all my family's investments without talking to my spouse first. I need to find that money. I push aside my privacy concerns and click into the depths of her web browsing.

I spend the next twenty minutes clicking through her daily browsing habits. Most mornings she would check her Outlook email account first thing. She'd send or return a few emails before moving on to the next part of her day. Nothing strange there.

She visited a site called Online Coach, which must have been some site for triathlon training. I click the link for the site, which takes me to a log-in screen. The web browser helpfully populates the saved login and password. The description at the top isn't what I expect. It's not a log of workouts tracked by miles of running, biking, and swimming.

> *Online Coach is a completely digital, professional service providing life and career coaching at your fingertips, 24-*

> *hours a day. Attain greater fulfillment in your life. Use our chat feature to begin now!*

Maybe she used it to coach her way to better sales performance? I close the tab. I have no interest in reading motivational speeches from some website.

I return to her email. I can't see any patterns here, just some shopping or driving directions. There were a few hotel websites where she made her reservations. She'd read the New York Times online pretty much every day. Typical stuff, almost.

It wasn't every day, but a few times each week, she'd visit NW Regency Bank. We didn't have an account there. Our banking was done through Oregon Transnational. The browser kept her username stored on the login page, but not her password. I tried the phone number trick. No luck. After answering some pretty basic questions, I reset the password through her email account. Thankfully, I know the name of her first pet, the high school she attended, and the name of the city in which she was married.

When I get into the account, I notice the total balance: $5,526 from savings and checking. This is a far cry from the $2.12 million Tina cashed out from our investments. Thank God we still have the life insurance from Goodwin Labs coming.

The NW Regency account was opened two days before the first of three deposits were made. The amounts were $200,000, then almost a year later $420,000. The final deposit that liquidated the investment account was $1.5 million. I looked back at the sheets from Paul and matched the dates. Each time she withdrew anything from Paul, she'd deposit it into the NW Regency account, then immediately withdrew a large amount in cash. The withdrawals were always less than $10,000, but still a lot of money to walk out of a bank with.

The rest of the account transactions were withdrawals—hundreds of them—including one for Online Coach for $39.95 each month. But that's not the one that stands out to me. On the third of every month, she would transfer $9,200 out of the account. It didn't say where it was going, but this was the same amount deposited into the Oregon Transnational savings account each month. This was the money I thought came from her paycheck. These were the funds I used to pay household expenses.

I opened a new tab in the browser and logged into our Oregon Transnational account. Eighteen months ago, the deposits were from Goodwin Labs, like I thought, but a month later, the origination of the deposit said TRANSFER: NWRB. They were coming from this new bank account, and I never noticed it.

If her paycheck wasn't going into our regular account or this new account, then where did it go? And where did these withdrawals go?

Where is the money?

My phone buzzes in my pocket. The screen reads, "Office Columbia Ridge." I look at the time. It's 3:21. I know why they are calling before I answer. Paige.

It's the office secretary.

"Mr. Bell, are you on your way? I've got this sweet little girl here, waiting for a ride home. At least, I think she's waiting for a ride home from you, right? She won't tell me anything. Doesn't talk much. I see that. Is everything good at home, Mr. Bell? I'll keep her company here until you arrive. Are you on your way? I'll tell her you're on the way."

CHAPTER 16

Online Coach, Session 1
Archive for client Tina Bell for any available provider at Online Coach

I don't know how I'm supposed to start this thing. I saw a shrink once, back in Nevada, but the state made all the foster kids do it. It was in person, though, not over chat.

Coach: *The chat takes some getting used to. We can switch to video anytime, just let me know. That's what you're paying your $39.95 a month for.*

No, that's OK. I can do a chat. It's probably better.

Coach: *Great. I recommend we start with a little about your background. What's your world look like today, and why have you decided to contact a coach.*

That's a lot.

Coach: *Take your time. At Online Coach, you can leave and resume your session at any time. You mentioned you were in foster care. Would you like to share about that?*

I lived with my mom until I was fourteen. Mom was an addict—heroin, painkillers, booze. Really anything she could get her hands on. She'd bring men to the apartment because they would bring her the drugs she wanted. I guess needed, really.

She'd always say, Steve or Rick or Trevor, he's going to be your new daddy. He's going to take care of us. These men would move into the apartment. It usually happened when she'd lose her job as a waitress or a telephone psychic or an office temp. I lost track of how many jobs Mom had. School was pretty easy for me, but when I came home, I was the responsible one. I had to get her up so she could make it to her night shifts.

Coach: *Tell me about your father.*

Nothing to tell. He might have been a senator, at least I like to think so, but he very well may have been the garbage man. Never met him, and I don't care to now.

Coach: *I understand. Please, continue.*

So, this guy named Trent moved in. Car salesman. Really nice guy. I couldn't figure out why he wanted to be with my mom. He was always at the apartment. He used to try to help me with my homework, not that I needed it. I'd just started high school. He'd tell me about how he'd sell cars to suckers. He called it, *giving intense focus.* You give this person every ounce of your energy, but not in some smug, slick salesperson way. Don't act like you like them; actually like and care about every part of their being. Send them your energy, at least until you make the sale, and then you can ease up. People would melt over that, he said.

So, we'd talk when Mom was at work, and he was always really nice. One night he made strawberry margaritas to celebrate a big month at the dealership. He offered me one. I'd never had alcohol before. I saw what it did to Mom, but it tasted good. I was surprised, and I had another. We were sitting on the couch, and he told me he thought I was pretty. And he gave me his intense focus. I didn't recognize he was doing it. Then he reached over, and it was like slow motion. He unbuttoned my top and touched my breasts. I'd gone to second base before, but that was with a boy my age. I was drunk from the margaritas, but I knew I definitely did not want this man touching me like that. I pushed him away, ran to the bathroom, and pretended to throw up.

He begged me not to tell Mom. She wouldn't believe me anyway, he said. He was right. She wouldn't believe me, so I didn't even try to tell her.

Sort of by accident, I told a volunteer at the Boys and Girls Club the next day. I sometimes went there after school if I didn't want to deal with Mom or her boyfriends. I was put into foster care the next week.

Coach: *Tina, I'm so sorry about what happened to you.*

Mom didn't fight for me. She said I tried to seduce Trent and that if I didn't show so much skin, this never would have happened.

Coach: *You know how wrong that is.*

Of course, I do. She was never a mother, and I blame her for how I am.

Coach: *What do you mean by that?*

When you're little, you learn from your parents or the adults in your life. You can't really help it.

Coach: *But how has that specifically impacted you?*

It means that I have an empty spot as a mom. It's like a foreign language. I can see it. I know it exists, but I'd rather just speak my own language. That mother's intuition or instinct? I wish I had that, but I just don't.

Coach: *The fact that you recognize what you're calling a deficiency is very telling about you.*

Yeah, what does it tell you?

Coach: *That you know yourself very well, and we can work with that. You're going to make great strides with us. I'm going to flag this topic so we can revisit it in the future. Is that alright?*

Sure. That's fine.

Coach: *Your intake form indicates your husband's name is James. Since we're still building a coaching profile to help you, it would be great if you could share a little about him. He's a stay-at-home dad? Not to sound old-fashioned, but that's an uncommon arrangement for a couple.*

James wouldn't have it any other way. Jaden, our oldest, was very much a surprise. I liked James, but I did not expect to have a child with him, let alone two more children.

Coach: *How did you meet?*

By accident. I had just ended a long-term relationship in

college with some loser, who in hindsight, was way too much like the guys my mom dated. I needed a break to get away. I convinced my friend Brenda to take a road trip. She had the car, so it was kind of necessary that she came. We went to a concert in San Francisco. She wanted to go home right after, but I told her I wanted to see the Redwoods and then the ocean up north. She got cold feet after we got there and left me in this crappy little town called Willits. I waited all day in this disgusting diner, fighting off advances from sweaty truck drivers. I needed a ride out of there, but not that bad. My options weren't great.

Then this guy came in—James. He was wearing this embarrassingly large backpack and his face was sunburned. He was hitchhiking down the coast. James was cute and innocent, but seemed a little out of his element, like this was his first time on his own out in the real world. I liked him. He was sexy and kind, too. I didn't intend to sleep with him. I'd never had a one-night stand before.

The next day I bought a bus ticket back home and resumed my summer in Las Vegas. I had big plans for my senior year at UNLV. I'd been recruited by this medical sales company, who had already offered me a job, pending graduation. My student loans were piling up, waiting for me to graduate and pay them off. This job was going to be perfect. The sales company couldn't say it outright, but they were looking for young, attractive women with long legs who could wear a tight skirt, low-cut blouse, and could rattle off stats about the latest pharmaceuticals. Doctors were much more likely to keep their appointments with women like that.

I had an IUD for birth control, so I didn't notice when I missed my first period, or my second. I was focused on finishing school. Being pregnant never crossed my mind. I didn't want a baby, and I didn't know the dad at all. He was some hitchhiker. How pathetic.

I was so far along when I found out that I never considered ending the pregnancy. But I couldn't turn into my mom, either—single and broke with some kid in tow. And I had that job offer. I knew they wouldn't take me with my round belly and swollen ankles. I'd look like a patient in the waiting room, not a sales rep, ready to flirt with the doctors to boost my numbers. I couldn't be a single mom and do that work. I needed help. I needed James.

Coach: *And he came through for you?*

Yes, more than any person in my entire life had ever done for me. When Jaden was born, I didn't have to convince James to be his dad. We got married, but it wasn't easy. I had to learn to love him as we were trying to raise a child and find some sort of balance. He is a good man, but he doesn't always listen.

We agreed early on how things would work between us, but as the years passed, I changed and wanted more from him. More from our marriage. I tried to express that to him. Our agreement of working and parenting wasn't enough for me.

Coach: *So, what did you do? How did you approach that?*

I did what many wives do. I found love elsewhere.

CHAPTER 17

Sleeping on my troubles didn't make them any better, and I'm keenly aware that each question I ask may uncover the true depth of those troubles. Financial concerns are a nightmare, but this is hardening my heart. I'm supposed to be mourning, not investigating the person I thought I knew.

As I comb through the computer and bank accounts, I've ignored my children, as evidenced by forgetting to pick up Paige at school, which is one of those absolute no-nos that you should avoid as a parent. Sure, we get distracted, but to forget your kid? That's next-level stuff.

I had a thoroughly uninspired conversation with Mason this morning about online gaming. He talked, and I listened while eating a bowl of cereal before school. At least we're talking. He's been spending more time with Yoseph, which I choose to think is a good thing while hoping that I don't get another drunken text for a ride home.

When I dropped off Paige, I chatted with her teacher before class started and asked that she contact me if Paige wasn't acting like herself. I think we're already there, the teacher's expression seemed to say. Of course, she's right. Paige is coping in her own way, and I'm not privy to the exact nature of that because I can't be inside her head. I carved out some dedicated time for her alone last night in a meager attempt to figure out how she was dealing with everything. We watched a movie, and I read her a bedtime story and tucked her into bed with her bear, Mr. Hugs. Returning to the basics felt good but didn't get me any answers.

The teacher promised to give me updates if anything changes, which is the best I can do.

I've not answered Christy's texts, and I'm sure she's getting annoyed. I haven't gone to the funeral home to pick up Tina's remains, either.

I'm adrift. My direction and motivation for the last twenty years of my life has been to raise the kids and make them into good little humans who can survive the dirty world around us. I could pick and choose what tools I used to shape them—discipline, structure, freedom, and craziness. They all had their place, but today, those tools seem inadequate to continue this same path. I have had the great luxury of time and money to mold my kids. But these luxuries are no longer options, and that has never been more evident than when I review our bank statement.

She stashed the money somewhere. She must have. I just need to find it, like Paul said. She couldn't have lost it. She wouldn't do that to me. This was just a misunderstanding. It had to be.

I thought our situation was terrible. Then it got worse.

* * *

The human resources lady at Goodwin Labs has a kind voice, but her words struck me like a knife to the gut. According to this woman, Tina resigned from Goodwin approximately a year and a half ago. She couldn't tell me anything more than her title and dates of employment, but she added that it was a voluntary separation. She then said that "considering the situation," she couldn't tell me anything more and wouldn't elaborate.

She transfers me to someone in the benefits department so I could deal with her life insurance.

"I see here that Tina is no longer with us," the man says.

"I'm terribly sorry about that. I didn't know her personally—big company and all. We don't see many of the external sales executives at HQ often, though. They're always on the road, making this place tick. Bringing in the big bucks. Needed, of course. Much needed for us, just never here at home base."

The situation sounds familiar.

"Since she voluntarily resigned, that means she was not an employee at the time of her death, so the life insurance policy was terminated. It's only applicable to active employees. She would have known that when she resigned, of course. It's in the handbook. We mailed all that out to her after the resignation, too."

No life insurance. He confirms the address was her secret P.O. Box in Woodlawn.

"Do you have any of that documentation?" he asks.

I tell him no, and he offered to send me some documents. I say yes, just in case I could learn something from it.

I was expecting a check for more than $2 million dollars—monopoly money. But that's why we had insurance. In case something happened to her, we'd be taken care of. The house. Bills. College for the kids. Did she know what she did? That by resigning from the company, she didn't have any life insurance? That she left us high and dry after cashing out our investments and stopping payment on the term life insurance? She had to have known.

"Do you know why she resigned?" I asked. It was a long shot. He already said he didn't know her.

"You don't know why she resigned? She was your wife," he says.

"No, I don't. I'm afraid I'm finding there are things about my wife I wasn't aware of."

"I know they did some shuffling when she left," he says. "Reorganized the department and moved some people around. Another employee… let me see if I can find it. He left at the same time, a lab guy. Oliver Tremblay, that was his name. He left about that same time."

"He resigned, too?" "You know, I probably shouldn't have said that. I do that a lot. Say things I shouldn't. I'm not sure why they even let me stay in this position sometimes—access to privileged information and all. I'm just on the benefits end. I hear things sometimes. Nothing official."

"Please," I ask. "If it could have something related to Tina, I need to know what it was."

There is a pause, and he puts the phone down. I hear a door shut, probably his office door for privacy. Why was this so secret? Then he is back on the line.

"There were some rumblings about a loss of IP. That's all I know."

"What's IP?"

"Intellectual property. Something about the IP created here at Goodwin going to another firm. At least, that's what I heard. I'm sure nobody is going to tell you anything about it. They keep things pretty hush-hush around here. Probably like I'm supposed to, but people tell me things when they are planning to leave the company. Retirements, mostly. They just want to unload to someone who will listen and often, that person is me."

"What does this IP thing have to do with Tina?"

"I have no idea, and maybe it doesn't. It was just something that people were talking about around the time she and Oliver quit. Probably just a coincidence. I really wouldn't put a lot of thought into it. They weren't even in the same department. I shouldn't have mentioned it."

But the fact is, he had mentioned it.

Why did Tina quit? But more importantly, now I know she was hiding it from me, and she took her first withdrawal of cash right when she left.

I was expecting money to fix this. Save us. Now, there is nothing. And if there is no life insurance money and I can't find the rest… I don't know what to do.

I pick up my cell phone. My first instinct is to text Tina to ask for advice. She was always a good problem solver. I catch myself before acting—embarrassed. I slam the phone down so hard on the kitchen counter that I crack the screen.

CHAPTER 18

I've had multiple occasions to be in the Columbia Ridge Academy principal's office with three kids attending the school. Once Jaden got into a scuffle with another kid at recess. Another time, Mason won an award for an essay he wrote about doing volunteer work. But each time, I knew exactly why I was coming in, unlike today. No doubt, I'm going to be read the riot act for being late picking up Paige a few days ago. I still feel terrible about it.

The assistant principal, Mr. Crowe, called and requested a meeting regarding Paige. In his voicemail, he said that Principal Woolworth had a report to give me and that I should arrive no later than two-thirty p.m. to discuss.

When I arrive at the ivy-covered brick school, I park in the back lot and rush through the rain to the student office's public entrance. The school's interior is all dark wood and glass, with marble floors that have been chipped and cracked from thousands of students walking the halls.

The student office is lined with mahogany benches on two sides that very well could have been church pews. The school doesn't have a religious bent, but it would be full Catholic if it did. Two women sit behind desks on their computers. The principal and assistant principal's offices are located in the back of the space. I introduce myself, and the receptionist gives me a guest pass sticker for my shirt.

Principal Gloria Woolworth, a squat woman in a blazer, waves me into her office. I sit in the chair in front of her desk. The office is cold and the rain outside pounds against the window. She does not close the door.

She sits patiently and waits, saying nothing as if I called the meeting and she's waiting for me to begin. So, I do.

"I'm sorry I was late picking up Paige the other day," I say. "It's the only time that has ever happened."

"Yes, punctuality is important, Mr. Bell. I appreciate that you recognize that."

"Of course."

"Paige has always been a good student," she begins. "Her teachers admire her, and her academic performance has been at standard or better each of her years here. Recently, her teachers have reported a change in her behavior."

"Her mother died suddenly. Of course, there's a change in her behavior," I say, recalling that I've already had several conversations with her teacher over the last few weeks.

"Quite right, yes. And understandable, too. I was so sorry to hear that." She looks down at several pages of notes. "She's withdrawn and doesn't engage in class discussions. She completes most of her assignments, but her work is sloppy. A bit disheveled. I've got it all right here in this report for you to take to her next school."

"Next school? She has several more years at this one."

Principal Woolworth gives me a puzzled look.

Out of the corner of my eye, I see movement at the doorway of the larger office. Standing in the entrance, holding a cardboard box, is Paige. Her thin arms struggle against the weight. There's no lid on the box. A paper totem pole she made in art class earlier this year sticks out the top. She's wearing her raincoat and boots, her backpack strapped to her shoulders.

I get to my feet, face flushed and confused.

Paige is crying, so I take the box from her hands. It's filled to the top with worksheets and other graded assignments. Inside are a dozen or more half-sheets of colored construction paper with notes and signatures from her classmates. Her pencil box, assorted books, and school supplies fill the remainder.

"They made me say goodbye to everyone," she sniffles. "They wrote me letters. I didn't know I was leaving."

"Yeah, that makes two of us," I say. I lead her to the bench, and she sets the box down.

"Why am I going to a new school, Daddy?" she asks.

Principal Woolworth approaches the bench where Paige is sitting.

"Maybe we should take this into my office?"

"Maybe you should first explain to me what the hell is going on here," I say, the anger and frustration evident in my voice, even as I try in vain to control it.

"Mr. Bell, if you'll please lower your voice and refrain from using foul language, we can continue this conversation calmly in the privacy of my office."

"Hold on there," I say. "You call me in here and ambush me. You have my daughter collect her things like she's being kicked out of school, and I'm supposed to just have a chat and walk out of here like this is totally normal?"

"Mr. Bell, if you insist on having this conversation here, in front of your child, we can certainly do that, but it is not my first choice."

We've drawn the attention of several parents in the hall waiting inside for the bell to ring to collect their children. Their conversations stop, and all I can hear are their shoes squeaking on the wet marble floors.

Christy Woods steps into the office. I hadn't seen her in the hall earlier. In fact, I've seen her less and less since the funeral. She doesn't ask what's going on or give me side-eye for raising my voice. She just sits next to Paige and puts her arm around her, taking control of the situation's emotions when I obviously can't.

"I'm waiting for Sophie anyway," Christy says. "I can stay with Paige until school lets out if you need to talk in the office and figure this out."

"That sounds like a very prudent thing to do, thank you, Mrs. Woods," the principal says.

Christy nods and a strand of wet hair falls across her cheek. She tucks it behind her ear, for a moment flashing the dark scars on her hand. She pulls the sleeve of her rain slicker down and covers her hand again.

I return to the office and Mrs. Woolworth closes the door, but we don't sit in the chairs.

"Mr. Bell, you can't ignore every letter we have sent you concerning your daughter's overdue tuition and expect her to continue to attend Columbia Ridge like the other students who have paid, do you?"

"What… what letters?"

"Please, let's not go down that path," she says. "I've dealt with deadbeats before and acting like you didn't receive notification isn't going to get you out of this."

I take a breath to control my anger. I try to ignore the deadbeat comment. I'm taken back to a very similar conversation I had several weeks ago with Ms. May, Paige's dance teacher.

"Do you have copies of the letters?" I ask.

She opens a folder and removes several letters with "Past Due" printed in red on the top of each. The letters were addressed to Tina and started last year, well before she died. Each was mailed to her P.O. Box in Woodlawn.

"How many tuition payments have we missed?"

"I'm not going to play this game with you," she says. "This is a private institution of higher learning with the utmost standards. A decision has already been made in this matter."

"Can you please reserve judgment for a moment and answer the question?"

Her scowl makes it evident that she's not familiar with being called out for her piousness. She swallows hard.

"Only because of your history with the school—having your two boys attend here—were you given this much grace, but you've taken advantage long enough. Mr. Bell, you haven't made any payments this year. None."

We had always paid the kids' tuition in full at the start of the year. Until this moment, I had assumed the same had occurred this year. I've never even seen a bill from the school since Tina set up the account and paid the bill.

"So, you're kicking my daughter out of school?"

"That's not the terminology I would use, but yes, we're expelling Paige from Columbia Ridge for non-payment."

"How much do you need to keep her until the end of the year? The school year is nearly over anyway," I ask, although I have no idea where I'd come up with the money.

"That's just not an option anymore," she says. "Maybe if you had responded to any of the letters or paid some of your tuition earlier, we'd be in a different place, but like I said, a decision has already been made."

"You know my wife died recently?"

"Yes, of course."

"You'll also notice these letters you sent were addressed to her alone. Not me, and not to my home address. I've never seen a past due letter or had any idea that Paige's tuition was not paid in full at the start of the school year like it had been for each of my children for a decade and a half. And now you tell me it's too late to rectify?"

"Mr. Bell, I've heard all the stories before. Parents making excuses for not paying. I'm sorry your wife passed on, but at this point, there's nothing I can do about Paige's expulsion. I'm sure you live in a neighborhood with a reputable public school for Paige. We wish her all the best."

And with that, it's over. We've gotten my daughter kicked out of school.

I exit the office. I can't help my lip from quivering. Paige is showing Christy her schoolwork from the box. Gone are Paige's tears, thanks to Christy.

Christy sees me and the water in my eyes. She can sense that something terrible has happened.

"I'm sorry, James," she says, reaching to hug me, but

then steps back. She looks over her shoulder to see who was watching us.

I pull Paige to me and wrap my arms around her.

"We're going to figure this out, kiddo," I say. "Everything is going to be OK."

"You mean I can stay at my school?"

"I'm sorry, no," I say. "But we're going to go home and make a plan."

At least home is something I can count on.

CHAPTER 19

Did you know there is a TV show that follows people who repossess vehicles? Banks or lenders give the repo men a list of cars to track down and legally repossess. They take cars, boats, and even planes, and then get paid a bounty. The show is exciting as they think up new ways to outsmart the losers who stopped making payments on their toys. Often the vehicle is some fancy, retrofitted ride that retails for hundreds of thousands of dollars. They have to follow the guy to the country club or wait for him to leave the car unattended somewhere before they snatch it up. It's fascinating stuff to watch from the comfort of your couch, far away from those types of people. You know, losers who don't pay their bills. If you haven't watched it, you should. It's probably on one of those cable channels you never tune to.

I didn't have to watch it on TV.

I wonder what the order to repossess our cars looked like? Because there didn't seem to be any sting operation in motion when they took them. They knocked on the front door and asked for the keys to the Mercedes and the Range Rover. They showed me the legal papers. I knew I hadn't made any payments, and apparently, it had been more than seven months since Tina had stopped paying for them.

I cried as Paige raced out to the car and pounded on the door as the repo man backed out of the garage. She just wanted her *Lady Ardella Dance* doll from the back seat. I didn't have the heart to tell her the car was never coming back. She was happy to keep her doll.

We're getting deeper and deeper now that she's gone—there's no income, and our safety net is nonexistent. Maybe I'm not doing the right things, but every time I try to figure out what Tina did, I see just how bad it is. I'm still numb. The days and weeks are all blending together. There is no money to be found, no answers to be had.

The cars are one thing. The Mercedes was mine, leased. The Range Rover was Tina's. It wasn't getting used anyway. I refused to let Mason drive it, despite his pleas.

But what hurt the most, by far, was the orange sticker on the front door—a foreclosure notice on our house.

I remember the day we moved in, back when the house seemed so big and empty. It smelled like fresh paint and carpet glue. The counters were polished to a blinding shine. The boys were excited to have their own rooms after sharing one in the small rancher from which we were moving.

Our saggy secondhand couch looked terribly out of place in this palace. We bought new furniture for the entire house on credit the next day. Tina's career was taking off, and she said we could afford it. She had big things planned. I believed her, and she came through. We made it a home for more than ten years until that orange sticker appeared on the door. I knew it was coming just a few days before, but it didn't make it feel any better.

I've got to give it to Tina. She's got one hell of a poker face. I had no idea. Good for her. She duped me again. She stopped the payments well over a year ago, right about the time she stopped paying for Paige's school. She lied to me the whole time. The deadlines to file for extensions or appeals had passed. It was over.

When I notified the post office that Tina had died, they redirected her mail to the house, giving me the first accurate look at how screwed we really were. We were so far behind on everything and there was no way I could catch up.

House. Cars. Columbia Ridge and dance. Jaden's on scholarship at the University of Oregon, but his credit card bill was going to Tina. She'd been paying that one up until the end. Nobody had come calling on that yet, but it's only a matter of time.

I'm putting all our current household necessities, like groceries, on a new credit card that I'll have to figure out how to pay off.

I canceled my gym membership for what good it did. I wasn't going any longer. The cable is off. No internet, except what we can pirate off Mr. Speight's Wi-Fi next door. His password is actually "GnomeSweetGnome."

With no money coming in, we're more behind every passing minute. And I'm exhausted.

My home is no longer my home. They gave us sixty days to move out, which was fifty-seven days ago. We're moving on to greener pastures in three days. OK, maybe not greener. The place we are moving into in three days is certainly not better by any account.

I pulled $2,500—nearly half of the money remaining in our savings account—and bought a rusty Ford F-150 pickup so we could at least get around town, and I could start my new job.

* * *

"You're going to have to move three of the tenants out by the end of the month," a man in baggy gray sweatpants with frayed cuffs says.

He pulls a pack of cigarettes out of his flannel jacket and pops one into his mouth. He doesn't light it. It just hangs there, dancing up and down on his lips as he talks.

"The pipes on the third floor have got to go first. You know, code violations, they say. People can't drink the water, says it tastes funny. Get those replaced and move everyone back in, assuming they want to come back. You hear?"

I survey the dark apartment we're currently standing in. My new apartment, or at least it will be in three days. The man with the dancing cigarette is Javier Rodriguez, the outgoing manager of the apartment complex, though the term 'complex' is misleading. It's an old warehouse in downtown Portland, converted into a cluster of low-income apartments with thin walls. These aren't the trendy apartments with tall ceilings and a classic industrial motif. The exterior walls are painted cinderblock, the pipes are exposed and wrapped in damp foam. The vibe is utilitarian, and you can hear the neighbor flush the toilet after he defecates, which you can also hear in stunning, gassy detail.

I used to work with Javier's cousin back in college before the kids came along. So, when I put out some feelers for a job, George Rodriguez called me. He was the only one to call me, and even he assumed I'd say no to him. The job was terrible, which was expected as I'm not a licensed contractor, and he still wanted to hire me.

George made me a deal. He owned the apartments and wanted to "class-up the place." He needed a project manager to supervise the work, and someone who could be a superintendent for the building. The project was extensive and would take eight to twelve months, maybe longer. For the duration, I could live rent-free in one of the apartments. The job meant unclogging toilets and snaking drains, cleaning the hallways, and making any needed repairs while the renovations happened. I'd manage the contractors, too. Simple enough.

This place is not exactly as George described, but I'd already agreed to it. I didn't have another option, and I couldn't find another place before we had to be out of the house.

"Where do the tenants go when we move them out?" I ask, opening a kitchen cabinet to reveal a mousetrap with a dead rat stuck inside.

"That's for you to figure out, big man. That's why George got you, right?"

His voice was tense. I was taking a job he thought was his.

I had already reviewed the project plans George had drawn up. The building was so substandard that it would require a complete gut and redesign to come up to code. Sprinkler systems, lighting, and electrical were just the beginning. There was certain to be structural damage, too. The difficulty level was multiplied many times over because tenants would be occupying portions of the building during renovations, which was not standard. George wanted the rent coming in, even as the walls were coming down. He assured me the plan was legal. I didn't ask many questions since I needed the job and the housing more than I needed it to be legal.

Javier gives me a half-hearted tour. Twenty-four residences on three floors. The renovation would cut the number of units in half. George would sell off the units as condos and make a bundle as long as we did everything on the up and up, which was no guarantee given the budget.

Javier shows me a "tricky" light switch in a first-floor apartment when I hear a rumbling of boots running down a wooden hallway above us. Dust and decay float down from the ceiling, from the pounding.

The boots stop abruptly. A loud bang follows, the distinct sound of wood splintering on a door frame.

Someone shouted, "Portland Police! We have a search warrant!" The noise of boots stomps above us again.

Javier shrugs his shoulder and begins a slow walk outside. He's not interested.

"Aren't you going to see what happened?" I ask.

"Nothing to find out. Cops finally raided the meth lab in 2D. And I, for one, don't want to be around when they drag that toxic stuff out."

"You knew about a meth lab? In the building?"

"Kinda hard to miss, bro," he says. "Hey, on the positive side, it's one less unit for you to clear out, big man. Good luck."

CHAPTER 20

"If you can't find a job, maybe you should start a professional packing business," Seth says, stacking a box in the back of the rented moving truck parked at my soon-to-be-former home. "This is some top-quality work here. Labels. Taped evenly. Uniform shape. The works. You sure you didn't have one of those cute PTA moms do this for you? Or maybe Christy Hayden—sorry, Christy Woods? I still can't believe you're friends with my ex-girlfriend after all this time."

"You dated her for a month, junior year."

"And what a glorious month it was."

"Well, if my packing impresses you, you should see how well I organize a pantry," I tell him. "You'd be so jealous. And, Seth, don't pander to me because you feel sorry for me."

"Hey, I was just wondering about those hot moms you hang out with now. I was sort of hoping to see a few here today."

"They're married and not keen on helping me out."

Christy had made herself scarce over the last few weeks since Paige was expelled. I didn't want to burden her with all my problems, so we hadn't been in touch. Our bi-weekly lunches had stopped abruptly, and I'm not afraid to admit that I've missed seeing her. I'm sure she is busy with end-of-year projects at Columbia Ridge.

Something must have changed with her schedule.

"Yeah, but married women need attention, too. You know what I mean?" Seth says.

"It's not like that."

"I can only imagine the tail you're spending your days with. Those yoga pants? Man…" Seth makes an hourglass shape with his hands to express his inner-caveman thoughts. "Like they're always going to the gym, but they don't need to. It's a wonderful thing."

"I was married, remember?"

"Well, you're not now."

"Careful," I retort.

"Yeah, I know, you're a Boy Scout. A guy can dream, though, right? I know you were 'just another mom' baking cookies and helping plan playdates, but it's a whole new world now. You're a single man. Granted, you have no job, no home, and are looking a little worse-for-the-wear lately, but still. You could be a hot commodity to some lonely lady in need."

"You should give inspirational speeches," I deadpan.

It's true the steady stream of well-wishers from the Stay-at-Home Tribe dried up fairly quickly. The women whom I occasionally spent my days with didn't stick around. Were they really my friends anyway? People moved on with their lives rather quickly.

I had a strong suspicion that some of those moms just wanted to come to the house to gather gossip about the widowed stay-at-home dad to share at their Bunko nights. I didn't want me or my family to be discussed, or worse, felt sorry for.

"Let's change the subject, please," I insist.

"James, my boy, you're a pathetic little man and have been since Mrs. Landkamer's second-grade class when you got beat up by a girl. If your best friend can't remind you of that, then who can? It's my job. So, you're good at packing and the ladies like you. Embrace it. We all have strengths. You should be glad you have at least one strength amongst your many faults."

"You're a jerk. You know that?"

"Obviously," he says. "But I'm in touch with my feminine side enough to love you still, stud."

I roll my eyes but appreciate Seth more than he knows. He's been here the past few days, sleeping on the couch. He volunteered to help Mason and me move our stuff out of the house. Jaden is still at U of O, and I told him to stick with the plan and take a few summer courses while training with the team.

Paige wouldn't be helping anyway, so I sent her to Shoreline with Mom. She was excited to spend some time with her grandmother. Mom had been insisting that Paige spend more time with her anyway, so it worked out. Paige was so close to the end of school when she was expelled that it didn't make sense to enroll her anywhere else. There's also no reason she needed to stay in Lake Oswego to watch all our possessions get pulled out of our house. Watching the cars leave was enough. Thanks to all this trauma, I'm fairly sure she will need therapy for years—and she's probably not the only one who will need therapy.

Seth wheels a dolly, loaded with boxes, up the truck ramp and deposits them in one of the few remaining open spaces.

"If my years in the Army taught me anything, and let me be clear, I didn't learn squat," he says. "But if I did, it's that you can always pack lighter. It's a good thing. Trust me."

"I'll try that with the kids. Something like, 'No, we're not moving into a rundown, tiny two-bedroom apartment on the third floor of a hellhole building with no elevator and a meth lab. And we don't own anything anymore, either. We're just packing lighter. It's a good thing.' Is that about the gist of it?"

"More or less," he says. "It sounded better when I said it."

Seth and I spent pretty much every waking moment together from the time we were old enough to play tag up until the day we graduated high school. His family lived four doors down on McArthur Street. When I ran my car into a ditch senior year, he was the first person I called. He pulled me out with his pickup and helped bang out the dent in the fender so my parents wouldn't find out. When we learned that his girlfriend, not Christy, was cheating on him with some guy in the school orchestra, I helped him steal the guy's cello, fill it with poop from the dog park, and then bake it in the hot sun so the smell really set in. Good times.

After high school, he enlisted in the Army and became an Army Ranger. He saw the world, at least the terrible parts of it. He did tours in Iraq and Afghanistan, so he wasn't coasting through his military career. He doesn't talk about it. He retired from active duty just a few years ago and moved back home to Shoreline and opened the Ranger, right across from my parents' inns on Laneda Avenue. Ironically, he sees my parents more than I do. I don't know if that falls in the pro or con category.

Mom and Dad both love him, and why wouldn't they? He's a man's man. Big, broad shoulders, dark hair, and a perpetual five o'clock shadow. He's in the Army Reserve now and could squish you like a grape if he chose to do so.

Seth called me after Tina died, and we talked. It was the first time we'd spoken at length in several months. He was working to build up business at the bar, and I was busy with the kids, and we just let time lapse too long. Yet, in my experience, time and distance don't impact guys much. A look or a nod of acknowledgment can take the place of a week's worth of discussion. So, you slept with your buddy's girl? She must have been the problem. You got drunk and punched your best friend over his insulting comments about your slow-pitch softball team? Well, he shouldn't have mouthed off. You didn't talk to your pal for years and developed a much different world view? That doesn't mean anything has changed between you two, right?

Guys don't need to talk it out. They just need to know who they can trust when the chips are down. These aren't the relationships I formed with the Stay-At-Home Tribe in the neighborhood, besides Christy.

Maybe that old saying is true that men and women can't be friends. If I could watch some kid one afternoon so a mom down the street could take her other child to the dentist, sure we're friends. But when her husband treats her like garbage, she can't come knocking on my door for comfort. People talk, and people would talk about that even if it were completely platonic. So, I need a guy like Seth.

After Tina died, Seth didn't ask if he should drive up. He just showed up, and I'm glad he did. My mom told Seth we were moving and when, and he just appeared unannounced. I teared up when I saw him at my door. He pretended like he didn't notice and handed me a growler of craft beer from the bar. We drank and talked about the Seattle Mariners latest losing streak.

I sit on the bumper of the truck and wipe the sweat from my brow. Seth sits next to me. It's almost noon and the house is nearly empty. I can see Mr. Speight watching from his driveway next door. I flip him the bird. I'm sure the old coot is just waiting until we drive away so he can cut off all the tree branches he claims are dripping sap on his magnolias. The Homeowner's Association president visited yesterday to find out when we were moving out. Jerk. I told him we weren't and slammed the door in his face.

"What did you tell the kids?" Seth asks, venturing into questions about the dark despair of my life.

"I couldn't very well tell them that their mom duped us all, spent all of our savings on God knows what, and left us with nothing but a massive hole of debt to dig out of."

"Yeah, I wouldn't have led with that, either," he says.

"I told them that we needed to cut way back on our expenses and that everything unnecessary had to go until I could find a new job. There's no hiding it, though. The boys know what happened, at least the broad strokes, and they might be old enough to understand it too, but I'm not talking to them about it. I told Paige we were going on an adventure, which is a total crock."

I have applied for seventeen jobs in the past month, which garnered me one interview with a landscape company looking for a project manager. The interview went off the rails when they asked what I'd been doing for the past two decades, which was pretty much the first thing they asked. I didn't get the job. I've also learned that you can't get unemployment if you don't have a job from which to be unemployed in the first place.

I got lucky with the apartment. It's a hellhole, but well… there is no but. It's a hellhole.

George Rodriguez said the job is only a few hours of work every week and that I'd be able to find full-time work somewhere else if I wanted. Considering the place's condition, I find that hard to believe, but it's all I've got at the moment.

The apartment is not in Mason's school district, but school is out in a few days. He'll need to do his senior year at a new school unless I can figure out a way the school will allow him to stay, which tears me up.

The same is true for Paige. Columbia Ridge isn't an option. I'll get her in somewhere, which no matter what, will be a far cry from Lake Oswego's finest private educational institution. Leaving her friends has been the most challenging part. The kids wrote her goodbye letters as she left and have already resumed life without her. One of her classmates had a pool party last weekend—a party we certainly would have been invited to had she not been kicked out. I saw the pictures on the kid's mom's Instagram and just lost it. I'm just thankful Paige didn't know about it.

Paige wants to know where she'll be going to school next year. I'm such an excellent parent; I told her it was a surprise.

I'm such a coward.

No more private anything for this family. Stock up on the Top Ramen because we're flat broke.

"What do you want to do with this stuff with a 'Tina' label on it?" Seth asks, pointing to a jumble of ten or twelve boxes yet to be packed into the truck. They were stuffed with Tina's belongings. I sorted and packed her clothes, shoes, books, file folders stuffed with papers, and other random things.

"I know I don't need any of it, and honestly, I don't want it either, but I can't just give it to Goodwill. I'll just stack it inside the bedroom at the apartment."

"In the room that you are going to share with Mason?"

"I couldn't have him share a room with Paige."

"That's not what I'm talking about," Seth says. "I'm just saying it's going to be tight in there. And, tell me I'm wrong, but it might be tough to move on, you know, emotionally, if all your dead wife's possessions are lining the walls of your new place."

"There is nothing new about that place," I say.

"You know what I mean."

"What am I supposed to do with it?" I ask.

"Dump it. Burn it. Toss it in the lake. What does it matter? You don't have any need for it, and it's only going to remind you of what happened."

He's not wrong.

"I think just living in that place will be reminder enough," I reply.

"So, we dump it? Remember, pack light."

But I just can't get rid of it. I gave everything a cursory glance when I packed it, but that's it. I need more time to go over it before tossing it in the trash.

"No, we stack it in the bedroom."

"Why?" he asks. "It's just more painful memories. You're just punishing yourself."

Again, he's not wrong, but what do you do when painful memories are the only ones you have?

CHAPTER 21

Online Coach, session 109
Archive for client Tina Bell

Coach: *You've been chatting with us for several months now. How have you liked the sessions?*

I've been going through a lot recently, and being able to talk, or at least type, about it has been very useful. I've followed your advice and am taking additional strides with the kids and my husband.

Coach: *That's wonderful. Please share more about that.*

I downloaded Snapchat. You know, that app where you send pictures and texts to people and then it disappears? I know it sounds silly and I'm certainly not the key demographic for the service, but Jaden and Mason use it constantly to keep in touch with each other and their friends. They don't send anything important, just blurry selfies with captions about their current activity. Jaden sends photos when he's working out at the gym at school. Mason sends them throughout the day. He's particularly fond of sending photos of coffee cups from this local coffee stand where James takes him on Friday mornings. It just helps me feel like I'm there, even when I'm on the other side of the country.

Coach: *Meeting your family where they like to dwell is key to a healthy relationship. How about your daughter Paige? How have you been communicating with her?*

She's too young for Snapchat, and James put parental controls on her phone so she doesn't venture into the dark parts of the internet. I text her. She's only eight, so she does voice-to-text to reply back. Often, she sends these long, rambling messages. Like a running commentary about what she's done during the day or the homework she hates. She likes to recap for me what happens on her favorite show—*Lady Ardella Dance*, too.

> ***Coach:*** *These digital communications are important, but what about in person?*

In person is much harder. I'm not at home as often as I'd like, and when I do come home, I want to maximize my time there, but James schedules these activities that feel more like I'm a guest intruding on some other family's vacation. We don't just grab a pizza and fall asleep on the couch watching a movie like normal people. James books these elaborate things, like last spring when he had the whole family take a professionally guided tour of bridges in Portland. We rode bikes all over the city with some poor tour guide from the historical society. Yes, the bridges were interesting, but learning about spans and traffic counts isn't my favorite way to spend my limited time with the family. It's like he saved up these things for us to do so we wouldn't be at home together.

> ***Coach:*** *Did you share your opinion with James?*

There's something you need to understand about James. When Jaden was born, we sort of flowed into this unspoken rhythm. He just took over the primary parent role. It was like there was something inside him that just knew exactly what to do. He was good at it, and I stood back and let him lead. I mean, it's not like I didn't try to help and do all the things that a mother was supposed to do, but he didn't need me and never allowed me to be a part of the parenting. He had his way, and it was settled.

I get it, I had a terrible childhood and no parent role model to emulate, but it's not like James' parents are perfect, either. They've got some major issues even to this day.

Home is James' turf, though. I could have pushed back more, but I felt like I was doing it wrong if my opinion differed from his. He was so confident in his way. Ironically, that's probably why I fell in love with him—his confidence. I didn't resent him for it, at least not at first. It was a relief. Eventually, I was ready to do more for our family, but I needed to keep working to pay for our lifestyle and he didn't want me to interfere with the world he had created.

Coach: *But did you express your displeasure directly with James? Have you told him how you feel?*

I tried, but it just never came out right. He made his opinion on my role abundantly clear.

Coach: *How so?*

Several years ago, a corporate headhunter contacted me about a position at a healthcare group in Portland. They were expanding and needed an executive to lead their community outreach programs, securing grants and donations from companies and wealthy individuals. I had met several of the board members through the years at industry conferences, and they thought I would be a great fit for the job. I agreed. It was a good job, a vice president role, and it was based in Portland. I would only have to travel in the state. No more nights away. I was very excited.

Coach: *But you turned it down. Why?*

Because of James. He didn't care about the benefits of the job—like me finally staying home. He only cared that I would be taking a pay cut. He listed off all the things we wouldn't be able to do if we couldn't afford it. Jaden's traveling baseball team was expensive. He was likely to be offered a college scholarship, but not if scouts didn't see him play at tournaments with good competition.

Paige was doing well at Columbia Ridge Academy, but if I took the new job, we'd have to move her to a public school. James hated that idea.

Mason wanted to take this trip to Australia with his senior class. Even with a year's notice, it was going to cost an arm and a leg. James wanted him to go on the trip. We hoped that Mason's grades would improve as a result.

Oh, and James also wanted to build some silly shop in the backyard so he could play with his old woodworking tools and build tables or something. He said he needed a creative outlet. He kept talking about wanting to do it, so I said yes because I thought it would make him happy. I justified the huge expense because it would include a small gym so Jaden could do his off-season exercise at home. James didn't need a shop, he just wanted it.

So I was stuck. Take the new job and rejoin the family, but

in doing so, I would be taking away so many of the things they each wanted to do. I just couldn't do that, so I turned it down.

My role in the family was to provide. If I didn't provide, what good was I to them?

CHAPTER 22

My alarm goes off at seven a.m. I roll over on the bare mattress and stare at the ceiling. I don't want to look around the empty master bedroom—my soon-to-be old bedroom. The one I shared with Tina for so many years. We shared it, even if she wasn't here most of the time. I wouldn't call it just my room, though; it was our room. The kids knew it was the parents' room, but it wasn't off-limits to them.

We never did the co-sleeping thing. The kids had their own rooms and beds, and for the most part, they stayed put. But some mornings I'd roll over and find one of them softly snoring next to me. To be honest, I liked the company because I was alone so much. If I discovered them in the middle of the night, I would give them a few minutes, make sure they were OK, then carry them back where they belonged. I did this to prevent a habit from forming, and it worked until recently.

Paige has been coming in here most nights since Tina died. She waits for me to close my door. Apparently, she thinks it takes me around five minutes to fall asleep, because that's when she sneaks into the room carrying Mr. Hugs. She slowly turns the doorknob, tiptoes over, and slips under the covers. I don't think she's coming in for her own comfort—she's doing it for me, even if she never says it. Kids are funny that way, at least the introspective ones. They see things that the rest of us adults just pass over. Too busy with day-to-day life, the stress and worry clogging up the processing power of our brains and hearts.

One morning I found her on the floor next to the bed, trying on Tina's jewelry and shoes that had been packed into a moving box. She knew that she shouldn't be messing with things that didn't belong to her. She looked guilty and certain she'd get in trouble. Maybe I surprised her when I sat next to her and explained what she was looking at. Mom wore hoop earrings only at social events, and always silver or white gold, never yellow gold. She had a ring with all the kids' birthstones it in, but she didn't like the fit on her finger, so she sometimes wore it on a chain around her neck instead. She had several bracelets but didn't wear them. They clanged on the desktop when she typed, and she didn't care for the sound. She had a few service pins from Goodwin. A one-year, five-year, and fifteenth-anniversary pin. The ten-year pin must have gotten lost.

Her wedding ring was there too—a simple band with a single, relatively small diamond. We couldn't afford much else at the time. Over the years, I told Tina that we needed to get the ring replaced or updated, but she insisted that the original was fine. The funeral home saved the ring for me in a little box before Tina was cremated. I put the ring back in the jewelry box, unsure of where else it should go.

I marked the box of keepsakes so I could find it easily if Paige asked for it. She needs to keep that connection to her mom. I wonder what memories Paige will have of her mother? When you stop making them, do the old ones just fade away? Maybe the memories will be held in those objects packed in the box.

When your parents live into older age like mine have, you make new memories every year, and the old memories fade. Those old memories become less important because they are mixed in with new ones. Updates. Will Paige be able to hold those memories of her mother as she gets older and time passes? And what is it exactly that she's going to remember? A few family events, maybe? Dinner at the table? Or will she remember watching her mom collapse into the water or getting wheeled into the emergency room? How about the absence of her at nearly every single meaningful event in her life? Will it be standing for endless pictures?

In any event, we won't be making any more memories in this house. Today is the end. Seth and I moved a significant portion of my belongings into a storage unit yesterday before he went back to Shoreline. He'd left the bar in the hands of his only other full-time employee—a woman who he wasn't comfortable being in charge for more than a few days. He needed to get back. So, Mason and I are on our own to move the remaining items. I won't be keeping much at the apartment, but nearly everything I still own—the things I need to live—is in the back of the rental truck parked in the driveway. When we leave here today, there's no turning back and nothing to come back to.

The kids and I made some great memories in this house. It's the only home that Paige has known. I vividly recall painting the bedroom that would become Paige's nursery. Tina's belly was beautiful and swollen at twenty-eight weeks. She shouldn't have been in the room when we painted, but the doctor said she couldn't travel anymore, and she was getting stir crazy just sitting around the house. It was only natural that she pitched in. She was happy then, just working away at a mindless project like painting. She was always happy when she was pregnant, but that changed after she gave birth. She would become withdrawn and isolate herself away from the rest of us or find a reasonable excuse to get out of the house or go back to work a little earlier than we had planned.

Today, looking back at it all, I wonder how many happy days she had. How many of them happened under this roof? I wonder if I missed them all.

* * *

I shuffle down the stairs, past empty room after empty

room, toward the kitchen, and a much-needed cup of coffee. I left the coffeemaker behind because I knew I would desperately need it this morning. Before I come around the corner, I smell it. The coffee is already made. I'm surprised Mason is awake, and even more surprised that he made me coffee since he doesn't drink it himself.

"I didn't know you knew how to work the coffee pot, Mason," I say as a joke from down the hall before stepping into the kitchen.

But it's not Mason in the kitchen. It's my dad.

He's leaning against the counter, holding a cup of coffee.

"We need to talk," he says.

* * *

"Hey," I manage to say. "What are you doing here?"

"Can't a father help his son move?" he deadpans.

"You're conveniently late for all that."

"Then my timing is impeccable, as usual."

I pour myself a cup of coffee and let the aroma fill my senses. It's thick and smells bitter. Dad always made coffee two or three times more potent than the average human could handle. Mom would fill her cup halfway with water before topping it off with coffee just so she didn't get knocked over by the taste and caffeine boost. I stayed away from coffee until college because I didn't know any better, and I thought that every cup was as strong as the stuff he made. It was a revelation when my fellow classmates introduced me to a good tasting cup.

"Strong as ever," I say, lifting myself up on the kitchen island to sit since all the chairs were gone.

"Is there any other way to make it?"

"As a matter of fact, there is, as I've told you many times."

"I like it this way."

I hadn't spoken to Dad since Tina's backyard funeral and his terrible reaction to Jaden's coming out. Dad and I didn't see eye-to-eye on everything, but this was one of those things that, even if I was struggling to figure it out, I expected him to get onboard and support his grandson. Especially the grandson he adored the most. It was no secret that Grandpa Mitch had a favorite. He didn't treat Mason or Paige poorly, but he went out of his way to be pals with Jaden.

Mom told me that Dad hadn't talked about Jaden with her, either. I'm not sure they had talked in depth much anyway, but the fact that she brought it up meant that something was amiss. He was stewing over it.

Reading Dad is fairly straightforward. He's not a simple man by any means; in fact, his intellect was exceptional. It made for many colorful debates on the front porch of the Westcott with guests who happened to disagree with him on any particular subject. He wasn't shy, that's for sure.

Darla and I had Dad figured out when we were kids. He operated in two modes. He was either completely on or completely off—no in-between. This meant he was open to discussing something or he would shut you down like nobody's business. If you wanted to ask for ten dollars to go watch a movie, you needed to know if he was on or off. This was pretty easy to figure out. If he was on, his face was relaxed and his movements had no particular purpose. Amiable. This was an excellent time to ask for your movie money.

If he was off, he wouldn't make eye contact and typically made himself scarce. He'd have an activity to occupy his time. He liked to sneak away to the beach with his rod and cast into the ocean for surfperch. It was a relaxing activity for most, but not for Dad. If you caught a glimpse of him, you'd notice his face was tight, teeth gritted like he was holding all his emotion in his cheeks. Not a good time to ask for movie money. Best to hit up Mom.

So today, Dad is definitely off, but he was still standing in my kitchen.

"Why are you really here, Dad?" I ask. "Because you

know plenty well that everything is already moved."

His face was taut. "Your mother asked me to come."

"That's not a reason. Why?"

"To help. I told you." He takes another sip.

"This is ridiculous. Let's just get it out there, OK? You've been distant ever since Jaden announced he was gay."

His face perks up. Bingo.

"That was an announcement? Fine time to tell the world that you like boys."

"Who cares when he did it?"

"It's not natural, James!" he shouts.

"That's what this is about?"

"How could you let this happen? Our Jaden, a gay."

"Let it happen?" I was exasperated. "What are you talking about? So what? It doesn't change him as a person. Our Jaden, remember. It's his cross to bear, and it hasn't been easy for him, either. Hell, he hid it from us. What does that make us? He's gay, but I didn't make him that way. Let it happen? That's absurd."

"Maybe if you didn't live in this palace with your fancy cars and expensive clothes that you'd have taught him to be a real man. Or if your wife didn't wear the pants in your marriage, maybe he would have turned out normal."

"Screw you, Dad. You have no right to talk to me like that, and even less right to talk about my son that way. That's our blood, our family."

"And you think that I can tell my…"

I knew what he was going to say.

"You're worried about what your buddies are going to say. Jesus. Who are you concerned about offending? That racist jackass Carl? Or how about alcoholic Tim? Fine company you keep. To be ashamed of your own grandson. You're a real piece of work."

"God didn't intend it."

"This has nothing to do with God. It has to do with a narrow-minded old man who should have stayed home and left well enough alone. At least in your silence, I could have assumed that you were trying to work it out in your head. But I see now that you've got it all figured out. Jaden's gay because we have money. Nice."

"*Had*," he pauses. "Had money."

"Thanks, Dad. That's helpful. By that logic, now that I'm poor, Jaden should start hitting on girls any minute now. Should we call him and see who he's dating?"

"Don't be so dramatic. He needed a male role model. A real man he could look up to. And it wasn't you, prancing around this house and letting your wife boss you around."

I've never hit my father before. I tackled him once when I was fourteen years old. We were playing football on the beach, tossing around the ball. I was big enough to take him down. I matched his height, but not his muscle. It was a playful tackle, and I landed on top of him. He pushed me off with one arm. With his teeth gritted, he gave me a look that said *that won't happen again.* He didn't leave or show anger, but I wish he had. He returned the favor several more times that day on the beach until I couldn't take any more tackles. My ribs hurt for a month. He wasn't about to be bested by his son.

When I left for college, we went toe-to-toe, shouting. But those were just words. We yelled—spittle flying in each other's faces. Mom stepped in. A cooler head. Would I have hit my father back then? No. It would have proven him right. Made him superior.

But today…?

I slide off the island, my fists balled up. Dad sets down his coffee cup. He knows what's coming. He asked for it. Maybe he wanted it. If ever he deserved to get cracked across the jaw, it was now. You don't walk into another man's home and challenge his manhood after belittling his child.

I take a step toward him but see movement out of the corner of my eye. Mason. I realize my teeth are gritted, and I must look just like Dad. I take a shallow breath and stop.

I'm not like him. There's a reason I am who I am, and it's not because Dad taught it to me.

"So, I'm not a real man?" I say, stretching out my hands to avoid making a fist.

"A real man would not have let this happen to our family."

"I let my son turn gay?" I can't believe the words I'm saying.

"Yes."

"Tell me, in all the days you coached Jaden, helped him with his swing or played catch during the summers. What did you do to what… stop him? You know, from 'turning' gay. What did you do, Dad?"

"I did those things," he says. "We played sports. I showed him what men do. You showed him that he can be soft."

"He's a 210-pound block of muscle. A third baseman on a Pac-12 baseball team, who happens to be one of the kindest people I've ever had the pleasure of encountering in my life. His sexual preference doesn't wholly define him. Who he loves doesn't matter to me, as long as he's happy."

"Love? What the hell do you know about love? You're alone. You've been alone your entire adult life. You chose it. Made it happen. That wife of yours? What a joke. You never listened."

I see red. My hands ball up to fists again, but I hold them at my sides. It would be so easy to pop him, and satisfying, too. All the pain and confusion of the last few months, I finally have someone to pinpoint that anger on. Someone who came forward to be my punching bag. He can belittle me because I don't need a defender, but my kids do.

"Dad, love means understanding, but I'm certain you don't understand," I walk to the side door and open it. The cold morning breeze hits my hot face. I turn to him. "Get out of my house."

"Your house? According to the sticker on the door, the bank owns this house. Another memorable achievement, son; you're the first in the family to get foreclosed on."

"Out." My voice is calm, but my heart is pounding out of my chest.

"Your mother asked me to come," he says, not moving from the kitchen.

"I wish she wouldn't have. Get out."

"Suit yourself."

He pours his remaining coffee into the sink, sets the cup down on the counter, and walks out without another word.

I gently latch the door closed behind him. My hand remains on the knob like I'm frozen in disbelief of what just happened.

Mason steps into the kitchen, his eyes wet.

"Why did he have to say those things, Dad?" Mason asks, his face contorted with emotion.

I don't answer right away. He'll remember what I tell him, and I want it to stick.

"Some people have a tough time dealing with things they don't understand. They lash out when their worldview is challenged. Please don't be like that, Mason."

"I won't. That's not how you raised me."

He walks to me and slips his arms around my waist. I pull him close, and he rests his head on my chest. We stand there together, in our foreclosed house, for a long time.

This isn't how it's supposed to be. I wish I could change it.

CHAPTER 23

My cell phone rings shortly after Dad leaves, which should be no surprise. He must have called her immediately after leaving.

"He's your father, James," she says in a tone that only comes from one parent trying not to bash their former partner when in all actuality, they'd rather let them have it. "He's just trying to come to grips with it all."

"There's nothing to come to grips about. It's not about him. I don't have to, shouldn't have to, convince my father to be a good man to his grandson. Jaden doesn't fit into his narrow world view. And get this… he blames me for it!"

"I heard. I wish you two could just see eye-to-eye."

"That would require him to open his eyes. Fat chance. He's straight-up wrong, and he's got to figure that out on his own. I think I need a nice long break from Dad."

"So, you won't reconsider the offer, then?" she asks.

My mind is still reeling from the earlier argument, but I'm sure I have no idea what my mother is talking about.

"Reconsider what?"

"He didn't tell you, then? That's why I sent him there in the first place."

"Mom, what offer? What are you talking about?"

"Oh, dear. That's not how I'd hoped it would go. Not one bit."

My mother has this annoying tendency to assume that you know what she's talking about when you have no context whatsoever. Like you're joining the conversation halfway through. Sometimes it's warranted, but other times, she just doesn't give you any information.

"You gotta fill me in here, Mom," I say the words I've said to her roughly four million times in my life.

"The Carriage House," she says with a sigh.

The Carriage House is not a house at all. It's not for carriages, either. It's a large garage turned storage building that sits in the rear of the Westcott property. The previous owners of the B&B gutted the storage building and added three rooms and a cramped workout facility for guests.

"What about it?"

"Your father can't rent out those rooms," she began. "They are detached from the main house and not that attractive. There is no sense of history to them like the rest of the house, either. One guest told Rylie Harrison that they felt like they were staying in a Motel 5. Not even a Motel 6, but a 5, James… a 5."

If you're keeping track at home, I don't know Rylie Harrison or why her opinion counts, but that doesn't matter to Mom.

"I'm sorry to hear that." Though it was still unclear where this was headed.

"You can stay at the Carriage House. That's why I sent your father to see you today."

"It's his inn, but your idea?" I ask.

"You know I'd love to have you at the Evergreen with me. And I've loved having Paige these last few days, but dear, there's no room, and the Carriage House is just sitting there, empty."

You'd think after what just happened with Dad, she'd have the sense to know a bad idea when it slithered in the door, but apparently not.

"We will not be staying at Dad's place. No way. I have a place, Mom, and a job. It's not much, but it'll be fine for a while."

"Seth told me about your job and that warehouse you're

calling an apartment. That's no place for my grandkids. You know that," she says, pleading. "Please, James, you don't have to do this. Take the offer."

I'm going to have to have a little heart-to-heart with dear old Seth about ratting me out to my mother.

"When the remodel is finished, it'll be a nice condo we can live in, and I can easily find work in Portland," I say.

There's no way I'm going to the Carriage House in Shoreline.

"There is work on the coast for you right now," she says. "I talked to David and Mary Ann Sever and Dale Lister. They have clients who need construction work done and would just love to have a professional like you manage it. You could be a construction superintendent or something."

Again, I have no idea who these people are. I haven't lived in Shoreline for two decades.

"Mom, thank you, but it's too late," I say. "The truck is packed, and we're moving into the apartment this afternoon. There is nothing you can say that would change my mind."

* * *

Later that afternoon, I park the moving truck in the small parking lot adjacent to the warehouse apartment. On my previous visit, the parking lot had been full, but that was in the evening. Today most of the residents would not be home from work yet, which I see as a very positive sign. These people are out and about, earning a living.

I'm going to be as positive as I can about the situation. I know the kids can read my body language, and if I'm down about the whole thing, there's no way they are going to accept it.

The apartment will be an adventure and a story we'll certainly recite for years. We'll tell everyone how we converted this dump into a fancy collection of luxury condos. Maybe this will be my niche. Portland is filled with buildings that could be converted into new downtown housing. I could consult on renovations or be the project manager. I could even roll up my sleeves and do some of the work myself.

I'm excited about the prospect of a new start. I get to do this thing all on my own and show the kids that nothing can get us down. I'm scared, yes, but prepared for the challenge ahead, too.

I pause for a minute and take a photo of the building. I note the cracked windows, graffiti, and the water dripping off the side of the building. This will be the ugly "before" picture that will make the "after" picture look astounding.

I follow Mason from the moving truck's ramp to the street-side apartment entrance. I'm lugging a box and he stops abruptly.

"Dad, it's blocked off, and the sign says biohazard," Mason says. "What does that mean? Like the zombie apocalypse?"

"Wouldn't that be lucky for you? Zombies in real life and not in a video game."

Mason reads the sign. I'm still holding the box, which is way heavier than it should be.

"We can't get in, Dad."

I read the sign. The city shuttered the building.

I try the handle. Locked. I try the keys from the ring I got from the outgoing manager, Javier. None of them fit. I loop around the building. It's locked up tight. Several of the doors are nailed shut with plywood—with no signs of life inside.

I call the warehouse owner, George.

"Nothing I can do, my friend," he says. "The city let us slide for quite a while, but with that meth lab business, there's nowhere to hide. They say the building isn't safe to occupy, and they booted everyone out. I'm sure I can get back in the game. Just give me a few weeks to get it all figured out. No promises on the timing, though. Might be awhile. But the job is still yours. I still need you."

I look back at the truck containing our most important possessions. The seeds that will start our new life. I look at Mason, his teenage angst turned to visible anxiety. Lastly, I look at the biohazard sign and see how much I was willing to compromise to be on my own.

"George, everything I own is packed into the moving truck or a storage unit, and I need a place to live. I can't wait around. I don't even have a place to sleep tonight. I have kids."

"I'm sorry, James, but there's nothing I can do. Is there somewhere else you can go? Family, maybe?"

Dammit.

CHAPTER 24

Online Coach, session 115
Archive for client Tina Bell

***Coach:** You have mentioned your mother a few times in our previous chats. How often do you see her?*

That's an easy question to answer. She's dead. The last time I saw my mother was when Jaden was a newborn. So, more than twenty years ago. I was still in Nevada, finishing up my degree. James was sleeping on the couch of my apartment at the time, taking care of Jaden pretty much around the clock. We weren't exactly romantic at that point. I didn't know what we were, but we were definitely not a couple. He was in charge of parenting, even back then.

Anyway, my mom showed up one night. I had not spoken to her once since I went into foster care. She never even called when I graduated high school—something she never did. She had no idea where I was for years, and then all the sudden she shows up when she becomes a grandmother.

Jaden couldn't sleep more than brief periods, but he'd always sleep longer if he was in his stroller. James would take him over to a park and walk for hours to make sure Jaden would stay asleep. Their walks would also give me time to study or sleep, whichever was more important at the time.

Mom knocked on the door when they were gone. I didn't recognize her at first. I guess in my memory I had pictured her healthy and happy, but she was anything but that. Her face was pale, and her skin seemed almost translucent under the dim light of the hallway. Her eyes were dark and sunken slightly into their sockets. She was coming down off some sort of high. Any beauty that had once attracted a string of men to her had long since faded.

She wanted to see her grandbaby, as she called him. She didn't even know his name. She forced this big smile that I'd seen before. It was all an act. There was no way I wanted this woman to meet my child, let alone have a relationship with him. She wouldn't be able to hurt anyone else if I could help it. When I told her no, her act dropped and she blew up at me. Screaming about how I never appreciated all she had done for me. How I owed her for my looks and smarts. That if not for her, I would be nothing.

> ***Coach:*** *I would attribute her actions to envy or resentment from the disparity between your lives. She had failed where you had succeeded.*

That makes sense. Eventually, she got to the reason for coming to see me. She wanted money. I assume for drugs, but I really don't know because I didn't ask. Somehow, she thought all my student loan money was cash or something that I could just give her. I explained to her that's not how it works, and that I had nothing except debt from student loans and, of course, medical bills from giving birth months ago. She called me a liar and a tease. She even brought up that creep Trent, who groped me back in high school. She said I ruined what the two of them had.

I just lost it and when she refused to leave, I dragged her out of the apartment. I wanted nothing to do with her ever again. I slammed the door and collapsed into a heap on the floor in tears. She died years ago. Overdose.

> ***Coach:*** *I'm sorry for your loss, Tina. Previously, we've discussed learning to accept your situation and finding someone to trust when you are in doubt. I know this was years ago, but did you confide in James after that night?*

When he and Jaden came back to the apartment, I wanted to hide it and pretend like it never happened. But as soon as I saw James, I couldn't hold it in. He sat and listened to me. I unloaded everything. All the bad stuff, all my childhood. All the things that I had never told a soul. I just felt like I needed him to know who I really was. He listened and understood. I wondered how a guy like James could even exist. He was a fantastic dad and was playing the part of a good husband, even when I was making him sleep on the couch.

Coach: *What did he say that stood out so much?*

He told me that I had value—value to him and value to our child. I didn't want our conversation to stop. I wanted him to be there for me and Jaden for good. I could not let him slip away. Our relationship changed after that night. We became a couple. He took me to Shoreline, Oregon, to meet his parents a few weeks later.

Over the years, I've gotten to know his family pretty well. His mom, Ramona, is a little nutty and his dad, Mitch, is a total grump if you don't know him, but they are good people.

I remember the first time I met them. I was a complete stranger, and they hugged me like I had come home from a long trip away. They asked me detailed questions about myself and seemed genuinely interested in who I was. Of course, they adored their grandson, too. Being with them felt like the home I never had. It was the first time I felt like I had any real family. These people, who I didn't know, were now my family. I wanted to stay. We've had our differences over the years, and sometimes I still feel like an outsider, but they are definitely my family.

James was different in Shoreline, too. He told me how he always wanted to leave the little town because he and Mitch didn't get along when he was younger. But the issues with his dad were between them, not Shoreline. James loves Shoreline, even to this day. Every spring break, summer, Thanksgiving, and Christmas, we end up in Shoreline one way or another. I don't always get to go because of my schedule, but James and the kids love it.

It's funny, I actually made myself a promise, way back when I first visited Shoreline. I knew the place was special, not because of the location itself, but because of the people. I promised myself that whatever James and I became, that we had to keep Shoreline close. I didn't have any idea how I'd do it way back then, but we've made Shoreline like a second home and it's been good for us.

CHAPTER 25

Shoreline, Oregon

I park the truck by the Carriage House in the alley behind the Westcott Inn. Seth, our welcoming party, is leaning against the fence. The courtyard of the Westcott is private, separated from the neighboring properties with tall, dark green arborvitae. Flowers flank a loose pebble and sand path that crisscrosses the mossy lawn. There's a wishing well off to one side and several private, but unused, seating areas adjacent to the main house.

I pull the ramp down from the truck bed and open the cargo door.

"You know, I agreed to load this thing," he says. "I never said I would unload it."

"All part of my master plan," I tell him.

Mason, who was none too happy with our change of plans, exits the truck and heads right into the Westcott through the wooden steps and large covered back porch that overlooks the courtyard. My father opens the door for him and intentionally avoids looking my direction.

"Your dad gave me the keys to the Carriage House rooms," Seth says. "He seemed unseasonably chilly about the whole thing, even for him."

"I bet."

I fill him in on my version of what Dad said in the kitchen this morning, which was news to him. Neither of my parents had given Seth the details.

"I'm sorry, James," he says. "That whole deal sounds out of character for Mitch. Maybe not for his generation, but Grandpa Mitch? Definitely not expected, and not with Jaden. But he's putting you up here at the Carriage House, so it's not all that bad."

"I haven't heard what the catch is yet. No doubt he's going to want something from me," I say, opening up the back of the truck. "We won't be here long enough to have it matter. As soon as I can find a new place and a job, we're out of here. The warehouse renovation job is still a go, just delayed a bit."

"Most people want to stay at the beach, not turn tail and run as soon as they get here. This was home for a long time," he says.

"It's not home anymore. And those vacationers only stay for a while. Then they go back to reality, too."

"This is my reality, buddy. I'm here for good, remember?"

He motions toward the Ranger, which sits across the street on Laneda Avenue. Seth has poured his heart and soul into the place, and it shows.

"I don't mean anything by it," I say. "It's just that I can't be here. We have a life in Portland to get back to."

"And from everything I saw, there is nothing in Portland that will be the same if the Bell family goes back. Your family is all here."

"When I go back, not if. It's not a question."

I don't need him piling on, too.

"Well, I'm glad to see you and the kids, even if you're not here to stay."

Seth and I unload what boxes we can into the converted building's storage area and separate the rest of the boxes for Paige, Mason, and me into different rooms. The building has three separate small suites with a queen bed, a table with two chairs, a couch, and a full bath. They are simple, clean rooms, but more along the lines of a roadside motel than a quaint bed-and-breakfast. I can see why Dad can't rent them out, they are bland and cheap. Not exactly a Motel 5, but not like the rest of the inn, either.

Seth invites me over to the Ranger for a beer after we empty the truck, but I decline. A beer sounds good, but Paige never came out of the Evergreen next door while we unloaded, and I need to go next door to see her and let her know we'll have to stay here for a while before we get back home.

From the Carriage House, I walk on the east side of the Westcott, through the Douglas fir and red alder trees that line the property closer to the street. I take the stone walkway onto Laneda Avenue, which is bustling with tourists ducking in and out of shops to avoid the wind whipping up from the Pacific Ocean. It's Friday, so weekend visitors fill the sidewalks holding ice cream cones and various purchases from cedar-shingled boutique shops.

The commercial portion of Shoreline covers six blocks centered on Laneda Avenue. Storefronts, restaurants, rental properties, a few motels, my parents' B&Bs, and the Ranger line each side. Only a few lots sit undeveloped. The largest one is across from the Evergreen, which is used as a farmer's market on weekends during the busy summer season.

I decide to clear my head and walk toward the water before going to the Evergreen to see Paige. A dozen vendors have set up booths and tables under pop-up tents at the farmer's market, preparing for the Saturday morning rush to come.

Shoreline is one of the few small towns on the Oregon coast that has successfully avoided the large commercial and residential developments that have taken over cities like Seaside, Cannon Beach, and to a lesser extent, Newport. No malls, no towering condos, but still relatively affordable for a middle-class family to spend a weekend or longer. It rings with small-town charm for visitors from June through September. Of course, it's still a beautiful place during the rest of the year too—if you don't mind the gray and drizzle of rain.

Besides the small shopping district, there's a bowling alley and a few restaurants just off the highway that pull in people who may have never taken the exit for Shoreline.

Commercial development is one of the things that my parents argue over to this day. My environmentalist mother is anti-development, but more than that, she is a proponent of returning some developed areas—where people already live—to their natural states. You might imagine this doesn't earn her many fans in the local community who see her as a hypocrite. She owns such a large piece of commercial real estate in the heart of Shoreline, even if it is the most environmentally friendly B&B on the Oregon Coast.

My father, on the other hand, was all for the development of new properties or growth. He even has his own side ventures. More people mean more guests filling his rooms. He doesn't mind the competition from additional hotels; he just worries about parking.

I can't help but admire what the town has become. Local government and businesses had worked together. They preserved the town's charm while allowing for more modern updates that welcomed more guests during the busy season and kept locals employed. The light posts were adorned with colorful banners about the upcoming Shoreline Kite Festival. Flower baskets overflowed with petunias onto flat, straight sidewalks packed with people, dogs on leashes, and kids riding scooters.

Laneda Avenue dead-ends at a roundabout and wooden boardwalk at the beach. A dozen steps lead down to paths through the tall grasses and the long sandy beach that makes up the Shoreline cove. Tall, rocky cliffs sit to the north, a lookout point from a state park popular for hiking. To the south, if you take the boardwalk, you can visit the shallow-port marina where visitors can buy crab or salmon fresh off the boat.

Tourists take selfies on the boardwalk. A couple on the beach try to get a hapless kite to take flight. Kids on rented bikes zoom off the wooden walkway and zip down Laneda

Avenue, ignoring everyone around them. I watch with a local filter, having seen it a thousand times before, its charm all but lost on me.

I turn right toward the cliffs, and before I know it, I find myself five blocks north and several blocks inland on streets filled with homes of locals, not vacation rentals. I'm standing in front of a small cottage house with peeling paint and a saggy roof—our old house on McArthur Street. The drapes are drawn behind cracked windows, but I know no one is inside. The house has been vacant for years. Under the carport sits an old Dodge pickup with four flat tires. Overgrown shrubs hug the corners of the house. It's a far cry from its former glory.

Decades ago, Darla and I grew up in this dilapidated mess, which was much more welcoming and well-appointed at the time. Surprisingly, the style is still in vogue, with wooden shutters and craftsman details under a long, angled roof. But moss covers the lip of the roof, and if there is any character hidden under this mess, it would take an archeologist to uncover it.

We all lived in this house until Mom moved out right before the divorce. I was away at school but would still return home for breaks and summer. After Mom left, Dad stayed at the Westcott most nights because he had to work at the inn without Mom's help. Darla had the run of the house until she left for school at Cal Tech. She always found somewhere other than Shoreline to stay during breaks.

While Dad still owns the house, he has let it rot. I sometimes wonder if he intentionally let the house fall apart to spite my mother, who absolutely adored it.

I walk to the small backyard, which is just a tangle of weeds. The metal clothesline Mom used in the warmer months has long since been abandoned and is leaning against the shop next to it. Seth and I used to hang blankets on the lines and make forts or see how many times in a row we could toss a ball up and over the line before dropping it.

I pause and gaze at the shop, with its metal sides and

roll-up doors on both the yard and alley sides. When I lived in this house, and when I wasn't at the Westcott, I was in that shop playing with my father's forgotten woodworking tools. The shop was lined with long benches covered in every tool imaginable for a craftsman to use—band saw, planer, joiner, drill press. And that's just on one side. I can smell the fresh-cut lumber just looking at the building.

But Dad never used any of it. He got much of the equipment from a guy who owed him money for some old debt. The guy couldn't pay, so he offered up his woodworking tools as repayment. Dad accepted, though he had no idea how to use them or any interest in learning. I, on the other hand, couldn't get enough.

I made picnic tables out of old fence boards and sold them at the farmer's market while I was in high school. I made enough money to buy my first car, then I started to craft chairs and small tables from reclaimed barn wood. When I had a little capital from those sales, I purchased new lumber from the hardware store and made picture frames for my mom's artwork. The frames sold like crazy, even if Mom's art didn't.

When Tina and I purchased our house in Lake Oswego, I dreamed of building a shop like this one. It's frustrating now, knowing that perfect little shop is gone, taken in the foreclosure of our home. I never used it like I should have. I was always waiting for the day when things slowed down a bit and I could focus on the hobby.

Seeing the old shop again makes me want to dig my tools out of storage and see if I still have what it takes to craft furniture or frames anymore. I push the idea aside. I need an actual paying job, not a hobby.

I step onto the small back porch. One of the boards gives way, and I catch myself on the railing, but my foot plunges through the deck. I carefully extract my foot and move carefully as I approach a window to peer into the kitchen.

There's rustling behind me.

"Hey, we don't want any trouble. Why don't you get the hell out of here?" a woman's voice says. "This neighborhood isn't for tourists, and this ain't your Air BnB."

The woman stands at the porch steps holding a baseball bat. She's in her mid-eighties, and her blue bathrobe flaps open in the breeze, revealing, well… too much. She's wearing a bra and underwear, and that's it.

"Mrs. Eifert?" I ask, focusing solely on her face and nothing below.

"Yeah, and who the hell are you?"

"James Bell. Ramona and Mitch's son? You remember me, right? You would make me no-bake cookies for my birthday every year."

"I make a lot of things. Why are you breaking into this house?"

"Just reliving a bit of the past, that's all."

I step around the new hole in the deck and closer to the railing, out of the shadows so she can see me better. Unfortunately, that means I can see her better, too.

Eyes up, James.

"Jimmy?"

"I go by James now, but yes. Jimmy Bell."

"By God. That *is* you."

She recognizes the openness of her robe and pulls the belt tight. I give a sigh of relief for that belt.

I would not have expected Cecily Eifert to be still living in the old neighborhood—or living anywhere for that matter. She was old when I was a kid. Her face is thinner, along with her curly white hair. She wears oversized glasses with chains linking them behind her neck.

Cecily and Perry Eifert were not only a fixture on McArthur, but in the town as well. She was a secretary at the elementary school, and Perry worked for the county water department. Their kids were a generation older than Darla and me, but we used to play day and night with their grandkids when they would visit during the summer.

"Let me take a look at you," she says and holds out her hand. Her eyes are dull with cataracts and age. "You look just like your father."

I'm not sure if that's a compliment or just a statement of fact or if her vision is even good enough to make that declaration. She's right, by any measure. I don't know if she even remembers my father or not.

"How are you, Mrs. Eifert? It's been, what, twenty-five years since I last saw you?"

"Your mother still comes over and visits me. More in the offseason when it's slow at the Evergreen, but we have coffee and catch up. Your father, too."

"That's great."

She launches into the Eifert family update. Perry passed on more than a decade ago. She rattles off a dozen names of her children and grandchildren. She lists who's gotten married or died, and how she's a great grandmother now. I catch a few grandkids' names, like Claire, Ian, and Aaron—the kids I knew during summers spent together.

"Since you're here, there's something you can help me with."

I follow Mrs. Eifert past the shop, through the back gate to the alley, and into her garage's side door.

"I've been collecting cans for the school fundraiser," she says, hitting the button for the garage door to open. The light reveals forty or fifty large black bags twist-tied at the top, full of crushed aluminum cans. "The can crusher on the wall here finally gave up the ghost after all these years, so I haven't been able to smash down these cans here."

She points to six garbage bins of uncrushed cans. I inspect the crusher and its black rubber handle. The metal contraption is screwed into a post. When you pulled it down, it would crush the can, then drop it into the receptacle below. The pin on the hinge had sheered in half, making it unusable.

"The volunteers are coming to pick these up, and I need to get these cans crushed and moved into the alley for pickup," she says. "Let me know when you're done. All the bags have to go out back because I won't be here to let them into the garage when they come."

With that, having unloaded my assignment, she exits the garage, leaving me no room to argue and six garbage bins full of sticky beer and soda cans to crush with my foot and stuff into trash bags. I consider chasing after her and telling her that I didn't come by for volunteer work and that I have things to do, but I catch myself. Why did I come down this way? Maybe because walking alone in my old stomping grounds feels better than stumbling through my present situation.

I set to work smashing the cans with gusto and scooping them into the bags. After half of the first bin, I slow a bit as my body weight alone can crush the cans with little effort.

It takes me more than an hour to crush the cans and bag them, during which time I try to figure out how I'm going to get my family back to Portland. I don't have the answer, but I have to admit it that it feels good just to smash something for a while.

Some of the bags look like they've been in the garage for years with dust and spider webs, but as per Mrs. Eifert's instructions, I move all the old, newly crushed bags to the small cement landing in the alley outside the garage door.

I use the hose on the side of the house to wash my hands before knocking on the backdoor to report my progress and then make my way back. No answer. Same thing at the front. I see Mrs. Eifert, sound asleep in her recliner with the TV on through the front window.

I try the knob. It's unlocked, so I reach inside and lock the door. I'm not sure why, it just seemed like the right thing to do. Mrs. Eifert doesn't stir. I close the door and make my way back to Laneda Avenue, limping slightly on a tender right quad muscle and aching foot thanks to my unexpected can-crushing chore.

CHAPTER 26

Laneda Avenue has quieted significantly from earlier, save for the patio in front of the Ranger where you can hear boisterous voices attempt to talk over the country music blasting from speakers. Patrons sip their drinks in cedar chairs surrounding gas fire pits illuminated by bistro lights and the last wisps of sunset. The vibe is upbeat and friendly. A cue ball cracks inside, breaking the racked set on the pool table. Seth is busy behind the bar, scraping foam off a beer pint, his attention on the packed house.

I contemplate going in for that beer he offered earlier. Maybe Paige could wait a little longer? Yet, my eye is drawn across the street toward the Evergreen. The inn's front porch is packed with people, but they don't look nearly as friendly as the bar crowd. I cross the street and climb the steps, weaving my way through a crowd of unhappy guests leaning or sitting on suitcases.

Inside, my mom stands behind the tall reception desk in the foyer, a phone to her ear. She waves me over and indicates that she's on hold.

"Elaina said she cleaned all the rooms, why would I check her work?" she says to me. "She's been cleaning for us for years now. I wouldn't have any reason to doubt that. And now I'm stuck with all these people, and they won't answer the phone at the cleaning service, and I can't get all these people in. There's no place to put them. And Susan is up in Seaside with her mother. I can't very well call her back, now can I?"

"I don't know, Mom," I said, trying to assess her frazzled state. It's always a puzzle with Mom. "Your maid didn't clean the rooms?"

"That's what I just said. You know Boyd and Demi would have never done this to me, especially not at the start of the busy season."

"They are your maids?"

"No," she exclaims. "They were before Elaina. I could trust them."

"And Susan?"

Susan Clark was one of my mom's business partners.

She turns her attention to the phone.

"Yes. No. Tomorrow?! That won't work, I have guests waiting now. They are literally tripping over each other here. Yes. No. Fine." She slams the phone down and looks at me. "Paige is next door with Mason and your father, so your evening is free… which is good because I need you."

* * *

I'm in the kitchen of the Evergreen two hours later, arching my back and twisting my hips, trying to ease the ache in my back and legs caused by the last few hours of spontaneous labor. I haven't cleaned hotel rooms since I was in college. When I get a chance to speak with this Elaina person—if Mom lets her back to work—I will give her a piece of my mind. My back has not been this stiff in some time, and that's after packing our entire house over the last several weeks.

The Evergreen Trail Bed and Breakfast has nine rooms, plus a suite where my mother lives. Today the B&B had a complete turnover, meaning every room emptied by eleven a.m. The maid, Elaina, was supposed to clean the rooms and have them ready for guests to check-in at four. Pretty standard stuff, but that didn't happen.

My mother and I cleaned each room in just over an hour and a half. The guests are now settled into their freshly cleaned rooms, preparing to open several bottles of wine we procured from Seth across the street. Hopefully, the free booze will help ease the inconvenience.

"Seems like you arrived just in the nick of time," Mom says, handing me a bottle of beer from the kitchen fridge.

"Why do I get the feeling you planned that stunt?"

"I'm not that devilish," she says as we settle into the sofa in the rear dining room.

"Make me feel useful, right?"

"I wouldn't risk the reputation of the Evergreen for that, but now that you mention it, that was rather convenient, wasn't it?"

"I don't want to be your maid."

"Of course, you don't. I didn't ask you to."

"Except you did, but never mind that. How did you get stuck with no clean rooms?" I ask.

"The guests were all one party and arrived for a family reunion of sorts around six p.m. The Clayton reunion. They booked their rooms last year. This was quite an embarrassment. I didn't check to see if the rooms were ready, though I seldom do since they are always ready. We usually have guests arrive before check-in time, but today they told me they would be later. I thought Elaina had extra time. If anything, I expected the rooms to be cleaner than usual."

"And she didn't touch them at all?" I ask, sipping the beer.

"Nothing. I was away most of the day with Paige. We hiked up Cliff Trail to the lookout point. I get back, and the group is early and waiting on the front porch. I find your father trying to get them to check-in to the Westcott. Unbelievable."

"He was trying to poach them?"

"Yes. The gall of that man. Unbelievable. Telling them that they all could easily be accommodated at his place since

I wasn't open and 'I didn't care about them.' I heard every word as I was unlocking the door!"

"So, you sent Paige over there to keep him occupied."

"Technically, he offered, but anything to get him away from my guests. So, I hand out the keys, and immediately, the whole group comes back down to the lobby and threatens to go next door because their rooms weren't clean. I about died right there on the spot. That's where you would have found me. Dead. Right there behind the desk. But you saved me. Where were you coming from?"

"I was recycling aluminum cans for Cecily Eifert."

"That sounds like an interesting story."

"Trust me. It's not."

"Well, it worked out. I have a feeling I will be comping the Clayton family at least a night for this fiasco, but at least they didn't jump ship and go next door with your father."

"Does that happen often? Dad trying to poach your guests?"

"Not quite so directly," she says. "He makes it a point to hang out on the front porch and make friendly with anyone passing by, including my guests, to let them know that the Westcott is always available for reservations."

"Does that work?" I ask.

"Apparently so," Mom replies and hesitates. "So, you two have made up?"

"Hardly. I just got here this afternoon, so no. I honestly have no interest in speaking with him in any case."

"My dear James, I am in a unique position to understand that point of view completely, but he is your father. You can't avoid him."

I do not have the energy to hash this out with my mother. I'm tired, I smell like stale beer, mixed with toilet bowl cleaner, and I have yet to see my daughter.

"Mom, the 'he's your father' line doesn't work here," I say. "He is Jaden's grandfather. That's where this went off the rails. You see that, right?"

"Again, I'm in the unique position to understand that,

too," she says, glancing away. She fiddles with the cream-colored tablecloth draped over the side table next to the couch.

"What do you mean by that?"

"A story for another time. But just know that your father—"

"You're going to defend him again, aren't you? After all this and he tried to steal your guests today? Why?"

"It's what I do. Always have."

"Not today. OK, Mom?"

She nods, undoubtedly plotting against me for a future effort.

"I need to go see Paige and get her to bed."

"I meant to tell you. She's already asleep, dear. You were up on the second floor, flipping room seven. Mason brought her back over and she's asleep in my suite. That's where she's been the last few days. There's an extra bed and quite comfortable. Her things were here, so I just tucked her in."

My brain quickly lists all the things that Paige requires to sleep in a new, strange room, and what that process would entail. The nighttime ritual has gotten rather extensive over the last few months.

"Did you read her a bedtime story? Brush her teeth? Talk about her day?" My mind is racing. "Did she decide what she would dream about? That always settles her down. Did she have Mr. Hugs? She needs that bear. She can't go to bed without him. Sometimes the blankets are too heavy, and she needs new ones or needs to be covered again after falling asleep. Did you do any of that?"

"Her teeth, yes. The rest, no. Maybe the bear… I don't know. I kissed her goodnight, and she was out before I left the room. It's her third night here. It's fine."

"Fine? No, it's not fine," I shout, suddenly ablaze with emotion. "Nothing is fine. No one here is *fine*, Mom!"

My cheeks flush red. I stand up to go see Paige. Obviously, Mom can't handle this. She doesn't know what

Paige needs, only I do. Why did I leave her here in the first place? We need to get back home… wherever that is.

"She needs her dad to go to sleep. She needs *me*," I say. "She's needed me every night of her life to go to sleep."

Mom grabs my hand as I attempt to leave. "James, sit," she states firmly. She pulls me onto the sofa next to her. "We're here for you. All of you."

"I don't know what you're talking about," I say. "I know that. I…"

There's sweat beading up on my forehead, and I'm breathing heavily. My vision is dark.

"James, have you ever had a panic attack before?" Mom asks, brushing my hair out of my eyes.

"No. Never," I say, gasping the words.

"I'm pretty sure you're having one now. Take a breath. Slowly," she says. She holds my hand.

All the emotions that have built up over the last few months percolate inside me. The pain and confusion of losing Tina. The anger for what she did and how she left us. A slow boil of unease. I'm alone, even here next to my mother.

This isn't the agreement Tina and I had made all those years ago. I did my part—I raised the kids, I kept the family together. Even at a distance, Tina played her role, too. How am I supposed to give our kids what they had without her? I can't do this alone. Everything is falling apart. We're not a family. We're not even under the same roof. I can't even manage that.

I've been kidding myself into thinking I could just find a job and everything would go back to normal. Nothing is going to be normal ever again.

But I don't say any of this to my mom. She wouldn't understand.

"James, you can't be this hard on yourself," Mom says. "You've done a great job with my grandchildren, and you have been dealt a terrible hand. It's not your fault, and you can't take all this burden alone. Losing a spouse like you did would break lesser men. You are not like that. You can get through this. You're an exceptional father and I'm immensely proud of you. Every single day I am proud of you. There is no reason you need to go through this alone. I know you don't want to be here in Shoreline right now, but maybe it's the best place for you. There is nowhere else in the world with more people who love you than right here in Shoreline."

Mom puts her arm around me and I fold into her, resting my head on her shoulder. I let myself cry until the tears won't come anymore.

CHAPTER 27

I spend the next morning cleaning rooms at the Evergreen for Mom after Elaina failed to show up again this morning. Afraid to show her face, no doubt. With the help of Mom's business partner Susan, the daily tidying up is relatively quick and straightforward, but backbreaking, nonetheless. We work on cleaning the rooms while Mom focuses on serving breakfast for the Clayton family.

"It's good to have you home, James," Susan says, loading sheets into the washing machines. "Your mother is worried about you."

I'd like to say that I'm worried too, but don't.

Susan is a tall woman with sharp features and short blonde hair. She wears worn linen pants, a tie-dyed shirt, and leather sandals as we work. Susan and Mom's other partner, Maureen Ellington, have been skirting the edges of our family for as long as I can remember. Always there, but not entirely inside. All three were the best of friends and successful business partners to boot. On holidays when we visit, Susan is usually in Seaside with her mother, so I rarely see her anymore.

Maureen left active involvement in the business years ago but still has an ownership stake. Mom was closer to Maureen than Susan in the early days. Maureen had helped organize the Evergreen remodel and hired me to do some of the carpentry work. She had a flair for art and decorated the guest rooms and public areas to match the eco-friendly theme. She was always at the Evergreen, day or night. No matter if there were guests or not, she was there, fiddling with something, always on the go. But she started to forget things, which were inconsequential at first. She'd forget why she had driven to the hardware store or how to repair a leaky faucet. Those early signs multiplied, and she was diagnosed with dementia in her early forties. Today Maureen lives in an assisted living center near Seaside, and Mom and Susan visit her several times a month.

Susan stepped up her commitment to the Evergreen when Maureen was unable to continue working. She couldn't take over the handyman role like Maureen, but she brought a carefree spirit that attracted guests. Her earthy-vibe was a perfect fit for the clientele. She honed the inn's brand as an environmentally friendly vacation spot.

Both of Mom's business partners were kind women who doted on the kids over the years and even sent gifts for their birthdays.

For what seems like the tenth time since I arrived, I must explain why the kids and I are in Shoreline.

"I'm not home," I tell Susan. "I'm just visiting until I figure out my next step."

"This place isn't so bad, you know," Susan says. "You should give it a chance. You might like it, and besides, your mother could use you around, if for no other reason than to gang up on Mitch."

"If anyone can handle him, it's Mom, and you know it."

"Strength in numbers," she says with a wink. "Ramona told me the news about Jaden. It hurt my heart to hear what Mitch did. I also heard how you responded. Not every parent would accept that kind of news with such understanding and continue as if nothing had changed. One's sexuality is so personal and private, and to be scorned for it? Trust me, it hurts. Jaden's going to need you to keep supporting him. It's not going to get any easier."

Susan says this matter-of-factly, as if relating to her own

experience coming out. Have I just been blind to the gay people around me? So caught up in my issues that I wasn't aware? I knew nothing of her personal life, except for her mother in Seaside. The way she's talking implies that she's sharing old information I already knew about her. I never considered Susan's sexuality—it's none of my business and had no impact on me. Why would I?

But she has a perspective on Jaden's situation, so I take the opportunity to learn.

"What's the hardest part?" I ask.

She pauses and leans back on the washing machine.

"Knowing that something you don't control makes you an outcast to some people. It's just who you are. And that ignorant people will always look down their noses at you, no matter how well you treat them. It's different now, though, at least a bit, more accepted in society for young people. I hope it's better for Jaden than it used to be. Your job is to love him, no matter what. He'll need that from you, James."

Thankfully, loving my child is the easiest thing in the world.

* * *

My body is not equipped to be a housekeeper. I hid it from the Stay-at-Home Tribe, but I hired out the housecleaning once a week to a little business that did several other houses in our neighborhood. My version of housework was a quick pass through the room. Grab all the stuff that shouldn't be there and stuff it in a closet or drawer. Done. The cleaners would come a few days later and fix what I missed. I have not come to terms with the absence of this type of service, but then again, at the moment, I have no house to keep so it's not really necessary.

I take Paige for a walk on the boardwalk after showering and changing clothes. Paige had made fast friends with the youngest Clayton, a nine-year-old girl named Morgan. I had to bribe her with a quick return so she would come with me without pouting. I'm not ashamed. I haven't seen her in days, and I want this to go well.

I explain to Paige that our plans in Lake Oswego didn't work out and that we have to stay in Shoreline for a bit longer until I can get us settled back home.

"So, we get to stay here for the summer?" she asks.

"I don't know how long it will be, but at least a few weeks," I tell her. "Think of it as an extended vacation."

"I want to stay all summer. Morgan is staying all summer, why can't we?"

"It's not that simple, Paige. We have a life in Lake Oswego, and we need to get back to it."

"I don't want to go. I want to stay all summer!"

I'm tempted to tell her that her friend Sophie and the rest of the Woods family will be here at the end of June for their annual Oregon vacation at Christy's mother's cottage. But I hope we'll be back in Lake Oswego by then, so I'll save that bit of information in reserve. Besides, she's got a new friend she wants to spend time with.

"Let's just focus on the next few weeks," I say.

I'm not exactly tripping over myself with housing options currently, but I'm also keenly aware that Paige has lost much more than just her mother, and she's struggling, too. She's going into the third grade and has lost all contact with her social circle—no more Columbia Ridge Academy. No matter what happens, I can't afford to send her there anymore. No more dance classes or Girl Scouts. Nearly all her possessions are packed into cardboard boxes. Having a new friend may be the best thing for her.

"It sounds like you found a good friend in Morgan," I say.

"She likes *Lady Ardella Dance* too," she says. This is the cartoon that's always on repeat on our TV. There must be more annoying shows on TV, but I just haven't come across one yet.

"That's great," I say, marveling at how kids can find the

smallest thing like a TV show and bond over it. "Where is she from? What city does her family live in?"

"I don't know, but they took a plane here."

"OK, so it must be far away. Maybe you can ask her sometime. I heard they are having a family reunion."

"Yeah," she says.

"Did you meet her parents?"

"Her mom and dad. They were nice."

"I tell you what, after I meet her mom, maybe I can take you two out for ice cream. How does that sound?"

"Great," she says, spinning in a pirouette. "That would be yummy."

Paige doesn't mention Tina, and I contemplate asking how she feels, but she looks so happy that I don't want to challenge it. She's content with staying in Shoreline for a bit longer, so if worse comes to worst, she will be OK.

So, for now, I'm pinning all my hopes for a happy daughter on Morgan, this random kid who happens to be vacationing where we crashed. No flaw in that plan at all.

Man, I can't even see normal from here.

* * *

I spend the afternoon online applying for jobs in Portland. I aim high for positions I know I'm qualified for—at least I used to be. Project Manager. Construction Superintendent. Construction Analyst, whatever that is. There aren't many to choose from so I broaden my search, knowing there is a sizable gap in my resume. I don't want to leave the Portland area, but I may not have a choice, either.

For any job, I'll need to explain all my years out of the workforce, and stay-at-home dad isn't going to earn me any street cred. Most of the jobs ask for qualifications or software certifications for programs that I've never heard of. I save the listings for roofers, carpenters, and drywall installers, too. My back and I aren't ready for them just yet, but I sense the time will come.

I call and leave a message for George Rodriguez in Portland, on the off chance that he has any employment leads. He was the only person to give me a shot when I put out feelers for work before, and maybe I'll strike gold again… or meth. Perhaps I'll strike meth again. My expectations are low, but sadly realistic.

My phone vibrates, and I'm surprised that George would contact me so soon, but it's not George. It's a text from Jaden.

Can U talk?

I don't return the text, but rather just click on his name and dial, happy that he reached out, but when he answers, it's not Jaden. It's Evan.

"The first thing I want to say is that Jaden is OK…"

CHAPTER 28

"Dad, there were three of them," Jaden says after Evan put the phone on speaker.

His words are muffled, like his tongue is too big for his mouth.

"One of them was from the baseball team, and no, I'm not going to tell the police who it was, even if Evan insists it's a hate crime and that it matters. I'm not going to be a victim and be painted with that for the rest of my life. I just want this to be over, and we both know going to the police won't make it over."

My mind reels as I try to come to grips with what he's telling me.

"I was down in the basement of our dorm, moving my laundry to the dryer, when they came into the room and threw a pillowcase over my head and—"

He starts to cry, big heaving sobs. I can tell there's something wrong with his mouth. He can't talk through the sobs and gasps. My heart is racing and tears are streaming down my face as I wait to hear the fate of my son. It feels like he's a thousand miles away, an impossible distance between father and son. My mind runs wild with horrible scenarios because I know something awful has happened.

Eugene was an awesome college town, completely centered on the school and was accepting of all types of people. Jaden said he was comfortable there and felt good to be out with his sexuality. I had never once worried about his safety or thought he could be a target of violence.

Until now.

Months earlier, we had decided it was better for Jaden to stay in Eugene over the summer rather than get caught up in the instability of our situation at home. As students on baseball scholarships, he and Evan both got rooms in a dorm for athletes. He was excited to get a job and train with the other players all summer. His scholarship was initially a nice bonus, but today, it's a blessing that means Jaden can stay in school without financial support from me, get his education, and get on with his life.

"They pushed me against the wall and called me a queer and a fag," Jaden says. "They tried to pull off my pants, but I kicked them away. They hit me in the face through the pillowcase and I…"

"His face is pretty swollen, and they split his lip open," Evan says, continuing Jaden's story. "Both knees are all scraped up and sore. But it's his ankle that's all messed up. He twisted it, and something snapped inside. They took an x-ray and now we're waiting to hear if it's broken."

"Jaden, I'm so sorry. You never should have been there. You should have been home with me," I say. "Damn it."

"I wanted to be here, back on campus. I'm just sore, Dad," he says. "I'm OK, really. I just need to rest a bit."

"I'll leave right now and come get you."

"And take me where? Mason said we don't have anywhere to go," he says.

He's not wrong. I wonder when he talked to Mason. Before he called me? No. That can't be right. We only got to Shoreline yesterday afternoon. That uneasy feeling creeps in again to deny the truth about our situation. I tell myself it's for his own good and that he needs to be with his family right now, but that's not entirely true. I need to take care of him, to father him. I need to help my boy, but I also need my mission back. My job. My purpose. With him here, I can fulfill that.

"We're better off without the place in Portland for now, trust me," I say. "We're spending the summer in Shoreline with your grandparents. There's a room for you here too, in the Carriage House. It's empty and ready to go. You can have it today."

That much is true. There's an empty room that Paige was supposed to take, but I'm sure, given the circumstances, Mom would allow Paige to stay at the Evergreen for a while longer.

They cover up the speaker, and I can't make out the crosstalk between the two of them.

"You want us to stay in the backyard of Grandpa Mitch's place? After what happened?"

My invitation was just for Jaden, not Evan, but if the boyfriend is the package deal that will get Jaden back to me, that's an issue I can handle. Forget the details. Forget my dad.

"Your grandfather and I talked," I lie. "It's all worked out. You don't have to worry about him. Just let me come get you. Alright?"

There is more crosstalk between them, which I can't hear. I can't believe I have to convince him to come.

"OK, that sounds good to us," Jaden says, clearly with some hesitation. "But you don't need to come, Evan will drive us. We just need to get this ankle thing figured out and get packed up."

"That's not your call. I'm your dad," I tell him. "I'll be there in a couple of hours."

"That's what I thought you would say," Jaden says. "And Dad, I don't want to duke it out with Grandpa Mitch. I just don't have it in me right now."

"Like I said, it's all good here. I'll let him know what happened and—"

"No, Dad, don't tell him what happened. I can't have him knowing what these guys did to me. It'll just make it worse. No way. If you tell him, we're not coming."

I hadn't considered that.

"Right, right, of course," I say. "I'll tell him you slipped or something. When do you get released?"

"As soon as they figure out my ankle."

"I'm on my way," I say.

"Dad, there's one more thing. I'm not coming back here, to school, I mean. Not now. Not after this. I… I just can't."

Now isn't the time to make such a big decision, but what am I supposed to say? Leaving school means leaving his scholarship. And he has no idea we can't afford to pay for him to attend anywhere else.

"It's OK, we'll figure it out," I say.

God, my lying is becoming habitual.

* * *

Jaden's face is dark purple and blue, with the majority of the bruising around his right cheek and eye socket. He doesn't look like he slipped, and I'm not sure how that story will play out. He looks like he was in a fight, which is pretty much what happened. The doctor said he fractured his tibia—the large bone in the lower leg—at the ankle. No surgery is required for now, but he'll need to see the doctor again once the swelling goes down. More than likely, he'll be in a boot for six to eight weeks at the bare minimum. If it doesn't heal, he'll have to have a screw inserted.

But I'm less concerned about his physical injuries. Jaden is sullen and quiet. He said next to nothing at the hospital or on the drive back to Shoreline. Embarrassed is the term if I had to put a descriptor on it. I didn't ask him anymore about the incident, other than what I learned on the phone. If he wants to talk about it, he will, and right now, he isn't interested. This isn't the Jaden who left my house for college, or even the Jaden I saw at the backyard funeral for his mother. He's standoffish and disengaged, which I understand, and it makes me hurt for him.

Jaden has always been a team guy, the social life of the party with lots of friends. Busy with life, both on and off the field. But he's always fit in, too. He was never the odd guy out or made to feel like he wasn't welcome, thanks to his athletic skills and outgoing personality. But he didn't let it go to his head, and he went out of his way to ensure that other people belonged—teammates, friends, or even straight-up strangers.

When he was twelve years old, we had a laser tag birthday party at a family fun center. It was this massive, old building that was converted with ramps and hideouts. Kids would run around under black lights with packs strapped to their chests. Their scores were displayed on a big screen TV after twenty minutes in the laser tag arena. The whole youth baseball team was there, plus friends from his school. It was a familiar scene for Jaden.

Yet that day, Jaden's birthday party wasn't the only one being held at the laser tag place. In the room next door, a boy was celebrating turning eight years old. The room size was the same, and the tables were decorated with the same cheap yellow tablecloths, blue balloons, and paper plates, but the contrast could not have been starker.

The other birthday boy was developmentally delayed. And while Jaden's friends leaped and bounced around the room like goofy twelve-year-olds tend to do, the boy next door sat quietly with one other child, who turned out to be a cousin.

From the hallway, I could hear his mom making panicked phone calls to the parents of kids on the invite list. One after another, she learned that no one else was coming to the party. This boy's party, meant for many, would only have two attendees. His reserved laser tag game would be a duel between the two cousins.

Jaden heard the mom in the hallway and did something more significant than any twelve-year-old should have done.

"Dad, would you be mad if I shared my party?" he asked me over the rowdy sounds of his friends.

I didn't immediately understand what he was asking.

"We have seats at the table and room on the next laser

tag game…" He then gestured to the room next door, and I knew what he meant.

I talked to the mom and gave Jaden a nod that it was a good idea. Jaden left his friends and went to the room next door and introduced himself. He said he was wondering if the boys would like to join them and share the party. He made up a story that he always wanted to have a party with another person. They would be doing him a favor, he said, and they could help him pick teams for the next game in the arena.

Jaden took the lead. He introduced them to his baseball team and school friends like they had known each other all their lives. The other kids had no idea what Jaden had done, and he didn't tell them about it.

Both birthday boys opened presents together, had cake, shared the Happy Birthday song, and shot lasers at each other in the arena. It was natural and completely unnatural at the same time.

When the party ended, the boy's mom hugged Jaden as grateful tears filled her eyes.

He looked confused and, to his credit, only said, "That was pretty fun. We should do double birthdays more often."

So today, as Jaden rests in his room at the Carriage House with his leg elevated in a boot, I wonder if he's feeling like that lonely birthday boy. Unwanted. Unwelcome. With no team and one friend.

I told him that he needed to tell the police, but he said it would hurt the entire baseball team due to the actions of just a few. He couldn't do that.

I had to respect Evan for trying to convince Jaden as well, but in the end, it didn't matter. He didn't tell anyone else what had happened, and he wanted to keep it quiet.

If it was a hate-filled player on the baseball team who did this to my boy, he didn't deserve to be let off the hook. But Jaden wanted the damage and pain to stop with him and not hurt his team, too.

I didn't raise Jaden to be so mindful of others as to harm

himself, but in the end, it's his choice, and it isn't my place to upend his life any more than it already has been.

CHAPTER 29

It turns out that Jaden twisted his ankle on the edge of an outdoor basketball court and smacked his head on a metal bench as he went down to the ground. That's what caused his bruised and swollen face and a broken ankle. At least, that's the story we are peddling to everyone, and he's a really good actor.

Mom makes him the special soup he likes—a chicken noodle mixture that she makes for guests when they don't feel well. Mom delivers it in several small, sealed dishes for his room refrigerator.

"Warm it up one bowl at a time, honey. It won't heal a broken bone, but it will fill up your stomach, and that's the next best thing," she says to him. "This is a terrible circumstance, getting hurt, but I'm glad to see all of you here together. I need to get as much of you as I can before you get too grown up and sick of us."

Jaden is grateful and diligently downs the soup while Mom sits with him. Mason promises to bring in his Xbox whenever Jaden wants to play. Paige picked out helium balloons from the store and gave him a card with baseballs drawn across the front.

It's been a few days of this. Jaden taking visitors, but staying in his room in the Carriage House, his foot up on a stack of pillows. Evan is making himself useful. He even volunteered to help clean rooms at the Evergreen, and Mom took him up on it since she had to fire the maid. He's much faster than I am, something my mother was not too subtle in pointing out.

Evan's a nice kid from what I've seen. After his actions at the hospital, and here with our family, well… he's welcome any time.

* * *

Jaden is asleep in his room, and I catch Evan alone in the courtyard behind the house, no doubt hiding from additional chores assigned by my mother. He's fiddling with his phone but puts it away when I approach.

"How's he doing in there?" I ask, gesturing toward the Carriage House.

"The same," Evan says. "Not exactly his normal self, but I guess that's because what happened to him isn't normal, either."

"I picked up those new pads for the arms of his crutches," I say. The hospital-issued pads were flat and hurt his armpits. "He should be able to get up and about a little easier now. Whenever he decides he wants to."

"You know he's not staying in the room because his crutches are uncomfortable, right?" Evan asks.

Yes, I know why.

"Mr. Bell… you told him that everything was OK between him and Mitch," Evan says. "If that was the case, then why hasn't he even come to see him? It's been days. I don't know the guy, but it's not hard to figure out and trust me, Jaden knows."

"He just needs some time," I say, sounding just like my mother and hating myself for defending my useless lump of a father.

"Jaden's body hurts, but his emotions hurt more, sitting there waiting," Evan says. "He won't say it exactly, but I know it's true. First, his mom and now this. It's a lot. I'm sorry for your loss, by the way, I never got a chance to say that to you before. She was a lovely woman."

I'm not sure why he calls her a lovely woman. How would he know that?

"Had you met her before?" I ask.

"Yes, a few times when she came to campus last year. We had dinner once, and she took us shopping at Walmart to pick up a few things. It's practically a requirement when parents visit campus. My mom loves doing it, too. You gotta make a trip for new deodorant, razors, and underwear. Moms love stuff like that."

"Right, right," I say. "Of course. Sorry, it slipped my mind that she was down there. Her schedule was so hectic."

No, I did not know that she went down to Eugene and had some special routine about going to Walmart.

Evan's phone buzzes. He glances at the text, then up at me.

"It's a guy on the team wondering how Jaden's doing. They keep texting. I told them he's going to be fine, but everyone likes him, so they're worried."

"They don't know he doesn't want to play anymore?" I ask.

"No, and he's not changing his mind, either. He's done."

"Would that change if the guy who did this was off the team? Would he feel more comfortable?"

"The guy *is* off the team. His eligibility was up this year. So, it wouldn't change anything."

"Then why was he still on campus?" I ask. "He shouldn't have been there to do this."

"He was still technically a student, even if he can't play baseball anymore."

I hate that this guy is getting away with assaulting my son. Now that I know he was in his last year of eligibility, I could look him up. There are only so many guys who maxed out their eligibility last year.

Maybe I could do something about what happened or prevent it from happening again. I set the idea aside. It would only hurt Jaden more to dig.

"Did this guy do or say anything to either of you to before this happened? Like during the season?" I ask. "Did you know he had a problem with your relationship?"

"No, he didn't say anything before this. Most of the guys knew, but nobody said anything. Honestly, it went way better than I ever expected it would when word got out. We were smart. We didn't act like a couple at team stuff. U of O is super liberal, so this attack was totally out of the blue. From the sound of it, the guys were probably drunk."

"I have a tough time just letting this go and not doing something to get justice for Jaden," I say.

"There's no justice to be had here," Evan says. "People are going to lash out and hate. It's the sad, sick world we live in. We don't need justice… we just need understanding and compassion."

"Like from Jaden's grandfather?" I ask.

"That would be a good start. Yes."

CHAPTER 30

Saint Ann Square is an old park three blocks north of Laneda Avenue, tucked between First Street and Seneca Avenue. It was once considered "off the beaten path" for resort-town tourists, with nothing of value for them to visit and inconvenient as well. But things change. The town installed a popular paved walking path along the beach, connecting the central commercial district to the square, thus eliminating a half-mile car ride to get there.

Access to the square made most of Shoreline a walkable community. The unintended consequence of this convenience is that tourists no longer visit the many small businesses inland along the highway, as they no longer drive by them. Not everyone is happy about it, and legal action has been threatened.

The streets that intersect at Saint Ann Square are lined with small homes and rental properties tucked between a handful of small businesses. The mist and sound from the ocean easily reach the center of the square, and even on a busy day, it's quiet and peaceful.

In my childhood, the square was just a basic park with a play structure and softball field funded and maintained by a local Presbyterian church, Saint Ann's. The church sat on the back edge of the land. Seth and I were there almost every day when the weather allowed. In ninth grade, I actually had my first kiss with Claire Eifert—Mrs. Eifert's granddaughter—under the pine trees by the park swings.

But over the years, congregants of Saint Ann's slowly left the church, putting it in a financial crunch familiar to many churches in small towns. The predominantly elderly congregation decided to sell much of the land adjacent to their building to continue operating their church in the red for the near future and complete needed repairs to their facility. Decades of salty sea air and coastal weather had taken a toll on their little church.

Saint Ann's Presbyterian was ready for changes, but Shoreline fought back.

The town—and my mom in particular—fought the sale with all they had. Still, it was private land, and the church wasn't technically doing anything illegal by abandoning the park and dividing it up into smaller lots. The biggest battle came when the church applied to re-zone the land from natural green space and a recreational area to resort and commercial lots to make way for new development. The town, encouraged by my mother, denied the change.

So, as the town and the church battled it out in court, the land sat vacant. Weeds and dust filled the former softball field. The church tore down the play structure for insurance liability reasons. Someone parked an old car on the lot and left it to rust in the elements. Garbage littered the ground.

Eventually, a court ruled against the town, and Saint Ann's put their newly divided lots up for sale, making sure to reserve a small section near their building for a private park for congregants.

These premium, buildable lots adjacent to the ocean were snapped up through an auction by an out-of-state real estate developer with deep pockets ready to cash-in on the opportunity. Soon, plans were submitted to the town planning department for a restaurant, a ten-story hotel, and a string of retail shops. The small little lots would be combined into one parcel for the hotel and concrete parking garage. The church worried about living in the hotel tower's perpetual shadow, but the sale had been finalized.

My mother was horrified. What would become of Shoreline if such a large hotel sprung up in the square? The sleepy little town would become just another tourist trap with boxy hotel rooms and too many saltwater taffy shops. Shoreline would be forced to invest in all manner of sewer and traffic infrastructure for the whole town that would only be necessary a few months of the year. The tax implications for locals would be sizable. Besides, according to my mother, developing the land wasn't in Mother Nature's best interest, either.

Another lawsuit was filed when she convinced the town to deny the permits in a last-ditch effort to block the development.

The town and the developer were tied up in court for years thanks to funding from a national environmental group. This all occurred, of course, during an economic recession that hit the developer hard. He had so much money tied up in the land deal that he was forced to sell off lots to finance the legal bills.

But no buyers came forward, and the price for the risky lots plunged. Who wanted to buy land that was always tied up in lawsuits with the town? Who wished to challenge the political muscle of Ramona Bell, the scrappy defender of Mother Earth, who was undefeated in her quest to stave off any development in Saint Ann Square?

Who was foolish enough to take her on?

Well, that one's easy…

My father, that's who.

* * *

Dad stands next to his pickup truck barking orders at a concrete crew, laying the foundation for Saint Ann Square's four-unit townhouse complex. For their part, the crew seems to ignore his instructions. He might be footing the bill for this project, but they take their orders from their foreman, not Mitch Bell.

Dad had somehow cobbled together enough money to purchase two of the subdivided lots and then convinced some banker to loan him the money to build four oceanfront condos with plans to rent them out year-round. The second lot, with four more condos, would be developed after the completion of the first project.

It was a far cry from the now-abandoned hotel tower project. The town relented on allowing the development when my father took the lead and convinced my mom to back off. The out-of-state developer still owns the remaining former park land, but those lots sit idle for now.

The idea behind the condo design is actually brilliant. The four units were self-contained, each with a garage, kitchen, living spaces, and a large open deck off the second floor and roof. Each had ocean views from multiple levels. At three-bedrooms apiece, the condos could easily fit a family. Dad had the architect design adjoining double doors between the units, so all four could be rented at the same time for large groups who wanted to be together in one space.

He said that most available rentals were one homeowner or businesses renting their own small space, but with his new condos, he could catch longer rentals at full capacity because of the adjoining room design. If smaller groups rented, the doors would remain sealed. After running the Westcott for so long, he said he knew what people really wanted and stuck his neck out to make it happen. Besides, he could always sell one or more of the condos if the design wasn't a hit.

If Dad saw me approach him and the concrete crew, he didn't give any sign of it. I lean on the other side of the truck bed and wait for him to notice me. It must have been a solid minute before he acknowledges me.

"Christ, James, are you just going to stand there?" he asks without turning around.

"You've ignored me in the Carriage House for quite some time now. What's a few more minutes?"

He turns around. His eyes are dark and tired. His usually clean-shaven face is full of several days' worth of stubble.

"Ignore you? That's rich. It's called giving you space to wallow," he says, opening the cab door and tossing a binder on the seat, then slamming the door shut with all of his might. "You're in my home, and I have to come to you?"

"Yes, Dad. When you're the jackass, you get to apologize. That's how it works."

"I have nothing to apologize for," he says, taking off his ball cap and scratching his forehead.

I wait, knowing he's angry and not nearly finished.

"I didn't make this mess," he continues. "I'm trying to help you. All I have ever done for you is try to help you, and *I'm* the jackass? No, son. Not me. You've got a lot of nerve."

I walk around the truck so I'm standing right next to him. I speak calmly, which I know from experience drives him crazy.

"Jaden can't figure out why his grandfather has suddenly forgotten about him," I say. "And I'm getting pretty tired of lying to him about you. Telling him it will just take you some time to sort out your feelings, then you'll come around, and everything will be normal again."

He leans in and whispers, "There's nothing normal about him. Not now."

Walking over to the square today, on the path my mom hates, I did not promise myself I'd be the bigger man because I didn't want to be.

I should stay calm and rational, but that wasn't going to turn the stubborn old man. I knew what was bubbling inside me would come out today, and honestly, I welcome it.

With both hands, I shove him against the side of the truck and hold him there. I'm only slightly larger than my father, but today those few inches are enormous. My forearm presses against his chest. I take a mental picture of the surprise and fear in his eyes. I press harder against him. My emotions manifest into physical action, and it feels right, it feels good. And no, I'm not sorry.

"That's the last time you say a negative thing about my son, you bigoted old fool," I say, my voice still calm, my face inches from his. "Not another word. Not another dirty look. You understand me? I've taken your garbage my entire life, and I'm not about to let it happen to any of my kids, not again."

The surprise on his face turns to disdain as he struggles to push me away. I continue to hold him against the truck. He stops pushing when it's clear he's outmatched.

The construction workers stop to watch but do not intervene.

He can't overpower me, so he turns to insults.

"What are you going to do, Mr. Mom? Send me to my room? Take away my video games? Isn't that what you moms do? God, who's the real gay here?"

I don't think, but at the same time, I know exactly what I'm doing.

I release him from the side of the truck just long enough to make a fist, cock my arm back, and smash my fist square to his jaw. He falls back against the truck and crumples to the ground. I stand over him, my heart pounding, my hands balled into fists.

I prepare myself for a fight.

I want this.

There's blood in his mouth. He spits it out on the ground, but he doesn't stand. He just sits there, looking up at me with tired, expressionless eyes.

The construction guys lose interest and go back to work.

"Guess I was wrong," he says. "I didn't think you had it in you. Let's put a point in your column, tough guy."

I don't need his ridiculous accolades. I don't respond or move to allow him up.

He holds his hands up in mock surrender.

"I'm going to stand up now," he says. "You going to let me up?"

I step back. I don't feel guilt or remorse. Should I? I only feel anger. I could pounce again in an instant.

"At least I taught you something," he says, spitting blood into the dirt below.

"That's the lesson you're proud of? That I hit you?"

"Whatever sticks. You stood up for yourself."

"What happened to you to make you like this?" I say exasperated. "What happened to the guy who coached Jaden, or the guy who took me camping on weekends when I was a kid? We spent days together. You weren't this guy. Not what you are today… this homophobic brute."

"The irony of you picking those damn camping trips as our father-son bonding is remarkably stupid," he says. "And you think you're so damn smart."

"Why's that?"

"You're kidding, right?"

He lets down the truck's tailgate, sits, and motions for me to sit next to him. Apparently, we're going to chat now.

* * *

When I was in elementary school—probably second or third grade—all the way to sometime in high school, Dad would take me to a small campsite in the dense woods of the Tillamook State Forest. At least once a month, we'd go, just the two of us. Just a tent, a fire, and whatever supplies we could carry into camp.

Those were quiet weekends. He taught me to use his compound bow and how to start a fire without matches. Occasionally, we'd grab our rods and fish for surfperch from the beach to fill the day. We didn't talk much at all. I would bring a book or homework and sit by the fire. Dad would take hikes and come back with a rabbit he shot with his bow. I learned how to skin and clean the rabbit, which is definitely a skill I have since let slip.

We'd hike in on Friday after school and stay until Sunday morning. Every time. Two nights with no contact from the outside world. It was the only time he was ever away from the Westcott on weekends.

He was always hard on me. No matter what I did, it wasn't enough for him, and he wasn't shy about telling me about how much I disappointed him. But on those weekends, he was different. Somber. He'd drink whiskey until he passed out most nights, but then wake up at first light to make breakfast—with no hint of a hangover.

"You had to have known about those trips. Well, I guess you're the only one who didn't. I figured you knew. Your sister did…" he says.

"Knew what? I don't understand. What am I missing?" I ask, honestly confused.

He just shakes his head in that, *I'm not going to spell it out for you,* way. He says no more on the subject.

I'm about to follow-up on what he said when he motions over to the condos.

"This project isn't the only one I started," he says. Apparently, Dad's not taking questions about camping. "I'd like to get rid of the McArthur house. I've kept it too long, and it's just a tax burden. I let it go. Didn't take care of it. Not much point anymore. Mrs. Eifert told me you were poking around there. Ironic, that is."

"I just happened by there one night."

"Yeah? Well, I want to update it and sell it."

"Well, good luck with that," I say.

I do not care about my father's real estate ventures.

"Stop being so proud for a damn minute and listen to me," he says. "I know you're hard up for cash, and I want to stop paying the taxes on that house. It was a mistake for me to keep it this long, and with these condos going up, I'd like to get rid of the burden. It needs a complete remodel. It's structurally sound but needs a new roof. The kitchen should be gutted and redone. Refinish the floors and with some paint the inside, it should be good. A little landscaping and we can put it on the market as a coastal cottage."

"You want me to remodel our old house?"

"What else are you doing except taking up rooms I could be renting at my inn?"

"No, find someone else," I say. "You've got the money, you're building oceanfront condos for God's sake."

"I can find someone else, but I'm asking you. Here's the deal," he says. "I know the current value of the house. Do the work, subcontract it, whatever, but get it done and ready to sell. Anything we make over the current value, and you can keep. I'll front the funds for the work."

I do some quick math and consider the cost of next year's tuition for Jaden and maybe even Columbia Ridge for Paige. I could cover those costs for a year if the house sold for enough. We could get back on our feet and return to Lake Oswego. The work can't be that complicated, and I could do most of it myself, or recruit the boys to help.

My dad still has blood on his lip from where I punched him, but remarkably, I'm actually considering his proposition.

"Why would you do this?" I ask. "Why now?"

"Like I said, I'm tired of paying the taxes on some empty old house. You'd be doing me a favor."

He seems sincere, and for once lately, he looks calm. It shouldn't feel like I'm making a deal with the devil, but it does.

If he needs me for something, then I have to get something more out of it.

"I need a better look at the place before I agree to it. But assuming it checks out, I have at least one condition," I say.

"And what would that be?"

"You need to go see Jaden. Be the grandfather you're supposed to be. Shove aside this anger with him. He's the same kid he has been his entire life. He deserves more respect than you're giving him."

"You're not in a position to be putting conditions on my generous offer," he says.

"But I did, and you're in no position to ruin your grandson's outlook on life. Those are my terms."

He gives a little chuckle and lifts himself off the tailgate. He touches his swollen lip. "I'm going to watch the Cubs-

Dodgers game on TV tonight in the den. I can't stop Jaden if he sits in there with me."

"This is a one-shot deal, Dad," I say. "This is my kid. Don't make me regret it."

"James, it's just a baseball game, don't get your apron in a bunch," he says and leaves me sitting on the tailgate.

CHAPTER 31

Sleeping is nearly impossible since I moved into the Carriage House. Several weeks have passed, and nothing has changed. I toss and turn every night, and it's not the room—it's this town making me lose it. I have no center here, no home base, and an intense desire to leave.

I've been in survival mode ever since Tina died. First the money, then the house, cars, and all that. Then getting the kids through the last bit of school. Each night, despite all of this, I've been unable to sleep. When my head hit the pillow back home, I was out, but not anymore. Not here.

I'm transported to a different place each night. The beach where Tina wades into the water in her green cap and black wetsuit. I see Paige watching each CPR compression of her mom's chest. Then I'm in a hospital room with Jaden and his battered face. I see a trickle of blood on my father's face in Saint Ann Square. I'm inside these terrible places every night. I can't escape. The only remedy is to stay awake.

I've been looking days, or more like just hours ahead, and have no plan for where the kids and I are going to land next. I've never been in such an unknown state. I reluctantly agreed to flip the house for Dad, but it's a short-term thing over the summer. You can't build any stability on that. It will go away like everything else. The unknown leaves me anxious and awake.

So, I walk the streets of Shoreline at night. I stroll up and down the narrow streets after sunset when the vacationers are tucked away inside their rentals, playing board games or completing puzzles. I see them huddled around tables, the dim light leaking out of their open windows. Moms and dads, shoulder-to-shoulder with their kids, smiles on all their faces. Family scenes, memorable not for the flash and bang but for the quiet togetherness. The time spent in between planned activities.

I pace. I don't sleep until my body can't stand to walk anymore, and all the families are gone from their windows. I think about my family. Not our version of the family today, but before, with Tina. Would that have been us around that table working the puzzle? Shoulder-to-shoulder with our three children? I know the answer, but I don't want to admit it. Why did Tina resist being there with us? How did I let it stay like that? Was it my fault?

Did I push her away or did she ever really want to be there?

The last photo I have of Tina was taken on the day she died. Taking pictures of the kids has become so routine, and I have thousands of them. I almost forgot I took one of her. Tina's in her wetsuit, standing on the beach, preparing to enter the water for the swim. Paige's arms are wrapped around her waist, holding her tight. Tina's eyes are closed, but she's smiling.

I want to look at that photo and be happy that Paige got to experience that moment with her mom before she was gone. I'd like to think that Tina died doing something she loved, tragic as it was. But I can't see those things when I look at this photo. I see someone withholding answers, who knows more than they are willing to share with their husband.

These unanswered questions burn inside me—the fire and visions that won't let me sleep. I have to figure out what Tina was doing before she died. Why did she do this to us? If I knew why, it would all be better and maybe I could sleep again. I could push her out of my head and take control of my brain when my head hits the pillow. I could stop pretending like I know what I'm doing in front of my parents and the kids.

The questions aren't going away, so when I'm not walking, I dig in search of answers.

* * *

The Rose City Triathlon Club meets every Saturday morning from late February to mid-October in various locations around Portland. Today they are meeting in Price Park for a bike ride on the river trail, followed by a run over the same path. No swim today.

It's six a.m., and the city is quiet. Last night, after pacing the streets of Shoreline, I drove to Portland for this gathering. I haven't slept.

The triathletes sit or stand in a circle doing group warm-ups. Arms. Legs. Neck. A woman in a windbreaker instructs from inside the circle, stopping at each person and checking off information on a list. *How many miles? How far did you go on your own this week?* She gently ribs those who were honest and haven't done their appropriate training regimen and praises those who put in their miles.

A dozen or so bikes are parked to the side, ready for the workout ahead.

The sights and sounds of the park and the athletes warming up take me back to the morning of the Tentpole Tri, and all those people passing Tina in the water. Watching her collapse and pulling her to the beach. I want to forget it, but I know I can't. That memory will be seared into my brain for the rest of my life.

This is my second trip to Portland this week. I drove back a few days earlier and searched through the storage unit for the box that contained Tina's planner and laptop. Her planner said she met this group each Saturday when she was in town. I don't know these people, but maybe she said or did something that would shed some light on why she drained our bank accounts.

Tina didn't have any close friends that she would chat with on the phone. She never went to her high school reunion or returned to Nevada for college alumni events. My friends were not her friends, either. The people in this park are the best chance I have of seeing who Tina was when I wasn't around.

I watch from under a picnic shelter not far from the circle of triathletes, trying to figure out how to approach the group. A newspaper in my hand disguises my purpose.

'Hi, I'm James. My wife had secrets and died. Can you tell me why?'

Yeah, probably not the best approach.

I search the faces around the circle, looking for someone familiar, and then I see him. The guy from the Gold Tahoe. White hat and dark sunglasses, I know it's the man who picked Tina up the day of the Tentpole Tri. He's wearing one of those skin-tight cyclist outfits with shoes that clip into the pedals.

On my nightly walks, I've made up stories about Gold Tahoe guy. How they had an affair or a secret family together. Oh, the laughs they had at my expense. How the stay-at-home dad didn't know anything. How they got one over on me. The gall of that man coming to my home the day of the race and picking up Tina. Like I wouldn't find out? Then he never reappeared after she died. Why? Who would do that?

He's stretching his right hamstring. For some reason, I think he'll jump up and run when he sees me approach him. I can't wait to see him scamper away in those goofy bike shoes.

My heart is beating in anticipation of the epic confrontation that is sure to come. I stand over him and he looks up, shielding his eyes from the sun, despite his dark glasses.

"Can I help you?" he says.

"Yes, I believe you can," I say, my voice less steady that I'd like. "You were sleeping with my wife, and I'd like to know how you live with yourself."

Do I know you?" he asks, his face twisted in a sour expression. "Not that it matters, I'm not sleeping with anyone's wife, except my own. So, thank you very much for that dramatic and completely unnecessary greeting at this ungodly hour."

The triathlon training group zooms past us on their bikes, leaving me alone with him and his overt disdain of me. He's in his mid-forties with a thin, tan face. He's an athlete. Fit.

"And now you've made me miss my group ride," he says, watching the bikes escape the park. "This better be good, pal. I'll never catch up to them now."

"My name is James Bell," I say. "My wife was Tina Bell."

The annoyance in his voice evaporates instantly. He removes his glasses to reveal light blue eyes, shaded under his cap.

"Oh my," he says. "James. Yes, I know you, or of you. I'm so sorry about Tina."

He extends his hand to shake but I back away. That's not going to happen.

"I don't know you," I say. "I don't know anything about you except that you drove to my home the day Tina died and took her to the Tentpole Tri. And also that you were sleeping with her."

"OK, James, wait. No, I wasn't," he stammers. "I mean, I picked her up, but that was it. I was her friend."

"A friend who I've never met?"

"Oliver Tremblay," he says, extending his hand again. "Nice to meet you."

That name. Tremblay. The benefits guy at Goodwin Labs mentioned him, something about him leaving the company when Tina left.

"So, you know me, but I don't know anything about you," I say, reluctantly accepting his handshake.

"I don't know anything about that. It wasn't my choice. That was all Tina."

"Forgive me if I'm skeptical," I say.

"Oh my God, I was not sleeping with your wife. Tina was my friend and co-worker, that's it. Nothing more than that. I'm happily married."

"And Tina?" I ask. "Was she happily married?"

He looks at me quizzically. "That's not something we talked about," he says. "Wait, isn't that something you'd know?"

"You'd think, wouldn't you," I say.

It was worth a shot.

"Why are you here? Just ask me what you want to know," he says.

He seems genuinely offended by my suggestion of an affair and is ready to be done with me.

"Why did you and Tina quit Goodwin Labs?"

"Quit? We didn't quit. Tina ticked everyone off and we were both forced to resign."

"That's not what the company told me."

"Well, that's what I'm telling you now," he says. "Hold up a minute. We're obviously not on the same page here. Why are you here in the park at this hour? How did you find me?"

I explain reading Tina's planner and that I didn't know who I might find in the park today. Of course, I didn't know that Gold Tahoe Guy would be here. He's annoyingly understanding of the whole thing. We find a table under the picnic shelter and sit. His funny shoes scrape against the cement floor.

"Let me start at the beginning," he says. "I worked in the laboratory at Goodwin Labs. She was in sales. All the medical devices we sold to doctors and hospitals were designed and tested in multiple labs before we released them for sale to the industry. That's how I met Tina. I didn't design any of our products. My job was to train the executive salespeople, like Tina, to use the items to teach physicians how to use them in an operating room. One day she noticed an Ironman race poster in my office, and we started talking about races. We became friends. That was it."

"Can you skip to the part where she quit?"

"She didn't quit. It wasn't voluntary," he says, then pauses, exasperated. "You're acting like you don't know any of this."

"Because I don't. Only recently did I learn she was keeping things from me. That I didn't know her like I thought I did."

"I'm sorry," he says.

Again, he's annoyingly understanding.

"Like I said, it wasn't a voluntary resignation. We all had these non-compete clauses and creation of ideas contracts. Meaning if we created something while working for the company, then the company owned it. Very common in the industry. And she had this wild idea for a new coronary stent."

"What's a coronary stent?" I ask.

"In the simplest terms, it's a plastic or metal tube a surgeon inserts into a vessel in the heart to keep a passageway open," he says. "Stenting is a very common procedure done thousands of times a day across the world."

"She had an idea for a new one?"

"Sort of. You see, when you put any foreign object into the body, there's a chance there will be some sort of immune response to it. Your body is like, whoa, what's this thing? Based on the reaction to the stent, the passageway could narrow again. It's not common, but it's possible."

"That would be bad, I get it," I say.

"Tina came to me with this idea. Now, here's the kicker. Goodwin Labs doesn't even sell stents. But she theorized it would be interesting if a stent could talk."

"Talk?"

"Yeah, like report back information on its performance. You know those black tubes that the traffic department places over the roadway to count cars? Each time a car depresses the tube by passing over it, it counts the car, which tells the department about the road's usage. Now imagine that the stent could measure blood flow, pressure, or how busy or slow the vessel is. The intent is to open the passageway, right? If the stent could report its performance to your doctor, you could head off trouble before it even begins."

"Makes sense, I guess."

"Tina took the idea to my boss, who rejected it outright. Too costly for too little gain, he said. Every new device costs millions upon millions of dollars to research, test, and market. They only bet on the sure things and this wasn't a sure thing. It was like building a better mousetrap. The old one worked fine, so why do we need another one? But she didn't give up. She knew surgeons from her work that wanted something like this. She was convinced it would sell and make a boatload of money if only some company would try it."

"But Goodwin Labs said no."

"Right, so she took it to a competitor, Hamilton Group. I told her not to; I told her it was reckless. That she was risking her career, and mine too, since Goodwin thought I helped her develop the idea."

"And they rejected it, too?" I ask.

"No, they wanted to secure the idea on a contingency, possibly for another purpose. Hamilton wanted a proof of concept developed before going any further. We didn't get a dime from them. But Goodwin found out about the conversation with Hamilton and that was enough for them to ask us to quietly resign."

"Why not just fire you outright and take the idea? Seems like that would be obvious."

"Agreed. I was surprised myself. But if they fired us, it would harm their reputation in the medical R&D community. It would be clear they let a potentially lucrative idea slip away. It's a public company, and the investors would get skeptical, but they could save face if we quit on our own. The company agreed not to enforce our non-compete and intellectual property creation clauses if we just went away. They wanted to pretend like they never rejected it, and in return, we didn't get sued."

My heart sinks as I realize why Tina had cashed in all of our investments. She was chasing the big payday.

"How much did you two invest in building the proof-of-concept stent?"

"Invest? Nothing. What do you mean?"

"What did you spend to develop the new stent?"

"We didn't."

"That makes no sense," I say. "Tina cashed out all of our savings and investments. Money set aside for our kids' college. Everything. She had to have used that money to build a proof of concept. It was several million dollars."

"When?"

"The first time she pulled money was almost two years ago now."

"She pitched to Hamilton Group around that same time. She didn't use that money on a stent," Oliver says. "And even if she had offered it, Hamilton wouldn't have taken her money. They wanted it all to themselves. And besides, a few million dollars is a rounding error in medical device R&D. It wouldn't have made a bit of difference."

The disappointment must have been evident on my face as Oliver turned away. I rub my temples. I've learned nothing, except why she left Goodwin Labs.

"I'm sorry about what happened to Tina," he says. "I should have called or sent a card or something, but I didn't know about all this. You've got to believe me. I hadn't even talked to her for months. She called me out of the blue and asked if I would give her a ride out there. I wasn't even doing the race and didn't even stay to watch. She said she had something to tell me."

"What was it?" I ask, wondering why he waited until now to tell me.

"She never said. She spent the whole ride talking about your kids. The one who plays baseball for Oregon. One of the boys was into robotics, right? And your daughter is a dancer."

I swallow hard, waiting for the rest, though it never came.

"And me? Did she say anything about me?"

"Sorry, man. No."

I'm embarrassed for even asking.

"There was one thing, though. I mean, it sounds like you didn't know, so I should tell you," Oliver says. "We talked about jobs for a while. She asked me about my new training gig. That was nice of her, considering everything. She said she had been job hunting for months, all across the country. She received several interviews and even a few job offers, but nothing worked out. Like, one of the offers she turned down was for a junior position."

Tina had been offered other jobs before but had turned them down without even talking to me about them, mainly because they were below her stature. Tina wasn't about to give up what she'd worked so hard for.

"But this junior position? Why didn't she take it?" I ask. "She had no job at all."

"She made it sound like the job thing wasn't a big deal," he said. "Like she already had something lined up, but she didn't tell me what it was."

I remember unpacking her suitcase for the last time. It was packed more for an extended vacation than for a business trip. She wouldn't need the same things if she wasn't working every day. What was she doing that whole time?

"Honestly, I can't remember every detail of this conversation," Oliver says. "It was months ago. And I didn't know it was going to be so important. I should have contacted you when I found out she died. I was waiting for a funeral announcement, but there wasn't one. I just figured the family wanted to stay private."

"I understand," I say. "But she should have just told me what had happened. All of it. We could have figured it out together."

"I know, I don't get it, either," he says. "Oh, and the other job she mentioned was a good one, but the main office was in Boston."

"Boston?"

"Yeah, but she turned it down because of the travel. She wanted less road time, and besides, she said she couldn't ask you and the kids to move from Oregon. She said it wouldn't be fair to put her priorities over the family's."

CHAPTER 32

I hosted a small gathering of parents at our house one evening last fall. Tina was traveling as usual. I wonder now where she was. Could she have been job hunting like Oliver Tremblay had suggested? In any case, my recollection of that night and the fight that ensued after is much different now, knowing that Tina was unemployed and hiding it from me.

I often hosted meetings or small get-togethers for parents who volunteered for school projects—it was a way to stay involved and busy. If I held the event at our house, I could be home with the kids, too.

Mason was in his second year of the Lakemont High School Robotics Club. I wanted to encourage his interest in something other than video games, so I had volunteered to lead the fundraising efforts for travel expenses to the regional competitions. They needed money for transportation and hotels for trips to Medford and, if they qualified, Seattle. Only now do I see the irony of raising funds for the well-off students of Lakemont when most parents could simply cut a check and cover the costs. We said we were doing it for the underprivileged kids. Today, Mason is one of the underprivileged kids.

Christy Woods, a married couple, and two other moms from the Stay-at-Home Tribe came over after dinner to outline the fundraising efforts, and of course, open a few bottles of wine. The business portion of the meeting took about fifteen minutes. We'd host a car wash with all proceeds going directly to the school. Students who needed a little extra help would sell over-priced chocolate bars.

The Wilsons left before the wine—they had kids at home to attend to. Christy and the other moms were content to drink at their leisure, having secured babysitters or had corralled their spouses into stepping up for the night.

Tribe members Amber Finch, Riann Mariano, and Christy stayed and indulged. I didn't then and don't now consider myself *one of the girls*. But as the wine flowed, the conversation eventually led to our spousal airing of grievances. The women would say their husbands were idiots who worked too much and didn't care about the goings-on in their homes. I didn't disagree. They claimed that running a household gave them little to no respect with their friends who had jobs outside the home. Although my experience aligned with theirs, I was still an outsider to these women—any man would be.

Eventually, the conversation turned to gossip about teachers and scandalous affairs in the neighborhood. The latest rumors were discussed and dissected for consistency. I wasn't much into gossip and busied myself with chores and cleaning up the kitchen. Christy was by my side. She had no love lost for Amber or Riann, either.

I was opening yet another bottle of wine when the living room went silent.

"Ladies, did I lose you?" I said, rounding the corner to see Tina standing by the front door with her wheeled suitcase.

The women looked at each other, like teenagers caught red-handed with a stolen bottle of booze. To make matters worse, Christy was standing right beside me. She took an awkward step away from me, instantly sending a signal that wasn't accurate.

"Tina, I didn't expect you tonight," I said, placing the wine on the coffee table, then kissing her on the cheek. "We were just discussing fundraising for Mason's Robotics Club.

Join us?"

I instantly knew that wasn't going to happen.

"A worthy cause for sure," she said, her face pale. Gone was the charisma that swirled around her. "Well, don't let me keep you. I have a lot of work to do. I'll be in the den. Ladies." She nodded at them, then briskly walked down the hall. I followed and she closed the door behind me.

"I'm glad to see you have discovered new ways to entertain yourself these days, James," she said. "I know how lonely it can be with just you and our children here. Nothing like a few drunk women to ease the pain."

"You're implying something that simply isn't true."

"Hard to defend yourself when I see it with my own eyes."

"See what? Four parents talking about car washes and candy sales?"

"It's fine," she said, erratically rearranging papers on the desk. "You know what? Forget it. I will. Let's just pretend I'm not here. You're good at that. You do what you need to do. I'll be out of your hair tomorrow. Go back to your women."

"You're being ridiculous," I said. "Nothing is going on with any of these women. It's not even eight p.m., and our children are upstairs for God's sake."

"No? You sure seem to spend a lot of time with Christy, don't you, James?"

She was slowly zeroing in on what she was really upset about.

"Yes, I do. We both have! With her husband Malcolm, too. Remember him? The pilot? You think I'm fooling around with Christy?"

A night at the lake in Expo Park with Christy flashed into my memory. But nobody knows about that night. Tina can't know and neither can the kids. They couldn't have told her because they weren't anywhere near the water. And besides, nothing happened.

"You know, you really should," she said.

"What?"

"She's really a catch. You are, too—no question about that. Still got the goods. I'm not surprised they are falling all over themselves to spend time with you. You're practically a single dad. Lonely women crave the attention of an attractive man."

"Where in the hell is this coming from? If you were ever here, you'd be sitting down on that couch right next to them."

"No, I wouldn't and you know that. You plan this stuff for when I'm traveling."

"Because you're always traveling!"

"There you go again, blaming me. Someone must have a job, James. And that someone is me."

I ignored the employment dig because we've had that fight before, and I didn't want to have it again. But this would have been the perfect time for her to come clean and tell me that she had lost her job. But she didn't, and instead, we argued about our marriage because we couldn't talk about what was really going on with her.

"It's true," I said. "I don't plan parenting activities like this for when you're in town because I'd rather spend that time with you and our kids, not wasting it on some meeting. The nights together are a precious few, Tina. You're spinning it into something it's not. How crazy is it that I actually want you here?"

"It's crazy, alright. Never did understand it myself."

In the distance, the front door opened and closed, our guests seeing themselves out. We both took a breath, knowing our voices carried enough for them to hear at least some of what we had said.

"You don't have to push me away, you know," I said. "It doesn't have to be like this."

"I'm not pushing you away," she said, looking away from me. "You've never given me the chance to be a part of this family. Not like you say you want it to be. It's always your way, and that's it. I can be here when it's convenient for you.

That's not pushing you away. It's reflecting the minor role you've given me. Playing my part, as you like to say."

"You want out of our marriage, then? Is that what you're saying?"

"Out? No, James. All I ever do is try to get back in. I'm trying now, not that you've noticed. It's all I've ever done, but you continue to hold me at arm's-length."

"You're welcome to come home anytime you'd like," I said. "There's no arm's-length there."

"You don't see it… what you do. I thought it was me. All this time I thought it was me."

She left me standing in the den. She took her still-packed suitcase and walked out the door, and I didn't see her again for a week.

CHAPTER 33

Online Coach, session 119
Archive for client Tina Bell

Coach: *You previously wrote that you found love elsewhere. I'd like to follow up on that. What do you mean exactly? Did you step out of your marriage?*

Did I cheat on James? I know he thinks so. He's constantly checking in on me when I'm gone. 'Where are you? When are you coming home? Put your schedule on the shared calendar so I can see every move you make.' It's a lot to take.

Coach: *You feel that keeping him current on your travel schedule is intrusive?*

I do, yes. I don't need him to know where I am at every waking moment. I'm not a child.

Coach: *Some might say he's showing an interest, and if you resist sharing these minor details, you may seem like you're trying to hide something.*

You know how many times I've gotten hit on in a hotel bar? Hundreds of times. After a long day of travel and back-to-back meetings in multiple offices, all I want is a nice glass of wine and a little peace and quiet. But what do I get? Pickup lines and horny businessmen who won't leave me the hell alone. I don't seek it out, but I'm also not going to sit alone in my hotel room and drink, either. But because I'm alone at the bar or poolside, I'm fair game to all these men.

Let me tell you, I've had my opportunities, and I've been known to flirt to get what I want. But I have never cheated on

James, so I have nothing to hide.

> **Coach:** *Honesty is important in our sessions, Tina. If you found your love elsewhere, you need to share that information to gain anything from these sessions.*

I should have been more clear. I found my love in my children, not another man.

> **Coach:** *Oh, I'm sorry for implying something that wasn't true.*

Trust me, I get it. If I were you, I would have expected an affair as well. But that's just not me. Did James have an affair? Or is he having one now? Maybe. I would understand if he is. It's probably with Christy Woods. He's a man, and while he's not a sleazy businessman in a hotel bar, he gets lonely, too. I know I'm not there for him like he needs. I wouldn't blame him. It would hurt, but I wouldn't blame him.

It hurts to even think about.

But my love and attention is focused on my kids, not James. The funny thing is, he doesn't even see it. He's like a gatekeeper who doesn't realize that everyone is just going around him and his gate to get through to the other side. Despite what he thinks, I don't need James to help me have a relationship with my kids. He wants to be the primary or alpha parent. Fine, be the alpha parent. I'll do my own thing.

> **Coach:** *The love of a mother is very important. What aspects of being a mother do you enjoy?*

I love seeing their faces light up when they are proud of themselves. James sends me these pictures of the kids' activities so I don't miss out on them. I have them all saved in a folder on my computer. And I look at them at night when I'm away. I look at them a lot. I've missed a lot in their lives. I want to be there more for them, and I'm working on that.

I enjoy spending time with them, particularly one on one. When Jaden went to U of O, I started taking trips to campus and not telling James. I didn't realize it at the time, but the reason I enjoyed the trips so much was because I was the only parent there. I didn't have a middleman between me and Jaden.

We would go to Walmart and buy supplies for his dorm. Simple stuff. Or we'd just do dinner at some funky restaurant in

Eugene. I had been waiting for years for Jaden to feel comfortable enough to admit that he was homosexual. It was pretty obvious to me for a long time, but he needed to do it on his own terms. Going to college was the thing that finally allowed him to be open about it. He decided to tell me, officially, over a plate of vegan enchiladas one night. I was honored to be the first person he ever told.

Coach: *I'm sure that helped him tell others as well.*

He's kept it pretty quiet. He'll tell everyone else, including James, when he's ready. He's only just found his confidence about it. I think he needs to live out and open in his new skin for a while before he takes on any more struggles.

Coach: *You think it will be a struggle to tell James?*

I hope not. Maybe it won't be hard with James, but it's going to be an uphill battle with Mitch, Jaden's grandfather, for many reasons. But that's a whole other story.

Coach: *OK, we'll note that for future sessions. I see here in our previous coaching sessions that you are still looking for work. Can you elaborate on your current employment status and job search?*

You mean how I basically got fired for trying to sell an extremely lucrative idea to my short-sighted, daft company, Goodwin Labs? Or how a rival firm thought so highly of my idea that they offered to hire me on the spot and lead the project? Is that what I should update you on?

Coach: *You sound upset.*

Well, I've been unemployed and most certainly unemployable for more than a year, so yeah, I'm a bit upset about the whole thing. And living in hotels, pretending to have a job, is expensive and exhausting.

Coach: *Pretending?*

I was forced to resign from my job at Goodwin Labs after pitching an idea to the Hamilton Group. Hamilton loved the idea and they wanted to buy it. I took that news back to Goodwin as leverage to get them to start work on this new medical device. I wanted to keep it at Goodwin; I didn't want to leave. Instead, they forced me out. They claimed they would not enforce my non-compete clause so I could work elsewhere, but it's been a year and none of the major firms will touch me.

One executive called me "toxic." Another headhunter told me that I'd be better off switching fields entirely because Goodwin bad-mouthed me all over the industry. They have deliberately prevented me from finding work. I have interviewed for a dozen jobs, but it feels like those interviews were mostly out of courtesy or obligation. They weren't going to hire me. Even Hamilton told me no, and after how I turned on them, I understand.

Coach: *But what are you pretending about?*

I never told James I lost my job. I'm pretending to go to work and bring in a paycheck. I've been faking it for over a year and draining our savings to do it. Work was the one thing I had to keep me on equal footing with James in our marriage. So, each week I buy a plane ticket to a different city and I pretend like I'm working. Today I'm in Toronto. Next week I'm going to be in Miami. I've become very familiar with Marriott Hotels.

James and I fought the last time I was home. I came home and there were three women—including Christy Woods—in my living room, drinking and having a grand time. I came in and saw them and I… I couldn't take it anymore. We argued, and I left.

Coach: *You need to tell James what happened. There's no getting around it. From everything you've said about your husband, I believe he will understand.*

I know, and I will. I just want to follow that bomb drop with the good news that I found a perfect job near our home that doesn't require extensive travel and will keep us living the same lifestyle. Once I find that job, I will tell James everything. In the meantime, I'm hiding my failure as best I can. I cashed in some of our investment portfolio to fund my year of travel and hotels. I'm also paying for the family's medical insurance out of pocket, which is outrageously expensive when you're unemployed. I had to buy that shop in our backyard for James. I know I'll be able to pay it all back when I find the right job. Besides, the rest of our investment portfolio is growing nicely.

I know one day we'll have a good laugh about all of this.

CHAPTER 34

Mason and I are in the McArthur house kitchen, surrounded by the stacks of soon-to-be kitchen cabinets we had picked up in Astoria earlier in the week.

Mason surprised me by showing interest in the house flip and having a knack for the work itself. He'd been rather useful over the last several weeks as we rehabbed the house. We are two weeks into a six- to eight-week rehab schedule for the flip. The best chance I have of selling fast is to get it on the market before the end of summer. Maybe one of the tourists would splurge and buy it on a whim.

There's a loud hum coming from the living room where Evan runs a sander over the hardwood floors. The threadbare green carpet has long since been tossed in the trash.

Jaden stands in the entryway on his crutches, much to my chagrin. I keep trying to send him away, but he keeps reappearing with his walking boot, crutches, and a paintbrush or some plants to fill the newly tilled flower beds. He's relentless. He says that he's coming over to give Paige something to do, as she has claimed him as her patient and is chaperoning him most of the day. Paige is splitting her time between her friend Morgan at the Evergreen and with us at the remodel. I admit it's nice to have them all under one roof for a while, Evan included.

It's been a week since I met with Oliver Tremblay in Portland, and I'm no closer to solving the Tina mystery. I've refocused my attention on the flip and our exit from Shoreline. Finish the house, sell it, collect the money, and then go back to the real world. Easy.

I pass Mason the drill, which he uses to assemble a section of upper cabinets. When Mason was younger, I tried to get him to work with me on some small carpentry projects. A birdhouse while in Scouts and a bench for the backyard. It didn't go well. He was more interested in his video games and didn't like being coached by his father. I ended up finishing the birdhouse, and he ended up quitting Scouts.

But today he's in a zone, assembling the cabinets and fitting them onto the studs on the kitchen walls. I showed him all the old woodworking tools in the shop out back and he seemed genuinely interested in learning how to use them—which was a delightful surprise. I promised we'd make something for him before we sold the house.

"When did you get so good at this?" I ask, holding a cabinet to the wall while Mason attached it to the stud.

"Very funny. You know I've never done this before."

"Have you ever considered learning a trade? You know, doing something with your hands? I think you might actually enjoy it."

We had discussed taking some classes at the community college next year after graduation, but nothing definite. Before Tina died, it was just fine to let him find his own way. He could stay at home, maybe find a part-time job. If we were lucky, he would enroll in college and eventually figure out what he wanted to do with his life. But that safety net is gone now. The luxury of having time to find one's self is no longer.

"Did you always want to be a stay-at-home dad?" he asks.

"That's a real question? You're not just deflecting so you don't have to discuss your career path?"

"Both."

"Fair enough. No, I did not always want to be a stay-at-home dad, but with your mom's career, someone needed to stay at home with you guys and that task fell to me."

"Yeah, but like, Yoseph's parents both work and he turned out fine," he says.

"You mean the kid who barfed in my office after a night of drinking?"

He shrugs, offering nothing else.

"It's a calculation that parents have to make. If you work, then someone else will be with your kids more than you are. You're raising your kids, but only before breakfast and around dinner. They are being monitored by someone else for the rest of the time. Should that person be you, a volunteer, or someone you hire?"

"Calculation sounds way too scientific," he says.

"Not really. It's a financial calculation, deciding if you can afford to live off one person's income."

"It's usually the dad who works."

"Trust me, I'm keenly aware of that. There's no question that your mom was the breadwinner in our house. She made good money and allowed us to live a comfortable life."

"What about now?"

"You're implying that living in a hotel room off the charity of family and having to do manual labor to earn your keep isn't comfortable? I'm shocked."

He chuckles. It's nice to see him smile.

"You know what I mean," he says. "What are you going to do now?"

"Like for work?"

"Yeah. You want to clean rooms for Grandma?"

"Not if I can help it," I say. "What about you?"

"I'm not good at cleaning my room or *any* room."

"This, I know all too well. What do you want to do after graduation?"

"You remember Craig Wilson from Robotics sophomore year?

"Sure, wasn't he a grade ahead of you?"

"Yeah, he just graduated. He got an apartment and got a

job at a coffee place. He said I could work there too, and I could stay with him. He's got an empty second bedroom. He wants a roommate."

"When did he tell you that?"

"Like, I don't know… a while ago. I didn't want to ask you, not with all this stuff happening here."

"Is that what you're doing now? You're asking me?"

"I don't want to just leave, Dad."

"Well, you've got one more year of school before you can make that decision."

"But where am I going to go to school, Dad? I could live there now. It's in Lakemont's district. The rent can't be that much."

"You're seventeen. You can't live in an apartment without a parent. You know I'm going to get you back to Lakemont. I'm working on that right now. It'll happen, don't worry. You don't get to be a free man just yet."

He smiles, a look of relief on his face. Did he need me to tell him it was going to be OK? I should know this.

I busy myself with the cabinet box and hope I told him the right thing. He's not asking for much, just to finish his senior year at his high school with his friends.

We work in silence and together, hoist up the last kitchen cabinet box to the wall and screw it in. The doors need to be stained and installed, but the new cabinets already make the kitchen look bigger and more functional.

"Mason, this isn't what I envisioned for any of us. If I had an immediate answer for you, I'd give it to you. We'll figure it out.

"I wish Mom were here," he says.

"I know, bud, me too."

If Tina were here, things would be different in a hundred ways.

* * *

I needed some time to think after my conversation with

Mason. I step outside to review the roofers' progress. Slower than they should be, so it seems. I'll need to make a call.

I step down from the back patio, over piles of old shingles and tar paper.

"Hey, you," a voice from over the fence calls. "Come around here, huh?"

It's Mrs. Eifert. I say a silent prayer that she hasn't misplaced the belt around her robe like the last time we met. I walk down the driveway and around the fence and find her fully clothed, pulling weeds from her garden. Perspiration dots her forehead below her white hair.

I recall the Eifert family used to grow an extensive garden every year, encircled with wire fencing to keep the deer out. Tomatoes, berries, carrots, lettuce, and squash. Seth and I used to sneak handfuls of raspberries and stuff them into our mouths when no one was looking.

The grand garden had long ago been returned to the earth, except for a small rectangle that Mrs. Eifert now kneels next to.

"Hand me that spade over there," she says, pointing to a gardening tool on a picnic table.

She takes the tool and pulls back a strip of dark soil next to a line of carrots. She carefully pulls out six medium-sized carrots, fuzzy with roots and earth.

"I can't eat these things raw," she says, tapping an index finger on her dentures.

"Why do you grow them then?" I ask.

"Tradition, and because growing them is the easy part. Drop the seed, cover with dirt, and wait. Anybody can do that. And besides, if you steam them, even I can handle the mush. And the deer don't bother with them for some reason, so I'm not wasting my time out here."

She places the carrots inside a wicker basket.

"I made $200 on those cans you crushed," she says.

"That's $200 for the school fundraiser, right?"

"Sure… the school fundraiser." She gives me a look that

says there was no school fundraiser. Looking back on that night—my first night back in Shoreline—it really didn't matter the reason the cans needed crushed. She asked, and I would have done it regardless of the reason. It gave me something mindless to accomplish, even if it was small and inconsequential. Helping a neighbor felt good, even if it was a con.

Maybe that's what I'm doing with the house flip, too. It keeps me occupied, focused. Having a goal that I can meet is a good feeling.

"You all are making quite a bit of noise next door, all day long," she says.

"We'll be done in a few weeks, and then it won't bother you anymore."

"I didn't say it bothered me. It's nice to see some life around here. Your little project has become quite the attraction in the neighborhood—lots of looky-loos.

"Oh yeah?"

"Nothing ever happens around here, Jimmy. You know that. It's always the same," she says. "Clouds roll in, mist strips everything gray, lawns grow crabgrass. That's it. So, when something changes, it's an event. Headline news."

"That's a particularly dark view of the town."

"The town, no. Life, Jimmy. Life. The world wants to pass each of us by. So, when something around us shows up one day and is different, people look into it. Like your project next door. It makes people wonder if they are somehow behind now. Passed over. Are they keeping up with the Joneses? Why don't they have new things, too? Does it mean they need to upgrade their house now? But no matter what they do, the mist comes in tomorrow and will start to strip away that fancy paint job and make everything gray again. The new thing that stood out before doesn't stand out anymore, and we're right back where we started. Everything uniform."

"I hadn't really thought about it in those terms before," I say.

"Because you are the one adding color to this gray neighborhood. Your father is too, in his own way, I guess, with that giant monstrosity he's building in Saint Ann Square."

"Monstrosity?"

"I agree with your mother, Shoreline doesn't need more condos. And condos that are built over a park, no less. Well, that's even worse. I don't care how much he tries to convince me; we don't need them."

"You've spoken to my father about the condos?"

"Amongst other things. He's a looky-loo for your project, too, you know? He was over there yesterday, poking around. I guess he owns the house, but still."

My father hadn't asked me about the house's progress once since I started work on it. I guess that's why.

"Do you see him often?"

"Not as much as your mom and not as much as before, but occasionally, yes."

"How do you mean, not as much as before?"

"Well, he used to spend quite a bit of time next door. I always thought it was his little hideaway where he could get away from the tourists at the inn. We'd chat over the fence. He turned me down for smashing those cans multiple times."

"I guess I'm just a sucker."

"Or maybe you're a nice man who helped an old lady?"

"Let's go with that instead."

"I've seen and heard you with your kids the last few days, Jimmy," she says. "You're not a sucker. All that noise I mentioned isn't all bad—laughter and conversation. I may not be able to hear the words you're saying, but I know the kids listen and want to be there. They want to work with you, and from my vantage point, that's a good thing. We need that around here."

"Once we complete the remodel, we're putting it up for sale, hopefully by the end of summer. We'll miss all the tourists coming to the Shoreline Kite Festival, though."

"A summer home, Lord, help us. We don't need another one of those. Sell it to a local, Jimmy, or maybe just keep it."

"I'm not really a local anymore. Haven't been one for a long time."

"Sorry, you're still a local, born and raised. You might have gone away for a while, but you're back now like you never left. This place never really lets you go."

I say goodbye to Mrs. Eifert and return to the house. I take a quick glance up and down the street. She's right. Everything with manmade color is bleeding into gray. Muted. The coastal weather having washed away the color on nearly all the houses, fences, and pergolas on McArthur Street.

As much as I want to fight it, this gray street does feel like home. It was for such a long time. Maybe it's familiarity or nostalgia, or perhaps it's because I'm a local, despite everything. But feeling like home isn't enough to get me to stay.

CHAPTER 35

The Woods family arrived in Shoreline as planned in the last week of June, moving into the spare bedrooms of Christy's childhood home. As was their practice, Christy's mom, Karen Ames, would stay with them for a week, then vacate the house until sometime in August when she'd return from stays with friends, travel, or whatever excursions she took while the place was occupied.

Christy and Karen get along quite well. In fact, if Karen didn't voluntarily leave Shoreline and allow the Woods family to stay, Christy would stay just as long and be just as happy. As an only child, Christy adored her mother, and the reverse was true as well. These days Karen spends her time volunteering for boards or advocating for causes around the Shoreline cove.

Her home sits north of the town, on the adjacent hillside overlooking Saint Ann Square. The single-story, post-modern home boasts floor-to-ceiling windows facing the ocean and a large, angled deck adorned with custom iron railings. The home's value had skyrocketed in the years since Christy lived here, despite no apparent attempts to update the interior or exterior for decades. Neighboring lots had sprouted many elegant vacation homes with towering rooflines, competing with each other for the best views of the cove. The Ames' house sat amongst them, but also several decades in the past.

After several weeks of radio-silence, Christy finally texted me with an invitation to their summer-kickoff barbeque. I accepted but could only convince Paige to attend with me. Mason, Jaden, and Evan had taken advantage of their day off from the McArthur project and left early for a day trip to Newport.

Upon our arrival, Paige and Sophie immediately ran off together, exploring the house, leaving me alone with Christy and Karen. Malcolm was nowhere to be seen and was not mentioned, either.

"Karen, you're looking well," I say, accepting a rather full glass of red wine. The summer evening is still warm on the deck and the breeze from the ocean nearly non-existent.

"Aren't you the charmer," Karen replies with a wink. "Well, I know better because I look at myself in the mirror every day. Being well is an illusion mastered by few and held by none."

"I don't think I've heard that saying before," I say.

"Well, you can't really claim that anymore, can you?" she says.

"No, I guess not," I say, sipping the wine.

We easily churn through the expected pleasantries. 'I'm sorry about your wife. How are you holding up? How are your parents?'

"Is your mother still on the planning committee for Shoreline's Fourth of July events?" Karen asks.

"Like always," I reply. "She just can't let it go. She's worried about the weather this year. The forecast is for rain and high winds—not a great combination for the festival. She's already had some room reservations cancel, too."

"Such a shame." She raises her glass. "Here's to the sun, surf, and just enough wind to loft the kites where they need to be."

"Agreed," I say.

We all clink our glasses in a toast.

Dinner is simple, and the same meal Karen has made since we were in high school—grilled chicken, a summer pasta salad, and watermelon. Nothing fancy, but it's savory and familiar. It's abundantly clear Christy did not get her culinary skills from her mom.

Paige makes a show of eating only the pasta from the salad, leaving all the actual flavor on her plate. The kids finish in record time and are quickly off together again.

I marvel at Paige. Just a few months ago, she was withdrawn and wouldn't talk about her mom, but today she's back to what looks like normal, at least on the outside. She still hasn't mentioned the day Tina died. I wonder why it seems as though she's only sad when she's alone around me? Am I dragging her down with me? Or could it be that she's hiding it from the world and only shows her true self when her guard is down? We've been together a lot at the McArthur house, but I need to make a point to spend more one-on-one time with her.

Karen opens another bottle of wine and refills our glasses again—my third. She excuses herself to the kitchen, leaving Christy and me alone on the deck. We sit in silence for some time, sipping our wine and watching the sun drop on the horizon. My head is a little dizzy from the wine, and I can see the same in Christy. The way she holds her lips in a pout and the extra tinge of water in her eyes. She was unusually quiet during dinner, her mind obviously elsewhere.

"Come on, let's take a walk," Christy says, not as a question.

She transfers our wine into tumblers with lids and confirms that Karen will keep an eye on the kids. She leads us down the rocky path between the hillside homes toward Saint Ann Square. The trail is steep in places, and more than once, she accepts my hand as we descend over large drops. By the time we reach the frontage road and cross onto the dunes, the sun touches the water. The low clouds have burned off, providing a perfect evening for a blazing orange Oregon coast sunset.

She continues past the ever-changing runoff stream that

weaves its way to the water. Past the carefully-built but abandoned sandcastles. A family, in matching shirts and jeans, rolled up to their calves, are taking pictures. A dog retrieves a tennis ball for its owner.

Christy finds a spot she deems suitable. We sit on the sand next to a large, weathered driftwood log. The remains of a fire sit in a shallow pit nearby. She continues to gaze toward the sunset. I lean on the log next to her.

"Your hands are rough," she says, taking my hand like she's never seen it before. "These aren't the hands of the guy I know."

"I've become something of a manual laborer in my return home."

She runs her finger over my palm, slowly examining the newly-formed calluses from construction work on the McArthur house. Her soft touch is playful and something I had only felt one other time on another beach years ago. She seems to sense the connection to the past, too—our minds in sync.

"We didn't do anything wrong that night in Expo Park," she says. "You know that, right?"

* * *

The Expo Park camping trip was a two-day family outing several summers ago. Jaden's premier baseball team was playing a tournament in Bend. Instead of forcing Paige and Mason to tag along and rent a hotel room, I decided to pack the back of the car with our camping gear and find a campground with a lake near the tournament. Maybe the younger kids would actually have some outdoor fun, not just play on their electronic devices by a hotel pool. Tina's schedule allowed her to stay the two nights, so I figured it would be a fun little weekend trip for all of us that she would actually attend.

We invited the Woods to join us since their son RJ was on the same team, and we'd all been traveling together for much of the summer for games. Sophie could keep Paige company, saving me from being her only companion.

We arrived in two cars and quickly set up camp. Jaden and RJ had both been Boy Scouts, making the initial set-up work much more straightforward. The sun was scorching overhead, and we took shelter under the shade of the trees. Anything to stay cool. The kids found the water immediately and played at the beach for hours, coated in layers of sunscreen.

I shouldn't have been surprised when I got Tina's text telling me that she wasn't going to make it. She had to be in Orlando by Sunday night for an early meeting Monday, so she wouldn't even come home to Portland over the weekend as planned.

> *So, there's no way I can go on your little trip. Tell the kids sorry for me.*

There was no apology to me, just the kids.

I told Christy, and she just laughed before telling me that Malcolm would also not be staying with us this weekend. He accepted a flight to Melbourne to replace one of his pilot buddies. Apparently, he owed the guy a favor and needed to pay him back.

This same scenario had played out for both of our families dozens of times over the years, and I quite honestly didn't give it much thought anymore. The working parents had more important things to do, which left us holding the bag. If it happened once or twice, maybe I'd take it personally, but it was routine, and we simply moved on. They weren't there—par for the course.

After a late dinner, the kids met up with the campground hosts for their nightly program. There was a big open field away from any lights that was perfect for stargazing. The kids would lay down in the field and identify the stars with large maps of the heavens. After stargazing, they did a bonfire while one of the hosts played a guitar.

With the kids occupied for a few hours, Christy and I stayed back at camp doing the usual chores of tidying up and getting ready for the night. Paige, only six at the time, still had trouble staying dry through the night, so I set up a mat in our tent and covered it in a plastic sheet I could quickly rinse and dry just in case. Christy worked on a s'mores treat she found on Pinterest and wanted to do with the kids. It involved chocolate chips, marshmallows, and strawberries in a waffle cone, then wrapped in foil and toasted on the fire. That didn't take too long to set up, and while we waited for the kids to come back, we cracked open a bottle of wine.

How we ended up at the beach is a mystery. Maybe it was the heat. Despite my sunscreen policy for the kids, I didn't do a great job applying the stuff myself. My forehead and arms were lobster red, and the alcohol only exacerbated my temperature. So maybe it was the heat or perhaps, something else.

Whose idea was it to go into the water when neither of us had swimsuits? I really can't recall.

"I can see your beet-red farmer's tan even in the dark, mister," Christy said after I pulled my shirt over my head and tossed it next to my shorts on the sand. I stood there in just my gray boxer briefs. Thankfully, the beach didn't have lights.

"At least it's red and white—team colors!" I shouted. "I can match the boys' baseball uniforms!" I stumbled in the soft sand and collapsed to my knees.

"Oh, no, you don't," Christy said, reaching down to pull me to my feet. "We're going in. You promised."

I struggled to stay up on my feet as Christy leaned against me, pulling off her shorts, but not her black underwear. I tried not to stare. She dashed out into the water, tossing her tank top and sports bra back at me. She quickly went under the water and called for me to join her.

Something inside me stirred. Christy was my friend, but her actions didn't compute with that. Most certainly, she was incredible and attractive, but I had never considered her anything other than a great friend, a great mother. Seeing her slim body bound away from me that night brought excitement and anticipation that I hadn't felt in a very long time. Damn the consequences, I wanted to be near her. I felt drawn to her and strode into the lake.

The water was cool, in contrast to the warm night air. Christy was bobbing up and down in the gentle surf caused by boats passing the swimming area in the distance. She was still touching the bottom of the lake when I half-swam, half-walked to meet her. She bobbed up with a large wave and allowed it to carry her backward, unbeknownst into me. I caught her. Her warm body pressed against mine. I wrapped my arms around her, ostensibly to catch her from falling back into the water. Her wet hair lapped back onto my shoulder.

I liked it.

She spun to face me; our bodies pressed together. The moonlight glistened in her eyes, and she smiled. Her hands moved from my waist, up my chest to my shoulders, then down my arms to my hands until we were arm's-length apart, but still holding hands. I had never touched her orange and pink scars on her left hand. They were rough, but certainly not the focus of my attention.

She allowed me to admire her slim, naked body. The nipples of her small breasts were hard from the cold water. She was beautiful, and the smile on her face told me that she knew the impact her actions had on me.

As I stared at her like a mesmerized schoolboy, I noticed a dark bruise on her ribcage. It was blue with ripples of purple and yellow and roughly the size of a baseball. Maybe she'd taken a line drive to the ribs at one of the games? I didn't think so, but I'd missed a few games recently.

She seemed to sense my glance and placed her right hand over the bruise, covering her breasts with her arms in turn. I couldn't look away, but she turned her back to me and pressed her body against me again. She could feel the arousal she'd encouraged in me. She placed my arms around her and pulled me against her tighter.

We never parted as we stood in the gentle waves for a few moments. My arms stayed wrapped around her; her hands encircled mine and encouraged me to keep close. My mouth drifted near her ear, her neck. Oh, how I wanted to explore the woman in front of me. At that moment in the water, nothing else mattered. I had been alone for so long in a loveless, transactional marriage that I wanted for at least one night to feel the touch of a woman. To make me feel like I was wanted and exciting, like I mattered and was desirable.

I'd known Christy since we were kids, way before we were both married. Never once had we been physically intimate or even approached a relationship beyond friendship. Had I been oblivious this whole time? Was she the aggressor, or was it me?

How easy it would have been to cross that line with her. Did she want to cross it, too? But I was not considering the consequences, the breach of trust with my wife, and suddenly it hit me like a ton of bricks. I can't do this to Tina, despite everything. Our problems wouldn't be resolved by creating more. I felt shame flash through my body. Maybe Christy did, too.

She turned toward me and placed her head against my chest for just a moment, our arms wrapped around one another. She pulled away, but not before running the tips of her fingers over my lips—a simple but forbidden thing for mere friends to do. If she shook her head no, I can't be sure. I reached for her, but she'd already moved away in the dark water.

All she said was, "I'll head back first."

We'd gone too far that night, down a path neither of us could tread, and one I never imagined was a possibility. I'd always been loyal to Tina. This was wrong and it shouldn't have happened.

By the time I returned to camp, Christy was already adjusting the foil around the stuffed waffle cones. She placed the treats near the coals of our dying fire. The kids had already returned from their program with the campground hosts.

"Dad, that was the best!" Paige said. "They gave Sophie and me a prize for naming all the stars."

She held up a little plastic helicopter spinner with a twisted rubber band.

"That's awesome, kiddo," I said.

"They had a little help," Jaden whispered, motioning toward him, Mason, and RJ.

"Thank you, boys, I'm glad you all liked it," I said.

"Where were you, anyway?" Jaden asked. "You were gone when we got back."

A moment of panic set in when I realized that we might have been seen at the beach. It was a dark, but clear night with a bright moon. The beach was a solid five-minute walk from camp and in the opposite direction of the campground hosts' activities, but still.

"Your father decided to cool off his sunburn in the lake," Christy said. "I tried to convince him that it wouldn't work, but he wouldn't be persuaded. Sometimes, even if you want something bad enough, there's just no possible way for it to work, and it's best to avoid the whole thing entirely so you're not tempted. Right, James?"

There was an added weight to her words, and I knew exactly what she was insinuating.

"Yes," I said. "That's right."

We ate the s'mores cones. The kids regaled us with what happened at the hosts' event. The stars were so bright but the mosquitoes were relentless, and they all were nearly eaten alive by the bugs, they claimed. We'd need Calamine lotion tomorrow before the first baseball game. Christy agreed to pick it up if I took the boys directly to the ball field.

Christy and I stayed on opposite sides of the campfire that night. We never ventured out of our separate tents after lights out, either.

The next two days of the trip were fun but subdued.

Christy and I avoided each other. Paige learned to skip rocks on the water. The hosts told ghost stories at another nightly event.

Christy was supposed to make dinner on Saturday, but she pulled a fast one on us and ordered pizza delivered from town. The boys got second place in the tournament, losing to a team from Northern California.

On Sunday, we packed up and never spoke of the trip again.

* * *

That memory is still vivid in my mind two years later.

"Why are you thinking about Expo Park?" I ask as the sunset starts to dip below the waterline into the Pacific.

"They keep us in this cage," she says, ignoring my question. "Self-contained in big houses. Burdened with responsibilities they could not handle, while feeling it necessary to belittle us for our mere contributions to just running the home. Just raising the children. And what do we do other than make sure their temporary home life is Instagram-worthy for them? How can they criticize something they cannot do? What gives them the right?"

We've had this conversation before. Every stay-at-home parent has, at some point.

"What happened?" I ask. "What did he do this time?"

I knew there could be long periods when Malcolm and Christy would argue. He'd somehow extend his working days by finding additional flights and not come home on his regularly scheduled breaks. Christy would tend to stay home, too, canceling our bi-weekly lunches or coffee adventures. She wouldn't talk to me about it. Was it too painful? Too close to home? Or was it that I, of all people, could sympathize with her and heaven forbid, make her feel better? Was she afraid of that closeness we shared that night but never addressed?

She seems to realize she's dropped her defenses and

allowed me to peek beyond her stoic façade.

"Oh, God. This isn't your problem," she says. "You've got enough problems to deal with on your own, and you're not having a breakdown like this."

If she only knew.

"I can't sleep anymore, Christy. I just walk the streets alone at night. People probably think I'm some creep, constantly reappearing each night on their sidewalk in the dark. We haven't talked in weeks. You don't know how hard it's been. One of my mom's friends called me a widower last week, and I burst into tears in the grocery store checkout lane. I had to leave the store."

"I'm sorry for that, James," she says. "I didn't mean to be so distant."

"No, I'm not blaming you at all. That's not why I said it. It's just that we used to talk and it made it easier. I miss it."

"Me, too."

"So, let's talk. What's going on? What happened?"

She pulls in a deep breath and holds her hands up in surrender. Not surrendering to my questions, but rather to the realization that she couldn't keep the information inside any longer.

"Malcolm left… for good. I'm alone, James, just like you."

CHAPTER 36

Christy and Malcolm met through mutual friends. Over the years, she'd told me bits and pieces of their story. Christy had just finished culinary school in Seattle and was working in a restaurant downtown. She showed potential as a creative chef, but she was young and pretty—two things that didn't signal instant success or respect. She was paying her dues as a junior sous chef, working twice as hard as her male counterparts just to get recognized with more work at the same entry-level pay. The promise of her own kitchen down the road was enough to keep her working twelve- to fourteen-hour days.

Tuesday nights were her one consistent evening off. On one of those Tuesdays, she reluctantly met with Malcolm Woods, a small regional airline pilot. He, too, was pushing himself for the chance at something greater down the line. They bonded over their struggles at the bottom, but neither sought out time for romance, not with their careers just beginning. Their paths were set and would not be derailed by a relationship.

Despite this, they made time for one another. They filled their little free time with dates around the city and eventually, moved into a small apartment together. It was work, in the kitchen or cockpit, then time as a couple. Malcolm was away a lot, even back then, due to the demands of his position. Yet, both were happy and focused on the next steppingstone of their careers.

Christy's time at the restaurant grew frustrating. She watched as two male coworkers were promoted above her. She knew these men were good chefs, but not better than her. If she wanted more, she'd need to make an opportunity elsewhere. She took a position as a full sous chef at an Italian restaurant near the apartment. The executive chef was a graduate of the same culinary school, and a female to boot. She was quickly recognized for her talent and work ethic with the title of chef de cuisine.

She'd wrangle the staff and iron out the wrinkles in the kitchen. She created a select few recipes and was recognized by her superiors, not with more work, but praise. She was happy.

Christy was reviewing the fresh produce that had just been delivered early one morning. They were short on onions, again. The simplest and cheapest item, but for some reason, they were always short in their order.

The delivery driver had just walked out the back door to his truck in the alley. If she hustled, she'd catch him and hopefully rectify the onion issue. When she turned, her foot slipped on the recently mopped floor. On instinct to catch herself, she reached for the only thing within her grasp—a lit burner of the gas cooktop, still waiting for a pot to be placed on it.

Had the burner not been flaming blue to heat the carabaccia—a Tuscan soup for which Christy needed those precious onions—the damage may not have been so extensive. But the burner was on. The middle and ring finger of Christy's left hand got tangled under the iron burner, holding it to the flames for a few agonizing seconds. That's all it took.

The initial diagnosis was second- or third-degree burns over eighty percent of her left hand. Her ring and middle finger would never fully bend again. When Malcolm arrived at the hospital, he was still wearing his pilot's uniform, having come directly from the airport. He cried with her and took her home.

The damage impacted the ligaments and tendons in her hand, forcing months of painful physical therapy to regain modest movement. She took the bus alone to those appointments with her arm in a sling to elevate her hand. The decreased blood flow eased the pain a little. The restaurant wanted her back right away. Her injury was considered worker's comp and the majority of her job could be done without the full use of her left hand, or so they claimed.

But Christy never returned to the restaurant. She locked herself in the couple's small apartment and waited for the nights when Malcolm would come home and stay a few days. She withdrew from the world and eventually, told the restaurant she wouldn't return. She never explained why.

Months later, Malcolm borrowed a dual-engine prop plane and convinced Christy to fly with him over the Olympic Mountains across the Puget Sound. She'd go anywhere with him, so of course, she said yes. Floating above the mountain fog, he pulled a small blue box from behind his seat and handed it to Christy. The ring was beautiful, and he proposed marriage.

She wouldn't place the ring on her damaged left hand, where it would traditionally have been worn, so she slipped it onto the ring finger of her right hand. She curled her fingers so the oversized ring wouldn't slip off.

They were married less than six months later with her mother officiating the small ceremony. Malcolm took a pilot's job based out of Portland so she could be closer to home, and they started their life there. Soon came RJ, and then Sophie sometime later.

Christy never worked in another kitchen, save for her own. She would build elaborate menus for the kids and ship them off to school with gourmet sack lunches that were the room moms' envy. She'd make grand meals when Malcolm would return home from his days away, but she did not cook for anyone other than her family.

* * *

"What do you mean, he left?"

Christy buries her face with her hands to hide her flood of tears. She doesn't respond for a long while, but I know this is why we are sitting on the beach right now. We came here so she could tell me this. I put my arm around her, pull her closer, and wait.

"When I asked you during coffee that day, if you and Tina were happy…" she says. "It was a cruel thing to ask. I said marriage is complicated, happy is not."

"I remember," I say.

"I asked because I wanted you to tell me that you were as unhappy as I was. That the perfect James and Tina Bell had a lousy marriage, so I could feel better about myself and what I'd done to my relationship."

I had suspected there was more to her questioning at the time, but I was only just then coming to grips with the reality of the marriage I once had and how painful it was.

"I don't understand. You said he left. What did *you* do to your relationship?"

"I let it go on for way too long," she said, pulling away from me and lifting the hem of her blue T-shirt, revealing a thick white brace wrapped around her ribcage.

"Christy, he—"

She nodded yes to the question that I didn't even have to ask aloud. He hit her. He hurt her. I think back to that night at Expo Park and the bruise on her side. How could I have thought that it was from a baseball? What sort of moron am I?

Again, I waited for Christy to find the words she needed to share her story, knowing that I was likely the first person she would have ever told.

"He loves me," she says.

"No, he doesn't," I say without even thinking. "That's not love. That's abuse."

Her sobs overtake her, and I wonder if I'm prepared to

have this conversation. My mind envisions ways to hurt Malcolm, to cause him pain that might bring some sick recompense for what he did to her. I don't want to make this conversation any more painful for her than it must be.

"Let me just get this out, OK?" she asks, her tone soft.

"Yes, of course."

"I left him the first time it happened. We didn't see each other for months, but he apologized, and he was so good to me after. He got us the apartment and asked me to move in with him. Despite everything, I missed him."

"You mean this started back in Seattle? That was so long ago."

She nodded.

"I'm so sorry."

She takes a deep breath and holds her hands out in front of her and looks at her scarred left hand and then toward me.

"No," I say, but she nods again, and now I know that what she told me about that kitchen accident years ago isn't true.

"He came home, and our neighbor Darrin was in our apartment. I was working on a new recipe for the restaurant, and I wanted someone to taste it. Darrin was a nice guy we sometimes said hello to in the hall, that's it. I should have known better than to ask Darrin over. I should have asked Malcolm first. I should have known that he would get upset. I was stupid. I'd even tried to get the lady across the hall to taste test for me, but she wasn't home, so Darrin was my only option."

"You can't blame yourself for what Malcolm did."

"I knew he had a temper, but I didn't know what it was like until then. If I hadn't made him so mad, it wouldn't have happened."

"It wasn't you—"

"Stop," she says. "James, I love you, but you just aren't going to get it, OK? You're the best man I know, and this sort of thing is so alien to you that you aren't going to get it.

I know you're trying to understand, but you can't. I've read all of this before. I've seen the battered wife movies; I know what kind of relationship I was in. I know that I could have sought help from a dozen different people or places, but I didn't do that, alright! I stayed. My choice."

I feel ashamed for trying to teach her that what Malcolm did was wrong. Of course, she knows that.

She takes my hand and closes her eyes while reliving the memory. "He was so nice to Darrin. They talked for over an hour about planes and basketball while I cleaned up the kitchen. I had no idea the rage that was inside him until Darrin left… He turned on the stove's gas burner and asked me to look at it with him. He said something didn't quite look right. So, obviously, I joined him at the stove to investigate, and that's when he grabbed my hand and shoved it into the lit burner… It's been so long, but I still remember every second of that night and the smell of my burning flesh as he told me that no woman of his should ever be alone with another man."

She took a minute to compose herself, reliving the memory again, probably for the thousandth time.

"He wrapped my hand in a wet towel and told me to go to the emergency room and tell them it was an accident. I needed to go to the ER. There was no question about it, and when I got there, I almost told the truth, but it hurt so bad and I just wanted them to fix it. To make it better. If I told them what really happened, I knew it would mean more questions and more people would know, and I couldn't let that happen.

"What was done was already done. Telling them that my boyfriend had hurt me wouldn't have made it go away… It was easier that way. Then he showed up at the hospital, back in his crisp pilot's uniform, like he had just arrived from the airport. For a split second, I wondered if I had imagined the whole thing—Darrin, the dinner, and what Malcolm did. But once we were alone, he asked me what I told the doctors so he could tell the same story.

"I didn't leave him. I couldn't. I quit the restaurant. I couldn't face them again. My coworkers were the only people I knew in Seattle, and I was afraid that I couldn't lie to them. I mean, what chef in their right mind gets a burn like that from a stovetop? Malcolm took time off work and took care of me and promised that it would never happen again. I thought that this was the turning point. He'd seen the damage that he'd done, and it was drastic, and he would never do it again.

"I hadn't left the apartment in over a month when he convinced me to go flying with him. He did propose to me, that part was true, but I didn't accept right away. I made him wait for months, and he asked me every day. Apologizing and then asking me to marry him. I gave in, and we got married."

"Jesus, Christy, I had no idea," I say, wiping tears from my eyes.

"Of course not, nobody knew. Nobody knows any of this, except you now. You're the only one."

It was late, and the sun was now gone from the horizon. The beach sand had lost the little warmth it once had held. Christy's arms were covered in goosebumps and a breeze was beginning.

"Do you want to head back inside? Where it's warmer?"

"No, I can't go back to my mom's house like this."

Then I think of an alternative. The McArthur house is still a construction site, but it's empty. We walk through Saint Ann Square, past Dad's condos, and an open-air restaurant. Christy crosses her arms against a chill. I'm afraid to put my arm around her, in the view of others, although I desperately want to. Is that what she wants?

Once inside, I grab the last two lukewarm bottles of beer from a cooler in the kitchen. We sit on the floor and crack them open. Christy's is gone in moments and I hand her mine, which she readily accepts.

"It didn't happen again for a very long time, and not like before. Sure, he'd get mad about little things, pressure me, but he'd just leave the house. He'd never hit me. He got help and saw a counselor for a while."

"The kids?"

"No, thank God. He never took out his anger on them. I'd never let it happen. He'd just leave, sometimes for days or weeks at a time."

"Tell me about the brace around your stomach," I say.

"I think it's bruised ribs."

"What did the doctor say?"

She gives me a look that tells me she didn't visit a doctor, and I should know better than to ask.

"What did you do to deserve it this time?"

"I had lunch with you."

Her words are like a lightning strike and I'm instantly furious.

"We've had lunch together several times a month for years."

"Yes, but you were married and not a threat," she says. "I'm not rationalizing it; I'm just telling you what he said. Once Tina died, it changed."

"That's why you've been so distant."

"Yes, that and you're mourning."

"Mourning, yes, but I needed my friend, too."

"I know, and I'm sorry.

I'm not comfortable with her apologizing to me for this, not after everything she's been through. But I don't know how to tell her. Whose to judge which pain is more?

"I never really thanked you for helping me with Paige that day when they kicked her out of Columbia Ridge."

"It was literally the least I could do."

"You've always been there for me," I say. "I'm sorry I wasn't there for you."

"It's not like that, and you were there for me… more than you know."

"So, he's gone?"

"I kicked him out. I boxed up all his stuff and had movers take it to a storage unit. He doesn't know that part yet. He'll come home when we're here in Shoreline."

"So, no communication between the two of you?"

"Not since I wrote a detailed letter to RJ and Sophie, telling them exactly what their father had done to me over the years. Every incident with dates and a few medical record notes from the times I did see a doctor."

"You said no one knew. How could you tell the kids? It must have crushed them."

"I said I wrote them a letter. For God's sake, I didn't give it to them. I gave a copy to Malcolm alone. I told him if he didn't leave and grant me an uncontested divorce, I would give the letter to the police, the airline, and the kids. So, even if he had some legal right to see them, they would despise him for the rest of his miserable little life. Give me some peace and leave, or else."

"Would you do that? Give the letter to the kids?"

"My kids don't need to be hurt by this," she says. "Of course, I wouldn't, but he doesn't understand that. The kids think he's working, which I'm sure he is. He just hasn't come home in over a month. I already met with a lawyer back home. They will serve him the divorce papers as soon as he shows up again."

"I'm going to ask you a really dumb question, but one you asked me after Tina died, too. How are you doing?"

"I feel more in control of my life right now than I have ever been. Yes, it's scary, and I don't know what's around the corner, but whatever it might be, it will be my choice. I'm in charge of what's next, not him."

"Can I ask you another dumb question?"

"I've never stopped you before," she says.

"Back on the beach, you said you loved me. Was that in the 'I love you, buddy, ole pal' kind of way… or something else?"

"What would it mean to be something else?" she asks.

"It would mean that I finally have the sense to see what's in front of me, and I don't want to let that chance go," I say. "That I don't have to hold it back, either."

"Then it's something else. Yes, I love you, James. I have for a very long time, but until now, I couldn't do anything about it except spend time with you as my *buddy, ole pal.*"

My heart beats a little faster with the words, and I smile.

"I have another confession," she says.

"Oh, boy, this night just keeps getting better, doesn't it?"

"It's about Expo Park," she says. She crawls across the floor and sits next to me. "I lied to you. I told you that Malcolm had to work, but that wasn't entirely true. I mean, he did have to work, but I never told him about the trip. I didn't want him to come."

"The bruise on your side?"

She nods.

"I didn't know Tina wouldn't be there. I didn't plan it, but we were alone, and I wanted you to know what he did. I don't know… I guess it was stupid, but I wanted to be reckless and carefree and let something happen that I couldn't come back from."

"But we stopped ourselves," I say. "We crossed a line, yes, but we stopped."

"I think that's when I really knew."

"Knew what?" I ask.

"That you were the real deal. I threw myself at you. You were drunk. Your guard was down. I was naked in front of you, and you still said no."

"I didn't want to say no."

"But you did."

I touch her cheek tentatively, allowing her to turn away. She doesn't. We lock eyes, and she invites me in. Her lips are soft and her kiss tender. It seems unreal to kiss someone other than my wife of twenty years. The way she holds her tongue on mine is foreign and exhilarating. Her smell fills my senses, and I want more. But she pulls back.

"I told you how I feel about you," she says. "And I don't regret it, but I need to know about you. Do you feel the same? Because if you don't, I understand, but—"

"Stop," I say. "You don't need to say anymore. Let's not

make it weird. Yes, I love you, too… ole pal."

I didn't realize it until I was asked to put words to it. Yes, I love Christy. Everything about her. That's not a question.

In response, she kisses me again. The weight of our confessions hangs heavy in the air. She wedges her head onto my shoulder. I can hear her breathe and feel her heartbeat against mine. A feeling of complete ease falls over me.

I'm sitting on the kitchen floor of my childhood home with the woman I love. This woman loves me, too. I close my eyes, and unlike each night since I came back to Shoreline, I instantly fall asleep, as does Christy.

CHAPTER 37

Shoreline survives on tourism and repeat tourism at that. Summer is always the busy season, but no time more than the Shoreline Kite Festival during Fourth of July weekend. It's the make-or-break weekend of the year. If the weather is good, then the rooms, restaurants, and shops are full, and the year will be a good one. If the frequent rains or winds are too high for kite flying, then every business owner will be playing catch up all season.

People don't just come for the weekend. Many families book a week before and a week after to grab the prime rentals and book their excursions. One bad weekend of weather won't sink anyone, but if it impacts two weeks of the busy season, businesses will be in trouble.

The festival's start is two days out, and the weather forecast for the three-day event looks bleak with high winds and a massive storm front. The Oregon coast knows a little something about rain and we've all learned to adapt, but the tourists? Not so much. The Oregon coast has never been a sun-bathing mecca like California. Think hoodies and sweatpants, not two-piece swimsuits. So, when the weather turns against us and people can't go outside, it matters.

The Westcott and Evergreen were booked solid for the holiday weekend by reservations made up to a year in advance. But today, both inns have several open rooms, due to late cancelations. The weather forecast and cancelations have put both of my parents in foul moods. They may not agree on much, but they both suffer financially when the weather doesn't cooperate.

Luckily, I have inadvertently escaped the wrath of my father. Mason and I were volunteered by my mother to help set up the large tents and canopies that house the festival check-in and storage spaces on the beach adjacent to the boardwalk. Dad has not done well with the situation, laying into anyone on the Westcott payroll for the smallest infraction. His housekeeper had already threatened to quit twice this week.

The kids and I have been lying low in the Carriage House for the last few days, staying out of sight of the guests, as per my father's instructions. The seclusion allowed me to catch up with Jaden. I was anxious to hear how it went with Dad when they watched the Cubs-Dodgers baseball game together. Thankfully, Jaden reported that he and Grandpa Mitch had a good conversation throughout the game, even after Jaden told him he didn't expect to return to school in the fall.

Dad, ever the pragmatist, told Jaden, "Your father is flat broke, and if you skip out on your scholarship, you'll be flat broke, too. Man up. Pack up and get back to school."

I was relieved that Jaden said he would consider it. I hope he will be up for it. I also hate to admit that my father was right—we can't afford to lose that scholarship. I wonder if my father would have been quite so direct about Jaden going back to school if he knew why he decided not to return in the first place?

Time may be the only tool available to heal the rift between Dad and Jaden. They agreed to watch another game together in the coming weeks.

It's been several days since Christy and I kissed, and I have to stop myself from thinking about it too much. We both agreed that night not to take things any further. I didn't want to take advantage of her emotional state, and we are still processing the confessions of affection we expressed. I longed to see her again but busied myself with the kids and now the festival. In turn, she had plans with her mom and Sophie. They'd even planned to visit Darla and Kevin's zipline business if the weather held out.

It seemed the weather was putting a damper on everyone in Shoreline.

* * *

The evening lights from the boardwalk shone down onto the beach, slightly illuminating the volunteers milling about the sand near the flattened canopies that had already filled with large puddles of water. The heavy coastal rains had drenched everyone.

Loose directions had been given to begin the construction process, but the work was slow, thanks to the wet and darkness.

"I would think that part of the tent rental costs would include the set-up, right?" I ask my mom in between swings of a large rubber mallet on the tent poles. She holds a large steel pole steady while Mason and I take turns wailing away on it.

"We got a reduced rate for supplying the labor," she says. "Gary over there is the owner. He's supplying the supervision."

Gary seems more concerned with draining his six-pack than how his canopies were erected for the festival.

One canopy's skeleton was nearly complete before Gary produced a two-man auger with a four-foot bit attached. The auger easily sliced through the hard sand, leaving a stable hole for the steel poles.

"It would have been nice to have had this at the beginning, Gary," Mom tells him as Mason and I drill the holes that another volunteer had measured and flagged.

"You told me you wanted to supply the labor, so I let you supply the labor," he says, taking a swig of his beer. "How was I supposed to know you wanted to use modern technology? I thought you were all eco-friendly."

Mom glares at him. If looks could kill.

We drill the holes for the remaining two canopies and drop the auger in the sand for Gary to drag back to his pickup alone.

My phone rings. It's Seth, but I decline the call as we huddle under the single finished canopy.

"Dad, I can't feel my hands," Mason says, rubbing them together for warmth and blowing on them to no avail.

"Put them under your armpits, you'll warm them up soon enough," I say, feeling the same burn in my cold hands that were still shaking from the vibration of the auger.

The rain has become so strong that all work stops and the volunteers now huddle under the tent.

"I think we should wait until sunrise to finish the remaining tents," Mom says, and no one argues.

My phone buzzes again, which means Seth left me a voicemail.

"Mom, how will the weather impact the Evergreen this week?" I ask.

"People everywhere have the Fourth of July off," she says. "They have their vacations planned, and every kid is out of school. That being said, they don't have to come here. Plans can change. The same thing happened five or six years ago. It wasn't rain, it was cold. It actually dusted snow in late June, which scared everyone away for weeks. We kept lean the rest of the year and we made it, but it's not so easy for everyone."

"How about Dad?"

"He's in the same situation I am, I'm sure. He'll figure it out. We've been here a long time and weathered a lot of storms." She winks at the irony of her play on words and continues, "I heard what happened at the McArthur house… I have to tell you, I was a bit surprised to hear that news."

The blood drains from my face, though given the darkness, I'm sure she couldn't tell. How could she have known about Christy and me? We were the only ones at the house that night, and I certainly didn't tell anyone. Christy promised the same. Could she have told her mom, who then blabbed it all over town? But why?

She must have noticed the confusion on my face. Clearly, I didn't hide it very well.

"The leaky pipe on the water heater… Duck Johnson has always done such good work for us. I couldn't believe he would let that happen."

Of course, she didn't know about Christy. I breathe a sigh of relief. The main water line into the water heater had pulled away from the unit and had caused water damage to the floor and some surrounding drywall. Still, it was a relatively minor issue considering the extent of the rest of the remodel.

"I don't think it was Duck's fault," I stumble to say. "The floor was already soft from years of the old pipes leaking. The new water heater was heavier. It settled and pulled away. It was my fault, really, for not replacing the subfloor like I should have."

She gives me a wary look. "Everything alright?" she asks in the way that only a mother can.

I want to tell her that I could be happy with Christy. That I found something there. It's strange and complicated, but maybe something that we've both known for a long time but never admitted. Mom was married and divorced before; she would understand. She, of course, never found anyone after she and my dad divorced. Never even dated anyone. And even though they divorced, they never separated more than one house apart. They're still close, like friends. Albeit friends who fight, but they spend holidays together.

"Yeah, I'm fine. It's just been a long few weeks—" I'm cut off before I give away any secrets about my love life.

Mason comes over, holding his cell phone. "Dad, I think you'd better take this."

CHAPTER 38

"James, I wish you would have answered your phone like ten minutes ago, man," Seth says.

Music and loud voices blare through the phone. Seth must still be at the Ranger, which makes sense for this time of night.

"Sorry, we were on the beach and—"

"Never mind that now," he barks in an unexpectedly brisk tone. "You need to get over here now. Your dad's drunk, and it just doesn't look good, man. There's gonna be trouble, and he's not interested in listening to me. Dude, I tried, but it only got worse."

I struggle to comprehend what he's saying. Dad is wasted? I can't remember the last time that happened. Not since I was a kid. He liked to drink, but always in moderation.

"OK, just tell me what happened," I demand, already heading up the beach to the stone steps leading up to the boardwalk.

"How soon can you get here?"

"I'm walking over right now," I say.

"Pick up the pace."

* * *

I cross the boardwalk and look up toward Laneda

Avenue to see a wet, empty street, except for a crowd two blocks down that I'm hoping isn't outside the Ranger. No such luck.

As I approach the restaurant, a crowd congregates on the sidewalk. I want to dismiss this as regular tourist activity, but it's pouring down rain, and none of them are dressed for the elements.

I push through the crowd on the sidewalk and past the blazing fire pits on the covered patio. Glass shatters just as a flicker of light spins inside the bar. I can't see the cause as the crowd obscures the windows.

I step inside. Seth is standing beside the bar, resting a golf iron to his shoulder. He sees me enter and nods toward the corner where the pool table and some old pinball games sit.

I scan the room. The place is still packed, probably thirty people or more. Couples and families on vacation, hiding from the rain. Every seat is full, or at least it would be if nearly everyone wasn't standing up to get a better look at the rumble going on around the pool table.

A broken light fixture above the table is swaying with one of the three green shades is smashed. Glass shards litter the table's worn felt, a half-finished game of pool remains among the debris.

Behind the table stands my father, glassy-eyed, holding a pool cue. On the other side of the table is Dad's friend Carl. The two men curse at each other and circle the table.

Some patrons line the walls and giggle at the old men and their stand-off. Rock music is blaring, drowning out the chatter, but the only thing holding anyone's attention is my dad and Carl.

"These two old bastards have been going at it for the better part of the last hour, chasing half my customers outside, many of whom have yet to settle up their bills, I might add," Seth says.

I worry less about the customers' bills and more about the dark look on my father's face. His cheeks are red, and he's sweating. He's angry and leering at Carl. I've seen this look on my father's face before—from memories I'd rather forget, from a time in my life I'd rather forget, too. Yet, even in our recent arguments, he didn't transform his face to this look of hatred. Whatever had happened must have been particularly bad to contort his face this way.

It's no surprise that Carl is the target of his anger.

Carl is a first-class jackass, always has been. When Darla and I were younger, he would order us to fetch him drinks and snacks when my dad was busy helping guests at the inn. Then he'd chastise us for taking too long.

"I'll break this over your head, you prick," Dad slurs, holding the pool cue in the air.

"Give me that cue, and I'll show you how a man handles it," Carl says.

Carl is about five-foot-nothing and possibly 140 pounds dripping wet. My father is a foot taller and has Carl by about seventy-five pounds.

Seth and I exchange a chuckle because if nothing else, this little fight-dance between the two men is kind of pathetic.

"Seth, what are they arguing about?" I ask.

"I heard Carl yell something about Nancy."

"What, did he get a girlfriend or something? That old coot? And Dad insulted her?"

Both men pause on opposite sides of the table, panting and exhausted from the effort. The air seems to come back into the room as they stop to take a breath. Some patrons sit down, quickly losing interest and returning to their meals.

I step back toward the bar, prepared to watch this old man fight simmer down from a distance when Carl lifts his pool cue above his head and charges around the table toward my father. Dad deftly steps aside. Carl's momentum carries him past my dad toward a high-top bar table full of beer bottles and baskets of chicken wings.

A man in a red shirt and a woman in a tank top who occupy the table's stools are both knocked to the floor as

Carl slams into the table. Carl's pool cue hits the woman in the face and a dash of blood appears above her eye. Still sprawled on the floor, she touches her hand to her forehead, a confused look on her face. Carl is crumpled on the floor next to her.

Red Shirt doesn't move to console the woman—who is presumably his wife—but steps over her and pulls tiny old Carl up by his belt and cocks his arm back, ready to unleash his balled-up fist into the older man's wrinkled face. Inexplicably, my father, who mere seconds ago dodged an attack from Carl, steps between the men like a peacemaker, only to take Red Shirt's fist to the side of his temple.

The blow knocks Dad into yet another table, spilling more beer bottles, cocktail glasses, and food onto the floor. All three men tangle in a confused skirmish. Seth and I both rush to break up the melee. Seth helps the woman with the bloody eye to her feet and ushers her toward the bar.

This act of courtesy enrages Red Shirt. It's possible at that moment he realized attending to his wife should have been his first instinct, not hefting an old man to his feet and punching my dad. Red Shirt pushes past both Dad and Carl, his fists still balled up. He zeroes in on Seth, whose arm is around the woman's waist. Seth's back is turned to the oncoming man, defenseless.

I step in to block his path, my hands in a defensive position. "Slow down, buddy. Let's figure this thing out and not make it any worse than it already is. My friend's going to get her some ice."

My peacemaking skills work about as well as Dad's.

I duck low as he attempts to swing his way past me to grab Seth. From one knee, I wrap my arms around his legs, squeeze, and lift. It happens so fast that I didn't realize I did it. Red Shirt falls hard onto his back. I climb on top of him, my left hand on his chest, my right hand at the ready, but he's out cold from hitting his head on the floor.

The entrance to the restaurant slams open as two Shoreline Sheriff Department deputies burst through the door. They see me on top of unconscious Red Shirt, a crying woman with a bloody face, and my father threatening Carl with a stool.

And that's how my father and I ended up in the back of a squad car in handcuffs.

CHAPTER 39

Shoreline doesn't have a real jail, at least not one in town. Apparently, my father and I are small-time criminals, and we're not worthy of a trip to the Tillamook County Jail. However, we are lowly enough to be placed in what the deputy affectionately called, "the drunk tank."

It's pretty much a jail cell and looks exactly like you'd imagine it would. The gray cinderblock walls are etched with blush-worthy pornographic images. Black bars constitute one open wall, complete with a sliding door that clanks when opened. Unfortunately, there's no skeleton key placed precariously on a hook outside the cell like you'd see in an old movie. Maybe if I had a long stick, I could just reach it… nope. I looked—no hook or key.

It turns out that if you tell the cops you aren't drunk, it doesn't do you any good. Who knew? When they forced me into the backseat of the squad car, they told me sober people aren't usually the ones fighting in a crowded bar. Fair point.

Seth tried to intervene and explain what happened, but the deputies had already made up their minds.

I recognized the cop who brought us in, Wayne Richards, although not until we got in the bright light of the station. He was the same year as Seth, Christy, and me, but even in the small school, we weren't friends. Now I wish we had been because maybe he could have gotten me out of this mess.

"Jimmy Bell," Wayne says through the bars, satisfaction

evident on his face. "Been a while, man."

I'm in no mood for a class reunion.

"That it has," I say. "How've you been, Wayne?"

"Not too bad. Good gig here on the force. Won't be a deputy long. Looking at County Sheriff in the long-term."

"Good luck, I mean it," I tell him, but my ability to chit-chat is gone. "So, how long do you think we'll be in here?"

"Tough to say. It's going to be a busy few days with the holiday. I'd settle in for the night. Since I gotta stay here with you two clowns, I won't be out on patrol tonight, so thanks for that. Gonna go put my feet up. You should just sleep it off. It's best for everybody."

"But I'm not drunk," I say.

"Cool," he says with a smirk.

The few deputies left on patrol are likely stretched thinner than usual with drunk tourists who usually occupy this cell. We're not a priority, even if we are locals. Yes, I feel like a local, at least for the moment.

No doubt, my mother will be raising hell about this injustice in the morning with the mayor, sheriff, or whoever else she can get ahold of from the local government on a holiday weekend. Wayne said he called her for us, but she hasn't shown up demanding our release.

No sign of Carl or Red Shirt, either. The criminal mischief must have ended when Dad and I were arrested, and those two got away clean. I'm still unclear about exactly what occurred at the Ranger. Why were Carl and Dad fighting? They'd never come to blows before.

"Who's Nancy?" I ask Dad, who is flat on his back on a steel bench.

"Leave me alone. And stop spinning the bed," he replies. The stench of alcohol emanates from his pores, making this foul-smelling place even worse.

I grab one of his legs and slide it down so it's touching on the floor.

"What the hell?" he asks but doesn't resist.

"It stops the room from spinning, and you're definitely

not in a bed."

He grunts his approval.

"Who's Nancy? Does Carl have a girlfriend? Wait… do *you* have a girlfriend? Is that what you were fighting about? I got arrested, Dad, you can at least tell me why."

"You got arrested because you showed up where you don't belong. I didn't ask you to come."

"That's just great. Thanks to you, I'll now have a criminal record for defending you, and you don't even feel the need to tell me why?"

He rolls over to face me. "So damn dramatic," he growls. "All the time. Never-ending with you. You know, James, the whole world doesn't revolve around you. I don't owe you any explanation. It's my business. I didn't ask for you to show up."

"No, Seth asked me to show up because you were destroying the Ranger, and Carl was having his way with you," I say, though the last part was not entirely true.

"Not what I meant," he grunts. "I didn't ask you to come back to Shoreline, period. You left a long time ago. Made it clear you didn't want to be here. Or be like me. And look where that got you. I didn't ask you to come home and cause all of this."

He turns his head away and says nothing else.

* * *

I'm not sure exactly when I fell asleep, huddled up against the corner of the cell. I'm awakened by the metallic clank of the door being unlocked and pulled open. My neck and back are stiff, and for a split-second, I don't know where I am.

"You're free to go," Wayne says. "Both of you."

"Why? Did someone pay our bail?"

"There's no bail," he says sheepishly. "You weren't charged with anything. Your mom made some calls. You can thank her."

I nod and stand, though a bit unsteady. Dad continues to snore.

"Wake him up," Wayne says. "He's got to get outta here to make way for the next round of drunks."

I look at Dad and try to remember when I was proud to be his son, but the memory is so old and faded that I have a hard time pulling it out of the archives of my brain.

"I'm not with this guy," I say. "If you want him up, that's all on you."

I step around Wayne, down the hallway, and through the unlocked door to a lobby with white tile floors and a hint of disinfectant. I expect to see Mom waiting for us, standing there tapping her foot with a worried look on her face or the phone to her ear, chewing out someone from the local government for arresting her son and ex-husband.

But it's not Mom waiting for me. It's Darla.

"You're an idiot," she says. "Come on, there's stuff you need to know."

CHAPTER 40

Darla's rusty Subaru is filled with dust and grime, no doubt from the dirt roads that lead to the forested property of her zipline business. The location is in the hills near Astoria, up a mile of pot-holed dirt roads that might sink uninitiated visitors. The company is successful, but like my parents' businesses, they are at the mercy of tourists and trends.

A box of sleek rack cards sits at my feet, advertising K&D Zipline—the kind you might see in your hotel lobby advertising a tourist trap. Several faded yellow harnesses with metal clips litter the backseat.

"Those are going in for repair," she says, motioning toward the nylon harnesses. "We lost two people last week."

"What? People fell out of the harnesses?"

She looks at me, incredulous. "I'm kidding. Geez, do you think we'd put people up there if it wasn't safe?"

"Well, no…"

"Big bro, have some faith. We haven't lost anyone yet. We've had plenty of unannounced visits from state OSHA. We're ship-shape."

We enter the highway, and she turns the car north but doesn't say where we are going. It's early, so the traffic is light. The weather cleared up considerably since last night's downpour, and I squint as the sun pierces through the tall pines. Maybe the Shoreline Kite Festival will be OK after all.

"Why am I an idiot?" I ask.

"Is that a question you ask a lot? It seems like you're pretty comfortable with that premise."

"You said—"

"I know what I said, and yes, I firmly believe that you are a serious idiot for so many reasons that I don't actually have the time today to tell you about all of them. Right now, my husband is the only person preparing for our customers on the busiest day of the summer because I'm here in stupid Shoreline, getting your thick skull out of jail. So, yes, you're an idiot."

"I'm sorry, I didn't know," I say. "How could I know? I don't even know how you found out where I was."

"James, there's like four people who live in Shoreline that I don't know, and those whom I do not know are friends with our mother. Couple that with the fact that you got arrested in your best friend's bar… well, it's not a giant leap to think that I caught wind of your shenanigans."

"Dad and Carl were fighting."

"Yeah, about that. It's the first reason you are an idiot. I mean, I have to start somewhere. There are so many choices."

"Enlighten me."

"The irony of what you just said. Well, I'll just leave it alone. No, I can't. Of course, you need to be enlightened, because you're an idiot."

I'm resigned to the fact that I deserve her verbal berating. I was the one in the drunk tank, even if I wasn't drunk and didn't cause the issues at the Ranger.

"So, Dad and our old buddy Carl were fighting, but you don't even know what they were fighting about," she says.

"Dad wouldn't tell me. Seth said it might have been about some woman named Nancy," I say.

She grimaces. "Nancy's not a woman. Nancy is your son," she says. "Carl called Jaden a nancy-boy because of his sexual orientation. It pissed Dad off, and he was defending him until you showed up and got the cops involved."

"No. That can't be it. Dad's been awful to Jaden since Tina's funeral. He hates him because he's gay. Just flipped a switch and decided that's the only thing that matters about him anymore."

"Has he been awful to Jaden, or has he been awful to you?"

"Both," I say. "He scolded me for allowing Jaden to become gay—like that's a thing. Then he ignored Jaden for weeks until I physically assaulted him, after which he offered me work on our old house and to watch a baseball game with Jaden on TV."

"You hit Dad?"

"Yeah."

"How'd that feel?"

"Not as good as I had hoped."

"Wish I knew," she says.

She pulls the car into a decades-old roadside fast-food joint specializing in cheeseburgers and shakes. The place has a gloriously greasy breakfast menu during the busy season, too. She orders breakfast burritos and coffee for both of us at the window.

"Seth talked to Carl after the cops left. The jerk came back to pay his tab. He asked him about Nancy. Carl, with no shame whatsoever about his rampant homophobia, explained what happened."

"I don't get it. Why would Dad do what he did to Jaden but defend him when someone else does it?"

"That's what family does. I can pick on you as my brother, but if someone else does it, they are getting a beat down."

"Oh, so sweet of you."

"Got to defend my idiot brother."

"Thank you for coming to get me, by the way."

"Don't make it a habit. And you owe me, like a lot."

"Why didn't you get Dad, too?"

"Because he would certainly not want to go where we're going."

She tosses the burrito wrapper into the backseat and shifts the car into drive. We enter the highway again, heading north, away from Shoreline.

"Are you going to tell me where we're going?" I ask.

"I thought you'd never ask," she says. "We are going to visit an old friend in Seaside."

* * *

The parking lot of the Grace Adult Care Center is half-full as Darla navigates the car into a spot near the glass-walled lobby. The beige building has two bland stories. If not for the small sign above the door, this building could have been an accountant's office or a nondescript government agency.

She shifts the car into park, exits, then takes a bunch of colorful flowers wrapped in white paper from the backseat and heads toward the doors. Halfway there, she stops and turns back, realizing that I had not left the Subaru's front seat.

She stands and waits, but I don't budge.

"This is the part where you get out," she says through the closed window.

I crack the door so she can hear me. "I'm tired," I say. "I slept on a concrete floor last night. I can wait in the car while you do whatever it is you need to do. It's fine."

She walks back to the car. "The only reason we're here is because of you, so get out of the car and come inside with me."

"Why? Who do I need to see inside there? What is it that you need to show me here? Why did we even have to leave Shoreline?"

She sighs and places the flowers on the roof of the car. She crosses her arms and displays her most serious face. "Do you want to know why Dad was so angry when he heard about Jaden?"

"Of course, but he's not here, so how's that going to

work?"

"I'll try again. Do you want to know why you got arrested last night?"

"Well, I think I know already—"

"You don't know. Trust me."

"Why is this such a big deal to you? What's with all the theatrics?"

"Because for some reason, the universe has conspired against you and kept things from you that the rest of us know full well. For some reason, this family secret is obvious to all who even tried in the slightest to look, but it's a complete blank for you. I can't explain it, and it still ticks me off. My pretty brother, dumb as a rock."

"What family secret?"

"Maybe you should get out of the damn car and find out."

This doesn't feel right. Like I'm walking into something I can never walk away from.

"Who's this old friend we're supposed to be visiting?"

"Now, there's an intelligent question," she declares.

"But you're not going to tell me. You just expect me to follow you?"

"I do. Here's why. Do you want to know why Mom forced Dad to take you on those stupid camping trips every month when we were little?"

"What? What are you talking about?"

"Come on, dummy, the adventure awaits. Let's go."

* * *

Darla checks in with the front desk receptionist. We wait a few moments before a woman gives us plastic visitor badges and leads us down a short hallway to a room marked "Family Visiting."

"They've just finished up breakfast," the woman says. "I'll check to see what sort of day she's having and let you know how we're going to proceed with today's visit."

After just a few moments, the door opens, and a woman walks through. She's thin and tall, in her late-sixties, with close-cropped silver hair styled meticulously. Her make-up is modest, save for the bright pink lipstick that seems oddly out of place for such a regal woman.

She's instantly familiar. Maureen Ellington, my mother's old business partner at the Evergreen.

She stops when she sees me. "Mitch? What in the world?"

CHAPTER 41

Maureen's expression is cold, pained.

Darla stands, drawing Maureen's attention. "Maureen, you remember James. He sure is the spitting image of his father, Mitch, isn't he?"

She gives me another once-over and nods to Darla. I look like my father, and Maureen was not pleased when she thought I was Mitch.

"Yes. Yes, of course," she says, dismissing me and embracing my sister. "How are you, my sweet girl? You look like a million bucks."

Darla and Maureen take seats in the visiting room and catch up. Darla must be a regular visitor. Their conversation is specific about patients in the care center and their various ailments and conditions. Darla speaks of the doctors and nurses as if she knows them personally.

Maureen stops mid-conversation and looks at me, sitting on the couch opposite. Her eyebrows narrow, unrecognizing, although I had been introduced moments earlier. I suspect that she again sees me as Mitch.

"It's James," Darla says. "He's a dope, but he's OK."

She nods almost imperceptibly.

"Do you have plans for the Fourth of July?" Darla asks.

"Nothing much, but we've received special permission to go on the roof during the fireworks display. One of the big timeshare places does it big every year, and we'll be able to see it from here. Can you imagine this lot of old farts on the roof?"

"You're not an old fart," Darla says with a shared smile.

"Oh no, I am not, but my fellow guests here certainly are."

They share a laugh.

"Would it be possible for you to show us your apartment?" Darla asks. "If it wouldn't be too much trouble. You've got that wonderful collection of art I was hoping to show my brother."

"As long as you'll excuse the mess, I've recently had to fire the maid," she says with a hollow laugh. "And I'm the maid!"

Maureen's apartment, just three doors down from the visiting room, is immaculate. It's smartly decorated with massive canvas paintings on nearly every wall. Lush floor plants dot the corners of the small living room. Adjacent to the sliding glass door is an easel with a half-finished painting of the Shoreline boardwalk. A worn, wooden table with paints and brushes sits next to the easel.

I take a closer look at the art. All the images are from the Oregon Coast. There is Haystack Rock in Cannon Beach, and the Tillamook Rock Lighthouse. A fishing boat is pictured docked at a marina in Newport. And, of course, there is a painting of the Shoreline Kite Festival.

"Did you paint all of these?" I ask.

"Well, I certainly couldn't afford to buy them for myself. I'm much too pricy," she says with only a hint of a chuckle.

There's a large painting hung above two sitting chairs of a sunset dropping low in the sky. In the foreground is Laneda Avenue, with several storefronts in the darkened shadows, almost an afterthought to the blazing sun. The same painting, slightly smaller, is in the living room at the Evergreen. I always admired that painting, but never considered who may have painted it.

"It's your art hanging in the Evergreen, isn't it?"

Although she looks at me, she ignores my question like

she hadn't heard it, then turns and begins to mix paints on the table. Darla touches my arm and beckons me into a dimly-lit hallway between the living room and bedroom.

"She does that sometimes… gets lost in thought or whatever they call it," Darla says. "I was hoping she'd stay with us for a bit longer. Some days are better than others. I hadn't anticipated that she would see Dad in you. I think maybe that threw her off a bit."

"It's Alzheimer's, right?"

"Yes, but that diagnosis is fairly recent. She has suffered from dementia for a very long time," Darla adds. "She manages fairly well here, and she still paints a lot. Most of the other residents here have one of her paintings in their apartments. It's so sad. She was such a lovely woman. I mean, she is such a lovely woman."

"Why do you come visit her? It seems like a regular thing," I say.

"You still don't see?"

"I agree that it's very sad, and it's nice of you to come, but why are we here now?" I ask.

She bites her lower lip, then takes and releases a deep breath. "To show you this. Come over this way."

We turn into the narrow hallway to see a collection of a dozen or more framed photographs on the walls.

The photos are like a tourist diary of the coast twenty-five or thirty years ago. The newly-opened aquarium in Newport. Haystack Rock. A seafood market on a pier. A fire on the beach. Drinks at a brewery in Pacific City. Then, there's an image of the sunset framed remarkably similar to the paintings at the Evergreen and in the living room not fifteen feet from here.

In fact, most of the photos have some elements hinted at in Maureen's paintings.

The photos are of locations I easily recognize and must be the inspiration for Maureen's paintings. But it's the subjects at the center of each picture that really stand out. Always the same two people—embracing, holding hands, kissing in one photo. They look very happy together.

Maureen and my mother.

* * *

Darla said it was best to leave Maureen to her thoughts. We make our exit quickly without saying goodbye, but not before I compare the photos to the paintings. Every painting had a corresponding photo. The key difference in each painting—Mom and Maureen weren't in the paintings.

"How could I have not known what Mom was doing?" I ask in the car as we drive back to Shoreline.

"I have my suspicions as to why, but that's not my story to tell. You're going to have to talk with Mom about that."

"But why did you know and not me? We lived in the same house, for God's sake."

"Same house, two different worlds."

"You've kept this from me for so long. Why?" I ask, suddenly angry.

"Whoa. No way. This is not on me," she says, matching my tone. "I didn't ask to be a part of it. There are several people, well at least two—our parents to start. They bear the responsibility for this, not me. It's not on me to explain the world to you, my idiot brother. You go and get arrested last night because Dad is fighting in a bar. And you have no idea why he's so mad? That's just dumb and I'm sick of it. I'm tired of acting like our childhood, our lives were something that they weren't. That our parents just decided to get a divorce one day out of the blue."

"What part of it? You said you didn't ask to be a part of it. What part?"

"Where do you think I was every time you and Dad went camping?" Darla says with tears in her eyes. "Not with you. Not with Dad."

"So, you knew, what? That Mom and Maureen were in a relationship?"

"That's what it was, but I couldn't have identified it as

that back then. I didn't know what was happening. I just thought they were friends, and I got to hang out with Mom and her cool friend Maureen at least one weekend a month for years. She was so happy."

"Darla, I'm sorry. I didn't mean to put this on you. It's just, well… it's nuts."

"I know. This is news to you," she says. "You've got to deal with it, too. What they did was messed up. How they divided us and expected silence about it. For what?"

"So, you knew everything?" I ask.

"How can I answer that question?" she asks, always with the literal answer. "I knew enough. You know, thirty years ago people didn't take selfies. Today, it's the norm. You stick out your hand and press the button. You get a blown-up version of your face and maybe the face of the person you're with but the background is usually blurry."

"I know what a selfie is, Darla."

"Well, when I was eleven, I didn't know what a selfie was because nobody did," she says. "Who do you think took those pictures on Maureen's wall?"

"So, you were there?"

"Yes, I was there, and I took every picture," she says. "While you were in the woods with Dad, I was with Mom and Maureen. And when the weekend was over, Dad wouldn't talk to me for days. He wouldn't even look at me. It felt like I had done something wrong. I was a little girl. I had no idea why he was so cold to me. Why he wouldn't hug me or want to play with me."

"Darla, I had no idea."

"Yeah, I know. You didn't see it. He still talked to you about sports and baseball, stuff he could keep at arm's-length. But I didn't like those things, and he had no idea how to deal with me. I think he was intimidated by me. But he also knew that I harbored his wife's secret, so he resented me."

"I want to tell you that you're wrong, that he didn't resent you, but I know Dad, and that's a disappointingly accurate description. I'm sure he did," I tell her. "He said something to me a few weeks ago that didn't make sense at the time. I mentioned the camping trips when we were arguing about Jaden, and he called it ironic. And he also said you knew the reason for those trips."

"I have never once spoken to Mom or Dad about those weekends, but yeah, I've got it pretty well figured out."

CHAPTER 42

I asked Darla to drive me back to Shoreline right away. I needed to have a conversation with Mom and maybe get some answers. I'm embarrassed about not seeing what was going on with my parents, and even more so that I was the only one who didn't know. Why was I kept in the dark? It just didn't make any sense.

Would Mom be honest with me if I told her I'd seen Maureen? She had to be. What would be the point of not telling me now? Is it a family secret if everyone knows it? Why did it have to be a secret?

I want to be frustrated and mad at both Mom and Dad. I can easily be frustrated with Dad, he's given me years of reasons for it, but Mom hasn't. But now I find out that she's been lying to me for years? How can I trust her? How can things go back to normal, and what exactly is normal now?

I'm also struggling to find a way to explain to the kids what happened at the Ranger yesterday and how I spent a night in jail with Grandpa Mitch. I don't know what they've been told, but since Mom had somehow negotiated our release, I can only assume that she gave them some version of what had happened.

I dread this conversation. I think back to the talks I gave the boys about drinking, drugs, sex, and other life lessons. This was part of the "Dumb Stuff To Avoid So You Don't Screw Up Your Life" dad-lectures that I'm so proud of. But

I didn't do a lesson on bar fights and jail time. Now I've given them a juicy nugget to throw back in my face any time they screw up. I'm never going to live this one down.

* * *

The terrible weather that had promised to ruin the first day of the Kite Festival didn't materialize. Sparse clouds dot the bright blue sky. It's warm enough to go without a sweatshirt, and I squint without my sunglasses. A slight breeze inland means the conditions are perfect for the festival on the beach.

Cars with out-of-state license plates clog the streets as soon as we exit the highway. The grocery store's parking lot is overflowing with tourists in shorts and sandals, snapping up supplies for the weekend at high-season prices.

Darla needs to get back to Kevin and the business. I promise her I will bring the kids up to the zipline course as soon as we have a free minute. I'm not sure when that might be with all the work remaining on the McArthur house, but I intend to keep my promise. If nothing else, I owe it to her. Maybe next weekend will work.

To avoid getting stuck in Laneda Avenue and Blackwell Street's congestion, she drops me off a few blocks away and I walk in.

Families fill the sidewalks, some carrying chairs and coolers toward the beach to watch the kite show's choreographed stunts starting at noon. A line of people wait for tables in front of the Ranger. If timed right, they might be able to enjoy both the show and their meal from the patio. Seth had wedged a few extra tables outside for just that reason.

Before finding my mom, I need to take a shower and change into fresh clothes. I smell like incarceration. I pass between the Westcott and the tall hedge of arborvitae dividing it from the property to the east. Rounding the corner, I see Jaden and Mason and a handful of boxes and suitcases in the inner courtyard. Next to them stands Paige, holding a box herself. I instantly flashback to that awful day at Columbia Ridge when Paige was expelled. She was removed from class and forced to carry the remains of her desk and school projects out the door. Her face is drawn, pale, and confused.

She sets the box down with the rest of the pile.

"What's all this?" I ask, motioning toward what must be all of our belongings.

"Grandpa Mitch said he needs the Carriage House rooms," Jaden tells me. "The people who canceled reservations showed up anyway, but he already filled their rooms. He gave them our three rooms."

"But we're in those rooms," I say, stating what was evident to all. My blood boils and my face flushes. A sheen of sweat instantly forms all over my body. The guests he didn't expect had shown up, and now we're taking up spaces he can rent. The almighty dollar rules the day.

"Dad, wait a second," Jaden says. "I can tell you're super pissed right now. I tried to call you, but you didn't answer. I told him it was fine."

It's true, my phone died overnight, and Darla didn't have the right cord for me to charge it.

"No. It's not fine, and you shouldn't have been presented with that option," I say. "You shouldn't have been consulted at all. I'm in charge of this family. Me, not you."

Jaden looks away, ashamed.

"Not cool, Dad," Mason says softly. "It's not like Jaden had a choice. Like with the meth lab, right? Didn't really work out there, did it?"

The mention of the Portland meth lab fiasco stings. If nothing else, we've been through worse. Mason must still be resentful of that embarrassment.

"Sorry, that came out wrong," I say. "Jaden, I'm angry and don't think it was fair of Grandpa Mitch to put this on you. I shouldn't have said that. When I'm gone, you're the adult. You've proven yourself responsible. I trust you, that doesn't mean I'm pleased with what is happening."

"I get it, Dad," Jaden says with a sly smile. "The slammer has changed you. Being locked up made you a tough guy, lashing out at the innocent free society around you. It's only natural. There'll be an adjustment period."

He smiles like it's a joke, but I know he's just lightening the mood.

"Very funny," I say.

"Yeah, how was the clink?" Mason asks. "You get one of those orange suits? Or join a gang?"

"I'm glad you two can see the humor in all of this. I'm certainly not there yet."

I lift Paige and she wraps her legs around me and puts her head on my shoulder. It feels good to have her little arms around my neck like she did when she was much smaller. She feels so big, like she grew up overnight.

"I've missed you, kid," I tell her. "It feels like I haven't seen you much at all lately. I'm sorry."

She doesn't respond, just hugs my neck a little tighter to acknowledge that she heard me and understands. I hold her closer.

"So, what's the plan, Jaden?" I ask. "Where is the wandering Bell family going to stay tonight?"

"Paige still stays in her room with Grandma, I checked, so no change there," he says.

Paige lifts her head. "Yeah, Sophie and I are going to watch the kites later with her mom," Paige adds, joyfully, releasing her grip on my neck and sliding down to the ground. "Her family bought front row seats."

She gives a little twirl to show her excitement. The festival is free, so I'm not sure where these front row seats could be, but I'm glad she's excited about it regardless. Christy hadn't mentioned this to me, but like Mason said, I've been in the clink.

"OK, Paige is taken care of. Next?"

"The bedrooms at the remodel are done, so you and

Mason can stay there," Jaden says. "You can still come back here to eat and stuff since there's no kitchen yet. That was my negotiation with Grandpa Mitch. It's just for the next few days while the Westcott is overbooked."

"But there are no beds there, man," Mason says. "We're supposed to sleep on the floor?"

"There are mattresses in the storage garage," Jaden says. "I already checked with Grandpa. We can use those."

"Alright, I wouldn't have thought of that. Good work," I reply. "That just leaves you and Evan."

"Right. I think… and don't be mad, but I think we're going to head out and stay with Evan's parents for a bit. He hasn't seen them all summer since we left campus, and we've only got about a month before we go back to school for practice. I know me being here has made this a little harder than it needs to be."

"You're going to go back to school? Are you sure?" I ask.

"I'm working through it. It's my school, and I belong there. For the most part, the guys on the team are pretty good. The ones who had a problem with us have graduated and gone now, so they are off campus. I'll be OK. And if I don't go back and play, I'll lose my scholarship."

"You don't have to go back because of that, Jaden. We'll figure out something else. If you're not comfortable going back, please don't do it because of the scholarship. I'll figure out the money. You don't have to play. You can just attend like a regular student."

"Dad, it's alright. It's something that I can do to help, and I want to play," he says. "I need to do a lot of rehab work on this stupid leg after I get this boot off. I'll be able to use the school's facilities to get back into playing shape and do physical therapy. I won't be able to play when the season starts, but hopefully by mid-season, I'll be set."

I marvel at the thought he has put into this decision. It's the right thing for him, but also a relief financially.

"I'm proud of you for facing that challenge," I say. "I

think going back to U of O is a good choice, but I need you to know that being here with us over the last few weeks was only difficult because of other people, not because of you."

"I know why you got arrested last night, Dad," he says quietly. "If it wasn't for me, that wouldn't have happened."

"Last night's issue was between two drunk old men, and I wasn't one of them. I just got in the middle of it by accident."

"I know they were fighting about me."

"Yes, but they're fighting their own battles with each other and the world only they see. It's a much larger issue than just you or any of us."

"He was defending me, Dad. He came and talked to me this morning after he couldn't find you. He said you left the police station before him."

"My ride back took me on a little detour. What else did he say?"

"Not much. He was worried about being overbooked and if we could vacate the rooms."

"All business, that guy."

I never wanted to stay at the Westcott, but I didn't have a choice after the meth lab fiasco. Now, the choice is being made for me again. This time, there is no way in hell we're coming back here. Once we pack up, we're gone for good.

"I want things to be back the way they used to be before Mom died," Jaden says, his shoulders shaking ever so slightly with a sob. "It wasn't like this."

Mason and Paige are sitting on a bench next to us in the courtyard and they both nod in agreement. I'm sad for them and disappointed in myself. It's my mistakes that have impacted them so much—it's my fault. I should have done more. I could have done better.

"Guys, I know this has been hard, and I'm blessed to have great kids like you three who love each other and stick up for each other. We're going to get through this, and we're going to be better for it. It definitely doesn't feel like it right now, not by a mile, but we're going to be OK. I promise you that."

Tears come to my eyes, and soon all of us are crying. With all the changes—losing the house, the money, leaving schools and friends—I know I haven't done a good job helping the kids through their grief over losing Tina. When you don't have a roof over your head or any means to support yourself, it's tough to deal with your feelings, let alone those of other people.

I've ignored their needs. I need to do a better job for them.

CHAPTER 43

"Homeless again, huh?" Christy asks, stepping onto the porch of the McArthur house. Paige greets Sophie at the front door, and they head to the rusty swing set in the backyard to play while Christy and I talk.

"It's kind of my thing now," I say.

"You're going to make it a habit?" she asks, a sly smile on her face.

"It's getting to be quite the routine around here. Keeps us on our toes, no doubt."

She walks past me on the porch and brushes her hand against mine. Not by accident, but also so no one would see the gesture but the two of us. I want to grasp her hand and pull her to me, but not with the kids around. This subtle touch tells me that she feels the same.

I explain to Christy what happened last night at the Ranger and how Dad had booted us from the Westcott rooms.

"So, you didn't talk to him about it?" she asks. "He didn't even tell you directly."

"No. Honestly, after last night, I'm just not sure that there is ever going to be a way to get through to him. I would have just gotten mad, and that wouldn't do anyone any good. I can't believe this is the guy who raised me. How can we be so different?"

I realize I hadn't told her about the trip Darla and I made to Seaside, which was the reason Dad talked with Jaden about the rooms and not with me.

If she's shocked or appalled, she hides it well as I retell the story.

"The best I can figure is that my dad started taking the camping trips with me every month and Mom filled in the time with Maureen, and they started, I don't know? Dating? An affair? I'm not sure what to call it. Then she stuck Darla in the middle. I need to talk to Mom and figure it out. I'm sure Dad found out, and that's why they got divorced."

"That's a lot of re-written history you got to experience in one day. That's got to be hard," she says. "How are you taking it?"

I shrug. "What's done is done. I can't change it."

"But that doesn't mean you don't want to understand it, though?"

"I'm not sure I see what you mean."

"James, it's just that you have this way of accepting these monumental things that have happened in your life and then just move on like it was meant to be that way all along."

"I'm not sure I follow."

"How can you not see this? Tina got pregnant and suddenly, your ambitions and dreams disappear, and you become a stay-at-home dad. No complaints. Life-changing. Your wife dies, and you lose everything. So, you find a job and a home, well… sort of home. When that falls through, you figure out something else and end up here, again with nothing. Now the entire history of your parents' relationship is in question, and you toss up your hands and say, 'what's done is done.' I just don't get that."

I've always considered my ability to roll with the punches to be an asset. I've adapted, and it's been best for everyone.

"All of that is true, but what else am I supposed to do?" I say. "I'm making the best of the hand I was dealt. I don't really appreciate being criticized for it."

"James, it's not criticism. In fact, I admire your ability to compartmentalize because I can't do that. I don't know how. I get stuck on something and can't move on mentally.

That's why I stayed with Malcolm for so long. I knew the bad, but I was afraid of the unknown. It took me a really long time to work up the nerve to finally leave him."

"You're really brave to do what you did."

"You mean to stay with him forever and then leave him without really confronting him about what he's done to me? That's not brave. I just hope my attorney is good. I never want to see him again. I don't know what he'll do."

"Still no word?"

"No, and I know that he's been served the papers—the attorney's office called and told me. So, I'm stuck waiting for my life-changing moment to end. I can't just go with the flow like you can. I can't move on."

"Maybe I'm just good at hiding it. The emotions, I mean," I say. "Just because I don't say it out loud doesn't mean that I don't feel it deep down inside."

Other than Christy, I've never had anyone I could really talk to about my struggles—not the other stay-at-home moms. I didn't talk to Seth, at least not about the marriage stuff. My friend circle didn't extend very far.

"James, we're in a different place now, OK? Just know that you can still talk to me about this stuff. I think right now, in this weird situation we're in, we need to tell each other everything. Good, bad, or indifferent. I know that I'm going to need you as I go through this mess with Malcolm, and I don't hold it together as well as you do."

She kisses me quickly, signaling the end of our discussion. For a brief moment, I'm not sure it happened because it seemed so natural and was gone in an instant. I want to hold her. To take her inside the house and lock the door, but that's not the place we're in. Not yet, and maybe not ever. I don't know. I want to be able to talk to her about everything happening in my life. Lord knows I can't do it alone.

I want to tell Christy that I forgive Tina for what she did. I may not understand it, but I need to forgive so I can really move on. I want Christy to know that I have things I need to work on personally, too. It's not just about compartmentalizing. I was not a perfect husband and casting all the blame for my rotten marriage on Tina is wrong. It will take time for me to work through those issues, but I want Christy by my side when I do it.

But I don't say any of those things. I keep up the fake wall that everything is fine, and Christy doesn't press me.

"I need to get going to the beach," she says. "I promised the girls front row seats to the stunt shows. You want to come?"

"I would, but I need to get this place habitable for the night."

"About that. I talked to my mom," she says. "She said you and the kids are all welcome to stay with us for as long as you need."

"That's very kind of her, but I have to decline."

"And why is that?"

"Two reasons. First, I'm about fed up with staying in someone else's territory. Even though this house is owned by my dad, at least he's not here to monitor me."

"You think my mom would monitor you?"

"No, but that leads me to the second reason. I'm not sure I could leave you alone if we were staying under the same roof. And with so many alert ears around, despite my best efforts, I believe I'd be discovered sneaking into your room after lights out."

"So practical." She gives me a wink. "Maybe I'll have to sneak down here one night then."

"I'll get you a key immediately."

As we round the side of the house so Christy can collect the girls, I hear their squeals and giggles as they ride the swings back and forth.

Standing behind the swing, taking turns pushing each girl, is Mrs. Eifert with a broad smile across her face. A container of chocolate chip cookies sits on the nearby sawhorse.

"This old swing set hasn't seen this much action in

decades," she says. "I just had to come over and join them. And I had these extra cookies I knew two hungry little girls would love to try."

The girls swing and munch on the cookies. I introduce Mrs. Eifert to Christy and explain that Christy is from Shoreline, too.

"Jimmy, don't let this aged exterior fool you. My memory is in tip-top shape. I got to know hundreds of kids when I was a secretary at the school, Christy and you included. And Seth, of course."

"You remember all those kids?" Christy asks. "That's amazing."

"Heavens no, and besides, I know your mother, Karen, from the school guild. I saw her just last week, and she told me you were in town for the holiday."

Christy laughs. "Of course, that explains it."

She continues to push the girls on the swings, alternating between the two of them.

"It's wonderful to see these swings get some use again," Mrs. Eifert says. "They've been just sitting here idle for so long—as long as this house has been empty. Several swing sets popped up on this street when the park at Saint Ann Square closed. Before that, all the neighborhood kids would just go there to play."

She's right. We were there all the time playing with friends. It was a different time, far out of the watchful eye of our parents. That wouldn't happen today, and not just because the playground is gone. You simply can't let your children roam the neighborhood freely, assuming if they stay within close proximity to home, they'll be safe.

"We were there all the time," I say.

"And now you'll be there again," she says. "All the time."

"How do you mean?"

"With those awful condos you're building, of course."

"That's all my dad, not me," I say.

"Oh, I just assumed it was you he was referring to."

"About the condos? How do you mean?"

"He and I talked a while back. You know, he would stay next door sometimes. Escape the tourists, he'd say. Right when he started building those monstrosities. We'd sit out here and chat some nights. Said he'd partnered with family to make it happen. You were a builder, and I just assumed. Guess I was wrong."

"I haven't built anything in a long time, if you don't count this," I say, motioning to the project behind me. "And Dad definitely didn't partner with me on the condos. My mom would have killed me if I had."

"Oh, I guess that's true, dear. She certainly fought it tooth and nail," she said. "She's a tough one."

Mrs. Eifert hands Christy the container of cookies. "Make sure these girls eat every last one of these cookies. They are too skinny," she says, then turns to the girls. "When you finish your dinner, of course."

They nod and giggle, knowing full well that they will inhale the cookies when given a chance. Yet, they promise to eat their dinner first.

Mrs. Eifert returns to her house, and we head inside so the girls can use the bathroom before heading to the festival.

"Why do you think she assumed you and your dad did the condos together?" Christy asks.

"She probably just got confused. Dad said he was going to remodel this house but never started the project. Then I show up and start work on it. She just got the conversations mixed up. I mean, she thought he tore down the playground, but the church removed it years before he bought the land."

"No, she might have been confused, but I don't think that is why," she says. "She said he partnered with… Oh, my God. James, that's it!"

She excitedly explains her theory about my father. It couldn't be.

"There's no way he'd do that," I reply, doubting myself as I say it. "He wouldn't have."

"If there's one thing I know to be true, it's that people

are capable of anything if they want it enough."

There's a pit in my stomach, and I feel as though I'm going to throw up. My gut says she's right, even if I want her to be wrong with every fiber of my being.

CHAPTER 44

"If you can find a seat on the patio, go for it, dude, but it's a bit packed because of the festival. Pretty sure you're going to be standing," Seth says, handing me a Rogue IPA that's thick and hoppy. "Are you sure you don't want to kick it back here with me? We're all caught up on orders momentarily, no thanks to my useless short-order cook who called in sick on the busiest day of the year."

"Thanks, I just need a few minutes and thought killing time with a beer would be nice before tackling the rest of my day," I lie.

"Cool, cool. I know how it is. You're welcome here anytime, except on old man boxing night. It gets a little rowdy. You know how it is."

"You're hilarious."

"If anyone gives you a dirty look, just call me over first so I can clear out all the glassware before you guys throw down, OK?"

"You'll be my first call."

A waitress gives Seth a new order to take into the kitchen. "Guess I better get to work," he says. He pats me on the shoulder and disappears into the back.

I'm not exactly in the beer-sipping mood, but I need to plant myself outside the Westcott without being noticed to see if my father leaves the inn. I've got to do a little digging, and he can't be around for it.

I settle into a spot standing next to a long table of rowdy college kids. They don't pay me any mind, and they aren't here to watch kites. I try to blend in.

It was an hour past guest check-in time, which is right about the time my father would typically stroll the boardwalk to stretch his legs in the afternoon. With the festival going on, the boardwalk is a nightmare. Still, I'm counting on my father's habitual routine to be enough to get him out of the Westcott.

I take side glances at the stunt kites to the west but keep an eye on the inn as I drain my first beer, then my second. Over an hour later, he finally emerges onto the porch and hands a set of keys to his front desk clerk before charging inland down Laneda Avenue.

I exit the Ranger and cross the street, rounding the building to enter the Westcott from the back. I go in through the kitchen. There's a narrow set of stairs for staff that are roped off from guest use. I ascend the stairs to the third floor, unseen by anyone.

There are three rooms on the third floor—all suites—but two have views of the ocean and modest balconies. But I'm not going to those rooms. Dad would never reside in a room he could make any money from.

I approach the door and punch in the four-digit code on the lock, praying that it's still the same after all these years. The light blinks green and the latch releases. I enter the room and shut the door behind me.

My father's bed is perfectly made, matching the exact specifications of the guest rooms. The bedspread corners are pulled tight, and a gray wool blanket is draped over the end. Three pillows, each of varying firmness, rest against the iron headboard. A round throw pillow adorns the center of the bed. I wonder why in the world my father bothers to make the bed in this way when he's the only one behind this locked door who will ever see and appreciate it.

A red wingback chair sits in one corner next to a handmade wooden end table. Well, that's a surprise. I'm not exactly sure what to make of the end table, considering I made it in our old woodworking shop on McArthur. My father keeps my work in his bedroom. Curious.

I move around the bed to my actual destination—his office behind yet another door.

My father's office is a cluttered desk, a few shelves, and a set of file cabinets under a dormer window. The office does not keep up the clean esthetic of the bedroom. It's a mess with papers and folders strewn about on the floor, the chair, and the desk itself.

I pause before entering. Am I really doing this? The more appropriate question is whether I think so little of my father that I *must* do this? But that one's easy. Yes, I do think that little of him.

I flip the light switch and start digging, knowing that I only have a short period of time before Dad returns from his walk. I have no vantage point from the window to see the comings and goings from the inn's front or back. Dad will immediately come back to this room upon returning to change out of his walking shoes. I probably have about ten minutes.

The file cabinets are a bust—I only find tax documents and legal filings for various lawsuits against the town and the showdown with my mom. There are some invoices for work around the Westcott, but that's not helpful.

One drawer was filled with records for frequent guests. Little note cards detail their room preferences—lighting, temperature, and wine selection during the wine and cheese hour. There are random notes about guest's families, political leanings, and the like.

Dad started keeping detailed notes on the guests after a minor disaster occurred. One husband decided to book a room with his mistress, and then again with his wife the following weekend. The staff remembered him but made an honest mistake by graciously thanking the couple for visiting two weekends in a row. So detailed notes are kept.

The desk drawers are unlocked but are void of anything

useful. Then, on the shelf, I spot a leather-bound accounting ledger.

Bingo.

* * *

I'm sitting in the wingback chair, legs crossed comfortably when I hear the clicking of the code being entered into the door. The nob turns and Dad enters, not seeing me at first. He's startled and takes a little jump backward when he sees me, though I wasn't trying to hide.

"James, what the hell are you doing in here?"

"Just some light reading," I say. "You know this chair is really quite comfortable, and I like the end table. Nice touch."

He sees the ledger on the table but ignores it. "I don't have time for your games, I have a business to run."

"All business. That's you, Dad. No question. Since the beginning. All business. Damn the rest of us."

"I don't know what you think you're talking about, but it's about time for you to leave," he says.

"Dad, I really, truly want you to make that happen. Go ahead. Make me leave, in any way you can." I stand, open my arms as if to say, "This is your chance, old man. Take your best shot."

"I'm not doing this with you," he mutters.

"I thought violence was the answer. No? Not anymore?"

He doesn't reply.

"I sometimes wonder, Dad. What would have happened between us if I would have bowed to the pressure you put on me and stayed in Shoreline to run this inn with you? What if I was under your thumb every day? Living by your set of arcane rules and world views."

"At least you'd have a steady job—a career to be proud of, unlike now."

"Sure, that's one way to look at it," I say. "But what about you? What do you have to show for all your efforts?"

"You're going to have to do better than that."

"Let me spell it out for you," I say with a certainty I've rarely felt since returning to Shoreline. "I know what you and Tina did, and I know that you no longer own the Westcott… I do."

CHAPTER 45

Mrs. Eifert was right. Dad made a deal with our family. Still, neither Christy nor I knew exactly to what extent. The deal he made wasn't for the condos, it was for the Westcott.

Dad's ledger showed large deposits into the Westcott accounts, matching two of the amounts Tina cashed out of our investment portfolio. This wasn't a secret he was illegally hiding. His accounting ledger said where the funds originated, plain as day.

My stomach churns with the knowledge of what my father did. The records show what happened, but I still don't understand why.

"Just tell me how it happened, Dad," I plead. "You owe me that much. You've seen your granddaughter kicked out of her school. We were evicted from our home. Our belongings were repossessed. We are homeless, for God's sake. And you had the nerve to scold me in my own kitchen about losing our house. What did you say? Foreclosure was a first for our family? Well, why do you think I'm broke? You said nothing! You watched it all happen and judged me? How did you think it was going to turn out? That you'd never be found out? How in the hell did you think you could get away with taking everything Tina and I had built?"

"She earned that money, not you," he asserts with little emotion.

"Screw you. That's not accurate in the slightest. We were

married, partners. We split our responsibilities like couples do. Just because I didn't bankroll our family doesn't make me a lesser part of it. It's not all about money and power, Dad. God, how can you not see that? What is broken inside you to make you like this? Never mind, I already know that, too."

He sits down at the foot of the bed, rubs his temples, and reluctantly begins talking.

"You've got it all twisted like you tend to do," he says. "Tina came to see me. I didn't seek her out. It was over two years ago. She said she wanted to strengthen your family connection to Shoreline. To do something for you. I didn't know what she meant at first. She said something about not feeling like part of our family, like an outsider. That maybe if you two owned a place in Shoreline, you could come here more. She said you were always happier when you were here."

"That sounds like a line of bull."

"Hey, you asked me," he says. "I'll tell you what happened. I can't make you believe me. I can't control that."

"She wanted to buy a place in Shoreline and never mentioned it to me?"

"That's what it sounds like, now doesn't it?"

"So how did you take nearly $2 million dollars from her?"

"Don't make it sound so sinister. This was legal, and we signed paperwork on it. We agreed that she'd be a silent partner in the Saint Ann Square condos. We knew your mother would be livid with all of us if Tina invested in the condos. So, Tina asked that we keep it quiet—to surprise you, too."

"The first $420,000 was a surprise for me, from our own investments?" I ask.

"She didn't seem to blush at it. It was a down payment for one of the condo units. It's still there. When they are done, the first unit is yours."

"More bull. $400,000 doesn't buy an oceanfront condo."

"No, it doesn't. It was a down payment."

"And you needed the down payment to keep building."

"Yes, because the costs just got out of control. With the attorney's fees and the environmental impact study that the town made me complete, the money was gone just as quick as it came. I couldn't keep building."

"So, you asked for more from Tina?" I ask.

"Not a first. I tried to get financing, but I was too far underwater. The banks wouldn't loan me the money to keep going. If I didn't get funds from somewhere, the original down payment she made would be lost. The project would have gone under."

"I don't believe you did this for her financial wellbeing. You threw good money after bad chasing your pet project."

"No, that's not what happened. I told Tina exactly what was going on. I laid it all out there for her in writing. She was a smart woman. She reviewed the books and decided it was a good bet."

"Not true. She didn't invest in the condos. She invested in the Westcott."

"She bought an ownership stake in the Westcott from me. She got something significant out of her investment. There was no way she'd lose. I moved that investment out of the Westcott to fund the final stages of construction on the condos. Everybody won."

"Doesn't exactly feel like winning," I say. "So, let me get this straight, she owns, or owned, the Westcott, not you."

"She put it in a shell company, but yes. Sixty percent of the Westcott."

"Whose names are on the shell company?" I ask.

"You know who."

"Yes, but I want you to say it."

"Tina and James Bell."

"And we own one of your condos, too."

"The majority share of one of them, yes."

"And you decided that it was best to never share this information with me, huh?"

"There you go again, twisting it," he says, waving his arms in frustration. "I was never going to keep it from you. When I went to your house the day you moved out, I was there in your kitchen to tell you everything, but you kicked me out before I could say anything. You said you didn't want anything to do with me, so I took you at your word."

"You have got to be kidding with this. Really? I seem to recall your focus was on Jaden's sexuality, not your investment partnership with Tina."

"Well, you know now. So, what's the difference?"

"What's the difference? I own this place, Dad. You weren't generous by allowing my family to stay in your crappy rooms in the courtyard. They were my rooms to have. Then this morning you kicked us out of them so you could rent them to tourists?"

"This place still has to turn a profit, James," he says. "You should know that. It was for your own good."

"Your version of what is good for other people is warped and dirty. It's no wonder Mom left you."

"Watch your mouth, boy," he spits. "I'm still your father."

"You stopped acting like my father a long time ago, Mitch," I bark at him. "I'm just sorry it took me so long to see and understand it. You only care about yourself, no one else—not me and my family. Not Mom. Not Darla and her family. Only Mitch."

"Everything I did was for your own good, or what Tina asked me to do," he says. "You can spin your own yarn about it, but I know the truth."

"I want to believe you, and if you hadn't kept it from me for all these months after she died, maybe I could believe you. We could have saved the house and kept the kids in school. But you lied and made a terrible situation ten times worse because of your own selfishness."

"You know everything now. I have nothing to hide," he says. "We can move on from this."

Was it remorse that flashed across his face? Or was it

hope?

"No, Dad, we can't move on from this. What you did to my family is unforgivable."

"You can't keep my grandchildren from me," he whispers.

I didn't expect that to be his primary concern, but I can leverage it.

"If seeing the kids is your primary concern, then you're going to have to earn back that right, and it's going to cost you. Dearly."

"Anything," he says with a nod. The bluster and fury he came into the room with are long gone.

Tina bought us a second home in Shoreline but didn't tell me. She then hid the transaction and purchased the Westcott. Again, not telling me at all. At the same time, Tina had already lost her job. Could she have wanted the Westcott to be our source of income? That can't be it. The inn is profitable, but nowhere close to what she was making at Goodwin Labs.

"OK, you told me what happened, at least your version of it. Now tell me why."

"Why what?"

"Tell me why she would agree to any of this? To put all of our money in this place?"

"First, I had no idea that she was cashing out your savings and investments for this deal. We never talked about your financial situation, only mine. I wouldn't have agreed to it if I had known how leveraged she was financially."

"Then why did she do it?" I ask.

"I already answered your question. Tina was an outsider to our family. She wanted a way in, and I gave it to her."

CHAPTER 46

Mom is in the kitchen of the Evergreen preparing trays of sliced meats, cheeses, vegetables, and assorted crackers for her guests' afternoon refreshment upon their return from the festival. She works in silence, focused on the simple task before her, one she's completed thousands of times. She doesn't see me in the entryway.

I wonder what she really thinks of me. Why would she hold her secrets from me for all this time? Why couldn't I know who she truly was? What was wrong with me? What made me untrustworthy? My own mother doesn't want me to know her.

Jaden's actions were similar. He hid his true self from me. Why?

Mom finally sees me. "Let me put these trays out, then we can sit out back and talk," she says casually, like she didn't have a care in the world. Like I wasn't again going to have my entire world turned upside down.

I head outside to the courtyard and grab a bottle of water from the metal bucket filled with drinks and ice meant for guests.

The courtyard is empty. All the guests are at the festival.

I sit on the soft cushion of a wicker chair shaded by an old wooden arch covered in ivy. The cushion's easy give is a stark contrast to the Shoreline drunk tank's hard floor where this incredibly long day started. I drink the water and let my body rest for a few minutes. I need it.

Mom is holding a glass of white wine when she eases into the chair across from me.

"I saw Maureen Ellington today up in Seaside," I say. "She thought I was Dad. Looked like she was going to deck me for a minute there."

She is not shocked by this news, which means she already knows Darla took me there.

"I'm not surprised by her reaction," Mom says. "No love lost between those two."

She leaves the comment with no elaboration.

"Thanks for bailing us out of jail," I offer.

"I had to pull some strings on that one, but it wasn't exactly a bail sort of situation anyway," she says. "As far as the authorities are concerned, it never happened."

She takes a long gulp of wine like she's pushing hard to get to the bottom of the glass.

We're nibbling at the edges of what this conversation should be about, though neither of us are willing to be the first to thrust into the heart of the matter. She's held her secrets this long, and I have a feeling she'd keep it up if given a chance.

"I went to Maureen's apartment, Mom," I say. "I saw her photographs. Pictures of you and her together. You know that stuff doesn't bother me—I proved that with Jaden—but what bothers me is that you lied to me. And it seems like I was the only one who didn't know. That hurts more than you can imagine, Mom. That you couldn't trust me? That I wasn't worthy."

"Stop," she says. "That's not… that's just not true. I didn't want to do it this way, James. You've got to believe me. I didn't want to hide who I was. Who I am. Not to my own children."

"Then, why?" I ask. "Why not just say it? That's all it would have taken."

"It's bigger than that. It's complicated."

"Then explain it to me because from where I'm standing,

you've lied to me for most of my life, and I can't figure out why that would be."

"This isn't easy for me," she says, her eyes wet. "Please don't make it any harder."

I try to temper my frustration. I need her to talk to me, not make her shut down.

"Mom, I'm not mad, I'm confused. This conversation won't change you and me, other than me getting to know who you really are. It's going to be alright. I just want to know."

She takes a deep breath and looks like she might bolt back into The Evergreen for more wine and delay this further, but she doesn't.

"Your father and I met when we were really young—only in high school. Things were different back then. It was the late 70s. The country wasn't like it is today. What you did and who you loved was expected to follow a set path forward. That never felt right to me, even when I was much younger, but I held those feelings down. I didn't want to be different. I couldn't be different. No, that's not right… I didn't understand how I felt because it didn't conform to what my friends said or did. So, I pretended I felt like them because it was expected of me.

"Then, I met your father. He was charming and smart. The first person who I felt like I had a real connection with. Intellectually, we were always on the same wavelength. We enjoyed the same things. We had mutual friends. We were a couple like it was supposed to be. We had all the stuff you'd expect to see from the outside, but something was always missing for me. But I didn't know what it was, and I kept those feelings to myself. This went on for years. I still didn't understand, or I wouldn't admit to myself what was really happening."

"Did you talk to Dad about how you were feeling?"

"Back then, of course not. Could you imagine? Yes, eventually, I talked to him about it, and it went about as bad as you could expect. But I'm getting ahead of myself. I was never with anyone except for your father. I was content with him, and I was satisfied that what we had was going to be enough. This went on for years. We married, and eventually, you came along. You were the best little boy. My little buddy and I loved you so much. Then we had Darla, and I was overjoyed. A boy and a girl. I thought that it couldn't get any better. I had a good husband and two wonderful, bright children. I had everything I was supposed to have. But that feeling was always in the back of my mind that I couldn't love your father how he wanted me to. I couldn't love him how he loved me."

She takes a moment to compose herself.

"And then I met someone else, and I finally realized that I had only been going through the motions, trying to be the person that the world said I should be."

"Maureen Ellington," I say.

"Yes. And it's not like you might… James, I don't know how to say these things to you."

"I'm not judging you, Mom. Yes, this feels awkward, but it doesn't change anything between us."

"OK. Alright," she says, forging on. "I felt like something broken was fixed inside me when I met Maureen. I finally had the emotions to fit the words I had been using in my marriage for fifteen years. I felt like, oh, so that's what love is supposed to feel like. Does that make sense?"

"Yes, it does make sense," I say, thinking of my feelings for Christy, which at the same time, makes me feel ashamed for not first thinking of Tina.

"Maureen was out with her sexuality, but very private. She had married a man too, in her twenties, but it only lasted a few years, and she was alone for a long time. She understood who she was much earlier than I did. So, I was in a very difficult spot. I finally knew who I was and what I wanted, but I was married with two adoring children and a husband who loved me. I couldn't tear that apart. That would have destroyed me. What that would have done to you and Darla, I couldn't imagine. I just… I had to keep acting married."

"What do you mean, act? You and Dad divorced. It ended."

"Yes, but not for a very long time. Years later. I was confused, frustrated, and I had decisions to make. Decisions that would change the course of the lives of everyone in our family. It wasn't something to decide on my own. So, I told your father everything. Every last feeling, emotion, and action. I laid it all out for him."

"This is what didn't go well."

"Right. It did not go well. I don't regret how I approached him, but the brutal honesty was a little much. You know your father. I knew he'd be furious. So furious that he might never speak to me again and take the decision entirely out of my hands. I'd sabotaged our marriage, and he'd be the one to end it. I was too scared to do it myself."

"And so, he ended it?"

"No, you and he went camping. A lot."

* * *

"I thought at first that your father was taking you and Darla and leaving town. But he wouldn't speak to me. He was so infuriated and embarrassed that his wife was interested in another woman. I didn't want to do that to him. I told him I still loved him, but just different from before. All he said was that he'd be back in two days. He grabbed his gear and took you camping."

I can't recall the first trip. They all run together in my memory. I never asked Dad why we went. It was just so routine. I never thought to question it.

Mom explained that Dad came back from that first weekend trip and proposed a compromise. He did not want to get a divorce. He loved her, no matter what. He loved her so much that he was willing to give up time so she could "figure this whole thing out." He thought that if he gave her one weekend a month to explore her feelings, that she would realize it was all just a fad. A passing fancy. He expected Mom to return to him.

This way Darla and I wouldn't have to be victims of divorce. And he loved her still. She loved him as well. That would be enough to make this strange arrangement work.

Mom and Dad made an agreement for the sake of all the years they had been together. She felt like she owed him.

So, they tried. Dad and I would leave on a Friday night and return on a Sunday evening. Mom and Maureen would spend time together while we were away.

"But Darla knew. Why didn't I?"

"Neither of you were supposed to know. Your father wouldn't allow it. It was his one condition—that you two never knew what we agreed to."

"But I saw the pictures, Mom. Darla was there."

"Shoreline is a small town. It's very difficult to find a place for your young daughter to go for a solid weekend once a month and have no questions asked. You were whisked away by your father. Darla would stay at a friend's house at first, but eventually, she didn't want to go anymore and I couldn't find a good excuse to keep making her. So, I kept her home one weekend, and she just hung out with Aunt Maureen and me. We had a wonderful time. Darla knew I was with Maureen when you and Dad were gone. Of course, she was too young to know the details then."

"But she did know, Mom. She knew she had to keep it a secret."

"I never asked her to do that," Mom says briskly, recoiling from the suggestion.

"But she did for years. Until this morning when she finally told me. Have you had this same conversation with her?"

She looks away.

"You need to," I say. "She needs to hear it from you. She feels guilty about keeping this family secret, even though everyone knew it but me."

"I know. I will," she says. "Soon."

Mom explained that Maureen's silly forgetfulness quickly became serious, and she was diagnosed with early dementia before turning forty.

"She wasn't herself anymore. She'd live in several worlds. Some days she'd think she was back with her husband. Other days, she'd think she and I were a full-time couple, forgetting our relationship's extremely unique circumstance. I told myself that I could continue in that relationship until you and Darla were out of the house, and I almost made it, too. You were in college. It was just Darla at home, and she already knew what was happening. Your father and I were not really even together anymore. He never thought the agreement we made was more than just a trial run. He thought I'd come running back to him after I explored, but I couldn't. And when Maureen started to get sick, he thought I'd come back to him but I didn't. Our lives had been divided for so long that there was no repairing it."

"So, you finally divorced Dad, even though you knew you couldn't be with Maureen because the illness took her and any chance you two had to be together?"

"Yes, it was the hardest thing I've had to do in my life, James, but I knew it was right to end it with your father. To be apart from him for good. I didn't do it so I could be with Maureen."

"But then you bought The Evergreen with Maureen and Susan, right next door to the Westcott?"

"I still love your father, James," she says. "It's just different now. He's a good man. Our lives have been unconventional for so long and I don't know it any other way."

"You've never really been apart, even after all of this."

"I'm not sure that's accurate. We live different lives. We don't agree on much anymore. He doesn't answer to me, and I don't answer to him. We're grandparents to four wonderful grandchildren, and we want them to know the good parts of Grandma and Grandpa Bell. There's just no sense in holding on to the past wrongs and slights at this point in our lives. Who can live like that?"

I ponder that—holding on to past wrongs. I think of Dad and Tina. I want to talk to Mom about it. Did she know that Dad is the reason our home was foreclosed on? Why we are flat broke? It's not possible that she would have allowed that and stayed silent.

It's improbable that Dad would have told Mom about the money or the new ownership of the Westcott—he's too proud. After thinking it over, I decide not to have that conversation with Mom right now. If she did know about it, it would hurt too much. For now, I want to avoid that betrayal. I may be burying my head in the sand, but I'm holding out hope that one of my parents is still a decent person. If I'm wrong, I'll delay knowing for sure, at least for a while.

I also want to tell her about Christy. She's just bared her most intimate secrets with me, and I feel as though I should respond in kind. I have a secret too, but one not nearly on the same scale as her own. I could ask for her advice. Just talking it out would be a benefit. I'm not sure how to date. I haven't courted a woman since college. Tina and I never dated. We simply had a child together and made it work.

I guess dating is not the right word, not for now. Christy is still married. That needs to figure itself out before anything between us can develop. At least that's what I keep trying to convince myself each night so I don't sneak away and go see her. Not yet. The time isn't right, and there's no rush. We both want the same thing. We just need time to get there.

"Mom, do you think it was a mistake for me to marry Tina?"

"Why would you ask such a question? Especially now that she's gone?" Mom asks.

"It's just that you married Dad so young, and it wasn't what you wanted. I married Tina, and while the circumstances were different, we too didn't exactly fit together, even if we lasted for nearly twenty years."

"You had a child together, there was something extraordinary there that held you two together," she says. "Of course, in the beginning it was hard to see you commit to Tina, a person you were still getting to know, but you made it work. So much so that you had more children together and built a life."

"But that's just it. Tina and I would never have been a couple if not for our children."

"You're thinking about it in reverse. You wouldn't have your three children if not for Tina. How could that be a bad thing? Were they a mistake?"

"No, of course not."

"Exactly. Just like you and Darla were not a mistake for your father and me, despite everything that's happened."

I can't help but question my choices, even if I agree that there's little to be gained in rehashing them.

"So, what happened with Maureen in the end?" I ask.

She doesn't respond right away, and I can see that she's struggling with her words. She picks up her empty wine glass again and shakes it like wine might reappear like magic.

"When it was clear that she would never recover from all that was ailing her, she ended it. During her lucid moments, she and I would talk. She thought she was protecting me by ending it. She said that I didn't have to live with what she would become. And she knew that I wouldn't end it, so she did it for me. She called it mercy for the sake of all that we had shared together."

"It must have been hard to accept that," I say.

"I didn't accept that. I still don't. Who is she to protect me from what I want?"

"But she moved to the memory center in Seaside."

"Despite my protests. But in the end, she needed full-time care. Care that I couldn't provide."

"Do you still see her?" I ask.

"Yes, but it's not the same. Susan and I go together. It's easier on Maureen when we show up as a friend group and not just me alone. She doesn't return to our days as a couple, just the friendship that the three of us shared."

"She really hates Dad," I say.

"I'm well aware of that."

"Were you and Susan ever a couple? She and I talked briefly when Jaden came out. She told me how difficult it can be. Because I didn't know anyone who was gay, or I thought I didn't. I never knew of the internal struggles."

"Susan and I were, and still are, just friends."

I blush despite myself. This is an immensely odd conversation.

Our attention is drawn to the sound of a screen door slamming closed and then Paige bounds down the steps of The Evergreen toward us. I look to see if Christy and Sophie are behind her. Maybe this is the right time to tell Mom about Christy. Will she know something is going on between us? I wouldn't put it past her. But as Paige gets closer, it's clear that she's alone.

"Hey, hon, how were your front row seats to the festival?"

"Great. They had the long dragons this year and had them fight in the air. It was cool."

Paige goes on to describe the elaborate dragon scene and each of her favorite kites. I've seen the festival performance every year since I was younger than her, so it's easy to take for granted just how mesmerizing the shows can be. I'm glad Paige has such enthusiasm for it.

"Where's Sophie and her mom?" I ask. "I thought you all were going to get ice cream at that place on Chinook Street that you like after the show."

"We were going to, but Sophie's dad said they had to go right away and didn't have time for ice cream."

My heart skips a beat. "Sophie's dad?" I ask, trying to quell the panic in my voice. Why would Malcolm be there?

"Yeah, he didn't have a seat, so he just sat on the sand," she says.

"And they left with him? Like they went back to Sophie's grandma's house?"

She shrugs.

I kneel in front of her and put my hands on her shoulders. I'm struggling and failing to stay calm. I'm mere inches from her face.

"Paige, it's very important. Where did they go when they left?"

She winces at the intensity of my question, ducking her head in an instinctual reaction.

"Paige, I need to know. Right now."

Mom interjects, pulling Paige away by the arm.

"James, you're scaring her. She doesn't know. What in the world has gotten into you?"

I know that Christy's abuse isn't my story to tell. I can't be the one to share that with anyone.

"Mom, there are things you don't know. Nobody knows. Christy filed for divorce from Malcolm, and it's not good. Let's just say that he's not supposed to be here, and there's no way Christy would willingly go anywhere with him right now."

"Oh, dear, that's awful. That poor woman is such a sweetheart."

Yeah, Mom, I know, I think to myself. I'm totally in love with her and now filled with dread over where she and Sophie could be and what Malcolm would do to them.

"Paige, I didn't mean to scare you," I say. "I'm sorry I did that. I'm just worried about finding my friend, and I think you might have been the last person to see them. Did she say anything when they left? Did they drop you off here in a car or did you walk?"

"Sophie's dad drove," she says.

"Can you remember anything that Sophie's parents said in the car?"

"I don't think so. They were just talking about traffic on the highway."

"Like the highway out of town?"

She shrugs again. She's eight years old. Why would an adult conversation have been memorable to her at all?

"You said that you guys didn't have time for ice cream, right?" I ask.

"Yes, because Sophie's dad didn't want to get stuck in traffic going home."

He's taking them home.

CHAPTER 47

Tina and I had countless dinners at the Woods' home over the years. While not refined and challenged in a professional environment, Christy's skills in the kitchen were exceptional, and she enjoyed cooking for friends and family. My version of cooking for guests usually meant something grilled on the barbeque, maybe a potato salad on the side. Not exactly gourmet.

So, Christy would cook and the couples would share a meal together. These occasions were the few times I had an opportunity to converse with Malcolm away from the bleachers of a youth baseball game. I know now that Christy's version of the man was sanitized for her own protection. Keeping her privacy meant maintaining her safety, too. I'm embarrassed that I hadn't seen who he was, despite our limited interactions. Even more so, I'm embarrassed that she didn't feel comfortable coming to me earlier.

Malcolm was always friendly and talkative. He treated his job at the airline like a badge of honor and often spoke about his time in the sky and all the destinations to which he navigated a plane. He always referred to himself as an aviator, not a pilot. He provided detailed descriptions of airports in foreign countries with crumbling infrastructure or inadequate runway length for maneuvering newer, larger commercial planes.

"They had to build new terminals for the new Airbus we were flying into South Asia," I recall him saying once. "Damn thing was so big, only the big boy airports could handle her. Here in the U.S., it was no problem, but in Asia? All kinds of trouble. It was a monster on the ground, but smooth in the sky. Only the best of us got those routes. Needed a special touch to squeeze her into those jungle airports."

Malcolm made sure I knew of his unique skills. He was important and necessary, like there was no one else in the world who could do what Captain Malcolm Woods could do. He also rarely missed an opportunity to mention his naval service flying F-14 Tomcats over Afghanistan. Was he trying to prove himself to the world, to me?

Malcolm created a shrine of sorts to his naval service in a basement room of the Woods' home. The walls were covered with American flags and prints of various aircraft. A glass case held medals and ribbons earned by his father. There were a dozen blue Navy caps with ship names stitched in yellow across them. A white dress uniform, in a clear garment bag, hung from a hook in the corner, ready to be pressed into service at a moment's notice.

He took me down to the room nearly every time Tina and I visited, though the wives were never invited. He'd break out the good scotch and pour three fingers for each of us, and I'd try not to choke when politely sipping the foul stuff.

It was on one of these scotch sipping visits when Malcolm opened his two-door gun safe and laid out his extensive collection of handguns.

I shot pistols with my dad for sport before I had kids, so I'm comfortable around firearms. Still, there was something about Malcolm's obsession with each piece that made me a little on edge. He was too comfortable. I attributed this feeling to my swimming head thanks to the three fingers of whiskey. But now, looking back on it, he treated those guns with an unnatural reverence, like they were a piece of him.

"This one was the standard issue," he said, handing me a fully loaded Beretta M9. "Just like my first in the service."

Malcolm's expression of admiration shifted to annoyance as I pressed the magazine release and pulled the slide to clear the chamber. I wasn't about to handle an unfamiliar weapon fully loaded in a crowded memorabilia room when tipsy on single malt.

"Looks like you've done that before," he said, taking the weapon back.

"Mostly hunting rifles, but my dad and I used to plink cans with a 9 mil Smith and Wesson," I said. "I'm a bit out of practice, though."

"Could have fooled me." He inserted the magazine and chambered a round before clicking the safety and storing the gun back in the safe, ready to be fired.

Had I missed any signs of his abuse that night, or any night? What did his love of guns mean? Was it just a hobby born from his military service?

But the guns in his safe are not my primary concern tonight as I race back to Lake Oswego, to the Woods' home. Would Malcolm hurt Christy again? What about Sophie? Could my concerns be completely unfounded? Has Christy decided to forget his violent past, take him back, and try to make it work? Why else would she ignore my calls?

Why wouldn't she answer? I have already tried her cell phone a dozen times, but it just goes to voicemail. No response to my texts, either. Maybe he took her phone?

Suppose they left Shoreline shortly after leaving Paige at the Evergreen. In that case, I'm probably thirty minutes behind them, assuming he drove them straight home, which is no sure thing. At this point, it's the only guess I have as to where they may be.

The heavy precipitation that missed Shoreline and the festival has now settled directly over Lake Oswego. My windshield wipers struggle to keep up with the torrent of water flying off my speeding truck. Despite the rain, pops of color from illegal fireworks dot the dark sky on both sides of the highway as people celebrate the Fourth of July.

I check my speed and realize I'm driving thirty miles per hour over the limit as I race off the wet interstate and onto side roads. I don't slow down until I reach the Woods' house.

Fireworks explode around the lakeshore, creating splashes of red and blue through the pines around the two-story, white brick home. The house is large and in a secluded hillside section of Lake Oswego. An iron security gate and brick fence surround most of the property. The house and yard are illuminated by a faint moon, obscured by the rain and landscape lights that shine upward through the wind-blown ornamental grasses across the manicured beds. The explosion of fireworks echo in the distance.

I push the call button on the security gate and wait for it to ring the house. The mechanical dial tone blares through the speaker as it attempts to connect. I anticipate Malcolm answering the house phone after looking at the live security camera video of me waiting in my car.

No answer.

I dial again.

Nothing.

I punch in the security code Christy had given me years ago in case of an emergency. I wonder now if Malcolm was the original reason she'd given me the code? Was she trying to tell me about him, even back then? How could I have missed it?

I wait for the gate to open, but it sits idle.

I try again, this time hitting "enter" after the code. The gate swings open, and I pull through toward the house. I park in front of the garage and march toward the door. I pause before knocking. I don't know what I'm walking into, and I have no idea what I'll say to Malcolm when I see him.

If only Christy would call me back.

I peer through the windows on either side of the front door, but the house is dark inside. I knock and ring the doorbell. No answer.

I circle around the side of the house, skirting a narrow strip of grass that gives way to a sharp slope down the side yard. The heavy rain and darkness mean I can't see the bottom of the canyon below the house. I hop over the locked gate and enter the backyard.

The living room and kitchen face the backyard. If anyone is home, those lights will be on. I mount the stairs to the back deck to see inside better. Nothing. No lights. No one is home.

I find a dry patio chair and contemplate my next move. I recheck my phone to see if Christy called. Of course, she hadn't. If not here, where would he have taken them?

I made a stupid mistake. Paige said they were going home. Home must have been Karen's cottage in Shoreline. I could have been there in ten minutes, not driven hours through this weather to an empty house in Lake Oswego.

I call Karen, who I know isn't home. She left town for her vacation days ago. She picks up on the third ring. I ask if she has heard from Christy today.

"No, but I'm about to board a boat in San Diego for my cruise. I was planning to call her soon," she says. "What's wrong, James? You sound very upset."

I set aside my concerns about Christy's privacy. I can apologize for it later. I unload everything that has happened between Malcolm and Christy—the divorce papers and the abuse, the sealed letter to the kids. I tell her about all of it in the hopes that she'll understand how critical it is that we locate Sophie and Christy immediately.

"James, I know they had some trouble, but I've never heard any of this," she says. "Are you certain? That son of a bitch. I'll kill him."

I appreciate Karen's reply more than she knows.

"I've seen the bruises with my own eyes," I say. "I just didn't know they came from him. I'm so sorry, Karen. We just need to find her. Is there any way to know if they went to your house?"

"You're closer than I am at this point, James. Can you

drive up there?" she asks.

I explain that I thought they were going to their house in Lake Oswego, and I've gone at least two hours in the wrong direction.

"I know," she says. "I'll call my neighbor and ask if anyone is home. Then I'll call you right back. James?"

I never get a chance to reply. I hear the whir of the security gate opening and see headlights flash across the yard. I hop over the fence again and come around the side of the house as Malcolm parks his Ford SUV in the curved driveway. I wait in the shadows. They can't see me, but my truck is parked in front of the garage, so they both know I'm here.

Christy sits in the passenger seat. The back windows are tinted, and in the darkness, I can't see if Sophie is in the vehicle, too. The car is still running, its wipers franticly flicking away the rain.

Malcom picks up a McDonald's soda cup from the console and takes a long drink from the straw. They stopped for dinner? Did I misunderstand what was happening? Did Malcom return so they could reconcile? Did they work it out over Quarter Pounders and a Happy Meal?

I can't hear their voices, but Malcolm raises his hand and points down in a stabbing motion, clearly indicating that Christy should stay inside the Ford. Christy is in tears with her arms clutched to her chest in a bear hug. Shallow breaths make her body jerk up and down.

I did not misunderstand the situation.

Malcolm opens the driver's door, fully illuminating the inside of the car. Mascara streaks stain Christy's worried face and Sophie is terrified in the backseat. Christy tries to reassure her as Malcolm gets out of the SUV.

I walk forward into the headlights when Christy sees me. She looks directly at me and shakes her head no. Malcolm sees this signal before he sees me.

"She needs to get out of the car and away from you. Now," I shout at Malcolm. "I know what you did. This is over."

"Who the hell do you think you are?" Malcolm spits. "You broke into my property and think you can command me or my wife to do anything? Not gonna happen. Get back in your truck and go, now."

I continue toward the car. If he doesn't allow her out, I'll just get her and Sophie out myself. We'll leave. The greater the distance between him and them right now, the better. But Malcolm steps between me and the car.

I stop cold as he enters the beam of light. Although back lit, I know what's in his left hand—his trusty Beretta M9.

"None of this is your business, James. This is my family. Why can't you just leave us alone? Every damn time you're in our business! Everywhere she goes, you're right there! No more. She's mine, not yours! This ends now."

"Are you going to shoot me, Malcolm?" I ask with courage I didn't know I had. "Put the gun down. I just want to make sure Christy and Sophie are safe. Are they safe, Malcolm? Safe with you and that gun?"

I hope asking him such a primal question will wake him from his blind rage. He wipes the rain from his forehead with his sleeve, but the gun remains at his side. Even at this distance, I can see his left hand is shaking. The barrel of the gun, pointed at the driveway, twitches from side to side.

"They are my family, not yours! Of course, they are safe. They are with me, like always. Now get the hell out of here—"

The passenger door pops open, and Christy emerges. He flits a glance toward her as she rounds the front of the car.

"Get back in the damn car like I told you!" he demands, but Christy doesn't stop. She closes in on him from the side.

He clearly wasn't expecting her to leave the car and stand up for herself. Her surprising movement distracts him from his focus on me, so I rush toward him as well. But I get only a few steps before he raises the gun and levels it at me.

"Not another inch. Either of you," he growls.

I stop immediately. I'm close enough to see his face

clearly. The well-maintained commercial pilot façade is lost. Dark bags hang under his bloodshot eyes and several days of unkempt stubble remain on his chin.

His attention darts back and forth between Christy and me.

Christy ignores the outstretched gun and charges at him, slamming her shoulder into his side. Remarkably, he doesn't lose his footing, though she falls to the ground at his feet. With his free right hand, he grabs her by the hair and holds her down on the ground. Christy is on her knees, her arms flailing and scratching at his arm above her.

There is movement inside the SUV behind him. Sophie crawls over the center console to the driver's seat. Malcolm is focused on holding Christy with one hand and keeping his gun trained on me with the other. He never sees Sophie. Somehow, Sophie pulls the gearshift and places the SUV in drive. It creeps forward, unnoticed by anyone but me.

Sophie lays on the horn. The blast lasted only a moment, but it's enough to startle Malcolm, who struggles to control Christy. He drops the gun and stumbles backward as the Ford continues to roll forward. Christy scrambles toward the gun, unaware that the car is nearly at her back. I close the gap between us in an instant. I lift Christy by her armpits, pulling her out of the path of the rolling Ford, which quickly passes over where Christy was kneeling.

The SUV runs over something with a thump. I quickly realize the thump was at least one of Malcom's legs. He writhes around on the ground in obvious pain, holding his leg with both hands.

The driveway's raised stone curbing stops the Ford at the edge of the grass. Sophie must have stepped on the accelerator as the engine begins to rev loudly. The SUV bounces over the curbing and starts across the yard directly down the grassy slope toward the canyon below.

"Sophie's unbuckled in the front seat," I tell Christy, who never saw Sophie climb over the seat. I scramble to my feet and race after the runaway vehicle. Christy follows.

Out of the corner of my eye, I see blue and red lights flash near the front gate. My first thought is fireworks, but the wailing siren tells me it's a police car. How did the police get here so fast?

I manage to not fall on the wet grass and reach the driver's side door, yank it open, and by some miracle, reach for Sophie as she launches herself from the driver's seat toward me. I pull her to my chest, and we tumble away from the SUV onto the hill.

The Ford immediately hits a tall rock outcropping below the landscaped yard and flips on its side before plummeting down the slope, end over end, into the canyon. Metal and glass crunch as it slams into the bottom of the canyon.

I take an unsteady breath.

"That was very brave," I tell Sophie. "Are you OK?"

"I-I think so," she stammers. "Where's Mom?"

Christy emerges from the top of the hill and kneels on the grass next to Sophie. "I'm right here, baby," she says as Sophie crawls into her arms. Christy then looks at me. "How are you? Are you alright?"

I sit up and do a quick check of myself—just a few bumps and bruises. "I'll be fine. Did he hurt you?"

The red and blue lights, now coming up the driveway, shine on Christy's face as she shakes her head no, yet the terrified look in her eyes betrays her real emotion. He hurt her, just as he's been hurting her for years. Physically. Emotionally.

The snapping sound of the Beretta echoes down the hill—once, then again. The sound is unmistakable, but faint through the sound of the police siren. I hear and feel two thuds impact near me. Christy and Sophie slide farther down the hill. Did he hit them?

"Christy!" I scream, but she's already too far away.

I feel a stabbing pain in my side as I roll behind a large rock outcropping and duck low.

Malcolm stands at the top of the hill, looking unsteady on one leg. He fires, then topples over onto his side. From his knees he grasps the gun with both hands, aims down the hill, and fires again.

"Malcolm, stop!" I shout, keeping my head behind the boulder. The words come out hollow. My breath is gone, and the pain in my side burns hotter.

An unfamiliar female voice, muffled against rain and distance, shouts commands to Malcolm. "Toss the weapon!" the policewoman commands. "Hands behind your head, now!"

He complies. The policewoman binds Malcom's hands behind his back and lays him face down on the ground. Only then does she look down the hill to see the rolled Ford, and the three of us climbing the hill.

"Are you folks all right?" she asks as additional police cars arrive. Soon the night is awash in colored lights.

We stand on the driveway as several police officers approach us. Malcom can't walk, so he is carried into a squad car.

"Christy, I'm so sorry for this," I say. "If I weren't here, this wouldn't have happened. He wouldn't have done that."

"No, James. Thank God you were here," she says, panic still in her voice. "I've never seen him like that. Just enraged. He forced us to go with him. To come back here. He wanted to act as if everything was normal. Who knows what he would have done to us? He shot at us, James. His own child, too. It's unbelievable. That's the man he is, and now everyone knows it."

"I'm just glad you are both safe," I say.

"Thank you for saving Sophie from the car. If not for you, she would have gone over the edge inside it," she says. "And thank you for coming for me, too."

She hugs me with Sophie sandwiched in between us. I release an audible wince at the pressure.

"Are you sure you're OK?" she asks, examining my torso. "Oh my God, James. You're bleeding."

CHAPTER 48

Online Coach, session 123
Final entry for client Tina Bell

Days before the Tentpole Triathlon

I guess all that interview coaching has finally paid off. I was offered a job in Portland today!

Coach: *That's fantastic news. Please, tell me more.*

It's a start-up medical technology firm that builds testing software for labs. I start next week as the Executive Director of Investor Relations. This is what I've been holding out for. The pay is close to what I was making before, and I'm getting in on the ground-level of this business. When it takes off, we will be set financially. I'll have to travel every month, but only a few days here and there. I will be able to spend more time with the kids and James.

I can finally stop pretending. I'm tired of lying and running.

Coach: *This will be a great burden off your shoulders.*

I just hope James will be happy about this new job and me being around more.

Coach: *Why wouldn't he be?*

I've been gone so long. This last year has been hard. Things will be different now. We'll have to learn to be together again. Mason graduates from high school next year, which means we'll only have Paige at home. James and I will have to be together, just the two of us. I'm hopeful, but nervous at the same time. I'm assuming he will be willing to forgive me, too. And that's a big question.

> **Coach:** *This is what you planned for, remember? And didn't you say you had a big surprise for the family, too? How did that go? What did they say?*

I haven't told James about the condo or the Westcott Inn. The whole thing didn't exactly go as smoothly as I had planned. When I left Goodwin Labs, I was sure I would find a new position very quickly. I made the decision, right or wrong, not to tell James. I pulled out some money and decided to ride it out. The months dragged and I couldn't find suitable work, but I was confident something would eventually come up.

Based on the coaching feedback I've received here, I know that coming home wasn't enough to repair my relationship with James. I needed to do something big. Then I remembered what it felt like the first time I went to Shoreline when Jaden was a baby. It felt like home and family. James always wanted to go home to Shoreline, so I decided to surprise him by buying us a condo there.

James' father Mitch was building several condos in this cute little town square. So, I put a $400,000 deposit on one of them. I swore Mitch to secrecy. I had to cash in some investments that I wasn't too happy about, but again, I needed to go big to show James and the kids how much I cared.

We could have a second home, and I would be able to spend more quality time with the kids no matter what job came along.

Unfortunately, Mitch completely mismanaged the construction of the condos and came crawling to me for a bailout.

> **Coach:** *What sort of bailout? Loans to family members can be tricky.*

Like everyone else, Mitch didn't know that I was out of work. He just assumed I had loads of money in the bank. This wasn't really a loan either, more of a purchase. One that set me back $1.5 million. If I didn't give him the money, my initial $400,000 condo investment would be gone. I couldn't let that happen.

If I told Mitch I couldn't afford it, I ran the risk of him asking

James for the money, and then I would have had to tell James that I didn't have a job. I had already been lying to him about it for over a year. I couldn't do that. Not yet. I needed to fix everything before I told James.

But today things have gone from bad to worse. Our investment safety net is gone—tied up in the Westcott Inn and the condo. Yet, the bills keep coming in. I have stopped paying the mortgage on the house and the payments on the cars. Paige's school tuition has also gone unpaid. The credit card bill went to collections. Paige's dance instructor has even started hounding me for past due payments for ballet classes. It's been a complete nightmare, and it's all my own doing.

I tried to shelter James from my job loss, but only succeeded by making the entire situation much, much worse. I've been distant and cold to him. I'm afraid if I spend too much time at home, I'll simply crack and spill everything to him. I know I have to tell him the truth, and now that I have the new job, I will tell him everything.

The Westcott gives us a safety net again. Mitch will run the inn, and we'll just see the profits. We'll stay in the condo on weekends and everything is going to work out great. All of this should be enough for James to forgive me.

Coach: *When do you plan to tell him all this news?*

I've got it all planned out. I'm flying home this weekend. I'm signed up to do a triathlon on Saturday. It's called the Tentpole Triathlon, which I've done before. It's this fun race at a lake, and I'm looking forward to it. When I'm back home, James and I will sit down, and I plan to tell him everything. I'll come clean about my job, the condo, and the Westcott. I pray he understands—he must. We can make this work and be stronger for it.

I'm ready to make some changes. It's going to be such a relief. I just want us to be happy, no matter what happens. I love James and want to come home and be with him and the kids for good.

CHAPTER 49

The Next Summer

"We've got three more orders of the lunch salmon at table twelve on the patio," Seth says, handing the order to a member of the Ranger's newly-expanded kitchen staff. "Tell the chef that we'll need to make a larger order for next weekend to make sure we don't run out again. And she was right—the crab tacos are a hit. We'll need to move them to the regular menu."

Business at the Ranger had picked up considerably with the addition of its new chef—Christy Woods. The local newspaper recently ran an article in its weekly Lifestyle section highlighting the chef's professional training, but long absence from the restaurant world. The Ranger had gone from "bar fare and salty nachos to a gourmet ocean bistro, which was alone worth the trip to Shoreline."

Seth took offense to the "salty nachos" comment. He loved those nachos, and besides, they helped sell more beer. But he had to admit, the beer and wine were easier to price high when the food experience was more refined. Credit went to Christy for all the upgrades.

Another waiter came on shift, and Seth transitioned his tables to him. He went to his office to change into shorts and a T-shirt. For the first time in years, he had agreed to attend the Shoreline Kite Festival's main event. Ranger Bar and Grill was the title sponsor, and he was expected to give a little speech to kick off the first show in the afternoon.

He'd spent hours thinking about what to say, but he couldn't get past his own thoughts on last year's festival. The rain and then sudden sunshine, the fight in the bar, and of course, what happened that night in Lake Oswego. So much had changed for everyone.

"Come on boss-man, we've got a pick-up to make on the way to the beach," Christy tells Seth. "I don't want to be late."

"You know, you should be doing this speech, not me," he says. "All of this is because of you. The new menu, the media coverage, the full tables for breakfast, lunch, and dinner."

"I can't take credit for the breakfast and coffee menu," she says. "You're not going to find me awake at six a.m. prepping for the early risers."

"Well, the rest of it is all you," he says. "Thank you. I know it's been hard for you."

She nods, not inviting a discussion about the painful past year. They both walk down the short hallway toward the noisy dining room, full of tourists and locals seeking lunch and refuge from the surprisingly warm day.

Their "pick-up" was waiting across the street on the porch of the Westcott. Sophie and Paige sit shoulder-to-shoulder on the steps, each holding a portable video game device, challenging each other to some digital contest. The girls are rarely seen without the other, and they wouldn't have it any other way.

Paige has recently begun to talk about her mother, at least to Sophie, but she won't discuss the day she died with anyone. However, tucked in Paige's bedside drawer is the last photo taken of her with her mom. They're on the beach before the triathlon began on that last day. Their arms are wrapped around each other. Paige sometimes sleeps with the photo under her pillow. Her new ballet classes in a tiny studio up in Seaside are the highlight of her week. When she dances, her angst and worry slips away, and she can be a kid again.

Mason and Jaden lean on the porch rail next to Christy's son RJ, who is on leave from the Navy for a few days. RJ is animatedly telling them about boot camp and trying to convince Mason to sign up now that he has graduated high school.

"Stop recruiting, RJ," Christy says. "Mason's already signed up for a community college in Portland. He starts next month."

Mason had enrolled at a school but had yet to decide what type of education he would pursue. His experience remodeling the McArthur house had piqued his interest, but not enough to start into a trade right away. He wasn't ready to set his future yet, but he was also sure that he wouldn't be going into the Navy with RJ, either.

Jaden looks nervously down Laneda Avenue for Evan, who should have already arrived at the Westcott. Evan spent the first half of the summer at home with his parents but committed to coming to Shoreline for a few weeks before they both returned to school and the baseball team. Jaden missed some pre-season games rehabbing his ankle last season, but he has since made a full recovery and was able to play in most of the league games. He was thriving at school and never regretted returning.

The front door of the Westcott swings open and the final member of the group arrives. His hair is speckled with sawdust and his shirt is damp with perspiration.

"James," Christy says, mounting the steps to greet him with a kiss. "You're late to the party."

CHAPTER 50

Malcolm's bullet went clean through my side, causing a world of hurt and some blood loss, but I was lucky that it didn't hit anything I couldn't live without.

The police had arrived so quickly, thanks to Karen. I hadn't hung up the phone with her that night when I saw Malcolm drive up. She was still listening through the phone I was holding in my hand. When she heard me call to Malcolm, she hung up and called the police in Lake Oswego, who dispatched a nearby squad car.

The home security video, Christy's statement, and the policewoman's eyewitness account of the shooting were enough evidence to convict Malcolm. He took a plea deal to avoid a trial for attempted murder and he was sentenced to more than seven years in prison.

Christy's divorce petition was granted before the deal was struck, unburdening her from his violent ways. RJ and Sophie were still struggling through what happened and the truth about their dad. Christy found Sophie an excellent psychiatrist, and she was making good progress with her feelings. Having Paige so close was helpful, too. RJ was stationed on the East Coast and was talking to a doctor on the Naval base.

Given all that had happened there, Christy couldn't move back to her house in Lake Oswego. Not just the shooting, but the years of torment by Malcolm. She and

Sophie stayed with Karen for a while, and I moved into the nearly finished house on McArthur to recover from my injury.

I had promised the kids that we would return to Lake Oswego, but none of them wanted to go back. Mason, Jaden, and I finished the McArthur house, giving the kids and me a place to call our own in Shoreline. Christy and Sophie moved in with us before the new year, after all the kids said we were really bad at keeping our relationship a secret. Fair enough.

Dad and I reached a reluctant agreement on the Westcott, of which I am still the majority owner thanks to Tina. He would permanently step away from management of the inn. He also moved out of his third-floor suite. He claimed leaving the Westcott was his desire in the first place and he wanted to focus on property development.

In a straight exchange, I swapped my stake in the Saint Ann Square condo for the deed to the McArthur house. After everything he did, it was really the least he could do for the kids and me.

He's made himself scarce around Shoreline, which I think is for the best for all of us. He has stopped by to see the kids occasionally, but only after notifying me first that he's coming. I usually lock myself in the workshop when he comes over.

I have zero interest in running the Westcott, and I never have. So, instead, I hired a full-time management staff. One of our first tasks was to write an agreement of cooperation between the Westcott and the Evergreen for some hotel services, both reducing costs for the businesses and partially offsetting my additional expenses due to hiring outside management.

Mom was all in on that one. She has welcomed the partnership and the ability for us to work on our relationship with no more secrets. We do dinners together every few weeks, and it's going well. Mom and Darla continue to be a work in progress, too. Old wounds don't heal overnight, but Mom is trying and that's good enough for now.

* * *

I found Tina's archive of her *Online Coach* conversations only recently when I was looking for records of her Westcott transactions.

The chats confirmed that Oliver Tremblay was telling the truth about Tina's resignation from Goodwin Labs. I am still angry that she didn't just tell me what happened. I would not have thought less of her or felt she was failing; I would have been her partner. She just never gave me that chance.

I read enough of the chats to understand that even after all the years we were together; I didn't know enough about my wife. I was an intruder reading the sessions, and I stopped several times out of guilt and shame. I hated reading that she resented me for being the primary parent and that she wanted a more significant role—one which I never gave her. She was right—I reserved the job for me alone.

There's nothing I can do now about these revelations, other than to make sure the kids know who their mom was and express to them how much they meant to her. I found her digital archive of our kids' photos. She saved every picture I snaped at every event. The kids and I went through them and talked about their mom. It was hard, but worth it. It meant a lot to the kids.

Tina and I both struggled with being partners in our marriage and with our kids, but we both wanted the same thing in the end, we just didn't know how to ask the other for it. I promised myself that as Christy and I build our relationship, I won't make the same mistakes again.

I misunderstood the agreement I had with Tina. I thought that if I took care of everything at home and she worked, we were even. But this division of responsibility didn't grant me the right to decide how she could parent or when she earned the right to have an opinion. I boxed her into a corner.

When she lost her job, it upset the balance in our marriage. Instead of working on it, she hid it until it was too late. Could we have fixed our marriage? Yes, I know we could have, but that chance was taken from us.

Marriage is complicated, happy is not. While I am coming to understand this, I also know that happy is what you make of it. You can't expect to be happy in your marriage if your partner isn't; that's selfish. And you need to be vulnerable enough to say when your happiness is threatened. Because only then can you both fix it.

EPILOGUE

I stand behind the closed front door of the Westcott, listening to the chatter of the most important people in my life. They are waiting for me to come outside so we can walk to the Shoreline Kite Festival together. I've been looking forward to it for weeks. But here, on the other side of this door, I can hear life happening. Joy, laughter, and love. People who want to be together. A family made from blood, but also bonds. I want to enjoy this simple moment before it passes.

After everything that has happened over the last year, I want just a moment to take it all in. To really appreciate what I have and what I could have lost. It's the quiet moments that I've come to want now more than anything. Sharing a meal with Mason. Watching Jaden play baseball. Clicking a bicycle helmet on Paige and watching her ride up and down the quiet street. Pouring a glass of wine with Christy, talking about Sophie and RJ, and deciding together what we'll do over the weekend.

These aren't significant monumental events that must be documented in a treasured photo album. They are the life that happens in between all those big moments. The life in between the stuff we tend to remember.

I brush the sawdust off my shirt and feel the soft scar on my side. My side aches, but I pushed myself hard in the woodshop over the last few days, completing orders. I've found that the market is thriving for handmade tables made of reclaimed wood. I'm busy in the shop most days and the kids often join me there. I've shipped orders all over the country. I may have to hire help to keep up and balance my time with the kids. I welcome the break from the work to spend time with those I love.

I open the door, step onto the porch, and into the rest of my life.

-end-

ACKNOWLEDGMENTS

Thank you first to Kellie Kolbet, my wife and first reader. Your notes and edits added a great deal of value and depth to this story. To my beta reader and friend Jessie Wuerst, I could not imagine writing a book and not getting your feedback—so very much appreciated. To Barbara Kolbet-Snyder, your insights and suggestions were amazing. And thank you for responding to my random texts about the story.

Thank you to Silvia's Reading Corner for copyediting and notes. So very extensive and helpful. Thank you to Dana Reinke at The Creative Catch for always being there for some design and graphics advice.

To Allison, Felicity, Blake, and Lock—thank you for inspiring me every day.

Part of the reason An Agreement We Made was so personal for me, was because it centered on relationships and several definitions of family. I'm a strong advocate for family being what you make it. Choosing your family binds you stronger to each other. The Bell family isn't atypical in that they can disagree, hide or ignore the reality of their situations—not always to their own benefit. Family is imperfect, but that's what makes it real.

A theme detailed in this novel was sexuality and I think it's worth an extra mention here. Several characters in different ways struggle with sharing their true selves to their family, or the outside world. Real experiences will certainly differ from the fictionalized accounts here. For those needing resources themselves, or as family members, I'd suggest reading "The Coming Out Handbook" published through The Trevor Project.

Finally to each of you, the readers of this story, thank you. If you enjoyed An Agreement We Made, please post a brief review on Amazon, Goodreads, or wherever you purchased the book. Reviews help independent authors like me find new audiences.

DANKOLBET.COM

Visit dankolbet.com to sign up for Dan's mailing list and be the first to hear about new books, sales, free content and events. You can also find Dan Kolbet Books on Facebook.

MORE BOOKS BY DAN KOLBET

Mr. Z's Toy Store Romance Series
Don't Wait For Me (Book 1, Christmas)
Better Not Love Me (Book 2, Summer)
An Easel For Avery (Book 3, Prequel Novella)

Off The Grid, a thriller

You Only Get So Much, a family saga

CPSIA information can be obtained
at www.ICGtesting.com
Printed in the USA
FSHW011055050321
79196FS